Praise for
NIGHT SHIFT

"*Night Shift* is an action-packed, sexy anthology that offers readers four unique and exciting stories by four of the most popular UF/PNR authors to date. This collection is an engaging read and well worth owning."   —Smexy Books

"If you are a fan of any of these authors or love urban fantasy and paranormal romance, then *Night Shift* is a must-read."   —Nite Lite Book Reviews

"If you're a fan of anthologies, you have to pick this up. You get paranormal, barbarians, magic, snark, and shifters. All four authors won't disappoint, and it's a great way to see more into the series you love."

—Happy Ever After, *USA Today*

NO LONGER PROPERTY OF
SEATTLE PUBLIC LIBRARY

RECEIVED

MAR 13 2021

BROADVIEW LIBRARY

RECEIVED

MAR 1 5 2021

BROADVIEW LIBRARY

Books by Milla Vane

A Gathering of Dragons Series
A HEART OF BLOOD AND ASHES

Novellas
NIGHT SHIFT

A
HEART
OF BLOOD
AND ASHES

MILLA VANE

JOVE
New York

A JOVE BOOK
Published by Berkley
An imprint of Penguin Random House LLC
penguinrandomhouse.com

Copyright © 2020 by Melissa Khan
Excerpt from *A Touch of Stone and Snow* by Milla Vane copyright © 2020 by Melissa Khan
Penguin Random House supports copyright. Copyright fuels creativity, encourages
diverse voices, promotes free speech, and creates a vibrant culture. Thank you for buying
an authorized edition of this book and for complying with copyright laws by not
reproducing, scanning, or distributing any part of it in any form without permission.
You are supporting writers and allowing Penguin Random House to continue to
publish books for every reader.

A JOVE BOOK, BERKLEY, and the BERKLEY & B colophon
are registered trademarks of Penguin Random House LLC.

ISBN: 9780425255070

First Edition: February 2020

Printed in the United States of America
1   3   5   7   9   10   8   6   4   2

Cover design by Rita Frangie
Cover photo by Claudio Marinesco
Cover lettering by viksof / Shutterstock
Book design by George Towne

This is a work of fiction. Names, characters, places, and incidents either are the product
of the author's imagination or are used fictitiously, and any resemblance to actual persons,
living or dead, business establishments, events, or locales is entirely coincidental.

If you purchased this book without a cover, you should be aware that this book is stolen
property. It was reported as "unsold and destroyed" to the publisher, and neither the author
nor the publisher has received any payment for this "stripped book."

To Jess and Jen,
thank you for holding my hand when I most
needed it.

To Cindy,
thank you for hanging in there for a very,
very, very, very long time. Like that
motivational cat poster, but a
million times better.

And to Marc Singer's loincloth,
I'm pretty sure that this is all your fault.

ACKNOWLEDGMENTS

This book was a long time coming, and there are many people to thank for it finally arriving. Many eons ago, I mentioned to Ilona Andrews that I wanted to write a dark barbarian romance, and she encouraged me to go for it. So I did. Then she gave my first novella a boost when she read it (not realizing who was behind the pen name) and gave my confidence a boost, too—which, frankly, was sorely needed. Confidence is sometimes hard to come by when writing.

And I have so many others to thank for it, too. To Jessica Clare and Jen Frederick, who read chapters as they slowly landed in their inboxes over the years, and who offered insightful feedback and much-needed cheerleading. To Cindy Hwang, my editor at Berkley, who waited a very long time for me to get my writing head in the game again, and whose faith in my work never wavered—even when mine did. Many others supported and encouraged me, because no one writes in a vacuum, and they know who they are. And if they don't, I'll tell them when I see them.

But there are also the ones that I don't see—the production editors and copy editors and cover artists and book designers, who I only meet in emails and in the margins of my manuscript. Thank you. And the readers, so many readers. Thank you so much to everyone who emailed or posted on Facebook and asked, "Where have you been? What are you working on?"

Finally, the answer to that is right here in your hands.

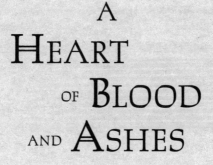

A

Heart

of Blood

and Ashes

CHAPTER 1

MADDEK

C ommander!" A young Syssian soldier called out as Maddek rode toward the bridge. "Something's got the savages on the run!"

Her polished helm gleaming beneath the early-morning sun, the soldier pointed across the river. Maddek slowed his mare, his gaze scanning the opposite bank. This was a grim stretch of the Lave. On either side of the swift-flowing waters, sparse grasses grew on stony ground that buckled and heaved into hills and ravines. The Farians' hunting party was camped in one of those gullies, hidden from Maddek's sight—though he knew well its location and had posted soldiers along the riverbanks, eyes covering every route out of the ravine that the savages might take when they finally attempted to cross.

Covered in the mud they painted over their translucent skin, now Farians scrambled their way out of the ravine using all of those routes—but not in concerted attack. Instead they were as gutworms wriggling free of infested dung tossed on a fire. Some carried spears and spiked clubs, but most had no weapons, as if they'd been surprised in camp and chose to run rather than arm themselves. Faintly Maddek heard their urgent hoots over the rush of the river.

"A trap jaw?" Maddek asked Kelir as the warrior rode up alongside him. If one of those giant predatory reptiles attacked the alliance army camp, Maddek would not have reprimanded any soldier for fleeing there, too.

His second captain cocked his head, dark braids brushing his shoulders. "Too quiet."

So it was. A trap jaw was silent until it rushed its prey. Then it often loosed a trumpeting roar—one that would have reached them even over the sound of the river.

A handful of savages scuttled nearer to the bridge, as if preparing to escape across the water, though this side of the river was no safer for them. Two dozen of Maddek's mounted Parsathean warriors and a handful of soldiers waited to separate the Farians' hairless heads from their hunched shoulders.

In nearly eight years of holding the Farians at the Lave, Maddek had seen savages run toward death many times. Never had he witnessed a Farian flee from anything.

"There it is!" a soldier cried out.

Coming up the stony path out of the ravine. A siva beast.

Maddek exchanged a look with Kelir as the soldiers snorted with laughter. Though as heavy as a yellow tusker and as tall as a mammoth, a siva beast was docile as a milk cow. Usually it waddled along, a plated dome of armor over its humped back and protecting the sides of its belly, using hardened beak and curved claws to rip open rotten logs and dig up roots.

Yet there were few roots and logs here. The jungle where the siva beast must have wandered from was three days' ride downstream.

A hard, bloody journey for the siva. Gaping wounds on its leathery neck and legs showed signs of attack. Gore dripped from its beak.

As did green foam. Maddek tensed. "It is poisoned."

Kelir had seen the same. "Silac venom."

Stung by one of the two-armed serpents that swam the Lave. The Farians had been right to flee. That venom first weakened the serpent's prey so it could be dragged from the riverbanks and drowned. Most animals stung by the serpent didn't escape.

And those that did, didn't truly escape. They only staggered away, until the weakness put them to sleep—and they woke as if brainless, unfeeling of pain and killing everything that moved. Eventually they starved or died of wounds. But the siva's armor protected it from an easy kill, particularly from the Farians' primitive spears and clubs, so the best chance of survival was to stay out of its sight.

The savages weren't out of sight yet. If the siva made noise, Maddek couldn't hear it from this distance. Silently it charged, tearing open a savage with curved claws as long as daggers. Its strong beak crushed another Farian's leg as the savage tried to run away.

Maddek heard those screams. He also heard a young Gogean soldier nearby, his face bloodbare as he watched the beast attack the Farians.

"So we . . . let the siva kill the savages for us?" He looked to his companions hesitantly, as if uncertain whether to be glad the beast tore their enemy apart.

Although that question hadn't been directed at Maddek, he answered it. "Then wait for it to attack our camp? It does not care if we are Farian or human. It will kill us all," he said. "There are enemies, and there are monsters. Always slay the monsters first, because enemies may one day become allies—but monsters never will."

As the Gogean soldier would have looked upon Maddek as an enemy only a generation past. Perhaps even thought him a monster.

Color stained the young soldier's cheeks as if realizing the same.

Maddek drew his sword. "Kelir?"

The warrior hefted his axe. "Ready."

To the soldiers, Maddek said, "Hold the bridge while we are across."

He took a dozen Parsathean riders with him. Their hooves thundered across the stone bridge. Immediately the siva found new focus, growling wetly as it charged Maddek and his warriors.

Had Maddek known he would be facing a beast maddened by silac venom, he'd not have ridden his favorite mare to the river this morn. Yet there was reason she was his favorite. Though tall and muscular as all Parsathean steeds were, she was also nimble as an antelope. With the barest signal from Maddek, she dodged the siva's swiping claw. As soon as they were past the beast, the siva's attention shifted to Kelir and the warriors behind him. Maddek's mare swiftly pivoted and sprang forward with a powerful thrust of her hindquarters.

The siva's soft belly was too low to the ground to offer a real target—any warrior low enough and close enough to cut it open might be crushed when the beast fell dead. Yet Maddek had seen that every time the beast struck with its foaming beak, first it reared back its head.

Sword in hand, Maddek launched from his saddle. The siva's neck muscles bunched as it prepared to snap at Kelir. A grunt tore from Maddek's chest as he swung at the beast's exposed throat, laying it open with one powerful slice of sharpened steel. Blood jetted from the fatal gash. Narrowly Maddek avoided a blow from flailing claws, rolling out of the way across the hardened ground and coming to a quick stop in a crouch—face to face with a Farian that hid from the beast behind a nearby boulder.

Muscles coiled, bloodied sword in his hand, Maddek made no move. The Farian held a bone blade in its long-fingered grip, yet the savage also remained motionless, near enough that Maddek could feel the hissing breath that issued from between its pointed teeth.

Mud covered its pale face. The savage's large ears shifted subtly—no doubt tracking his warriors' movements by their sound. All had fallen quiet behind Maddek. Waiting for his signal.

A signal would not come. He'd given an order that as

long as the savages remained on this side of the river, the alliance soldiers and Parsathean warriors were not to kill them except in defense of their own lives. Maddek cared not if the Farians overran the territory south of the Lave, from the Bone Fields to the Salt Sea. He would leave them in peace. Yet if they crossed the Lave, they would die.

Many *did* die. But this one hadn't lifted its blade toward Maddek, so it would not.

Slowly Maddek backed away, gaze never leaving the crouching savage. His mare nickered softly behind him. Eyes still on the Farian, he swung up into his saddle.

Kelir laughed at him as they rode toward the bridge. "Now you wait for that savage to attack our camp?"

Poking at him with the same words Maddek had said to the young soldier. Maddek grinned, for despite Kelir's teasing, he knew that the warrior would have made the same choice. Perhaps the savage would cross the river with intention of raping and killing every human it encountered. But Maddek would not kill even a Farian for what it had not yet done.

If the savage crossed the river, however—then Maddek would tear its head from its shoulders.

His attention was caught by the mounted figure watching them from the opposite end of the bridge. Enox, his first captain—who ought to have been at camp, sleeping in her furs after a night spent along the river.

Silver beads glinted in her dark braids as she cast him a dour look. "A thousand warriors you have at your command. Could you have not sent them to kill that beast instead of taking it upon your own head?"

Never would Maddek send warriors into a battle he was not also willing to fight. Nor would Enox. If Maddek had not been upon the Lave this morning, it would have been she who led that charge and felled the maddened siva. "Warriors accompanied me across the bridge," he pointed out. "It is no fault of mine if my mount was fleeter than theirs."

Her snort echoed Kelir's. Yet she had not come to reprimand him, Maddek knew.

Drawing his mare alongside hers, he asked, "What brings you?"

"Dagoneh has arrived with a company of Tolehi soldiers," she said, reining her horse back toward camp. "And a message for you from the alliance council."

Maddek frowned and urged his mare to keep pace. "What message?"

"He would not give it to me, but is waiting to speak with you."

Unease slithered through his gut. Not many years ago, he'd delivered a message from the alliance council, too.

Maddek had assumed command at the Lave eight years past. In the six years following, not once had Maddek journeyed home to the Burning Plains, until his parents had requested from the council a three-year leave, so that they might find him a bride and see him married. In his absence, Iova of Rugus had assumed command of the alliance army. Before even three seasons had passed, however, the alliance council bade Maddek to return to the river with a message for Iova—the Rugusian king was dead—and to resume command while that realm's affairs were sorted. Iova was to have returned when all was settled. Yet despite the passing of a winter, she had not.

Now the alliance council sent another message, and Dagoneh would not tell Enox what it was? That could not bode well.

Yet Kelir's mind had taken a happier route. "Perhaps they have finally found you a bride."

His parents. Though Maddek had returned to the Lave, a bride for him they'd still intended to find—one who might strengthen ties between Parsathe and the five realms that made up the alliance. A royal daughter, or a noblewoman.

Very likely a woman like Iova, who was not only a fine soldier but also aunt to the dead Rugusian king. If Iova had been younger, or if she'd had a daughter, Maddek suspected that he would already be married.

For all that it would be a marriage designed to strengthen

the alliance, however, never would his parents choose a bride unsuited to him. Though finding a warrior among the noble houses might prove too difficult a task, no doubt she would be honest, never lying or speaking with sly tongue, for she would become Maddek's closest advisor. If from Toleh, then she would be educated by the monks, with a mind both clever and fair. And as befitted a woman who might one day be a Parsathean queen—and if she wished to gain his mother's approval—she would be tall and strong and a skilled rider, and possess a heart that burned with fire.

Such a woman Maddek would be eager to meet—and take to his bed. For he'd been celibate after assuming command at the Lave eight years past, mindful of his parents' warning that when the High Commander of the Army of the Great Alliance asked someone to share his furs, there was not much difference between an invitation and an order. And during his short return to the Burning Plains, he'd taken no lovers. Not when his parents were already seeking a bride. Touching anyone else seemed a betrayal of the vows Maddek would make to that woman, and it mattered not that he hadn't yet met her.

A fine thing it would be, to finally fuck something softer than his fist.

So it was with anticipation that he rode into camp, where Parsathean tents made of mammoth hides and tusks housed the alliance army. Dagoneh had brought with him a hundred soldiers . . . as if expecting Maddek to leave with a large number of Parsatheans.

As Maddek would, if there was to be a wedding.

Yet there was to be no wedding. He entered the commander's tent with Kelir and Enox at his sides, and one glance at the Tolehi man's face told Maddek that he was not to receive news about a bride.

Dagoneh still wore his armor, yet had removed his helm, revealing his shaven head. Uncertainly he looked to Enox and Kelir before returning his solemn gaze to Maddek's. "Perhaps we might speak privately, Commander?"

As if fists had clenched around his lungs, Maddek told him tightly, "There is nothing you can say that they cannot hear."

Yet what Dagoneh did say, Maddek seemed not to hear. Not through the roaring in his ears.

Yet Enox must have also heard what Maddek could not accept. Fiercely she advanced on the captain, as if the sheer threat of her approach might force him to retrieve what he'd said and shove it back into his mouth.

"That cannot be truth," Enox spat. "It *cannot*."

"It is." Grave and steady was Dagoneh's reply. "Ran Ashev and Ran Marek have returned to Mother Temra's embrace."

Ran Ashev and Ran Marek. The Parsatheans called them their queen and king.

Maddek called them Mother and Father.

All fierceness leaving her, Enox fell to her knees on a keening wail. With her fists she pounded the ground as if she might reshape the world, as Mother Temra had. As if she might shake her queen and king free of that goddess's eternal grip.

A harsh sobbing breath came from beside Maddek before Kelir threw back his head. The warrior's howl of grief sounded as if torn from a bloodied throat.

Maddek's own howl swelled in his chest, yet it seemed there was no release for it, the grief too deep, a cavernous hollow that had suddenly opened within him.

"How?" So empty was his voice, he knew not how Dagoneh heard it.

Yet the captain must have. With grim regret, the other man shook his head. "I have no answers for you. My message and orders from the council were so bare, I suspect they were sent to Toleh in great haste."

"And the messenger knew nothing more?" Maddek asked hoarsely.

"Only rumor that your queen and king were killed in Syssia. But I know not if it was bandits or beasts or illness, whether in the city or the outlands." Voice deep with apology, Dagoneh spread his hands. "I am only to assume command here and send you north to Ephorn."

To stand before the alliance council and learn what had killed his parents.

What had killed his queen and king.

In his heart yawned a great and painful emptiness, yet unreal it all seemed. Maddek knew the dangers that might befall a warrior . . . but could not imagine what had befallen them. His queen and king had been so strong, and such clever warriors. Unbelievable that they might survive Anumith the Destroyer, only to be killed by bandits.

So he would demand answers of the council. And if it had been bandits, Maddek would hunt down every single one of them.

Answers . . . and vengeance. It seemed that purpose was all that moved his feet. Each breath was a hot, shuddering agony. Maddek emerged from the commander's tent and a blurred sea of Parsathean faces was all he saw—warriors drawn by the sound of Enox's wail and Kelir's howl.

Three times he tried to say the words that needed to be said. Each time they broke on his mother's name. Yet it was enough. Understanding and grief slid like a blade through the warriors standing before him, shearing hearts open as Maddek's had been. On a deep breath, he gathered that purpose again.

Answers. Vengeance.

If they were to be had, then Maddek would have both.

In stronger voice, he called out, "Riders of the Burning Plains, make ready to fly north!"

The Parsathean army started out silently on their journey, grim-faced and grieving. Riding hard, never did they pause to hunt for meat or furs; their saddles were their dining halls, the cold ground their beds. Even battle-hardened muscles ached, yet no complaints had issued from the warriors' lips.

As the days passed, grief softened and song returned to

the Parsatheans' tongues, ballads that spoke of lusty warriors and legendary rulers—and of the goddess Temra, who
had broken through the vault of the sky and reshaped the
world with the pounding of her fist, forcing life to sprout
from the earth's barren face. Temra, whose loving arms
welcomed the souls of the dead back into her eternal embrace.

But silver-fingered Rani had carried Maddek's parents
into Temra's arms too early.

Though sorrow lay like stone upon Maddek's features,
even his granite mouth smiled again when the warriors told
their ribald jokes. Though his deep voice did not lift in
song, he felt the rhythm through his blood like the beat of
war drums. But his grief did not soften; instead the burning
need for answers and vengeance hardened around his be-
reaved heart like steel.

A full turn of the moon passed before the white stone
wall surrounding Ephorn's great city became visible in the
distance. Maddek often heard Ephorn's soldiers claim that
glimpsing the walled city from across the plain was akin to
gazing upon a shining mountain.

Maddek agreed that Ephorn could be mistaken for a
mountain—a pale squatting one, built upon a hill of its own
dung.

Walls should not swell any soldier's breast with pride.
Those walls symbolized fear, not strength. Ephorn and the
cities of nearby realms had built their walls because they
feared each other and feared their common enemies: the Parsathean riders to the north and the Farian savages to the
south. Yet the walls had not stopped generations of rulers
from conspiring and warring among themselves, had not
prevented the Parsatheans from invading and raiding their
cities, and had not saved them from the Farians who raped
and slaughtered their citizens.

And a generation past, those walls had not stopped Anumith the Destroyer, who'd crushed the cities' stone defenses as easily as he'd torn the hide tents in the Parsathean
hunting camps.

Walls were not strength. The alliance that had formed between the riders of Parsathe and the five southern realms in the wake of the Destroyer—*that* was strength.

That alliance was also why Ephorn's gates opened for Maddek upon his approach. The city that would have barred a Parsathean's entrance a generation ago now invited him in. The citizens would not as warmly welcome the Parsathean army that rode behind Maddek, however, so only three warriors accompanied him.

Beneath the shadow cast by the white wall, sallow-cheeked children played between mudbrick houses that only saw the sun at midday. No breeze stirred the stale air but for the wind created by the swift passing of Maddek and his warriors, their mounts' hooves clattering on the cobblestone road.

Visible beyond the clay-tiled roofs rose the shining blue spires of the citadel—and it was at the citadel where the splendor of Ephorn was put on display. In the great courtyard beyond the fortress's outer gates, lush gardens breathed their perfume into the air. Fountains splashed into gleaming marble basins. Market stalls boasted pots full of colorful spices and hung a dazzling array of silks. At the open tables, mead flowed like rivers to wash down mountains of roasted meats.

It was the city that never hungered or thirsted. Some said Muda herself favored Ephorn, so its fields always yielded a bounty and its wells never ran dry.

Maddek could not claim to know whether the goddess of law cared for crops and water, but he thought her favor had been helped along by Ephorn's location. Centered among the four other southern realms that made up the Great Alliance, Ephorn had not been raided or attacked as often as the cities on the borders. And most roads—along with the trade they brought—took a central route through the region instead of crossing Parsathean or Farian territory, so the merchants of Ephorn bought from foreign traders on the cheap and sold their wares to the other realms at a profit.

But perhaps they called that the goddess's favor, too.

Maddek passed through the citadel's inner gates and dismounted at the base of the Tower of the Moon—the tallest of the four great towers within the fortress. With sheer walls of seamless white marble topped by a sapphire spire that pierced the sky, the tower had served as the royal keep until the Destroyer had slaughtered the royal family. Afterward, though many nobles still lived, no one had taken the king's place on the throne. Instead the city had come under the protection of the Court of Muda and the fortress became the seat of the Great Alliance.

Here Maddek would find the answers he sought.

He glanced over at Kelir, who still sat on his horse. The big warrior's head was tilted far back as he took in the height of the tower.

A doleful expression settled over Kelir's scarred features when he noted Maddek's gaze upon him. "I have held the tales of Ran Bantik close to my heart since I was a boy. One day, I would have told them to my own children. But now I know them all to be false."

Tales of the legendary thief-king of Parsathe, who had long ago united the tribes that rode the Burning Plains. "Why false?"

"No one could have scaled *those* walls to steal the pearl from Ephorn's crown. Easier to scale a wall of greased steel."

"So it would be. But a man does not become a legend by performing feats that others deem easy," Maddek said.

"Climbing that wall would not be difficult. It would be impossible."

Maddek agreed. But a man also did not become a legend by doing what others deemed possible. "Is the feat not as impressive if he climbed the stairs?"

"How can it be? Shall I tell my children how Ran Bantik gasped for breath when he reached the top? Shall I describe how he must have clutched his burning chest as he stole the pearl?"

"If Commander Maddek were to race to the upper chambers, he would not be gasping for breath—and neither would I." This came from Ardyl, who had also dismounted and now looked up at Kelir with a frown creasing her black-painted brow. "Perhaps if you more often ran beside your horse instead of always sitting on him, you could also reach the top unwinded."

Kelir looked to Maddek as if for help, but Maddek had none to offer. Instead he could only laugh his agreement. Kelir's saddle would wear thin before his boots ever did.

"When I see the keep, I do not think of Ran Bantik," Ardyl added as she took Maddek's reins. The warriors would not accompany him inside but would remain in the courtyard with the horses. "Instead I wonder what sort of fools the royal family must have been. They built a majestic tower honoring the moon goddess, though it is by Muda's favor that they all prosper."

"What insult could that be?" Kelir frowned at her. "Vela gave birth to Muda. What daughter would not see her mother honored?"

Ardyl's response was a glance at the silent warrior mounted a few paces behind him. Danoh's feud with her mother was almost as legendary as any thief-king. Many Parsatheans claimed the only time they'd ever heard Danoh speak was when she yelled at the older woman.

Grinning, Kelir bowed his head to acknowledge Ardyl's point.

Movement on the tower steps drew Maddek's attention. A seneschal in blue robes approached—a wiry Tolehi man with shaved head and pursed lips.

Omer. Maddek knew him well. He'd first met the seneschal as a boy, visiting the tower while his parents spoke to the council. He'd spent a full morning in an antechamber with Omer watching him as an antelope watches a drepa—with trembling limbs and pounding heart, fearing the raptor's sickle claw that would spill steaming innards to the ground.

Though a sickle claw from Maddek's first drepa hunt had already hung from the leather thong around his throat, he hadn't spilled the Tolehi man's innards. Instead he'd eaten his way through a platter of roasted boa.

Maddek had pleasant memories of that morning, and of every meeting since. Even if the seneschal did not.

"Commander Maddek." Omer imperiously swept his hand toward the tower entrance. "The council is ready to receive you, if you are ready to be received."

The doubt in the seneschal's tone suggested that Maddek could not be. "I am."

The older man sniffed as Maddek joined him. "If you wish, I will escort you to the bathing chambers first."

Grinning his amusement, Maddek climbed the steps. "I do not wish."

There was no shame in smelling of horse, or in wearing the grime of camp on his skin. The duty of serving the alliance and protecting their people left his warriors covered in sweat and filth, and he would not pretend a warrior's work was a clean work.

As it was, the council ministers should be grateful he always washed away the blood of battle, or he would have faced them dripping an ocean of it.

With a sword's worth of steel in his spine, Omer tipped back his head to meet Maddek's gaze. "I would offer a robe so that you could clothe yourself before meeting the ministers, but we do not have any large enough to cover your mountainous expanse of flesh. But did I not see a mammoth's pelt rolled up and tied to your beast of a horse?"

Not a mammoth's but a bison's—and it was too warm for furs. The last frost had melted during their journey north, and Maddek no longer used his furs except to sleep on.

He said simply, "I am already dressed."

In red linen folded over a wide belt. The inner length of cloth hung to his knees. When it was raining or cold, he could draw up the longer outer length and drape it over his shoulders, but now it fell almost to the ground, all but concealing the soft leather boots that protected his feet and hugged his calves. The outer length of linen was split to allow for ease of movement, but unless he was riding or fighting, it concealed his skin as well as a southerner's robe did . . . from the waist down.

On this day, the sun was high and warm, so he needed no other covering—whereas Omer wore enough for two men.

The southerners did not just wrap their cities in walls. Their soldiers wrapped their bodies in heavy armor even when they were not in battle. The citizens wrapped themselves in cloth from neck to ankle, even on days when they needed no protection from the cold or wind.

An entire life they spent wrapped, as if for a funeral pyre.

Maddek spent his life as he lived it. For a full turn of the moon he had been traveling, so he was dressed to ride. He did not anticipate a fight, so he wore no armor, and his chest was bare aside from the leather baldric slung across his shoulder to carry his sword. No black paint darkened his brow. The only silver upon his fingers was the family crest circling the base of his thumb; he'd tucked away the razor-tipped claws that would drip with blood by the end of a battle.

Although he was a commander of the alliance's army, if Maddek had arrived looking as he did after a battle, he doubted they'd have let him through the gates. Many southerners within the alliance still believed the Parsatheans were little better than the Farian savages. The riders were still called raiders and thieves—and uncivilized.

Maddek had never known the raid. By the time he'd been old enough to mount his first horse, the alliance between Parsathe and the southern realms had been firmly established. But if civilization meant cowering behind walls, if it meant wrapping every bare stretch of skin in linens, then Maddek preferred to be a barbarian.

In a god's age, when their civilized walls were crumbling to dust, when the names of their civilized cities were forgotten, Parsathean seed would still grow strong amid the ruins.

Omer gave Maddek's bare chest a despairing glance before sighing and continuing across the marble floor inside the tower's entrance. In silence they walked, until they reached the anteroom outside the council's chamber.

There the seneschal quietly said, "It was with great sorrow that I learned what befell Ran Ashev and Ran Marek. They were always the most welcome of the council's visitors. Of those who knew them, there can be not one who does not grieve for them now."

Maddek inclined his head but made no other response, except in his gratitude to draw the red cloth up over his shoulder and drape it across his chest.

He had not yet learned what had befallen his parents. Maddek would not press Omer for answers, however. The questions that burned within his breast would be asked within the council chambers.

Nothing had been left unasked or unsaid between mother and father and son. Every Parsathean warrior knew life was too uncertain to leave important words unspoken. And since leaving the Lave, much time had Maddek to think upon what came next, beyond answers and—if needed—vengeance. To think upon what his parents would have wanted of him. When Maddek had last seen them, his queen and king spoke of finding him a bride and of strengthening the alliance between Parsathe and the southern realms.

Nothing was left unsaid, but there was much left undone. So Maddek would see it finished in their stead.

CHAPTER 2

MADDEK

The tower's former throne room lay beyond gleaming doors carved from ivory. Such a grand entrance had likely once opened into an opulent royal chamber, but the council's was starkly decorated. Instead of a throne, six bone chairs sat behind a long crescent table. Those chairs did not belong to any one minister; like the moon, their positions shifted, so that no member of the alliance always sat in the center or at the ends of the table.

Each member had an equal voice and a council minister who spoke on behalf of their home. The alliance between Parsathe and the southern realms formed after the Destroyer had marched through these lands. Former enemies and rivals, now they were bound together by a common purpose: not to stand against the Destroyer—it had been too late for that—but to stand against the warlords and sorcerers who sought to conquer the shattered remains the Destroyer left in his wake.

But for one, the same ministers sat on the council as the last time Maddek had come before them. On the far left was

Nayil. The Parsathean minister also only wore a cloth over
his belt, with the longer length draped over his shoulder, but
Maddek doubted that Omer ever chided the older man for
his lack of clothing. A queen's age past, in battle against one
of the Destroyer's warlords, Nayil had lost his right hand,
and a poisoned blade had withered the strength on his left
side. He'd stopped wearing a warrior's braids and had grown
his beard long. Yet his quiet and formidable power never
waned, and his patience and loyalty were endless.

For those reasons, Maddek's parents had considered
Nayil their closest friend and advisor. They had fought the
Destroyer together and helped form the alliance together.
Now the older man's expression brightened at the sight of
Maddek, but grief lay heavily on his lined face, and he ap-
peared to have aged ten years in the three seasons since
Maddek had last seen him.

Maddek bowed his head in Nayil's direction. In his role
as an alliance commander, he should not show more respect to any one minister over another—but he *did* respect
Nayil above all others and would never pretend otherwise.

Beside him sat the Gogean minister, Kintus, whose
sharp expression often matched the words on her scythe of
a tongue. As the southernmost realm, Goge would suffer
more than any other if the Farian savages were not checked,
yet its every contribution to the alliance had to be pried
from the woman's begrudging fingers.

Unlike Parsathe, where everyone was taught to ride and
hunt and fight, in the southern realms only a small number
of citizens became soldiers. So the cities contributed a few
squadrons to the alliance's army and made up the difference with goods that the council deemed were of equal
value. For Goge, that meant sending grain for every Parsathean warrior and horse.

Kintus looked upon Maddek now with a bitter scowl,
which he imagined was the same face she would wear if
anyone requested air to breathe while they passed through
Gogean lands. But he would ask nothing of her. Everything
his army required while traveling through Ephorn would

come from the woman to her right—Pella, Ephorn's minister and one of Muda's high priestesses.

Pella did not sit on the court while serving on the alliance
council, yet her gray hair was still sheared closely to her
bronze scalp. Over her wrapped linens she wore Muda's
robes, the heavy cloth dyed the deep orange of that goddess's ever-changing and ever-burning fire. Thin gold chains
circled her neck, her wrists, and her ankles—signifying the
law by which she was always bound. Yet those chains were
malleable. Pella herself often seemed forged of steel, and
Maddek appreciated her all the more for it.

He could not feel the same toward the Syssian minister
who claimed the seat beside her. Bazir had been appointed
to the council by his father, Syssia's regent king. Bazir's
moonstone eyes also marked him as a son of the House of
Nyset and a descendant of that great Syssian warrior-queen,
but there was nothing of a warrior that Maddek could see
in him.

Bazir had strength enough in his linen-wrapped limbs.
He had skill with a sword and upon a horse. But he had not
a warrior's plain speak—his tongue was as slick as his blue
silk robes, and his every word stank of indolent rot. He had
not a warrior's honor, which demanded that he fight in service of his people. Instead he was driven by self-interest,
just as his father was. From the moment Zhalen had married the last living daughter of Nyset's bloodline, his seed
had corrupted Syssia's ruling house with selfish ambition.
Zhalen did not look upon Syssia's abundance of riches as a
gift from the gods, as did the rulers and citizens of Ephorn.
Instead the regent king took Syssia's wealth as his due,
owed to him by virtue of his superior position and birth.

So did his sons. Bazir gazed upon Maddek now with his
usual unconcealed disdain—a disdain that frequently
deepened to frustration when Bazir realized his opinion
touched Maddek not at all, except to amuse him.

As if Maddek would ever be touched by the contempt of
an overindulged sly-tongue. If the Parsatheans still raided
their neighbors, Maddek often thought he would lead his

warriors against Syssia first, simply to watch disdain give way to terror in Bazir's pale eyes.

That would amuse Maddek even more.

Never would he ride against the man at Bazir's left, however—Gareth, the Tolehi minister who'd served as a captain under Maddek's mother in the alliance's campaign against Stranik's Fang. With steady hands and a steadier heart in battle, Gareth had also proved himself a quietly stubborn and thoughtful addition to the alliance council—and it was his son Dagoneh who had taken over Maddek's command on the Lave.

Maddek was unacquainted with the last man at the table. Rugus's new minister was hardly more than a boy. But Maddek needed no name to know who he was. Those moonstone eyes spoke for him.

So did Pella. "Commander Maddek, you have not yet met the newest member of our council—Lord Tyzen of Rugus."

Of Rugus now, but originally of Syssia. With those pearlescent eyes, Tyzen must be brother to Bazir—and also brother to King Aezil, who had gained the Rugusian throne following King Latan's death by poison. That king's murderer had not been discovered, but everyone who spoke of it suspected that Aezil had been responsible.

So now two of Zhalen's sons sat upon the council, and another son ruled Rugus—and their reins were held by the regent king of a rotten house.

This could not lead to the stronger alliance that Maddek's parents had been fighting for.

With calm elegance, the youth inclined his head toward Maddek. "Commander."

Maddek merely looked upon him. Though as tall as his brother, with the same dark hair and bronze skin, Tyzen did not appear to have even reached his bearded age. Perhaps he fully shaved his jaw, as most Parsathean warriors did. But Maddek suspected that nothing yet grew in.

Eyes ghostly pale, the boy regarded him with undisguised curiosity, as if oblivious to the insult of Maddek's silence.

His brother was not oblivious. Bazir's disdain darkened to anger, a flush rising over his cheeks.

Smoothly Pella spoke before Bazir could. "We mourn your queen and king with you, Commander Maddek. And we are sorry a messenger could not have been more fleet."

Maddek bowed his head. "Silver-fingered Rani has flown them back into Temra's arms, so not even the swiftest horse could have changed their course, Lady Pella. It is as it is."

And there was a distance to be crossed. The news had to travel from Parsathe to Ephorn, then from the council to the banks of the Lave. A full season would pass between his parents' deaths and Maddek's return home. That could not be helped.

Yet now he could finally learn what had befallen them. He looked to Nayil, but before Maddek could speak, Kintus's sharp voice pulled his attention to her.

"We knew that you would return home upon receiving word, Commander, but we did not expect to see an entire army behind you. Have you withdrawn every Parsathean warrior from the Lave encampment?"

Maddek met the Gogean minister's gaze squarely. She would demand this answer of him *now*? Before he could speak another word of his queen and king?

But a season had passed since their deaths, and Kintus already knew what had happened to his parents. Those questions would not burn in her mind as brightly as they still did in Maddek's—and when Kintus looked at him, she likely saw him only as the alliance's commander, not a son.

So he swallowed his questions for the moment. "I have."

"Why would you do such a thing?"

Irritation tightened Nayil's weathered face as he looked to the woman beside him, but it was Pella who said, "Lord Nayil has already explained that every Parsathean must be present when their tribes gather to choose their new Ran, so that they may raise their voices in support or opposition."

That did not satisfy Kintus of Goge. "Could not the warriors have sent word of their choice, instead? Could not the numbers have been taken at the encampment and counted among the voices?"

Maddek stared at her, disbelief and disgust rising sour to his tongue. "You would have me toss each warrior's voice into a sack like a kernel of corn and carry it north, so that it arrives indistinguishable from the voices I carried with it?" Perhaps that was what civilization meant—in the southern realms, their kings and queens were chosen for them. Individual voices mattered little. But if civilization demanded silence, Maddek would *never* see the same happen to Parsathe. "They *all* come."

Though his tone must have told her the matter was closed, still her mouth opened again.

Gareth of Toleh stepped in. "The boundary was not left undefended, Kintus. When we sent the message to Commander Maddek, my king also sent one hundred soldiers. Even with the Parsatheans absent, there are still a large number of alliance soldiers at the encampment, including a squadron of your own Gogean warriors. Their number can hold the river."

Kintus's bitter gaze swung back to Maddek. "And if the savages come in such great force that they overwhelm that number? What do we do then?"

Anger fired his tongue. "Then you will do as you have done for ages, and cower behind your walls," he told her. Her eyes snapped wide and she looked to Nayil in outrage, but Maddek had not finished his answer. "You ask what to do? The savages will never stop coming, and they will never gather in such numbers that we can destroy them all. They will *always* be a threat, yet Goge does not have enough soldiers to fight them, even though you have had a full generation under the alliance's protection to grow and harvest new warriors. Instead you made them into farmers and relied upon another wall—a wall constructed of Parsathean flesh and mortared by Parsathean blood. You did nothing to strengthen your own flesh and blood. I suggest you begin."

"We did nothing?" Her thin lips pinched, two dull spots of color burnishing her cheeks. "You look well fed, Commander. Your giant horses appear fat. And the grain you gorge yourselves on is *our* flesh and blood, you reeking, brutish—"

"Kintus." A sharp word from Pella stopped the tirade. Her steely gaze met Maddek's. "In your opinion, Commander, are the defensive forces on the river sufficient to counter the savages' attacks?"

"They are."

If they hadn't been, Maddek would have requested more forces before leaving.

Pella accepted his answer with a simple nod. "The agreement between our people states that each member of the alliance must be allowed the opportunity to settle their affairs and to establish new rule when internal disruptions of this nature occur. Following King Latan's death last summer, the Rugusian commander left the Lave encampment early, as did most of the Rugusian soldiers. That ruling house is now settled. So Rugus can send additional reinforcements to the Lave until the Parsatheans have settled their affairs and their warriors return."

A self-satisfied smirk curled Bazir's mouth, his moonstone gaze smug as he regarded Maddek. "Rugus is under another obligation—providing guard to the Syssian court," he said before looking to Pella. "The council approved the contract. Do you not recall? It was only done this past winter."

"I recall the contract." She frowned at Bazir before looking beyond him to his brother. "Can Rugus not spare a company of soldiers, Tyzen?"

Solemnly the boy shook his head. By all appearances he was at ease, yet his hands were curled into fists, his knuckles white. "Syssia's regent has recently demanded that my king's every available soldier be sent to his city."

Bazir's pale gaze flicked to Maddek again. "We believe the extra guard will be necessary."

The heavy silence that fell across the ministers then felt like a burden of things undone. It weighed hard and sudden upon Maddek's heart, and for a long breath, that great muscle seemed not to pound.

Then it began beating again, faster and hotter. He looked to Nayil.

"What felled our queen and king?" he asked, and his voice was quiet, but every Parsathean knew that quiet simply preceded the rage of a fire, the fury of a storm, the clash of a sword.

He saw the hardening of Nayil's face, the rage already burning. But it was not the warrior who answered him.

Pella said, "Before we begin, Commander Maddek, you must understand that all has been satisfied by alliance law."

"*What* has been satisfied?" Not he.

Eagerly Bazir leaned forward to tell him. "This winter past, your queen and king came to Syssia to discuss strengthening the alliance through your marriage to one of my kin. While there, your king assaulted a woman of the household, and was slain when *my* father defended her honor—"

Without haste, Maddek started for him.

Bazir scrambled back, bone chair clattering to the floor in his rush. His pale eyes finally darkened with fear—but the sight didn't amuse Maddek as he'd thought it would. Instead he only saw red.

He did not reach for his sword. He left his silver claws tucked away.

With bare hands he would tear this liar's head from his neck, rip out his sly tongue, and stuff it down the ragged blood-spurting hole of his throat.

The crescent table stood in his path. The ministers were already scattering—Gareth thrust the boy behind him as if to use his own body as a shield against Maddek's wrath, and Pella grabbed Kintus's arm as if to haul her away before the table was shoved aside. But Maddek simply leapt onto the carved surface, then over, his muscles coiled like steel springs, his gaze fixed on Bazir's bloodbare face. The man's pale eyes darted right and left, searching for escape.

Instead of escape came rescue in the form of Nayil's wasted hand upon Maddek's arm.

Nothing else in that tower could have made Maddek pause. Only out of the deepest respect did he halt.

And Nayil knew that *halted* was not *stopped.* "If you value your life, leave us!" he snapped at the cowering Bazir. As if Nayil was uncertain of the depth of Maddek's rage, the warning in his gaze shifted to the brother. "Leave us, Tyzen."

Maddek would not have touched the boy. Any fool could see that the youth had not shared Bazir's smirking pleasure when his brother had spoken the foul lie. Instead he'd turned his face away, as if shamed.

Ashamed of his brother or ashamed of what their father had done, Maddek cared not. The boy would have neither brother nor father to be ashamed of much longer.

A murmur from Pella sent Gareth and Kintus from the chamber after the two brothers. With bloodrage in his eyes, Maddek's gaze followed Bazir's hasty retreat through the ivory doors. The sly-tongue's escape now mattered not at all.

Maddek *would* find him again. He would rip that lying tongue from between Bazir's smirking lips.

He could hardly believe that it hadn't yet been done. With a throat scoured raw by grief and rage, he looked to Nayil. "You were friend to my queen and king. Tell me why he still lives. Tell me why Zhalen does. It could not be my absence that stayed your hand. You would not wait for me to avenge their deaths and to silence the lies that would stain their names."

"There will be no vengeance," Pella said, but Maddek's gaze did not stray from Nayil's face. "We could not prove any lie. Indeed, part of the story was corroborated by a minister on this council."

"A minister?" An incredulous sneer twisted Maddek's mouth. "Zhalen's son?"

"By me." The older man's eyes were steady on his. "Your parents came to me and asked what I knew of the House of Nyset. They had received a message from a woman within the household that put forth the possibility of marriage to unite our people."

"And what did you tell them?"

"To avoid Syssian royalty as they would avoid a nest of

starving drepa. But your parents said they knew what Zhalen and his sons were, and went."

"That is only corroboration that they journeyed to Syssia. Not that my father assaulted a woman."

Simply speaking the words was like acid burning Maddek's tongue. His father would *never* touch a woman other
than his mother. To do so would be to betray his vows and
be known as the most cursed and cowardly of all warriors,
an oathbreaker.

Pella shook her head. "The incident was also witnessed
by the Rugusian guards—"

"And upon Rugus's throne sits Zhalen's murdering son,
who has most reason to support his father's lies! And you
say this matter is satisfied? It is *not* satisfied." Nor was it in
Nayil's opinion, Maddek saw from his face, yet the older
man still held his arm. Still held him back. "What of my
mother? Was she also murdered by these treacherous curs
when my father was?"

For she would have fought to the death at his side—or
to avenge him.

Renewed rage sparked in the older man's gaze. "She was
held as an assassin and interrogated for three turns of the
moon before she tried to escape."

Interrogated. Maddek could not speak.

"She killed Zhalen's eldest son during her escape attempt,"
Pella added solemnly. "Her sentence was the same as any
who had been found guilty of assassinating a Syssian royal."

"What sentence?" he asked hoarsely.

"Beheading."

Maddek closed his eyes. His queen, his mother—bound
and beheaded, forced to endure not a warrior's honorable
death but a criminal's shameful punishment.

Not a single wall would be left standing in Syssia when
Maddek was done. Not one.

His eyes opened. "I will have Zhalen's head." The man
could hire every guard and mercenary from every realm
west of Temra's Ocean. It would not save him.

"You cannot seek vengeance for this," Pella said firmly.

"Disputes between alliance members must be settled by the council—"

"As my father and mother's dispute with Zhalen was settled?"

"That was not a dispute between the realms. Theirs was a personal attack made against a member of the House of Nyset on Syssian soil. Zhalen had the right to administrate the laws of his city, just as you could enforce Parsathean law if he attempted to kill someone while in your territory."

"There was no attack. There are only lies."

Pella did not deny that. "The incident has been investigated. By alliance law, it is satisfied. All reports support Zhalen's claim that his actions were justified—and he has also lost a son. Blood has been shed on both sides. To seek vengeance beyond the law is an affront to the gods."

"An affront to the gods?" Maddek's harsh laugh echoed through the chamber. "Only to *your* goddess. Her brother Chaliq rages with me."

"So he does." Her gaze was steely as it held his. "But that is the way of Justice. He serves himself. Law serves the people—and it is by alliance law that this matter has been resolved."

"Alliance law is not Parsathean law."

"Then by your own laws. If Zhalen set upon your parents, as you believe, then your queen and king were challenged and defeated. The council could have allowed Zhalen to take Parsathean lands for his own—a suggestion that was at one point put forth by him."

Maddek might have welcomed that. For if it had been done, then Maddek would have soon been meeting Zhalen and issuing a new challenge.

And if it had been done, so too would the alliance council have met him on the battlefield. "You would have *allowed* him to take Parsathean lands?" The fury of his gaze burned into hers, and even steel could not long withstand heat of this intensity. "Parsathean lands are not the council's lands to give. We are not a province under rule of the alliance. The alliance is an agreement between our people—

and treachery breaks that agreement." Pella and her devotion to Muda did not sit at that crescent table alone, however. Maddek met Nayil's gaze again and could see no weakening in the older man, nothing to distrust. Yet Zhalen still lived. "You stand with this decision?"

Grim resolution lined his face. "Our queen and king wanted nothing more than a strong alliance—"

"They were betrayed by that alliance. I have no more use for it."

"You speak in haste and rage and grief." Admonition firmed the other man's voice. "Your parents would still have the agreement between our people and the southern realms be honored."

Haste and rage and grief did not change the truth that prompted Maddek's response. "What honor is there when we stand in alliance with their murderers? Do you speak as their friend and fellow warrior? Do you speak as a Parsathean? Or do you speak for this council?"

The older man's jaw clenched—likely holding back his own words of haste and rage. After a moment, he said evenly, "I took a vow to serve our people and to serve this alliance. And I speak for both when I tell you we *cannot* weaken now."

Pella's gold chains clinked softly as she folded her arms over her chest, her eyes tight with dread and fear. "Word is that Anumith the Destroyer is returning from across the western ocean."

"Rumor," Maddek dismissed. He had heard the same word. But not a day of his life had passed without hearing someone speculate upon the Destroyer's return.

"This news has come from many sources," Nayil said quietly. "You were a babe too young to know the terror and evil he brought upon us, but Pella and I remember well. So do Kintus and Gareth. Now with the monasteries of Toleh at our side, with the strength of Ephorn and Syssia, with Rugusian steel and Gogean seed—perhaps more might survive his march through these lands. More might live."

Bitterness rose to Maddek's tongue again. "What life

would it be when every breath drawn is of air that Zhalen still breathes? As a son, I cannot let their murders go un-avenged. I cannot be part of an alliance that will turn their gaze from truth and say that justice has been done."

"And what of your people? You are not only a son. You will be a king."

"Parsathe has not yet spoken."

"They will. As one voice." Nayil's was certain. "You *will* be Ran Maddek—and we must have a king who does not put himself above the needs of the people by turning his back on the alliance."

And Maddek could not turn his back on his mother and father. "Others could lead. Your daughter is strong. Enox would be a fine Ran."

"She is and she would be," Nayil agreed. "But so would many others. The tribes would argue and put forth their own candidates, and we would be divided instead of strengthened by the choice we must make. You are the only one who would have the consensus of all. You are the only one who already does. Do you think these discus-sions have not already taken place? They have. You are the voice we will choose to speak for all of Parsathe, Maddek, and is this how you would serve us? Is this how you would honor your mother and father—by destroying the alliance and abandoning your people?"

"It is Zhalen who destroyed the alliance when he struck my father down."

"Not in the eyes of the law." Pella's response was not without sympathy, but her gaze and her tone were steel again. "And if you touch Zhalen or his sons in retaliation, the alliance will move against you as an enemy."

Maddek inclined his head. "If that is what must be, then so be it."

On a heavy sigh, Nayil closed his eyes, then looked to Pella with a silent request.

She answered with a bow of her head and more solemn words for Maddek. "I will leave you to speak with your advi-sor, Ran Maddek. I understand what a blow this must strike to your heart. But the alliance *must* survive if we are all to survive—and it cannot if your vengeance rips apart the agreement that binds us. No one will trust the Parsatheans to hold to alliance law if their Ran raises himself above it."

"Your words are not unheard, Lady Pella," was his only response. It was all Maddek could give to her now—the reassurance that he respected her enough to hear and consider everything she had said.

Upon her retreat, Nayil sank heavily into one of the bone chairs. With a gesture he invited Maddek to do the same, but Maddek could not sit. He prowled the length of the chamber instead.

"Held and interrogated for three turns of the moon?" Maddek would not lay accusing eyes upon the other man, so he looked to the ivory ceiling instead. If Nayil had known what had occurred, his mother would never have been imprisoned for so long. "How did their absence go unnoticed?"

"We knew they were journeying in search of a bride." Weary self-recrimination filled the response. This was a question Nayil must have asked himself repeated times. "No one in Parsathe thought them missing, only traveling. I thought their silence was unusual but never suspected the truth. I believed they had simply not sent a message—or would not, until they found a bride for you."

"What of this girl? There are no more daughters of Nyset. Are there?"

Only a woman of Nyset's blood could inherit Syssia's throne, which was why Zhalen would never be more than regent. Nor would his sons, despite the moonstone eyes that marked them as Nyset's descendants. Their own children would not carry the same mark; it only passed through the female line.

Zhalen's wife, the warrior-queen Vyssen, had given birth to five sons. But she had borne no daughters and was the last female in that bloodline. With no one to claim the throne after her death, Zhalen clung to her power and his position with an iron fist.

Nayil shook his head. "A lure, perhaps. There have been

whispers of a female heir, but I know no one who has seen her with their own eyes. I've spoken with the girl who claimed your father assaulted her. She is a cousin to their late queen, but through the male line. Nyset's blood does not run through her veins, and she has no claim on the throne. As a bride who would strengthen ties within the alliance, she would not have suited our queen and king's purpose. As a woman . . . she was too weak in spirit and body to have suited your parents' purpose. Or you."

Another liar, then—though if weak in spirit, perhaps forced to lie by Zhalen.

"And the warriors who traveled with them?" A Parsathean queen or king was always accompanied by a Dragon—six warriors whose only purpose was to protect the Ran and carry out her or his commands. As they had both been named Ran, his parents had two Dragons.

"Also sentenced for conspiring against the House of Nyset."

Sentenced? "Silenced. So they could not speak the truth of what happened."

Nayil inclined his head in agreement. "That is often how Zhalen quiets dissent within his city. It follows that he would do the same to them."

"Our queen and king and two Dragons murdered." A dozen warriors, who were also mothers and fathers, sons and daughters. Maddek stopped pacing, his chest a ragged ache, his family's silver crest burning around his thumb. "How can I let this remain unavenged? I cannot."

"You must."

"The alliance has run its course if this corruption and betrayal can stand and the council stands with it, because *nothing* will stand if our allies cut our legs out from beneath us."

"And what would you put in the alliance's place? Warriors are stronger when they stand together—and Parsathe is stronger if we stand with the southern realms. Even if one of those realms is rotten."

"Only one? With Aezil on Rugus's throne, Zhalen's rot

will not be contained within Syssia—and some say that Aezil is worse than his father." Not only murdering his cousin to gain his throne, but also studying dark magics and seeking power through blood sacrifice. "These are the kings we stand with?"

"If we must," Nayil replied. "Kings rise and fall. It is not for them that we fight, but for the people who live under their rule."

That was truth. So was Maddek's reply. "Then it would be better for all if I took Zhalen's head."

"And if your vengeance destroys the alliance—"

"Then we will remake it anew."

For a long moment, only another heavy sigh was Nayil's response. Then the older man said, "You will be *my* king, Maddek. I hear your words—and I hope you hear mine when I advise you not to make any decisions in grief and rage. If you must vow to avenge them, I advise that you also do not speak an oath in haste. Silver-fingered Rani has taken your parents, so nothing can change their course; only yours can be determined now."

And his course might determine the course of every Parsathean. Maddek inclined his head. Though his heart yearned for blood, he could not deny the wisdom of the man's words.

"Your journey home will pass through another full turn of the moon," Nayil continued. "Use that time to reflect upon the path you will take. That is my advice to you: think hard and well upon your next steps."

"I can promise that." Another harsh laugh escaped him. "I know not how I will think of anything else."

"Nor I. I have not these many days and nights." A rueful smile curved Nayil's thin mouth before a grave weariness flattened his expression again. "When you are Ran, you will speak for every Parsathean. Perhaps you should let every Parsathean guide your voice—for Ran Ashev and Ran Marek were not only your parents but also our queen and king. When we gather, we can tell our brothers and sisters what befell them. We can tell them of the council's investigation and of the lies we suspect. We will tell them the consequences of vengeance and the threat of the Destroyer. If they demand blood, I will stand with you."

That was also wise advice. "And if there is not a consensus?"

"Then it is your place as Ran to speak for us. We will abide by your decision. So think upon what it must be. Think upon it as a son and as a king."

He would try. But he was not a king yet. Only a warrior.

Now his warrior's heart grieved anew. His parents, too, had been warriors—and every warrior knew death would one day come. If not by steel, then by claw or plague, or the ravages of age. Countless dangers could have befallen his parents. Before Maddek had arrived in Ephorn, he hadn't known what danger it had been, but he could have accepted any of them.

He could not accept treachery and dishonor.

And Maddek had believed that in the council's haste to send word, they simply forgot to tell the cause of his parents' deaths to the Tolehi captain who'd borne the message. But now Maddek understood.

If the queen and king had sickened, or been attacked by bandits, or become a meal for the fanged beasts that stalked the Burning Plains, such information would have been passed along, too. But the council had not told Maddek what Zhalen had done because they had not wanted him to charge north with the Parsathean army at his back and with vengeance burning in his heart.

Yet vengeance burned hot, anyway—and only one thought stoked the furnace of his mind.

Someone would pay.

CHAPTER 3

MADDEK

With Pella's blessing and the resources of Ephorn at their disposal, the Parsatheans made camp on the plain north of the walled city, where there was fresh water and ample grazing for the horses—and where the riders would be near enough to the city to enjoy its abundant pleasures.

For two days and nights, naught but music and laughter and feasting filled the camp. But the mead tasted bitter and the meat like ashes, and Maddek found no enjoyment in any of it.

He could not begrudge his warriors' light hearts, however. A full turn of the moon had passed since the Parsatheans had left the Lave encampment, and tomorrow morning would see the riders hard upon the road again. All preparations had been made, supplies renewed, mounts rested. Around the fires, some warriors already slept. Others were intent on drinking and fucking until barrels and bodies ran dry, though the morning would come upon them doubly hard.

Those at Maddek's fire slept. Only he was awake, sitting

upon his furs and staring into the flames until his eyes stung. At the base of his first finger now rested his father's silver crest, which Nayil had retrieved from Syssia during the inquiry into the queen's and king's deaths.

These crests were often all that were returned to a warrior's kin. As leader of the Parsathean army, Maddek had collected hundreds of fallen warriors' rings and sent them north to the Burning Plains, so their families would know that silver-fingered Rani had flown them into Temra's arms. Even now, within his first captain's satchel were dozens more, each one belonging to a Parsathean warrior killed while battling the Farians—and each night, as was the first captain's duty, Enox polished those rings until they gleamed.

Nayil had cared for Ran Marek's in the same way, but never would the silver shine bright again. Age and use had scuffed the surface and worn thin the image stamped into the metal—a firebloom's petals, the mark of his father's tribe. When Maddek had last seen it, Ran Ashev's crest was equally worn, the winged dragon of Ran Bantik's line no longer standing in sharp relief, its stamped edges dulled by time. That same dragon decorated Maddek's own crest, its wings cradling a firebloom, and on either side of the mark was etched his parents' names. But although his father's ring now circled his finger, his mother's did not lie beside it. Her family crest had not been among the belongings Zhalen had returned to the alliance council, though his mother's sword, shield, and the silver claws she wore into battle had been.

Stolen, then. The thief-king himself would not have taken a silver crest from a warrior's thumb, whether enemy or friend. Yet Zhalen had dishonored his mother even in that small way.

And Maddek had been forbidden to raise his sword against him.

Throat aching, he swept the pad of his thumb over his father's crest—remembering another night, another fire, and his father's words to him then.

Wars are fought on battlefields, my son. Yet it is in throne rooms where wars are lost—or won.

But his father had been wrong. Maddek had spent the past ten years upon battlefields. And he *had* won. Battle after battle, season after season, until few threats to the alliance remained, until even the savages could be held back by a small company of soldiers on the river Lave. Wars were not won or lost in throne rooms; they were won or lost upon the bloodied edge of a warrior's sword.

Throne rooms were where a man was told he could not wage war upon those who most deserved it.

But Maddek *would* have Zhalen's head. He *would* hold Bazir's wriggling tongue between his fingers.

He *would* have his vengeance.

And he *would* honor the life's work of his mother and his father. He *would* strengthen the alliance. He *would* be the king his people needed and deserved.

Temra help him see a way to do it all. For he could not.

Heart heavy, Maddek closed his burning eyes. He opened them again at the sound of approaching footsteps. Silently came Etan, one of the warriors posted on watch. With him was the one whose feet made noise—a tall, slender woman in dark robes. Maddek knew little about women from the southern realms who were not soldiers, and he could not always recognize their origins in the differences marked by their manner and dress. But this woman wore her dark hair in two braids that started at her temples and wound around the back of her head in a crown before falling straight down her back as a single thick braid—in the manner of a Syssian.

Etan crouched beside him. "This woman claims an urgent need to speak with you. She would not give her message for me to pass on."

Maddek studied her for another moment. It was a bold request, yet the woman did not appear bold. Instead she fidgeted, her fingers twisting together while looking all around with wide eyes, as if she expected attack to come from the darkness surrounding the camp.

Finally he inclined his head. "She may speak."

At a word from Etan, the woman took the warrior's place, her robes settling around her on a waft of anise perfume. Someone from within a noble house, then. A servant or a lady's companion but not a lady herself. Her robes were roughly woven rather than of silk or fine linen.

Her hands trembled but her gaze was earnest upon his. Firelight gleamed in the darkness of her eyes. "Commander, do you wish to avenge your queen and king?"

Her words were dull knives shoved through his ribs. Was this woman sent here by Bazir to mock him? For the Syssian liar must know that Maddek had been forbidden to take his vengeance.

Quietly he said, "Upon that matter, you will hold your tongue if you wish to keep it in your head."

Even in the dim glow of the fire and the darkness of her skin, he could see the bloodbare fear that bleached her cheeks.

Her voice trembled as she continued. "I know how you might have that vengeance against the one who lured your parents to Syssia."

His eyes narrowed. Few people—and only fools— would have spoken after such a warning. This woman did not seem a fool. She only seemed terrified.

And she spoke as if reciting lines given to her, for although her words were full of conviction and purpose, she had barely enough courage to sit at his side.

He studied her more closely. An old scar bisected her left eyebrow, but he could see no other injury. Her nose was straight, her teeth strong and fine, and she had moved easily beneath her robes and wrapped linens. If she had been forced to come here, she had not been compelled by a beating. "Who sent you to me?"

Some of her agitation eased. Her eyes held his steadily, earnest again. Eager to offer the words, then—yet still relieved that he knew these words were not her own. "I represent someone with no love for Zhalen. Someone who would like to see him destroyed more than you do."

A harsh laugh shook him, and Maddek gestured to Etan that he was done. "No one wants that more than I do. Now leave me be."

"There is a daughter," she said quickly as the warrior bent to take her arm. "A woman of Nyset's bloodline."

His gaze shot to hers again. "What do you say?"

"You may not touch Zhalen or his sons," she said, her breath coming in panicked spurts as she pulled against Etan's hands—as if afraid of being carried away before her message was delivered. "But there is a daughter. An heir with moonstone eyes. It was she who sent the letter that brought your parents to their end."

A daughter. Purpose hot and fierce rose in Maddek's chest. He stopped Etan with a lift of his hand. "Where is she now?"

"A full day east of Ephorn, on the road to Toleh." Now courage rose in the woman, hard anger lighting her eyes and her soft fingers curling to fists. "Where Zhalen is sending her to be married to that old lech of a king."

So that Zhalen and his offspring would sit upon the thrones of three realms within the alliance, spreading his corruption. But not if Maddek took Nyset's heir and prevented the marriage. "How many soldiers serve as her escort?"

"A dozen, perhaps."

Sudden anger hardened his tongue. But it was Maddek's first captain who replied, and her thoughts echoed his.

"This woman is either a fool or a liar," Enox said from her furs. "Send her away."

"A dozen," the woman repeated firmly. "There *is* a wedding caravan with a large escort that travels the main road to Toleh. But Zhalen believed that party might attract thieves. He sent his daughter on the southern track so she might pass through the hills unmolested."

That made more sense than sending her with so little protection. The richly appointed caravan would act as a decoy upon the main road, while Nyset's heir took a route less traveled, less likely to be a target for bandits.

Or a target for Parsathean raiders.

"They left Ephorn separately only one day past," the woman insisted. "That can be verified by the guards at the east gate. Now, please"—fearfully she glanced over her shoulder, to where Ephorn's great white walls gleamed—"I must return before my absence is discovered. I have told you all that I can."

All that she had been instructed to. But Maddek would not detain her. The fear in her glance had appeared genuine enough—and he could not know whether she'd had any choice to play the part she'd been given.

But that part was over. Now the choices were his.

He looked to Etan. "Escort her back to the gate."

Maddek waited until they were beyond the glow of his fire before speaking to Enox—aware that every warrior who had been sleeping nearby was listening. All of them had awoken when the woman arrived.

All of them yearned to avenge their queen and king as hotly as he did.

Sitting up, Enox drew her heavy furs around her bare shoulders. Her keen eyes searched his face. "What will you do?"

To the woman who had lured his parents to their deaths? "Toss her rotting corpse over Syssia's wall."

Slowly she nodded. "Do you wish for me to take a handful of warriors and fetch her to you?"

A cold smile touched Maddek's mouth. "No."

That was the only answer Enox needed—and was the one she likely expected. Maddek would pursue Nyset's heir himself.

Wry amusement curved her lips before she eyed the warrior bedded down on Maddek's right, who had been following their exchange with sharp interest. "Kelir, you and your five will accompany Ran Maddek and serve as his Dragon."

Ran Maddek. It marked the first time any of the warriors called him by the title that had belonged to his mother and father. But it was not Maddek's title yet. And wouldn't be, unless all of Parsathe claimed his voice as theirs.

Enox met his grim look with a lift of her chin. She had never liked hearing him called *Commander*. That was the alliance's title, not a Parsathean's. "When you find Nyset's heir, please add my greetings to yours."

Maddek would—a greeting given by the sharp edge of a blade. As soon as Zhalen's daughter was within his grasp, he would make her pay for her treachery.

Vengeance *would* be his.

CHAPTER 4

MADDEK

At dawn, the riders of Parsathe struck hard for home—
with Enox at their head. The same dawn saw Maddek and his Dragon guard upon the road to Toleh, a
half night's journey already behind them.

But a half night's journey for the Parsatheans was a full
day's for a bridal caravan, and that train of soldiers and
wagons was in Maddek's sight by the following morning.
Another ten days of travel lay ahead for the caravan—and
its escort would not know until too late that the bride had
not arrived in Toleh with them.

Before they were seen, Maddek veered hard south
through the trees that rose tall on either side of the road.

Riding alongside him, Kelir cast a doubtful glance over
his shoulder—toward the caravan, though it was already
out of sight. Over the thunder of their horses' hooves, the
warrior called out, "Are you certain we can trust the Syssian woman's word?"

"We will soon see!" Maddek called back.

Because he could not be certain. But everything she had

told him before begging to return to the city held the ring of truth. If Zhalen had hidden the daughter away until she was of marriageable age, then he would not likely expose her now, before she had fulfilled her purpose.

But Kelir's concern was not unwarranted. What better way to lure Maddek to an ambush than by placing a path to vengeance in front of him?

Yet even an ambush would be welcome. Eagerly Maddek would meet an attack and spill the blood of anyone who challenged him.

By midday, they reached the southern path. The road's soft earth had not seen recent passage. So either they were ahead of the daughter or no daughter was coming.

But if there was to be an ambush, it would be Maddek's. The forested hills provided cover. A steep and narrow stretch of road offered a strong position.

All was quiet but for the chittering of birds and small feathered lizards that raced about on two feet. Infrequently came the howls and screams of the predators that prowled these forests and the heavy tread of the giant reptilian beasts that foraged the treetops.

The midday sun began its slow slide west. Shadows lengthened. But the Syssian messenger had not spoken false, for as evening gold began to gild the clouds, Danoh's signal sounded from her post high above the road, the trilling chirp of an infant drepa.

A dozen soldiers—ten mounted, and two driving a carriage. Harnessed to it were four horses too light-boned to pull such a burden over such a rough road for such a distance. Little wonder they lagged so far behind the caravan— and Maddek would not have to worry that those horses would outrace his mare. Unlike a Parsathean's mount, the carriage horses had been chosen for their elegance rather than their strength.

That was also what it meant to be civilized. And for it, they would lose a bride to a barbarian.

Maddek bade his warriors to remain behind him and urged his mare onto the road. He came over the steep rise as the soldiers and carriage reached the narrowest part of the path, hemmed in by the thick growth of conifers and ferns on either side. The horses strained against their harnesses to pull the weight of the carriage up the incline.

Shouts rose from the soldiers, crossbows swinging up to their shoulders. But they did not look to another soldier for an order.

They waited for one.

Waiting for word from within the carriage, Maddek realized. By Temra's fist, he prayed it was that murdering dog-king, Zhalen.

His prayer was not answered. The man who poked his head through the carriage's curtained door was not the father but another son. Maddek would have thought it was Bazir but for his hair, lighter and longer than the sly-tongue's. The smirk was the same, as were the moonstone eyes.

Maddek called out, "Give to me Nyset's heir!"

Zhalen's son barked with laughter. "Or what? You have been forbidden to harm me, raider!"

So he had been. Maddek allowed a smile. "When they find your meatless carcass and the bones of your soldiers scattered across the road, they will believe you fell to the apes. Not to men."

Another bark of laughter was the only response before the son disappeared into the carriage. The soldiers looked to each other uneasily. Syssian men, not Zhalen's hired Rugusian soldiers.

Maddek met the eyes of the nearest one. "I am Maddek, High Commander of the Army of the Great Alliance, son of Ran Ashev and Ran Marek, rider of the Burning Plains of Parsathe," he told them. "You will lower your weapons before you take another breath, or the warriors behind me will make certain it is your last."

They obeyed, as Maddek knew they would. They were soldiers, not warriors—and one warrior might follow another, as his warriors followed him. But soldiers followed orders and Zhalen's son had given them none. So they would obey Maddek's orders, instead.

He urged his horse forward again, then abruptly halted when Zhalen's son emerged from the carriage, jewel-encrusted daggers at his belt, a gleaming sword in his right hand—and with his left, dragging a woman out with him.

Nyset's heir. Last in the bloodline of the legendary warrior-queen.

That blood had thinned.

Ineffectually she struggled against Zhalen's son, the sleeves of her blue robes riding up to reveal arms that were nothing but linen-wrapped twigs. Her legs folded beneath her when her sandaled feet struck the ground, and Maddek glimpsed ankles that appeared as fragile as a fawn's. A black veil covered her dark hair but was thrown back from her face. Sitting in a crumpled heap at her brother's feet, she glared up at him with features pinched and sallow.

Then she turned her head to meet Maddek's eyes and a shiver raced over his skin, as if he had stepped into an icy wind.

He had heard tales of the legendary Queen Nyset—of how the moon goddess Vela had once walked within her, and of how part of that goddess's power lingered in her blood. He had heard that the warrior-queen's moonstone eyes possessed sight beyond what was seen. Listening to those tales, Maddek had always felt the same cold, as if he approached something beyond the reach of his ken and his mind gave warning that these were not matters for mere men.

For he could not deny the existence of the gods and goddesses—but in Parsathe, those gods did not influence their daily lives as they did in the temple-studded cities and villages of the south. The riders were given life at birth by Temra, who had reshaped the earth by the pounding of her fist. And they were taken at death by silver-fingered Rani, who flew them back into Temra's arms. Every day between birth and death they lived by their wits and their strength, not by the whims and favor of the gods.

That was how Maddek preferred to live—without the gaze of the gods always upon him. And when Zhalen's sons looked at him with their moonstone eyes, he did not shiver.

When this woman looked, it was as if a goddess looked *through* him. As if she peered down to his bones.

And approved of what she saw.

With her piercing gaze upon him, a slow smile curved her lips. "You had best do as the Parsathean commands, Cezan. Give me over to him and depart in haste like the coward you are."

Her voice was not weak, but bold and amused. Then was sucked in on a sharp breath when Cezan released her wrists and backhanded her across the mouth.

"You will be silent, Yvenne!"

Maddek stiffened. Nor was he the only one. Each of the Syssian soldiers went rigid—because perhaps her brother had forgotten that this would be Syssia's queen, but they had not.

And she was bound, he saw now—her wrists tightly tied, palms together. Her pearlescent eyes were still upon him, her mouth still smiling despite the blood trickling from her battered lips.

That pale gaze finally left Maddek's to slide down his mounted form. "Do you see that he is dressed for battle, brother? Black paint upon his brow, drepa-skin guards upon his shoulders and arms. And those silver claws will rip out your throat."

Cezan's fingers fisted in her thick hair, dragging the woman to her feet. "You *will* be silent."

Though her neck twisted awkwardly and she stumbled unbalanced against her brother's side, she did not heed his warning. "Dressed for battle, but he wears no breastplate. Do you know what that means, brother?"

"It means I will run him through all the easier."

Yvenne's amusement only deepened. Standing, she barely reached Cezan's shoulder. "It means the Parsathean has no fear of you. He does not respect you enough to armor his stomach or his heart. It is an insult that you do not even recognize without being told. And he *will* defeat you. Without effort. So you had best leave me here with him and flee as quickly as you can."

That was all true. His blood pounding slow and hot, Maddek tore his gaze from the woman and looked to her brother.

"This is what you would take to your bed, barbarian?" Irritatedly pushing his sister behind him, Cezan lifted his sword and regarded Maddek with insolent disdain. "She is a foul, treacherous, ugly stain upon our house."

"I will have her," Maddek said, though he had no intention of taking her to any bed. Instead she would never sleep easy again. "And your house will know my vengeance."

Cezan laughed. "Will you make her repay your mother's screams? Will you do to my sister all that we did to your queen?" His vicious gaze left Maddek and swept his Dragon. "You will need more male warriors—"

Abruptly his pale eyes rounded, mouth open in an agonized rictus. From between his gaping lips, a gout of foamy blood spurted over his chin and splattered down the front of his robes.

Shouts rose from the soldiers, horses snorting as their riders tensed, searching for the source of attack. Gaze scanning the trees, Maddek spun his mount to the side. None of his warriors had struck the man—though, like Maddek, they had been on the verge of it. If one more word had been spoken of their queen, they might have killed him. But someone had beaten them to it.

Had someone else come for Nyset's heir—?

Swiftly Maddek reined his mare back around just as Cezan fell to his knees, moonstone eyes rolling in their sockets.

Behind him Yvenne stood with her brother's bejeweled dagger clasped between her bound hands. Crimson dripped from her fingers and was a spreading stain down the white linens wrapping her forearms.

"I warned you to run," she told Cezan flatly before placing her foot against his back and shoving him dead to the ground.

All was silent but for the uneasy stamp of hooves that echoed the uneasy hearts of Syssian soldiers.

She looked to the nearest. "Did you witness that it was me and not the Parsathean who killed him?"

The soldier stared back at her wordlessly.

A weary sigh lifted her chest, but her voice only strengthened. She turned so that her moonstone gaze swept all of the soldiers. "Did you see that it was me? Did you see that I used the dagger he was fool enough to put within my reach?"

"Y–Yes." Visibly trembling, the soldier bowed his head. "My queen. We did not know you truly lived—"

"I am not yet queen. And as I was kept veiled and hidden, you could not have known. What is your name, soldier?"

"Jeppen, my lady." He sounded on the verge of tears.

"You and your fellow soldiers will have my gratitude, Jeppen, if you always speak the truth of what happened here." With her sandaled foot, she nudged her brother's body. "We could leave this for the scavengers, but it would likely turn their stomachs. Instead you will take him directly to the alliance council, so they might see the wound in his back to corroborate your story. Do *not* take him first to Zhalen or Bazir, for my father and brother might decide to make another story of it, and you would not be long for this life."

The soldier had gone deathly pale. "Yes, my lady."

Maddek tensed when two soldiers clambered down from the carriage and approached the woman, but it was only to collect the body.

"Put it on one of the horses," Maddek told them, and they paused, as if in confusion. Patiently he said, "Unharness the horses from that overheavy carriage and ride them. But leave one."

The elegant creature was not sturdy enough to carry a Parsathean soldier for a full turn of the moon, but Nyset's heir must only weigh a feather.

Her skinned and bloodless corpse would weigh even less.

The soldiers looked to Yvenne, who nodded. Hastily they began unharnessing the horses.

"Now, Jeppen—I suggest you take the advice my brother

did not, and flee. Without me!" she said sharply when the
soldier reached for her, as if to swing her up onto the horse
behind him. "I stay with the Parsatheans willingly. Tell the
council that, as well. Though they likely will not believe it,
hold to that truth. And I will return for you and the others
as queen, Jeppen." Her voice softened now. "Tell them all
that I will come. My father's rule will end."

"Yes, my lady," he said thickly.

Her pale gaze returned to Maddek, but she still spoke to
the soldier. "Go now. Directly to the council. Stop for nothing."

Immediately they complied, with Cezan's body draped
over the back of the last horse. She did not turn to watch
them leave. As the sound of their pounding hooves retreated
down the hill, she tossed the jeweled dagger to the ground
and stood with her arms dangling loosely in front of her, long
blue sleeves concealing her bound and bloodied hands.

"I am yours to do with what you will, Ran Maddek," she
said.

What you will. That will was vengeance. But although
Maddek still rode that purpose, his anger seemed unseated—
completely thrown by this woman.

Nor was it only he. When Maddek glanced back, his warriors appeared in turns bemused and bewildered, looking at
each other as if to confirm what they'd seen had indeed just
happened before their eyes.

She waited silently.

His gaze upon her again, Maddek dismounted and approached her. "You throw yourself upon my mercy?"

"Do you have any?"

"No." Not for her.

That seemed not to disturb her. She held out her bound
hands. "Will you free me?"

"No." So easily had she plunged a dagger into her brother's back that Maddek would not soon trust those hands,
bound or not.

"Perhaps for the best." Her sudden grin revealed straight
white teeth. "I am treacherous and foul and ugly."

Treacherous, yes. Foul, he knew not. And though not ugly as her brother had claimed, she was a thin and sickly-looking thing, with a yellow tinge to her brown skin. Not just sallow but dull, as if never touched by the sun's glow. Despite her natural color she was as pale as the children who lived beneath the shadow of Ephorn's wall.

And those eyes. Maddek wanted to look away from her eerie, piercing gaze but could not. Both the desire and his inability irritated him.

She had no similar trouble, however. Easily she glanced away, turning toward the carriage and sweeping aside the curtain.

Maddek's sword in her path stopped her from reaching inside.

"No threat lies within," she told him. "Only a satchel that holds my wedding robes."

"You will have no need for clothes."

Her dark eyebrows arched, eyes widening. Her head tilted back as she gave him a searching look. "Perhaps I will not," she finally said. "But these raiments have been passed through a line of Syssian queens. Should they fall into the hands of travelers who happen upon this carriage, and those travelers wear them, my father might recognize the robes and punish them for theft—or try to create a story in which I was set upon by bandits, and use it as an excuse to raze innocent homes and villages. Just as he used a false story to justify killing your father."

Fierce elation gripped his heart. "A false story?"

Her pale gaze locked to his. "Your father did not touch me or any other woman within the house."

"Tell the council."

"To what purpose?" She gave the blade in front of her a significant glance. "Anything I say will be doubted. They will believe that you threatened my life and forced me to lie. Only one of Justice's swords could confirm my truth—and when have you ever seen Chaliq's judges in Ephorn? Can you imagine one in Muda's court?"

No. Chaliq's wandering judges did not often venture into

Muda's cities, because the entire world trembled when Law and Justice were in discord.

The world should be trembling now. It should tremble until his queen and king had been avenged.

And Maddek was finding his anger again.

Perhaps Yvenne saw it. Carefully stepping back from the carriage, she asked him, "You came for me, Ran Maddek. With what intention, if not marriage?"

Marriage to a woman who had lured his parents to their murders? Everything within him revolted at the thought.

"I have no *intention*," he spat. "I *will* visit my wrath upon you." Sheathing his sword, he stepped closer until his height forced her head back, her pale gaze never leaving his. "I would have my vengeance upon your father and brothers all, but on this day I will settle for you. My queen and king traveled to Syssia at your request. Is that true?"

On a deep breath, she inclined her head before meeting his eyes again.

Though her gaze did not waver, a tremor shook her when Maddek gripped her bound wrists and raised her fisted hands to his mouth. "Then perhaps I shall start by biting off the fingers that wrote the treacherous message."

"And finish what my father began?"

That was not the response he expected. Frowning, he glanced at her hands as she unrolled her fists and spread her fingers.

Two were missing from her right hand—the first and second fingers, leaving only her thumb and two weakest fingers. The stumps appeared evenly matched, as if they'd been severed above the knuckle with a single blade.

"Your mother did not kill my brother Lazen when she attempted to escape," she said. "Though it was with the bow she made that *I* killed him, while trying to help her flee. My father made certain I could never draw a bowstring again."

That was what a treacherous liar would say to save herself. But there would be no escape for her, just as there had not been for his mother.

His gaze on hers, Maddek suckled her brother's lifeblood

from her remaining fingers, then licked between the stumps and down her bloodied palm. Her breath shuddered, clammy perspiration dotting her upper lip. His tongue pressed against her inner wrist, above the crimson-drenched ropes. Her pulse thundered through her veins.

Her blood raced as quickly as his did. But soon hers would spill onto the ground.

She swallowed thickly before telling him, "If you intend to kill me, I only beg that you do it quickly. My life has been a torment. I pray my death will not be."

The fear in her voice did not please him as much as the taste of her brother's blood did. The fear *should* have pleased him, for she had been the reason his parents had entered that drepa's nest, and so she was the reason he had to speak the words, "Was my mother's death quick?"

Shadows passed through her pale eyes. "No."

Anger speared through him anew. "A beheading is not quick?"

"That was how it ended." A heavy rasp deepened her reply. "But that was not how her death began."

She was fool enough to tell him this? Did she hope her words would spur him to rage, to a quick end? She would not have that wish.

"And so it will be for you," he said. "Very long, very slow, and all the pain that was visited upon my mother and father will be visited upon you." Releasing her wrists, he gripped her slender neck in one hand, the silver claw at his thumb pressing into the vulnerable flesh beneath her jaw. "Now I only have to decide where to start."

In a voice strained by the pressure upon her throat, she told him, "By taking me as your wife."

Maddek laughed.

Her laborious swallow worked the muscles of her throat against his fingers. Her moonstone eyes were steady on his. "If you truly wish to destroy my father and brothers, take me as your wife. Nyset's line passes through the female and I can claim the throne when I have reached a queen's age— or when I bear a child."

His laugh fell silent, his body still.

"As my husband, you could take everything of value to my father. And when Zhalen is not a regent king, who will care if you claim his head? When I remove my brother Bazir from his position as council minister, who will care if you kill him? Not I. I would do it myself if I could."

His gaze skimmed down her trembling form. "I could simply rut upon you until you bear a child."

"You could. But without marriage, you have no claim on the child. Without marriage, you cannot share my throne."

"What do I care of your throne?"

"Because as long as my father sits upon it, you will have a weak and rotted state at Parsathe's southwestern border. If the Destroyer comes, my father would turn against the alliance in an attempt to save himself, my brother Aezil would join him, and together they would strike at your people first."

Or perhaps they would not wait for the Destroyer. Zhalen and his son ruled the two realms on Parsathe's southern border, so perhaps they believed the Burning Plains might be easily taken.

And perhaps that was why Zhalen's daughter wished to be Maddek's bride. She would wait until his back was turned and bury her dagger between his ribs.

Even if she killed him, never would her family conquer his people. "All of the realms could band together and still they would not defeat our warriors."

"This I know." Again her throat worked, her voice hoarsened by the pressure of his fingers. "Just as I know that it would be my people who would suffer because of my father's ambitions. Better peace and a strong alliance than war between Syssia and Parsathe."

As his parents would have wanted. But they deserved more than peace. And they deserved better than a son who would ally himself with the woman who'd conspired against them. "You only hope to save yourself now that you will not marry Toleh's king and spread your father's poison there. But you will *not* have Parsathe."

"I do not want Toleh's throne. I want my own. But I cannot take it alone, for my father and brothers will not easily let it go. I need your strength and seed to claim it." Her breath wheezed harshly through her lips but her gaze still held his. "And it would be more painful for my father to see you seated upon Syssia's throne. He despises the Parsatheans. He has never forgiven the raids that weakened his family's holdings in Rugus before the alliance was established. It is your people he blames for not being directly in line for the Rugusian crown, and for having to marry a Syssian to secure the power he believes he deserves. If a Parsathean took that power from him now . . ."

It would be humiliation on top of vengeance. Against her father. Against her brothers. Maddek's eyes narrowed. "Why would you take part in this?"

Sudden fury burned in her gaze. "Because I hate my father more than you ever could. My brothers, too—except for the youngest. You wish for vengeance? It is *nothing* compared to my wish. I will not rest until they are dead."

Then she had made a fine start by killing her brother. But although her anger spoke to his, Maddek did not trust it. His hand tightened. "Yet you lured my mother and father so that your regent could kill them?"

"I did not beg them to come for my father's sake. I begged them to come for *mine*." The force of the word vibrated through the silver claws at his fingertips. "I wrote to them that an alliance between us would be beneficial to both our peoples but I needed help to escape Zhalen. I did not know my messenger had been found out until too late."

His gaze searched her face for truth. He knew not if he saw it but the pressure of his fingers softened.

She dragged in a long breath to say, "That is why my father killed your parents—to stop a marriage between us. Your parents came to see if I could earn their approval. And I would have. But my father wanted me to marry Toleh's king because that old man is more easily controlled. Never could my father control you."

The last was truth but Maddek could not believe the rest.

"You lie now to save your life. My mother would never approve of such as you." Even if this woman genuinely had sought an alliance, she was not what his mother would have chosen. "You are not strong enough to be a Parsathean queen."

Now her breath shuddered and pain flittered through her eyes. "She did say that upon meeting me."

"Is that why you conspired in their murder—her rejection pricked your vanity?"

"What vanity?" A laugh shook through her. "I know my strength is nothing. I am small. My muscles are soft. Yet I could lie beneath a man even of your size and bear his children, and that is all I need to do. That is all my father would have me do. But I could be *more* for you." Her amusement faded with every word and now she looked at him solemnly. "And your mother said that I was not strong enough upon *meeting* me. She believed differently after knowing me."

Only during a short time could his mother have known her. "During her captivity? While she was interrogated and tortured?" Rage came upon him full again. "You will never speak of her. Your lies defile her memory."

"I would not lie to you," she immediately returned. "Your mother told me that as your intended bride, I can never speak with a sly tongue or break an oath."

She would use these words against him, too? She would claim that his queen and mother had loved this treacherous woman enough to give her to Maddek as a bride? The woman's own bloodied fingers betrayed her lies, for his mother's silver crest did not sit upon her thumb.

His heart a ragged and gaping wound, he grated out, "Do you *ever* speak of my mother again without my asking you, I will rip out your lying tongue. I vow it."

Instantly her expression froze. Her gaze searched his for a long moment before she said thickly, "As you say."

He let go of her throat, then immediately dragged her closer. With his hand wrapped around the back of her neck, he lowered his fierce gaze to hers. "If I take you to wife, your life will be as a dog's. All you will know is pain and you will wish yourself dead."

Equally fierce, she said, "All I have *ever* known is pain. So use me to avenge your queen and king, if you must. Through your vengeance I will also have mine. To see my people freed, to see my father and brothers destroyed, I will bear *anything.*"

So would Maddek. But marrying her would not be a burden only he would bear. A Parsathean married but once, and those vows were never taken lightly.

And if he was named Ran, she would be queen.

He could hear the echo of her voice telling the soldier that she would return. Her promise that her father's rule would end. That was the voice of a woman who cared for her people. But would she care for his?

As if reading his doubts upon his face, she boldly claimed, "I will be a strong queen. I come from a line of strong queens."

That was true. "But they were warrior-queens," he said, and could not stop the mocking curl of his lips. "You are not."

Her gaze did not falter. "Wars are not won with swords."

"Are they won in throne rooms?" His bitter laugh sounded between them. "They *are* won with swords and you are a fool to believe anything else."

Yvenne regarded him without response for many breaths— in the same way Maddek might study a fractious mount while deciding how best to make it settle: a firm voice, a gentle touch, or a sweet bribe.

She must have chosen the bribe, for she said, "Our children will be born of the legendary warriors of your line and mine. The blood of Nyset runs in my veins. Do you think your people will not be proud to see Vela's pearled moon in our children's eyes? To claim such blessed ancestry for their own?"

They would be. And when he looked at her, even in anger and hatred and knowing the manipulative lies upon her tongue, he saw not how scrawny and sickly she was. He saw a woman shrewd and bold. He saw a queen.

A queen who would be *his*.

With that knowledge, his loins tightened when he looked upon those eerie eyes. Goddesses were beyond his ken but he could not deny the strength of her bloodline—a strength that would mingle with his own.

He wanted that strength. That blood.

His fingers tightened on the back of her neck. "Then lie upon the ground. I will take you to wife, but only after you are bred."

It would all be for naught if they married and he discovered she was barren.

Her breath caught, eyes flaring wide. "You would have me now?"

"Now." Because the need was urgent and hot upon him. Dragging her closer, he let her feel the rise of hot steel.

Let this be vengeance. For now.

Though it did her no good, her bound hands shoved against his chest. "You court the wrath of Vela."

Because the goddess had been forced by her brother Enam, the sun god. During that rape, the twins Law and Justice were conceived, and now Vela cursed those who forced themselves on another.

Maddek had no intention of forcing her. He intended for her to submit. "You have already consented to be the vessel for my seed."

"And I would consent to lie beneath you now. But I have not yet had my moon night."

The goddess Vela demanded a virgin's blood as her due, and so both men and women took their first lovers beneath Vela's full, shining face. On his own moon night, Maddek had shed a crimson drop for the goddess with the prick of a silver claw against the base of his throat.

"You never have taken another to your bed?" If true, it would be a tennight before she could take him.

But that would be for the best, too. If he fucked her in haste, Maddek could not be certain any child was his.

"No." A laugh shook her body against the heated length of his. "Zhalen guarded my cunt more closely than his horde of gold. I only needed a child to take the throne from him."

"And you could not lure a guard?" He studied her sallow features. "Perhaps not."

Her laugh only deepened, and the sound forged the steel hardness of his cock thicker and longer. "What man ever cared for a pretty face over opened thighs? But what would come of it? My father had to approve every morsel that passed my lips. If he ever suspected I was with child, he would make certain I drank the half-moon milk."

The same drink that his female warriors took once every moon cycle to prevent a pregnancy. In small doses, it did. But given a large dose while already with child, it would force the woman to miscarry.

Her piercing moonstone gaze caught his again. "I need no husband to be a queen, Maddek of Parsathe. What I need is a warrior's protection and his seed. If you can provide that, if you can help me destroy my father and my brothers, then you will have your vengeance and the strength of my throne behind you."

Vengeance, and an alliance free of Zhalen's corruption. He only had to shackle this sickly, treacherous woman to his side for the rest of his life.

Or for the rest of hers.

With his heart burning in his chest, he told her, "Then let it be done."

CHAPTER 5

YVENNE

Anger and hurt had lived together within Yvenne for so many years that she no longer knew the difference between them. Rage was the bite of the bindings around her wrists as Maddek dragged her to the horse her soldiers had unharnessed from the carriage. Fury was the pain shooting through her knee as she stumbled after him.

Now the hurt was all the sharper because, for a short time, the anger had gone. For a short time, she hadn't felt hunger gnawing at her belly. She hadn't felt the phantoms of her severed fingers or the itch of healing scars upon her back. Even the agony of her once-shattered knee had been nothing, though the stiffened joint had collapsed when Cezan pulled her from the carriage.

All the pain and anger had vanished when she'd looked upon the man who would be her husband. When she'd seen that his dark gaze did not falter as he met her eyes. When she'd seen the arrogance and confidence of that bared chest and the strength of steely muscle. When she'd seen the leather guards over her shoulders and arms, the black-painted brow, and the silver claws that declared war upon her father without speaking a word.

He was everything his mother had claimed he was—fierce and proud and strong, savagery contained through sheer will.

His mother had also said he would be a great king. Ran Ashev had not spoken false, but Yvenne had not listened closely enough to her words. Now she cleaved to them. He *would* be a great king.

But *now* he was only a warrior. A warrior who had not come to marry her but to kill her.

So pain and anger returned—though deeper than before. There was a new hurt to add, because her own heart had betrayed her. She had hoped for too much.

By this age, one would have thought she knew better.

But she would not yield to despair. For although her heart had betrayed her, it was still beating within her chest. And she would be married. She would be free of her father. She would have her vengeance.

And she *would* make a king of Maddek.

Abruptly he released her wrists and she almost staggered into his broad back—though if she had, her slight form would have scarcely made an impact against his. Her eyes were barely on level with the tips of the black braids that were gathered in a thong at his nape and fell in a thick rope to the points of his shoulder blades. Bronze skin flowed over rugged plains of muscle that hugged the valley of his spine. Silver-fingered Rani's winged dragon decorated the carved ivory face of the scabbard that sheathed the curved sword slung across his back from shoulder to opposite hip.

The horse whinnied, shying nervously away at his approach. His big hands were gentle as he calmed the animal, his silver claws gleaming against the horse's russet coat.

Hoofbeats pounded up the road—a mounted Parsathean warrior, perhaps one that had been scouting within the forest and was now joining the others. Two wolves ran at the heels of his horse, which was so tall and muscular it could have carried upon its back the horse Maddek soothed now.

The rumored size and strength of a Parsathean steed had apparently not been exaggerated. Nor were the size and strength of the warriors who rode them.

There were six warriors in all, four men and two women. All wore armor similar to Maddek's, with spaulders and vambraces bound in pebbled drepa skin to guard their shoulders and arms, and their chests bare—except for one of the women, who wore a binding around her breasts. But aside from their armor and their dark coloring, they appeared not much alike in features or in age. And if they had different temperaments, Yvenne could not tell, for at the moment they all regarded her with the same expression. Each one studied her as curiously as she did them—though perhaps for a different reason. Yvenne wondered what sort of warriors had been chosen to serve as his Dragon.

They likely wondered why she was not bleeding and screaming.

But although they all seemed filled with questions, they deferred to the barrel-chested warrior whose broad axe hung heavily from his wide leather belt. A ragged white scar cut across his left eye and cheek.

Allowing him to be the first to question Maddek. He must be the head of the Dragon—the one who led the others.

"Are we bringing her with us, then?"

"We are." Maddek didn't turn away from the horse. His deep voice was pitched low, as if not to startle the creature. "She claims the message to our queen and king was sent in hopes of forming an alliance through marriage. She claims that she was not part of a plot to murder them."

She claims. He could not have stated his doubt more clearly.

And Yvenne could not fully explain, because he'd vowed to rip out her tongue if she spoke of his mother.

She did not doubt that vow, and she dared not lose her tongue. It was the only shield she had, and the only weapon—though now she had to wield her words more carefully than in the past.

She had not known how difficult it would be to always

speak the truth. Nor had she known that truth could seem to implicate her rather than prove her innocence.

Ran Ashev had warned Yvenne that Maddek would come to her in anger. But the queen had assured her that as soon as Yvenne spoke her truth, Maddek would hear her.

But she never had a chance to speak it. Nor could she now.

So she would say what truth was allowed. "I would not have sent my handmaid to the commander if I believed he would have reason to kill me rather than marry me."

The scarred warrior shared a quick glance with the woman mounted beside him. "You sent the Syssian woman to our camp?"

"I did, after my brother Tyzen informed me of the council's meeting with the commander. My handmaid pretended an illness so that she could remain behind in Ephorn and seek an audience with you."

Now the woman beside him spoke. Unlike the other female warrior, whose square face was undecorated, silver rings pierced her eyebrows and the upper curves of her ears. "She said you *lured* our queen and king."

"I only sought an alliance. I confess it was your commander I lured with those words. I believed anger might bestir him more quickly than an unsubstantiated claim of my existence."

They looked to Maddek then, but his back was still turned to them, his focus on the horse though it had finally calmed under his hands. Perhaps listening to her words— or waiting to hear those of his fellow warriors.

Yvenne pressed on before he silenced her again. "These many years my father has kept me hidden away. You have seen that even my soldiers had no real knowledge of my existence. I had hoped for rescue by your queen and king— but it is you who have rescued me, instead, from my father and from an unwanted marriage. For that, you have my endless gratitude."

And saying, she bowed her head—and *was* overwhelmed by a rush of gratefulness. For these warriors *had* saved her.

They looked at each other uneasily. Perhaps because they were unused to a queen bowing to them. Perhaps because they'd only saved her with the intention of watching her die. Perhaps because of what was yet unspoken.

The warrior who rode with the wolves spoke it. "You hope to marry Ran Maddek?"

Yvenne would not hope. She simply *would*. "If he gets me with child, upon its birth I can claim my throne. For that, I need no husband, but I *do* need protection from my father. And if we are married, your commander can be the one who removes my father from that seat. Zhalen will have no power, nor will my brothers—and the alliance council can have no argument if he then avenges the murders of your queen and king."

Fierce pleasure fired through the scarred warrior's expression. Through all of their faces, Yvenne saw. They yearned for vengeance as he did.

As she did.

The warrior looked to Maddek. "Is this your intention?"

Back stiff, Maddek inclined his head. And he only said, "Her wedding clothes are in the carriage," but that was answer enough. "Ardyl, you will tie her satchel to your saddle. Remove any weapons you find."

"And beware any vials," Yvenne added. "Syssians are best known for poisons."

With a sharp grin, the pierced woman dismounted and started for the carriage, along the way scooping up the jeweled dagger Yvenne had thrown to the ground.

"So that is why you almost mounted her while we watched," another warrior spoke up—the only one who wore furs over his shoulders, despite the warmth of the day, and who looked to be the youngest of them. "To get her with child."

"Toric and I will turn our backs if you wish to continue," the leader of the Dragon said, a jesting note to his words now.

No humor lightened Maddek's voice. "She has not yet had her moon night."

"That is unfortunate." His brow creasing, the scarred warrior looked her over from his height upon his horse. "The sooner you are with child, the more quickly Zhalen loses his throne. Will he come for you, my lady?"

"Yes," Yvenne said. "He will pursue us relentlessly."

One hand still upon the horse's neck, Maddek turned to glance at the warrior before meeting her gaze with the burning coldness of his. "I told your soldiers I would visit my vengeance upon you. Will he not believe you dead?"

"He will assume what Cezan did—that your intention in taking me was marriage. I am far more valuable as a bride than as a corpse."

His dark eyes did not waver from hers. "Your only value is in the pain it will cause your father."

Yvenne wanted her father to suffer, too. But if that was the only value Maddek saw in her, then he would never be a king worthy of the title.

Yet for now she would speak to the warrior in him. "As soon as the guards alert the council, Bazir will send soldiers after us. In two days, we will have all of Rugus and Syssia upon our heels."

And all of Rugus's and Syssia's territories lay between them and the Burning Plains.

Maddek looked to the scarred warrior. "What say you, Kelir?"

"They will expect us to race north and rejoin the army, finding safety in those numbers. But it will be difficult to catch them. Enox rides hard."

"So she does." Maddek looked to the gray-haired male warrior who had not yet spoken. "Banek?"

The older man replied slowly, as if weighing every word. "If we continue east, we will travel ahead of the news from the council. We could ride east and north through Rugus, then over the pass at the head of the Fallen Mountains."

Which would take them to the Burning Plains, though they would have to travel west again to reach the heart of Parsathe.

The second woman spoke. "West. To the sea."

The Boiling Sea, which marked the western edge of Syssian and Gogean territory.

"And through Syssia as we originally planned?" Kelir asked before glancing quickly at Yvenne. "But without a flayed corpse to toss over the city wall."

Her brows rose and she looked to Maddek. "That was to be my corpse?" At his nod, she pursed her lips. It would not have pained her father to see her dead, but it would have angered him terribly to know that his attempts to secure power in Toleh had been thwarted along with her marriage. Losing a son, though? "I wish I had thought to flay Cezan and do the same."

A snort of laughter came from Ardyl. "You still can. If we ride west, no doubt we will overtake the guards who escort his body."

The warrior with the wolves did not laugh. "And the guards would tell the council—and Bazir—of our direction. We cannot go west upon this road."

Kelir nodded his agreement. "Or by the same route as the bridal caravan. That road is too heavily traveled and there are too many eyes to see us. They know we will travel home. But there are many paths north, and it is better not to reveal the one we take."

"Yes." Maddek stroked his silver-tipped fingers down the horse's neck. "We will go west to the sea."

With satchel in hand, a frowning Ardyl mounted her horse again. "Through Syssia?"

"Through Goge," he said. "Any time lost spent traveling south can be recovered on the ship that will take us north across the water. Then east to Kilren."

The Parsathean city built after the alliance had been formed. Yet more than a city had been built after the formation of the alliance, Yvenne knew.

"What of the Syssian outpost?" Which lay north of Syssia, at the western edge of Parsathean territory. "If they realize the route we've taken, my father's soldiers might intercept us."

A hard smile touched Maddek's mouth. "And attempt to take my bride?"

He hoped for such an attack, Yvenne realized. Because it would be in Parsathean territory, and he could retaliate according to Parsathean law. The alliance council could say nothing, because they had called it justified when Zhalen had retaliated for a similar personal attack.

Her chest tightened. Before an attack came, she needed to be pregnant and married to him. Or he would have no use for her.

And no reason to allow her to live.

The hard triumph in his smile said that he was thinking the same. It mattered not to him how he avenged his parents, as long as he did. And he could easily be rid of her if Zhalen ordered his soldiers to move against them upon the Burning Plains.

No doubt he would take her to his bed during their journey, because he would be a fool to place all his hopes on an attack from an outpost. But if that assault came, no need to marry her or to help her secure her throne.

Anger and pain rose together, hot and aching in her throat.

In five winters, she would be a queen's age and could have taken her crown without issue. If she had possessed the strength of her foremothers, she could have easily killed her father—or escaped and waited the five years before approaching the council. She wouldn't have needed protection or to throw herself upon the mercy of a warrior who had none.

But she did not possess that strength. Only courage and wits and rage.

The heat of the last seemed not to touch Maddek. Dismissing her, he looked to his warriors. "We will ride south through the forest until we reach the ridge path that will take us to Goge."

Trepidation gripped her heart. Yvenne had not expected an easy journey, but she had thought it would be upon a road. "*Through* the forest?"

"Yes." He turned those cold eyes upon her again, contemptuous as they swept her from head to foot. "If you did not rest within your carriage, you'll wish you had. Because it will be unlike any ride you've ever known."

"That is truth. For I have never sat upon a horse."

Utter silence fell over his warriors. Disbelief crossed their expressions, followed by humor—as if they thought she must be joking.

Then a harsh laugh ripped from Maddek and he looked to the others. "Yet she hopes to be a Parsathean queen?"

Their laughter joined his, and although theirs did not hold the same scorn, humiliation burned in her face.

Yet she had nothing of which to be ashamed.

She turned her gaze upon the warriors. Few people could look directly into her moonstone eyes without wavering, and they proved no exception.

Their laughter came more uneasily and they averted their eyes even as she said, "My father imprisoned me in a tower chamber from the day of my birth. There was not much opportunity for riding."

Uneasy laughter fell to shamed silence.

Maddek was not shamed. Instead their reaction seemed to anger her would-be husband. Expression hardening, he told the warriors, "Make ready for the ride."

There could not be much to make ready, but as they turned their horses away and rode a short distance down the hill, she realized that it was a signal to leave them alone.

Watching his face, Yvenne waited.

She had been told he was handsome—and indeed, it seemed to her that he possessed the finest face she had ever seen. So fascinating to look upon, his cheekbones high and jaw strong. A bold, straight nose sat over wide, firm lips. The black paint upon his brow deepened the intensity of his dark stare. He wore a short beard, which was unusual in Parsathean warriors—but he had been traveling and grieving, so perhaps there was reason he was not clean-shaven.

His gaze still did not falter from hers. Even Ran Ashev had confessed she found it difficult to meet Yvenne's eyes for any length of time. Yet earlier Maddek had looked into her eyes and not only held her gaze—he had been aroused by it.

He was now, too. She saw it in the flush of his skin, the flaring of his nostrils.

Yvenne had little experience with men beyond her own family and what her mother had described of them—but she was no stranger to punishment and recognized when one was upon her. This was arousal born of anger, not desire. Maddek intended to please himself by humiliating her.

Coming closer, he looked down upon her. His big hand gripped a thick bulge through his red linens. "You will ready me for the ride, and ease this discomfort since I cannot ease it between your thighs."

She would have wagered her throne that he had ridden without complaint under far worse discomfort than he suffered now. But she had agreed to serve as the vessel for his vengeance.

"How would you have me ease it?"

His burning gaze fell to her mouth. "I think I should not trust your teeth."

She smiled up at him, displaying how very sharp and strong those teeth were. "Perhaps not."

"Your hands, then."

"And will you untie me?"

Slowly he shook his head, his gaze still holding hers.

"Then you will need to unfasten your belt for me," she told him reasonably, "for I cannot unfasten it with my hands bound."

His color heightened, his anger heating. Because he'd expected her to balk, she realized.

She never would. Best he learned that now.

Gaze on hers, he crowded closer. And by Vela's moonglazed sword, she could feel the heat of his body through her robes. The sheer expanse of him seemed to swallow the world. Her head tilted back so that she would not look away from his eyes, and his head was bent as he held her gaze. Challenge burned between them.

He did not unfasten his belt. When he gripped her hands and drew her even closer, she discovered that he'd simply gathered up the linen.

She could not stop the shudder of her breath when her fingers wrapped around his heated length. Temra had been generous upon his creation, and his steel cock burned like a brand between her palms.

His teeth gritted. Disgust? Pleasure? Yvenne knew not. She only knew his anger as it filled the distance between them.

Sensing it, her own rage rose—anger at him, for being this man who had made her heart betray itself with hope. He had already closed his ears to her. Now he would punish her?

She lifted her chin. "What now, warrior?"

"Stroke me," he said with clenched jaw. "As if your hands are a sheath that I would fuck."

A sheath. Her fingers circled him. The grasp of her right hand was weak, but her left hand was still strong. Upward she stroked his length, his skin softer than she expected, her fingers both sticky and slick.

"A sheath wet with my brother's blood," she told him, and watched the hot flare of his eyes. "Does that please you, warrior?"

It did. Because although he gave no answer, his thick cock responded with a pulse against her palms, growing harder in her grip. Down she stroked, feeling an answering pulse deep within her body, a rising liquid heat as unexpected as it was sweet.

This was not punishment at all. For as strong as Maddek was, she did not think he could have stopped her now if he'd wanted to. She might serve as a vessel for his vengeance, but his pleasure was in her hands.

So she took her pleasure in this, too. Pleasure in knowing her own vengeance would soon be had. Pleasure in the steel of his cock and the strength of his arousal. Pleasure in the heated response of her body. She was uncertain whether she responded to his strength or to the unexpected power she wielded over him—but it mattered not.

She'd had so little pleasure in her life, she would take this and be glad of it.

He sucked in a breath through gritted teeth. "Harder."

She did and then gave him more. "Do you know how it felt to slip the dagger into Cezan's flesh, to feel his lifeblood spill over my fingers?" The groan low in Maddek's chest said he imagined it, but he could not possibly take the same pleasure as she had. And would not take the pleasure he *should*, because he had forbidden her from telling him anything of his mother. What Cezan had done to Ran Ashev was not the only reason Yvenne had slid that blade through her brother's ribs and into his heart, however. "Today he hit me. But a year past, he threatened to silence me by stuffing my mouth full of his cock—and it was also only fear of my teeth that stopped him."

Maddek's lids had grown heavy, though he still held her gaze, but upon hearing her, his eyes met hers again fully.

Now the anger there was not only directed at her.

She stroked him harder, faster. "Fortunately for Cezan, he did not ask for my hands instead, as you did. I would have ripped him apart." Gently her fingers slid down to cup his sac. "But you, warrior—I will take your seed as often as you like. I care not how you give it to me. Upon my mouth, my hands, or deep inside me."

A tremor worked through him. Still his gaze burned on hers.

Her fingers worked the length of his shaft and her voice worked upon the furnace of his heart. "I *will* be your queen, warrior. And I look forward to the full moon, when the blood and the wetness upon your cock are not my brother's but mine, after you have thrust your sword into my virgin sheath and spilled your seed. For when that seed takes root, we will have the vengeance we both desire."

The tremor that worked through him turned into a violent shudder. His chest lifted on a great breath and his thick length pulsed into her hands, and she held his gaze as she used the wetness of his spend to continue stroking him.

Until he pushed her hands away, his teeth clenched as if her touch were now too much to bear.

Smiling up at him, she raised fingers pearled with his seed to her mouth, and licked them as he had licked Cezan's blood from hers. The lingering metallic flavor of that mingled with the salt of his spend.

Maddek's seed and her brother's blood. Yes, she took great pleasure in drawing both.

His eyes heated again, watching her. Still he said not a word, but his gaze finally broke from hers when he stepped forward and his hands circled her waist.

Easily he lifted her astride the horse. A glance down the road revealed that his warriors had all turned away from them.

And her anger was not completely spent. As his hands slid from her waist, she snatched the point of his beard in her sticky, bound hands and dragged his gaze back to hers.

"Treat me as you wish when there are no eyes to see, warrior," she hissed fiercely. "But when we are with others, you will treat me as your queen."

His eyes narrowed. "I will treat you according to your worth."

"You fool," she said, and did not balk now, either, though the anger in his eyes burned hotter than she had yet seen. "I am to be your wife, and as such, I am under your protection. If your people see you treat me as a dog, though I am a woman you are obligated to protect, then they will not trust you to care for *them* as you should. They will not trust you to fulfill any obligation."

"They will not care of obligations when they see you. They will only see the daughter of the man who killed their queen and king."

That was what *he* saw. "I will make no secret of my hatred for Zhalen. I will tell them you saved me from an unwanted marriage to Toleh's king and won me to secure a new and stronger alliance between our nations. I will say I was abused and controlled by my father and brothers. That is not something the Parsathe look kindly upon, is it?"

Maddek gave no answer, but he did not need to. For the Parsathe took care of their own. Abuse and neglect were not tolerated.

"Their hatred of my father will not extend to me unless you allow it," she told him. "No one even knows of me to hate me."

"Perhaps they will never know of you." Coldly he pried her fingers from his beard and placed her hand upon the horse's coarse brown mane. "Hold fast, daughter of Zhalen. Because if you fall, my warriors and I will not halt for you. We will leave you for the beasts of the forests to find—or your father."

A fate more terrifying than anything a beast might do. "And what of your vengeance?"

"It is already in motion. Zhalen believes I have you, and he will come for me. Your throne and bloodline would sweeten my vengeance, but you are useful to me as a wife or a corpse." He paused and his deep voice took on the solemnity of a vow. "And know this, Nyset's heir—if you are too weak to keep up, if the Syssian or the Rugusian soldiers take you, I will not come for you. I will not risk my life or my warriors' lives to return for you. So you had best hold on."

Abruptly he left her, collecting her horse's long reins before mounting his own with an easy leap onto its back. He tied her reins to his saddle.

Without looking back, he urged his horse down the hill.

Yvenne's heart leapt on her mount's first step. She jolted forward, almost falling over its neck.

Yet they were only *walking*. She had no hope they would not set a much faster pace through the forest. Desperately she twisted her fingers in the long mane. She had held on her entire life.

This would be no different.

CHAPTER 6

MADDEK

With their strong hearts, the Parsathean horses could have run through the night—if they ran upon a road. But the forest had deepened, the uneven ground rising steadily as they climbed through the foothills toward the ridge separating Ephorn's lands from the Gogean plains, and soon their mounts were snorting with effort. Foamy sweat lathered their coats.

And even the strongest heart could not give a horse eyes to see through the dark.

Maddek slowed and dismounted. By torchlight he and his warriors walked, leading their mounts—except for Yvenne, who looked to have collapsed over her horse's neck, clinging to its dark mane with her face buried beside her bound hands.

Her mount seemed as exhausted, delicate head hanging low and sides heaving.

Kelir was studying that small horse as well. His gaze met Maddek's and the decision passed between them unspoken.

They would halt for the night. Maddek gestured to Fassad, who sent his dogs in search of water.

The hounds returned quickly, then led Fassad to a stream that tumbled down the rocky hillside. Maddek followed its path upward until he found an outcropping of boulders that would provide cover for their camp. The trees did not grow so thick here, though there was still little sky to see through the canopy—and no grazing available. They would not have let the horses forage, anyway. Instead their mounts would be kept close and quiet, so as not to attract the predators that hunted in these hills.

They would make camp, but the horses came first. Maddek untied Yvenne's reins from his saddle, and in the dim torchlight he saw that she had lifted her head but had not yet made a move to dismount.

The others were looking her way, as well—at the frail and sickly queen who could not ride. As she had never been on a horse before, she likely didn't know how to care for one.

"I will tend to her mount," Maddek told them before leading his to the stream. His mare would not bolt even if charged by a tusker, so he left the horse to drink her fill.

With his gelding waiting behind him, Banek had paused beside Yvenne. A blade flashed in his hand.

The back of Maddek's neck tightened, but the older warrior's posture was not tensed for attack, and his voice was pitched low as he told her, "My lady, let me help you."

Carefully the warrior slipped the dagger beneath her bound hands. Long strands of coarse hair floated to the forest floor.

The horse's mane. More strands were caught between her fingers—glued by dried blood and Maddek's seed—but she still had not uncurled her fists.

Even in the firelight, Maddek could see how her face paled when Banek gently pried her cramped fingers open.

Carefully the old warrior picked away clumps of mane from her palms and fingers. "Can you walk, my lady? It will help ease the stiffness."

Her reply was tight, so strained it was barely more than a whisper. "I will try."

Yvonne did not look over at Maddek's approach, but Banek did. As did the other warriors.

For the first time in Maddek's life, he saw reproach and censure in the warriors' eyes. He could almost hear it upon their tongues.

He probably *would* hear it upon their tongues when they had a moment alone. Or more damning—they would give him their silence.

Yvonne had spoken true. His people would think poorly of him if he visited his wrath upon her where they might see. Although his warriors also yearned for vengeance against her father and brothers, they had taken her word as truth. Perhaps they only believed her because Maddek had not killed her. Or perhaps they had recognized something in her he could not.

But queen or not, bride or not, she was a woman under his protection whom he had not protected.

Maddek could not treat her as a bride in front of his warriors and as a dog while alone, however. He could not pretend in that way. It would be as if speaking lies through every action.

So a choice needed to be made. Either he would take Yvonne at her word and accept that she had not plotted to kill his parents—or he would kill her for her part in that plot now.

Maddek could not force aside doubt—and he could not believe her claim that his mother had chosen her to be his wife. But if he would have his vengeance, then she must be his bride. So until she gave him reason to believe otherwise, he would also accept that she had only sent a message to his parents in hopes of forming an alliance.

And Temra be merciful if he ever discovered that she had spoken false, because Maddek would not be.

His gaze upon her pinched face, he told Banek, "I will tend to her. Our mounts—"

"Will be mine to care for this night, Ran Maddek." Respect returned to the older man's voice as his blade slipped through a dark cloth tied around Yvenne's waist.

Her veil, Maddek realized. At some point during the ride, she had fastened herself to the horse's chest harness by the leather strap that passed over the withers.

That would not have saved her if she'd slipped from its back. Better to fall clear than to slide beneath the horse's belly to be dragged or trampled by its hooves.

As soon as she was cut free of the horse, Maddek sliced through the bindings around her wrists and tossed the blood-stiffened ropes to the ground. His hands circled her narrow waist. She truly weighed a feather, the points of her hips softened only by the thin silk of her robes.

Cradling her slender form against his chest, he carried her upstream of the horses, to the very edge of the circle of light cast by the torches. Her body shook against his, though the night was warm. It must be fatigue and pain that made her tremble.

They could not travel at a slower pace. But Maddek could not let this happen again.

Beside the stream bed, he set her upon a flat stone. After rinsing his hands in the icy water, he cupped his palm and carried a handful to her lips.

She drank eagerly, her tongue flicking out to catch the last drops clinging to the side of his hand.

Licking those drops as she had earlier licked his seed and her brother's blood from her fingers. But there was no challenge burning within her moonstone eyes now. No arousal. Only exhaustion.

He ignored the hardening of his cock and brought her another palmful to drink, then wet the rags of her veil and began cleaning her hands.

Maddek could feel her gaze upon his face as he wiped away the blood and seed and hair. "The only remedy for a new rider's pain is to move the muscles that have stiffened. No matter if it hurts all the more when you do."

Fatigue thickened her voice. "I will bear it. I daresay the

pain of freedom is far more tolerable than the comfort of prison in my tower chamber."

So it must be. "It will be worse when you awaken, so it is best to stretch the muscles now. The stiffness will pass after a few days of riding."

Chin sinking low against her chest, she nodded. But despite her agreement, there would be no walking or stretching. Even as Maddek watched she fell asleep, slumping sideways upon the stone seat.

After wetting the rags again, he slid his arms beneath her legs and shoulders and carried her to camp. The horses were staked together near a large clump of trees, eating grain from their bags of feed. Maddek's warriors had laid out his furs beside the shelter of the large boulders. With Yvenne in his arms, he sank down upon them.

"We will leave at sunrise." At his announcement, he saw their surprise—and their approval. Usually they would set out at first light, long before the sun rose above the horizon. But one look at the woman in his arms told them why he allowed the extra time. "Take your own rest," he added. "I will keep watch."

For Maddek would not sleep. Vengeance blinded men. Tonight his eyes needed to remain open.

So he kept them open as he finished washing her hands. He still had doubts, but not everything she had spoken was a lie. She'd said her father had locked her away, and indeed her brown skin was as sallow as if she'd never seen the sun. She had also said her fingers were severed after killing her eldest brother, so that she could not draw a bowstring again.

Battle always left a mark. So it did here, when he looked with open eyes. The skin over the stumps of her missing fingers seemed thin and pink, as if only recently healed over. The remaining fingers were soft, but for a slight thickening at the tip of her third finger. A callus common to archers, though hers was not as rough or as hardened as a warrior's. Newer.

By the light of the torch, he unwrapped the bloodstained linens from her left wrist to elbow. Pale lines marked the thin skin at the inside of her forearm. He and every other Parsathean warrior wore leather vambraces to guard their forearms, yet he still recognized those stripes. They were from a bowstring snapping against the skin like the lash of a whip, and signaled a new archer who had not yet mastered her technique. By the appearance of her scars, the string had struck hard enough to break skin—and by the number of them, had made her bleed over and over. They indicated that she had recently learned to use a bow with a hard taskmaster to push her.

A hard taskmaster, as Maddek's mother had sometimes been.

Had Ran Ashev come to care for this woman? While imprisoned and tortured, had his mother tried to help Yvenne because she cared for and trusted the frail woman—or had his queen merely used Yvenne for her own ends?

Using her to aid in an escape that resulted in Ran Ashev's beheading.

His heart aching fiercely, Maddek wrapped Yvenne's forearm again. He knew not what to believe. He knew not what to trust. Did he betray his parents by keeping this woman alive? Did he risk his people by aligning himself with her?

Those answers were not visible upon her skin. But with open eyes, he saw what needed to be done. He saw how to best serve his parents and his people. He would use Yvenne for his own ends. He would protect her.

But he dared not care for her. Not when doubt still lived within him. Not when her claims might still be exposed as lies.

Not when his parents were still unavenged.

CHAPTER 7

YVENNE

Yvenne woke to darkness and a hard hand clamped over her mouth. At her back, a steely form held her tight, heavy arms and legs locked around her own. Panic struck, terror increasing when her struggles moved her captor not a bit.

A warning hiss of air in her ear made fear drop away. *Maddek.* It was Maddek who held her.

Heart pounding, she halted her struggles. Not all was darkness. Through the canopy of trees, the sky had lightened. Shapes and shadows resolved as her eyes accustomed themselves to the night.

Something huge moved through the dark. Yvenne stiffened again as a deep lowing sounded from high overhead—and close. So close. The noise was answered by another resonant call. The tread of heavy feet shivered through the ground. A dozen shadows passed. Some blocked all the light from above, others were smaller. Beneath the dim sky, she had the impression of smooth dappled skin, long necks and longer tails.

Giant reptilian foragers. But they were not foraging now. Instead the herd moved quickly through the forest.

Yet Maddek's tension did not seem like the simple tension of avoiding the bull or a protective cow with a calf. Because even after the foragers passed, still he held her silently, his back against the boulder, his hand over her mouth as if he expected her to startle or scream.

A nervous snort and the stamp of hooves drew her gaze to the horses staked near the trees. Restless, they were all in motion, pulling at their tethers.

Then settling as two forms flitted around their legs. Fassad's wolves. As if their presence were a calming hand from the warrior himself, the horses went still.

Except for Yvenne's mount. The wolves only agitated the smaller horse more. It reared against the leather lines, its panicked neigh ringing through the forest. Behind her, Maddek's body stiffened, and Yvenne realized that what she had thought was steel tension was only the resting hardness of his form.

Now he was tense.

A tremor shook the ground. Another.

Not the foragers returning.

Right hand still clamped over her mouth, Maddek released her waist and signaled with his left. Through the dark, a form peeled away from a tree. Silver rings glinted upon her face—Ardyl. Even as the earth shivered again, the warrior darted toward the horses.

Not to calm Yvenne's mount, as she thought. Instead Ardyl's blade flashed and sliced through the tether. The warrior melted into the shadows between the other horses as Yvenne's broke away, whinnying and wildly tossing its head.

A roar ripped through the darkness. Though Yvenne had known a predator must be out there, never had she heard anything so loud as that roar. Instinctual terror jolted through her limbs. Maddek's arm wrapped around her stomach again as if to prevent her from bolting, his broad palm muffling the fearful whimper she couldn't halt.

The frantic horse screamed, wheeling around on its hind legs to run. Too late. Thunder seemed to shake the small clearing and death rushed out from the dark. Huge jaws clamped onto the horse's hindquarters and tossed the animal off its hooves with a vicious shake of its thick neck.

Hind legs useless, the horse thrashed on the ground. Its shrill neighs pierced the night. Huge talons pinned the barrel chest and with a mighty clamp and twist of jaws, the horse's neck broke.

Silence fell. Shaking uncontrollably, Yvenne watched as the trap jaw lifted its broad head, snout raised to snort the air. Her mother had described the giant reptiles to her before. Never had she imagined the predator's sheer size, the powerful haunches that seemed to overbalance the small arms, or the massive teeth. Never had she imagined its smell, thick and eye-watering, like a chamber pot left unemptied for a full turn of the moon. Its unblinking eyes searched the clearing, but although the trap jaw seemed to look directly at the other horses, even at Yvenne and Maddek, they were either not seen or deemed no threat—or the beast decided one horse was enough.

Lowering its enormous head, the trap jaw clamped giant teeth around the dead horse's shoulders and lifted the heavy animal. Legs dangling limply from its mouth, the predator carried the carcass from the clearing, its steps thunderous.

Maddek's big hand slid from her mouth to curve around the front of her throat—a calming touch, not to choke. "A bull," he told her softly, his deep voice low in her ear. "We might have killed it but that outcome is never certain. Better to lose a horse than a warrior. And better to lose one mount than to lose them all."

Yvenne had not questioned that. "Yes," she whispered.

His broad thumb stroked the line of her jaw. "You will take the half-moon milk this morn."

The drink that would force her menstrual blood to flow. Not to prevent pregnancy, as it was usually used, but to prove she was not already with child.

As would be best. Yvenne knew not what lies her father

would say to separate her from Maddek, and although she would go to him a virgin, not all women bled on their moon night. The half-moon milk would leave no uncertainty.

She nodded into his hand. "I need rags."

"I will speak to Ardyl and Danoh," he said. Then his body shifted behind hers and a wave of pain crashed through her every limb.

Only gritted teeth stopped her agonized scream. Frozen in place, she breathed shallowly. Everything hurt, as if her muscles were springs coiled to the breaking point and beaten with a steel rod.

Another agonized hiss escaped from between her teeth when Maddek's strong arm easily lifted her to her feet.

"You must walk." His voice was low but implacable. "Though it hurts."

Though it hurts. That was how she'd done everything her entire life. So she would this, too.

She shuffled toward the stream—and a laugh escaped her when she realized that, for the first time in as long as she could remember, her shattered knee ached no more than any other part of her. She was like a broken doll, put back together.

Put back together stronger.

Crouching beside the stream was a new agony, but she forced herself to sink to her heels and stand a handful of times before finally settling in to wash. The linens stained with her brother's blood had dried into an itchy and hardened cast around her forearms. Yvenne rinsed them as best she could. Her satchel held new linens but it seemed foolish to wear anything clean now, when travel would just soil it again.

Arms wrapped in wet cloth, she shivered while hobbling back to where the warriors had gathered in a circle to break their fast.

Fassad was skinning three lizards. Yvenne recognized their type. Scavengers, they often swarmed Syssia's refuse piles. With dark green skin lightly covered with scraggly dun feathers, they were the size of a dally bird—and she hoped as tasty.

The warrior offered Yvenne an apologetic look as he gave her a skinned leg. "We do not risk a fire this morning."

Raw, then. Her mouth already watered and her empty stomach had not a care.

She sank her teeth into the white meat and her entire body revolted. Never had she tasted *anything* so foul, as if the fresh meat had already rotted. But she chewed, gagging, then forced herself to swallow.

The warriors ripped into theirs. She did not even wonder if the manners of Parsatheans were as uncivilized as she'd heard, for there must be only one way to eat this lizard: as quickly as one could. Yvenne wished to eat as quickly as they did. But she could not manage the great tearing bites and swallows that Maddek took. Her throat would not allow her, revolting harder the bigger the mouthful she took—and the tiny bites she managed, she battled to keep down.

A throat cleared. "Do you see beyond what is seen?"

Her gaze flew to the young warrior who had asked it. Toric, who still wore furs over his broad shoulders though the others only wore the leather spaulders that served as light armor. The same braids fell back from his forehead, and his clean-shaven face was broad, his dark eyes holding hers—for the barest moment, before his gaze dropped.

All of them were looking to her. Each had finished with their lizard. And were waiting for her to finish, too, she realized.

So the Parsatheans' manners were not so different from a Syssian's—but their faces were. Oh, all the features were in the same places and the coloring was similar. Yet rarely did Syssians so plainly wear their thoughts and emotions. Fear, anger, even joy were hidden away.

These warriors concealed little. Now they watched her with undisguised curiosity.

"No," she said, returning her gaze to Toric. "Though my mother could, I have not that gift."

And was sorry for it. Her mother had taught her what lay beyond the walls of their tower chamber by using that sight.

After her death, seeing beyond the reach of her own eyes would have helped Yvenne many a time.

She might have known why Maddek had come for her.

"Not *that* gift?" Eyes narrowed on her, Maddek wiped his fingers on the red linen folded over his wide belt. "You have another?"

She met his gaze and he did not look away. "Not a gift as you mean—nothing that will benefit our alliance." Not after Zhalen severed her fingers. "I do not possess the goddess's sight. But I believe Vela has mine. I can feel her looking through me, seeing what I see."

Uneasiness seemed to pass through the warriors as they frowned and exchanged glances.

Kelir spoke. "Always? Even now?"

"Yes." Such a familiar touch at the back of her mind that Yvenne hardly noted it.

"She looks through you as she looks through a priestess?" That came from Banek, the older warrior who had shown her such kindness the previous night.

Yvenne could not answer him directly, for she had no knowledge of what a priestess did, only of what her mother had told her about the goddess. "I hope Vela also looks through them. I hope not all she knows of humans and men is what I have seen."

That thought appeared to unease the warriors, too—apart from Maddek, who only studied her with that unwavering gaze. "And what of your brothers? Their eyes are the same as yours."

"Yes. But they do not have Vela's sight."

"It is said that Aezil does. It is said that before taking Rugus's throne, he sacrificed one of his own eyes to gain the sight."

"That is said," Yvenne agreed. "I have no knowledge of its truth, however. Only that he *has* lost an eye. But my brother Tyzen, who serves as Rugus's minister, has seen no evidence of such dark magics. Thus far, it is all insubstantial rumor—perhaps even one started by Aezil himself, so that his missing eye would not be viewed as a weakness but as something to fear."

"You trust that minister's words?" Maddek's tone said that only a fool would.

"I do." Always would she believe her younger brother. And Tyzen had not said the rumors were false—only that he had not seen evidence of their truth. "I also believe Aezil would attempt that sacrifice if it gave him the power to see as my mother did. But it would not be Vela's sight that he would gain. He would need to appeal to another god. Stranik, perhaps—and we know his priests did the same."

The same priests that the alliance's army had defeated ten years before. She knew that Maddek had witnessed the horror of exactly how those priests had appealed to their god with the blood of Farian children.

Now darkness moved across his expression before his features hardened again. "Did Aezil poison King Latan?"

She took another bite of lizard and forced it down. "He did—after he, Lazen, and Cezan killed every heir that stood between my father and Latan. And then my father bragged of his success in finally securing the Rugusian throne for his line."

"Did Zhalen also brag when he murdered our king, and then our queen?"

His father and mother. Her chest tight, Yvenne simply nodded.

Sheer rage and grief seemed to take hold of his body. Rigidly he stared at her, eyes hot with loathing.

Ardyl's voice pierced the burning silence between them. "Is it true what your brother said—that Zhalen set his male warriors upon our queen?"

Bile that was more sour than the meat shot up Yvenne's throat. Anger tightened her fingers upon the bone.

"I cannot speak of her," Yvenne said.

Expression like stone, arms braced over his broad chest and feet squarely set as if prepared for a blow, Maddek told her, "This you may answer."

"Yes, he did," Yvenne spat with the force of all the hatred inside her. "He set upon her himself. As did his personal soldiers. As did my brothers Lazen and Cezan. There were many reasons for me to kill them both, but that was the most recent. So I rejoice in their deaths and their blood on my hands."

Eyes closed, face drawn into tortured lines, Maddek bowed his head. As did the others. Which was not just grief and rage, she realized. It was gratitude. Respect, because she had taken the vengeance they had not.

But an arrow through Lazen's throat and a dagger in Cezan's back had not been enough. It would never be enough.

Kelir's gaze was like fire. "Would that we had known before we let his carcass go."

Yvenne might have told them. But Maddek did not seem prepared to rescind his vow to tear out her tongue for speaking more.

"Where is Vela's curse upon them?" Ardyl's anger was directed toward Yvenne but seemed meant for the goddess instead. "If she sees as you do, then she would have known. By Vela's law, a rapist is cursed and should be punished. We have encountered those who have been marked and broken by her power. Yet Zhalen is not?"

Her rage echoed Yvenne's at a younger age. Now she gave the same answer Yvenne's mother had.

"Vela can only touch those who have invited her in." Such as those who quested for her, or the Nyrae warriors, or the priestesses who tended her temples.

Though even if an invitation was given, the goddess did not always accept. Yvenne's mother had prayed for Vela's strength, as had Yvenne.

But now she was glad the goddess had not answered and avenged Maddek's parents or her own mother. For instead Yvenne would do it herself.

Perhaps *that* was Vela's answer.

Ardyl's gaze finally fell away from hers, her voice bitter. "Then why does she not touch the nearest priestess and break Zhalen?"

"Because she does not need to," Yvenne said softly. "My father's curse is here. *I* am his curse." She looked to Maddek. "You are his curse. Are you not?"

"I am," he said gruffly, voice thick with emotion. New rage, new grief, new purpose.

Holding his gaze, she said, "I prefer to believe that Vela's gift is to allow us the satisfaction of breaking him. Will you not visit pain upon my father, agony as he has never known?"

His eyes gleamed. "I will."

Hanan's ruddy staff, how the bloodlust in his gaze spoke to hers. This was not only about vengeance, however, but also law and justice. Heart thundering, she looked to Ardyl again. "So you see. *We* are her curse. As are all rulers and citizens who do not allow such offenses to remain unpunished."

"And unpunished they will remain if we wait here much longer. We must ride," Maddek said to her, and reached for the lizard leg in her hand. "Discard the rest of that. You can hardly choke it down."

"Do *not* take it from me." Fiercely, she yanked it away from his reach. "I cannot remember the last time my belly was full. I *will* fill it, even if with this. I will finish it as we ride."

If she was to ride. Her horse was dead. Perhaps Maddek meant to leash her behind his mount and force her to run.

It mattered not. She would finish her meal while being pulled along the ground.

His dark eyes searched hers before he nodded. His gaze swept the others. "Ready, then."

The warriors broke from the circle, heading swiftly for their mounts. Yvenne could not move so quickly. She hobbled after Maddek, but when impatience darkened his expression and he bent as if to lift and carry her, she stopped him.

"You said I was to walk to ease the stiffness," she reminded him. "This is my only opportunity, unless you intend to drag me behind your horse."

"Do not tempt me," he said, but no heat was in it. Swiftly

he saddled his mount, fastening his rolled furs and satchel to the back.

Without ceremony, he gripped her waist and lifted her astride, then leapt up behind her.

And Yvenne was sorry her horse had been eaten, but this was much better than desperately clinging to its mane and praying she wouldn't be jolted from her seat as they raced through the forest. Never had she felt more secure than with Maddek's hard chest at her back and his arms at her sides. When his horse abruptly moved forward, she had no fear of falling.

With Maddek behind her, she had no fear at all.

They only went a few steps, to where Danoh stood beside her mount, sorting through a leather pouch tied to her saddle. Already astride, Ardyl joined them, a pile of rags in her lap and a vial in her hand.

At a glance from her, Danoh shook her head.

Uncertainty crossed Ardyl's decorated face when she looked to Maddek. "We have the half-moon milk but not the sleeping draught that accompanies it." Her gaze shifted to Yvenne's. "We have neither of us needed to drink it of late."

Because they had neither been intimate with a man of late, Yvenne understood. So there could be no pregnancy to prevent.

"Is it not effective without the sleeping draught?" Maddek's voice sounded behind her. Now that they were mounted, the top of her head came to his chin—their heights more even than when they were standing, but he still towered over her.

The two warriors exchanged an uneasy glance. "It is effective," Ardyl said. "But unpleasant."

"Then the sleeping draught matters not."

Ardyl's gaze turned withering. "You say that only because you have never taken the half-moon milk."

Neither had Yvenne, but she had little choice. "I will take it now so there can be no doubt that any child I conceive is Maddek's. You and the other warriors will be my witnesses."

With a heavy sigh, Ardyl nodded and poured a small measure of white liquid from the vial into the cap. "If Vela truly looks through your eyes, my lady, I pray that she will be merciful upon you now. And upon me for giving it to you," she added wryly.

Though the potion looked like milk, it tasted nothing of the sort, but rather chalky and bitter. Yvenne swallowed it down—and used the lingering bitterness in her mouth to mask the foul flavor of her next bite of lizard.

Danoh mounted her horse, then looked to Maddek. "Carry her as a babe this day."

His big hands circled Yvenne's waist again. Abruptly she found herself sitting sideways upon the saddle, with her legs dangling over his heavy thigh, her side against his bare chest, and his steely arm secured behind her.

Ardyl held out the rags. Yvenne hesitated, the lizard leg clutched in her left hand. She could not grip that bundle with only the weak fingers of her right hand.

Maddek took them instead, and her face flamed when he wasted not a moment parting her silk robes. His hand delved beneath her breechcloth. His callused fingers scraped the soft inner skin of her thighs, and she braced herself for some new humiliation as he had tried to visit upon her the previous day.

But he only tucked the rags securely against her and withdrew his hand, then gripped his reins.

"Let us ride," he said.

CHAPTER 8

MADDEK

Many warriors joked that an enemy could attack a Parsathean camp on the half moon and find half their army so deeply asleep that even the clash of swords would not wake them. In the morning, the women emerged from their furs with rags so bloodied, it seemed as if they'd fought in a battle—but it was simply that they had passed their menstrual blood in a single night rather than a handful of days.

Now Maddek understood why female warriors always took the potion at night—and why they drugged themselves with the powerful sleeping draught.

Rigid against him, Yvenne had curled forward with her arms crossed over her stomach, her skin sweating and cold. Not a sound passed her gritted teeth, not a single whimper or moan, but Maddek thought he could measure the depth of her pain by the shortness of her breaths. The faster and harder they hissed through her teeth, the greater the agony.

He ought to have waited until they had the sleeping draught. He ought to have heeded his warriors' warnings.

And never again would he ask Yvenne to drink the potion. By Temra's fist, he vowed it.

But this time could not be undone.

It was midafternoon when they emerged from the forest and onto the high ridge that overlooked the Gogean plains. Finally able to travel at full pace, the horses raced along the ridge track.

Though her stiff form had been jostling against him, Yvenne abruptly went lax in his arms, her head lolling forward against his bare chest.

Sudden dread gripped Maddek's throat as he let loose his reins to press his palm between her small breasts. Her thin ribs still rose and fell. Her heart still beat, stronger than he expected to find within a body so frail.

He tipped her chin back, examining her face. Her eyes were closed, her lips softly parted, her teeth no longer clenched. Though her brow was lightly furrowed, serenity claimed the rest of her features. She slept, then. Or had fainted from pain and exhaustion. Either was better than still enduring the half-moon milk.

Without slowing pace, Maddek shifted her limp body more securely against his. Dread returned when he saw the crimson stain that soaked through her robes and into the linens covering his thigh.

Chest tight, he glanced back at Ardyl but did not wait for the warrior to catch up to him. His mare was already responding to the pressure of Maddek's legs, the unthinking directions more effective than a pull on the reins.

Slowing, he rode closer to Ardyl's mount and lifted Yvenne's slight form to show her the blood.

"Is it too much?" It seemed too much. Maddek was certain that even his deepest wounds from the savages' knives had bled less than Yvenne did now.

Ardyl shook her head. "Likely she was close to her natural time."

About to begin her menses, anyway. So the half-moon milk would not have been necessary to ascertain whether she was already with child.

But Yvenne had spoken true again—taking the potion erased all doubt. Maddek would have known she wasn't pregnant with another man's child, first when she needed the rags and again if she bled when he bedded her. Yet Zhalen could have said she wore rags for show and faked her menses. He could have said Maddek had mistaken her virginity. Now the Dragon guard bore witness and the effectiveness of the half-moon milk could not be denied. So she had not taken the potion to prove herself to Maddek, but to prevent any outside claim on the child.

She was always thinking forward, he realized—as the commander of an army did. Trying to outmaneuver her father.

Perhaps trying to outmaneuver Maddek, as well.

Her mind was a shrewd one. To know how she thought made Maddek ever more wary, but it did not mean she lied. He had known many shrewd Parsatheans who never spoke false, and whom he respected over any others. His parents. Nayil.

But they had been raised to honor truth; Yvenne had not. Only a fool would swiftly trust a woman with a mind such as hers.

The mind of a queen.

His queen, whether he would have chosen her or not.

It would be no hardship to bed her. Despite her brother's words, she was not at all ugly—and with her eyelids closed, he could study her face more easily, for it was difficult to tear his gaze from those eerie moonstone eyes when they looked back at him.

Now her long eyelashes cast fanned shadows against her cheekbones. Thick black hair was drawn back from her forehead in two braids, but the plait at her nape had come undone and fell over his arm in a heavy curtain of curls. The dark eyebrows that always seemed to be arched when she gazed at him had little curve in sleep. Only her lips were curved, pink and full and soft.

Everything else about her features seemed as straight as her eyebrows—and almost painfully delicate. Not just thin.

He suspected she would still appear delicate even after the hollows in her cheeks filled.

Maddek also suspected what had put those hollows there. Yvenne had eaten more of that foul-tasting lizard then he had, though his body was twice the size of hers. He'd only taken enough to stave off hunger, yet she had carefully stripped the leg down to the bone, even after the cramps had turned her stomach to stone, even though she looked as if she might vomit while chewing every bite.

Because she could not remember the last time her belly had been full.

Maddek would see it kept full. He would see the sickly, pale cast upon her skin disappear.

Skin that was soft everywhere. Between her thighs, she had been smoother than the silk of her robes, as had been the wisps of curls upon her mound. He could still feel that softness upon his fingers and his own hardness in response.

His gaze fell to her lips, her cheeks. Already she was not so sallow. Instead a flush rose beneath her skin, no longer tinged yellow but pink. Perspiration dotted her upper lip.

Too hot. The sun glared down, unblocked by the canopy of trees—and if she had been locked away for these many years, or kept beneath a veil, then her skin must be as tender and as new to the sun as a babe's.

Frowning, Maddek drew up the outer length of his red linen and draped it over his shoulder, shading her face while she slept.

He did not know if he could trust her. But he *would* protect her. With his own life, if need be.

But for now, she only needed a bit of shade.

CHAPTER 9

YVENNE

I t was full dark when Yvenne woke—still cradled in Maddek's arms, though his mount no longer ran. Instead they had slowed to a walk, the motion gently rocking her against his hard chest.

Rocking against her right shoulder rather than her left. She had been turned while she slept. Or perhaps the warriors had stopped to rest the horses and when they resumed their travel, Yvenne had been lifted into his arms again, facing the new direction.

The rags between her legs felt less bulky, as if only one or two folded cloths were tucked against her instead of the great wad. So they had changed those, too.

The agonizing cramps had passed. Nothing but a dull ache remained. That was not so bad. *All* of her body was a dull ache.

Maddek's arms tightened when she lifted her head. "We still ride," he told her, as if thinking she might be disoriented from sleep and would roll off the horse as she would her bed.

In the dark and seated sideways against him, she could see little of his features. Just the shadow of his strong jaw above the thick column of his neck. It must not yet be midnight, for the faint glow of the waxing sickle moon on the northwestern horizon still touched him. She faced that moon—so they were riding south and west.

The other warriors rode behind them. She could not see past Maddek's great form but could hear the clomp of their horses' hooves.

His big body shifted as he turned to unfasten one of the satchels tied to the back of his saddle. A moment later, a wineskin and a packet of waxed leather dropped into her lap. The scent of cooked meat wafted up, sending her dry mouth instantly to drooling. Her stomach grumbled ravenously.

"Thank you," she said hoarsely. Her throat was parched and raw. The wineskin only held water, but she did not care. Her first sip was the sweetest ever taken.

The meat was cut into thin strips. Perhaps because the Parsatheans had been in a hurry for it to roast—but they had roasted a fine amount. Venison, by the rich flavor. Yvenne believed she could have eaten an entire herd, but Maddek had given her so much, her stomach was well filled before she could even finish the packet.

"Enough?" he asked when, try as she might, not another bite could be taken.

"It is." She folded the packet again. "May I save the rest for later?"

He made a grunting sound that might have been assent. His rough fingers slid against hers when he took the packet and tucked it into one of the pouches fastened to the front of the saddle.

Where she could easily reach it again without asking him for more.

The realization made her throat close with emotion. Her voice was thick when she asked, "May I use this water to wash or ought I conserve it?"

She felt his dark gaze upon her face but did not look up

to meet his eyes. After a moment, his answer came. "Wash as you like."

She carefully rinsed her greasy fingers before wiping them dry on her robe—which was so filthy, Yvenne was uncertain whether her fingers came away clean or dirtier than before.

Oh, but she cared not at all. She was filthy and aching and happier than ever she had been.

So happy that she might weep from it.

But a queen did not cry when there was someone to see her tears, so Yvenne turned her burning eyes to the land-scape that lay ahead. They rode upon a rocky ridge over-looking a broad expanse of grassland. Beneath the faint moonlight, she could make out the silhouettes of hump-backed beasts. Short-haired mammoths or their gray-skinned cousins, perhaps—or the bulkier, plated lizards that roamed the plains, though most of those did not move in herds and usually remained near the shores of lakes and riverbanks.

She tied the wineskin to the front of the saddle. "Where are we?"

He gestured north, where a faint silver ribbon unwound in the distance. "There lies the Ageras."

Which marked the border between Goge and Ephorn. They traveled now on the Gogean side of the river, which emptied into the Boiling Sea—and where they would find a ship to take them to Parsathe.

"When will we reach Drahm?" The port city lay at the mouth of the Ageras.

"In a quarter turn, if we travel at a quick pace."

Seven days, perhaps. Her gaze touched the Ageras again. "We will take the river road?"

"Yes."

"Do we ride through this night?"

He shook his head. "A village lies not far ahead. We'll take our rest when it is in sight and purchase a horse there for you tomorrow morn. My mount has a great heart but we travel too fast and too far to carry two. Especially in this manner, for although you weigh but a feather, that feather is uneven and more difficult to carry."

So she could imagine, as it was more difficult to ride in this manner, too. "Shall I sit astride, then? It would not be so uneven."

Maddek's arm circled her waist and lifted her. Awkwardly Yvenne swung her left leg over the horse's neck, breath hissing through her teeth as her stiffened muscles screamed a protest. She settled into the saddle and for a long moment, pain blinded her as her hips and inner thighs seemed to tear apart, stretching and adjusting to the new position.

She almost cried out when Maddek's palm flattened against her stomach and forced her up to sitting instead of curled over the horse's withers.

The deep, soothing rumble of his voice moved through his warm chest and into the aching muscles of her back. "This pain will be but a few more days."

Wordlessly she nodded.

Beneath her, the horse's stride was long and smooth. Yvenne had no reins to grip, so she leaned back against his chest and braced her hands on the heavy thighs alongside hers. Beneath red linen, hard muscles became as iron—but he made no protest and did not push away her hands.

His manner had completely altered since the previous day, but Yvenne would not mistake his care and protection for a deeper change. Still he doubted her. Still he believed she might have taken part in his parents' murders.

But she would win him over. Just as she had his mother.

At the beginning, Ran Ashev had doubted, too. Enraged and grieving after her husband's death, the Parsathean queen had wondered if Yvenne's message had been designed as a lure. Yet Ran Ashev had also seen firsthand the tower chamber where Yvenne was imprisoned and the punishment she'd received for writing that letter. When the two women had met, a fevered and healing Yvenne had not even the strength to leave her bed.

Where Yvenne's frailty had stirred sympathy within Ran

Ashev, however—and had lent truth to Yvenne's claims—
in Maddek, her weakness only stirred contempt. As if he
believed strength of body outranked strength of mind or
will.

Truly, Yvenne had expected more of him. But that more
would come. For now, his anger and grief burned too hot to
attempt persuading him to her truth. He would reject her
every explanation.

And although his disbelief was a disappointment, perhaps she ought to have anticipated it. Through her mother's
eyes, Yvenne had followed a young Maddek from the Burning Plains to the banks of the Lave. She'd learned how
fierce he was in battle against the savages, how shrewdly
he'd commanded the alliance's army, and how deeply he'd
grieved each time another warrior was lost. For years, she'd
known what kind of man he was.

But Maddek had not known her. It was not so surprising
that he did not immediately trust her.

Yvenne would teach him who she was, then. Slowly.
Carefully. If he realized that earning his trust was her purpose, he'd disbelieve her every word.

So tonight, she would not speak of anything that gave
him reason to doubt. Let him become accustomed to hearing truth from her tongue—then he might not be so inclined to rip it out.

And let him discover that he and she were not so very
different. "The warriors who travel with you—they are your
Dragon?"

A slight hesitation. Then, "They are."

Oh. How unexpected. She'd thought he would say they
were not, because only a Ran was protected by a Dragon
guard. So it was not strictly true that they served in such a
capacity. Yet she also knew Maddek would not lie.

"Even though you have not yet been named Ran?"

"So I would have not yet called them my Dragon," he
replied—and that explained his hesitation, she realized.
Just as what followed explained the response he'd given.
"But it is what they would call themselves."

In this matter, then, he would weigh his warriors' voices more heavily than his own. Never would her father have done the same. Zhalen's own opinion was the only one with any significance.

And for that reason, her father would never inspire the same loyalty that Maddek did. "I suspect that these warriors would serve as your Dragon even if you never became a Parsathean king."

Maddek grunted.

Whether that reply was agreement or dissent, Yvenne couldn't decide—but he did not seem displeased by her observation. "My mother once told me that no matter how many times the raiders from the Burning Plains invaded Syssia before the alliance, nothing the Parsatheans ever stole from us equaled the value of what Queen Nyset took from your people in return."

Another grunt, but this one clearly dismissive. "You've heard false. Never did that warrior-queen lead a raid against Parsathe."

"I said nothing of a raid. It was not silver or iron that Nyset took from your people, but something she saw with her moonstone eyes."

Amusement and interest deepened his reply. "What of value could she take with those?"

"She watched Ran Antyl." The successor to the thief-king, Ran Bantik, who had become a legendary queen in her own right. "And Nyset saw how much better it was to lead a people—as Parsathean queens and kings do—than to rule over them. So that is what Nyset did. That is what all my foremothers have done."

"And is that what you will do, when you are queen?"

"It is."

His hard laugh stirred the loose tendrils of her hair. "Leading means nothing if your people will not follow. Should they follow you because of your moonstone eyes? Your brothers' eyes are the same color."

"It would not matter. But for Tyzen, my brothers would

not even attempt to lead. They would try to rule over them, as my father does."

"And how will you inspire your people to follow you? Your mother and foremothers were warrior-queens. You cannot even sit a horse."

"That hardly matters. If it meant freeing my people from my father's rule, I would crawl upon the ground. Whatever I must do, I will do it. My people will see that, and they will know that every step I take is a better direction for us all."

"If you wish to free them, better to raise a sword against your father than to crawl at his feet."

"Certainly a sword is *easier*. That is why I would ally myself with you, to see your blade take my father's head." She glanced back, hoping for a glimpse of Maddek's face, which revealed so many of his thoughts—but she had no good view, only shadows and the broad mountain of his shoulder. "Surely you do not believe that one must be able to hold a sword to lead. Would you not follow Nayil?"

That council minister would never hold a sword again, yet Yvenne knew how deeply all Parsatheans respected him.

"I would," Maddek said, but instead of the solemn reply she'd expected, another laugh rumbled against her back. "Though I do not always listen to him as well as I should."

"No?"

"He said that the ruling house of Syssia should be avoided. That everyone born of Zhalen's blood was as cunning and vicious as a starving drepa." Some of the humor leached from his voice. "Yet now I take Zhalen's daughter as my bride."

"Oh." Yvenne would lose her tongue if she told Maddek that his mother had heard the same advice, yet would have given Zhalen's daughter to him as a bride, anyway. So instead she offered another truth. "Nayil is not wrong. If I had not been born into my family, I would make great effort to avoid us, too."

She thought he might have smiled at that, though she could not see his face. Because silence fell between them, but it was not uneasy or tense. Instead it was the comfortable quiet of two people in agreement.

Everyone of Zhalen's blood *was* vicious and cunning.

But Zhalen's blood alone did not pulse through her veins—or through her brothers'. Only Yvenne and Tyzen had been raised by their mother in their tower chamber, however. Her older brothers had not been so fortunate, and it was not just Zhalen's blood that had poisoned their hearts. It had been every moment he'd spent with them.

She might have told Maddek so, but this time it was he who broke the silence.

"And what of your father's personal guard?" The hardness of his voice told her that he was thinking of his mother's rape. "Are they loyal to him, as a Dragon is?"

"Some are loyal to my father. Others are loyal to his gold."

"They are not Syssian." It was not a question, for Maddek must have seen how the Syssian soldiers responded to Yvenne. Never would a Syssian have kept Yvenne—or Queen Vyssen—imprisoned as her father's guards had. A single word from either woman would have secured their freedom. But her father's mercenaries cared nothing about Nyset's heirs.

"Most are from Rugus," Yvenne said. "Many fought with him at the Battle of Fourth Ridge, when he held the pass against the Destroyer's warlords, and when he smote the Smiling Giant. Those soldiers came with him when he married my mother."

"How many?"

"Fifty in my father's personal guard, made up of his most loyal soldiers." Before her death, Queen Vyssen had counted them each day—monitoring their movements, their conversations, always seeking a weakness in Zhalen's security. "Two hundred more serve as the palace guard. There are no Syssian soldiers within the royal citadel. They are instead charged with protecting the city walls and the Syssian outlands."

"Against what threat?"

"The barbarian raiders from the north, of course," she said dryly, and felt another laugh tousle her unbound hair. "My father claims the alliance will not long keep the Parsatheans at bay."

"I will only come for him and his guards," said Maddek.

"My people will be glad to hear it. Though, in truth, even if there was no alliance, the greatest threat to Syssia would come from Rugus."

"From your brother Aezil?" There was no surprise in his voice.

Yvenne nodded.

"Does your father not recognize the threat?"

Her father was not so blind. Only arrogant. "He does, though he would never admit to it."

"Then why place Aezil on the Rugusian throne? Lazen was next in line. Why did he name the second son—and the greater threat—king of another nation?"

"Lazen cannot be king," Yvenne reminded him happily. "He's dead."

Slain by the only arrow she'd ever drawn with the intent to kill. But Yvenne could not risk saying that without also risking her tongue. Maddek still doubted her part in her brother's death, for the alliance council had been told that Ran Ashev had slain Lazen, instead—and that was why his mother had been beheaded.

But if he was thinking of that failed escape now, Yvenne could not tell. Maddek only said, "He was not yet dead when your father gave Aezil the Rugusian throne."

"My father convinced Lazen that Syssia was the greater prize." Which was truth, but it was not Zhalen's true purpose in giving Rugus to his second son. "And if he had named Aezil the successor to the Syssian throne, my brother would not have waited for my father to vacate it."

"Zhalen fears his own son?"

"With good reason. In the alliance council meeting, you heard of the contract between Syssia and Rugus, in which every available Rugusian soldier was sent to protect my father?"

"I did."

"I suspect that Aezil agreed to send Rugusian soldiers to Syssia not to protect my father but so that, when the time is right, my brother might more easily take the Syssian throne."

"Is your father such a fool?"

"No. But he must weigh that risk against the risk of allowing Syssian soldiers near the tower—and the risk of my people discovering that Nyset's heir is alive and nearly a queen's age, and rising up against him. And my brother has only been king a few seasons; most likely he'll wait to secure his power in Rugus before trying to conquer Syssia. No doubt my father believed he would have time to allay that danger." Yvenne shrugged. "It matters little. When Zhalen is dead, I will purge the Rugusians from the ranks of the palace guard—and purge Syssia of my father's legacy."

Maddek only offered another indecipherable grunt. Probably thinking that *she* needed to be purged from memory, too. Perhaps it was best, then, to turn his mind away from how much he distrusted her, and toward something every Parsathean appreciated: their horses.

Particularly since, if Yvenne was to be riding her own mount tomorrow, she needed to learn more about them, too. He had mocked her because she could not ride. That didn't mean she never would.

Trying to find the horse's rhythm, she studied the bobbing of its big head. Its long ears were turned forward but flicked back as if to catch the sound of her voice when she said, "What is his name?"

"Whose name?"

"Your horse."

Sudden humor lifted his voice. "It is a mare. And she has no name. We do not name our horses as we do not name our swords."

Because they were only tools. But the horses did not lack for care. From what Yvenne had seen, the Parsathean warriors tended to their mounts better than they tended to themselves.

"Fassad named his wolves," Yvenne said.

Maddek grunted, a disapproving sound. "They are but dogs."

"Fassad says they are wolves."

"They are tamed."

So were the horses. "And named."

"And he will mourn them all the deeper for it when they are lost—and a warrior's hounds and horses will *always* be lost on the battlefield."

"Or in the forest." As Yvenne's had been.

"Yes."

"You have said you will treat me as a dog," she reminded him. "I hope you treat me as Fassad treats his, for it is better than any queen could hope for."

His laugh was a deep quake against her back. "That is true enough. Though I vow it will not be the same. For Fassad does not do to his dogs what I will do to you."

Upon her moon night. No, she supposed it would not be the same at all.

And her would-be husband must be thinking of what he would do. His hardness rose behind her—but although he could not be comfortable with his cock pressed between them and her bottom rocking against his arousal with the horse's every step, this time he did not demand that Yvenne ease his need.

Nor did she wish him to. Not here, in front of the others.

Yet she liked knowing that he hardened against her for no other reason than the thought of having her in his bed. Yesterday his arousal had been fired by his anger and his desire to punish her. He did not seem angry or inclined to punish her now, however.

And despite her own rage the previous day, she had known unexpected pleasure while touching him. She would like to know it again—but she had little hope Maddek would give it while he believed her responsible for his parents' murders. Any pleasure she would have to take for herself.

As long as he did not hurt her when he took his.

Her breath shuddered as his broad hand suddenly pressed against her stomach. But not to hurt her—or to please her. In a low, rough voice, he said, "Tomorrow when you ride, you must tighten these muscles. Straighten your back. Do not be as a sack of meat sitting upon your mount. Instead move as one with her."

Yvenne tried but didn't feel as one with the horse. Instead she felt as one with Maddek, for it seemed there was nowhere he did not touch: her back pressed to his chest, her hips cradled between his thighs, her legs dangling against his.

He must have approved her new posture, because he gave no instructions to adjust it. Instead he said, "Do not rely upon your hands for balance. The steadiness of your seat is all you need to stay mounted. You should be able to ride with a sword in one hand and a crossbow in the other, yet still command your mount's speed and direction."

A laugh shook through her as she imagined herself doing anything of the sort by tomorrow. "Perhaps within a few more days."

His answer was the barest tensing of his thighs. The horse immediately responded, moving faster. Yvenne desperately gripped his legs as she was jolted and bounced in the saddle.

His voice hardened. "You strike like a hammer upon your mount's spine." Forearm across her stomach, he raised her higher against his chest, until she was rocking smoothly with him. "Feel her rise and fall through each stride. Sit tall and use your hips to rise and fall with her. You have no stirrups, so let your legs hang loose, steady your weight upon the insides of your thighs, and find your balance. Do not squeeze her sides with your legs to remain seated."

Though loosening the secure grip of her legs was terrifying, Yvenne did as he commanded. Her balance shifted, her weight sinking deeper into her seat. Pain shot through her stiffened hips when she tried to move as he did, but she gritted her teeth and persevered, until the pressure of his arm around her waist eased and she was not relying on his strength to keep from bouncing upon the horse's back.

"In that way," he said approvingly, and the horse slowed to a walk again. "We do not often travel at that pace, but you must know how to ride at it."

Breathless from exertion, Yvenne nodded. "It was easier," she panted, "on the first night. When my horse was running."

And was probably the only reason she had remained on its back. Had they trotted, she'd have bounced off before they'd traveled a sprint.

"Running is smoother," he agreed.

As was walking. Though she still did not feel as one with the horse. "I have heard legends of Parsathean riders who truly became one with their mounts."

"No." They had slowed, yet his arm remained around her waist, holding her securely against him. "Though it is almost a truth."

"How?"

"Because we are as silver-fingered Rani." Lightly he dragged the tips of his silver claws up over her forearm. Amusement deepened his voice again when a shiver raced through her. "There is no greater warrior than she."

That was not what Yvenne's mother had claimed. "It is Vela who is goddess of warriors."

"And Rani is the finest of them all. The strongest warrior, the keenest hunter—for no one has ever defeated her, and no one has ever escaped her. When she comes for you, it is the end."

For she was death. On that Yvenne could agree. "Yes."

"And after Rani claims you, she flies upon her dragon to deliver you into Temra's arms," he said, and each word seemed to swell through Yvenne's chest. "That is what the warriors of Parsathe do—we are as silver-fingered Rani, delivering our enemies into Temra's arms. And when we ride into battle, one with our mounts . . . it is as if we fly."

Heart thundering, Yvenne whispered, "I would do that. I would learn to ride simply for that."

"Would you? Race into battle, even if it is into death?" His silver claws grazed the side of her throat before he pressed forward against her back and said roughly, "Hold fast to her mane. Crouch low over her neck."

She did. Maddek's legs tensed and the mare sprang forward. Then they were racing, racing with the wind whipping tears from Yvenne's eyes and the warriors racing with them, all around her, the hoofbeats pounding like the pounding of her heart.

And it truly *was* like flying—though not into Temra's arms. Not when Maddek held her so tightly in his. Everything hurt, yet there was no pain. This could not be like death.

Not when Yvenne felt alive for the very first time.

CHAPTER 10

MADDEK

For two days they rode beneath a blue sky shimmering with the heat of a glaring sun. On the third day, they started out when dawn was a distant gleam upon the jagged teeth of the Fallen Mountains to the east. Above the flat grasslands to the west, sullen clouds swept toward the riders on a hot wind swollen with the promise of rain.

That promise was delivered before midday. A deluge fell in torrents from leaden skies. Blinded by the downpour lashing his face, Maddek bowed his head against the onslaught. His mare did the same, head hanging low as she walked, her great hooves wading through the muddy slop of a road.

They traveled too slowly. Yet a faster pace through the slop risked injuring the horses' legs.

Any other day, Maddek would have found shelter and waited for the storm to pass, but they could not delay. No doubt yesterday Cezan's body had been delivered to the alliance council. Bazir would immediately send word to his father in Syssia and brother in Rugus, but would also order his soldiers in all directions to search for Yvenne. She and Maddek's warriors were but a single day's ride beyond the bridge over the Ageras—barely three days ahead of any soldiers sent in pursuit.

That lead would not last. Not at the slow pace they'd traveled the past two days, after purchasing a mount for Yvenne. Not at the much slower pace they traveled now.

A powerful gust flapped Maddek's sodden linens against his legs, the heavy weight of his braids whipping his shoulders. Swiftly he looked back, half expecting that Yvenne's slight form had been blown out of her saddle.

But she still rode tall—taller than any of his warriors, who sat low in their saddles, heads bent and bodies braced against the wind. Loosely she held the reins in her two-fingered hand. Her left hand she'd wrapped around the saddle's pommel, anchoring herself.

She did not return his gaze with a questioning arch of her eyebrows, as she had almost every time he'd looked back at her in the past few days. Instead her eyes were closed, her face lifted to the rain, her mouth curved into a soft smile.

Another gust tore at her black hair, the long strands streaming out behind her in a wet silken banner. Heavy over her slim shoulders lay the homespun cloak he'd purchased for her at the same village where he'd bought her short-backed dullard of a horse. The coarse cloth was saturated, water dripping in a steady stream from the hem—just as it dripped from her exposed brow, her nose, and her chin.

Frowning, he glanced at Banek, who rode beside her. They traveled the road two abreast, with Maddek and Kelir in the lead. Banek and Yvenne followed a few paces behind. The older warrior had appointed himself as her companion these past days, patiently teaching her how to sit a horse—and, by unspoken agreement, serving as her guard while Maddek rode ahead. It was Banek who alerted Maddek when she needed to rest or eat, and it was Banek who reminded her to drink often beneath the hot sun.

Yet now she was soaked from head to toe and the older warrior had his face down.

Maddek looked to her again. He had to raise his voice over the short distance and driving rain. "Draw up your hood, Yvenne."

At the command in his tone, each of his warriors snapped to attention, faces lifting and bodies tensing before the words themselves registered. When his meaning sank in, they all looked to her.

As slowly as if waking from a dream, she opened her moonstone eyes. Yet *slowly* was not how she rose from sleep—Maddek knew that well. The past few mornings when he'd roused her, she awakened instantly, her clear gaze piercing him through to his bones.

As it did now, when she regarded him with amusement arching her brows. "Shall I shield myself from the elements as well as you do, Commander?"

Beside him, Kelir snorted out a laugh. Banek grinned. For Maddek wore nothing but his belted linens—and had not even drawn the outer layer up over his shoulders. There was no need, for the storm had formed over the Boiling Sea. He had known baths colder than the wind and rain were.

Yet she had never known the wind and rain at all—or the sun. The heat of the past days had burnished her face, her skin as tight and as hot as if she suffered from a fever.

"When you have a warrior's strength, you may ride as bare as you wish," he told her. "I have no use for a frail wife who falls so ill she cannot be bred."

Her amusement hardened like stone. "I have no use for a husband whose performance in bed can be diminished by my cough."

A cough would not stop Maddek from burying himself between her soft thighs. Had they not needed to wait for her moon night, he'd have already spent each day riding her, spilling his seed within her silken sheath until his vengeance took root. But he only said, "Draw up your hood."

Not one of his warriors would have argued. Yet she slowly shook her head, pale gaze never leaving his.

"The rain feels sweet upon my face," she said.

Her sunburned face. Yet perhaps the downpour against her heated skin was not the only reason it was sweet. The first day upon her horse, she had lifted her face to the warmth of the sun in the same way, though it burned her. Because she'd never known it before. Just as she'd never known the rain.

He held her gaze for another long moment, an odd tightness squeezing within his chest. Finally he nodded and faced forward again.

And the lashing rain *was* sweet against his own heated skin. How a treacherous, sickly woman warmed him so quickly, he knew not. By all that was rational, he should not desire her as he did. Not the woman who might have lured his parents to their murders. Not the woman who had so coldly plunged a dagger into her brother's back.

That memory still sat unsettled in his mind. She had skewered her brother as easily as one skewered a roasting pig, with no emotion and no warning. Certainly Cezan deserved to die—and over the course of his life, Maddek had seen far more blood shed, and spilled much of it himself. Yet that had been in the heat of battle.

Yvenne had been as ice.

But the fires of vengeance burned hot in his own blood. When he'd first looked upon Yvenne, he had no thought but to kill her. The moment he'd agreed to take her as a bride, however, little else but bedding her filled his head—of getting her with the child that would hail Zhalen's end. If she had not been a virgin, he'd have been upon her so often that any soldiers in pursuit would have been at their backs now.

Bedding her would only slow them further. Though Maddek yearned for vengeance, he could not let its fires blind him. Only a sevennight remained until the full moon. She would be beneath him soon enough.

"She has steel in her." Kelir's voice was pitched too low

to carry to the riders behind them. "More steel than her horse does."

That was certain. For although she was new to the saddle, Yvenne had not slowed them. Had she been upon a Parsathean horse and they'd set a brutal pace, no doubt she'd have clung like a burr to its back. Just as she had the first eve.

Her horse had less stamina than she did. Maddek had known upon a glance that it was a poor mount, with a stiff stride and shallow chest. The gelding couldn't maintain a pace faster than a jog trot for any distance, and even before the mud had slowed them, the gelding's walk had. Instead of the Parsathean horses' swift and smooth ambling gait, it lumbered along on ponderous steps. Yet there had been few horses to choose from in a village full of farmers who placed higher value on heavy, laboring beasts. Maddek bought the gelding with the intention of trading it for a more suitable mount at the next village. He'd found no better selection there, however—or at any of the settlements they'd passed.

"I should have taken the dun stallion," he said now. Though smaller than a Parsathean steed, the dun had been the only horse they'd seen worth having, but its fiery temperament wouldn't have suited a new rider.

Eyebrows drawn and braids dripping with rain, Kelir frowned. "You'd have put her on that fire-breather?"

"I'd have ridden him."

"And you'd have given your mare to your bride?"

Maddek inclined his head.

Disbelief burst from the other warrior on a hearty laugh. Amusement lighting his eyes, he said, "I suppose putting her on your mare would be easier than teaching your bride to ride. She would not even need reins to guide her mount, because that mare would follow you like a dog."

So the mare would. Her dam had also been his mount, killed by savages upon the river Lave when she'd been little more than a spindly-legged foal. Recognizing that she had the same steady strength as her mother, Maddek had raised her by hand. When it had come time to ride her, he'd never known a horse better suited to him, or with as much courage and ferocity in battle.

Though for that same reason, better not to ride an untested horse. If he did, Maddek could not be as certain of protecting Yvenne. Fighting to control a panicked mount made it harder to fight anything that threatened her.

But he said nothing, and Kelir cast a speculative glance behind them. "For her third day upon a horse, she does well."

"She stays on."

"From dawn until nightfall."

Maddek grunted, a grudging agreement. For Yvenne did not ride well. She was nowhere near to it. But she possessed an abundance of fortitude. And ever since Maddek had held her against him and they'd raced beneath the night sky, she'd been determined to have her own mount—not just to ride it, but to care for it. She'd insisted on tending to her horse even at the end of day, when her stomach grumbled loudly enough for the entire camp to hear and her limbs trembled with exhaustion and pain.

That effort earned her more respect from his warriors than any skill upon a horse could have. Maddek suspected that Yvenne knew it would win them over.

But even if she manipulated them all, her effort wasn't false—and it took a toll. Each night when Maddek retired to his furs, she was already there, sleeping so soundly that she didn't stir when he pulled her against his chest and wrapped his arms around her frail form, shielding her with his body as they slept. The previous eve, she had not even finished her meal first. Her eyelids had drooped with every bite, and she'd finally put it aside, crawling into bed with her dinner half eaten.

And by Hanan's weeping staff, she slept so hot, a warrior needed no fire to help warm his bed. Maddek would have thrown off his furs if it wouldn't have left her uncovered.

After her moon night, Maddek could throw them off without hesitation. For it would be he who covered her then.

A white flash of lightning split the gray clouds ahead. Maddek's gaze shot over his shoulder again. Yvenne's horse was placid and dull, but even the most docile of mounts sometimes bolted during a storm. With tension gripping his body, Maddek waited for the crack and rumble of thunder.

When it came, her mount tossed its head, snorting. Releasing her pommel, Yvenne leaned forward and stroked the thick neck. Her lips moved—soothing the gelding with a murmur, though her face was pinched with unease, as if she feared the horse would panic and throw her. Her pale gaze darted to Banek, who looked on and nodded his approval.

When the next crack of thunder sounded, the horse's ears flicked, but that was its only reaction. It continued plodding steadily along the muddied road.

Maddek looked to Kelir. A frown pleated the other warrior's brow as he studied the woman and horse—a frown that deepened when lightning flashed again. Grimly, Kelir eyed the thundering sky. "Do we take shelter and wait for it to pass?"

They should. But this storm would not slow anyone who pursued them.

Maddek shook his head. "We press on," he said.

CHAPTER 11

MADDEK

The storm's fury abated midafternoon. Abruptly the rain stopped, clouds parting to reveal Enam's glaring yellow eye. Beneath the sun's burning stare, steam rose from the sodden earth, forming a heavy mist that crawled over the ground and swirled around the horses' legs. The cracking thunder and howling wind subsided, replaced by the increasing roar of the Ageras as the road bore north and began to run parallel at a distance from the swollen riverbanks. Across its hazardous waters lay Ephorn—and farther north, Syssia.

Maddek's gaze scanned the opposite bank. No travelers were in sight on the road that followed the river on Ephorn's side.

Even if a company of Syssian soldiers gathered there, they would pose no immediate threat to Yvenne. Any soldiers in pursuit might come along the road behind them, but not from across the Ageras. To everything but the creatures that dwelled within the river, the swift waters were unnavigable and uncrossable. Only three great stone bridges spanned its width, and they'd been built by the gods themselves—one bridge far to the east, in Toleh. Another almost two days' ride behind them. And the third in the port of Drahm, where the mouth of the river spilled into the Boiling Sea.

A fourth bridge had once linked the roads on either side of the river, but only one of their party had ever seen it.

Hoofbeats quickened behind him as Banek urged his mount forward. The gray-haired warrior pulled up even with Maddek, who turned in his saddle to look at Yvenne. Her sandaled heels against its sides, she was gently nudging her gelding forward as well, but her plodding mount did not respond.

Her horse's reluctance drew grins from the warriors behind her. Each one of them had sat upon mounts as stubborn. Some more so—at least the gelding was walking.

Toric called out his advice. "Dig your heels in, my lady!" When she hesitated and glanced back at the young warrior, his grin broadened. "Your little feet won't hurt his ribs. It'll be nothing more than a tickle to wake him up and move him along."

Nodding, she pressed her heels tighter. The horse didn't respond, and when pain whitened her cheeks Maddek signaled to the four warriors. Immediately they urged their own mounts forward to flank Yvenne, ready to catch her if the horse bolted. A short word from Fassad sent one of his gray dogs darting in to nip at the gelding's hocks.

Her horse broke into a bouncing trot. Maddek watched as she used the momentum of the gelding's stride to rise in the saddle as he'd shown her—though at obvious cost. Her narrow face stiffened, her full mouth pressing into a thin, bloodless line.

"Still saddle sore," Banek said quietly.

And still limping every time they dismounted, still hobbling each morning after she woke. But there was no cure for the pain except more riding, until her muscles became accustomed to the exertion.

"The old crossroads lie ahead," Banek continued as Yvenne's horse drew up between Maddek's and Kelir's.

The scarred warrior leaned over in his saddle, ready to catch her mount's bridle before it ran past, but she deftly slowed the gelding to a walk again with a light touch on her reins. "I should like to see what remains."

Banek's glance conveyed what he did not speak aloud: that Yvenne needed a respite from the road. But she was not alone. After a half day spent trudging through mud, the horses needed to rest and graze.

Maddek nodded. "How far?"

"Only a sprint."

The distance a good horse could race without slowing. The gray-haired warrior pointed ahead at a grassy mound that, through the mist, Maddek had taken for a stony hill. But instead of a natural rise, it was rubble—ruins that had lain abandoned for a generation.

"*That* is one of the great bridges?" Yvenne stared ahead wide-eyed.

"And the trading town that stood at the crossroads," Banek said in a voice heavier than Maddek had ever heard from him. "Once this road passed straight through."

But after the Destroyer dropped the bridge on the town, travelers had been forced to go around the rubble. Now the route beyond the ruins couldn't be seen past the curve in the road.

An ideal place for bandits to stage an attack, then.

Maddek studied the mound, searching for movement, then looked to Yvenne as she leaned forward in her saddle to peer past him, her pale gaze studying the older man's face. "Did you ever visit this place before the Destroyer came?"

"I did." A faint smile pulled at Banek's mouth. "On a raid."

"So far south?" Ardyl asked from behind them. After escorting Yvenne to Maddek's side, the four warriors had not yet fallen back—nor would they now. Not when there was a tale of the raid to be told.

"What did you take?" That from Kelir.

"We heard a load of Tolehi iron was traveling along this road to Syssia, and we ambushed them just beyond the bridge." The older man chuckled. "We had no more trouble stealing the load from its escort than we did stealing Maddek's bride. But still we returned home empty-handed."

That bride leaned forward again, as eager to hear the tale as Maddek's warriors were. "What happened?"

Banek's face reddened. "We were not satisfied with taking only what we could carry. So we took the entire load, which was too heavy even for oxen. Instead the train of wagons was drawn by a kergen."

Which were often used for labor in both Toleh and Goge. The single-horned beast stood taller than a mammoth, and although docile enough to be ridden, more often it was harnessed and used to haul plows or to drag boulders.

"Never has any beast moved more slowly." The old man shook his head. "But it was just as well, for we spent so much time gathering feed for it that we could not ride swiftly, either. Almost a full turn of the moon passed before we reached the Syssian border—and it was there we lost the load, when the queen herself rode out to meet us."

Yvenne sucked in a sharp breath. "My mother?"

"Hers," Banek said, meeting her wondering gaze.

Awe shimmered in Yvenne's pearlescent eyes. Beside her, Kelir seemed no less impressed. "Queen Venys?" he asked.

The gray-haired warrior nodded and his eyes broke away from Yvenne's to gaze unfocused at the ruins ahead. "A handful of soldiers came with her, but she was still at a distance when she left them and approached us alone. Our raiding party was three dozen warriors strong, yet when we saw who was coming, many of us believed we should flee. We decided to stand our ground instead. If we'd known then how powerful she was, we would not have been foolish enough to remain. But we didn't know. This was before she severed the Destroyer's arm."

The only warrior known to have injured the sorcerer—until the Destroyer used his dark magics to heal his wounds and create a new arm.

"She was slain in that battle," Yvenne said softly.

"And yet renewed a hope that had been faltering. To see him *bleed* . . ." Voice roughening, the old man shook his head and fell silent.

Until Fassad spoke behind him. "Yet you fought her?"

Ardyl huffed out a laugh. "He still breathes, so apparently not."

Banek cast an amused glance at them before looking to Yvenne again. "She rode closer, and that was the first I saw her moonstone eyes—so much like yours."

"Not like mine," was her quiet reply. "She had sight beyond what is seen."

"That must be how she found and intercepted you," Toric said to Banek.

"Yes," he agreed. "And never have I seen such a figure. Taller than Fassad, and as easy upon her horse as Ran Ashev ever rode. But it was not only that we could see at a glance what a strong warrior she was. When she walked, the earth did not tremble beneath her feet, but seemed as if it should. And she looked upon us with *such* a gaze . . . I did not know whether to fear her or to love her."

"Love her," Yvenne murmured, and gave a wistful sigh.

Surprised by the soft longing in that breath, Maddek looked to her.

Her pale eyes met his—and for the first time, it was she who faltered and cast her focus beyond him. Not merely glancing away, but unable to hold his gaze.

Beside him, Banek continued, "All of Syssia loved her. And it was plain to see why. She could have slaughtered us. Instead she said that we could continue unmolested through all of Syssia—and take our spoils with us—if a warrior of our choosing could shoot a better arrow than she did."

Yvenne's eyes remained fixedly upon Banek, as if she were aware that Maddek's gaze had not yet strayed from her face and was determined not to look at him while he watched the expressions that flitted over her features. First amusement appeared, replaced by disappointment that pleated her brows. "That seems akin to cheating. She would not miss."

"Is that how you lost the spoils?" Ardyl asked. "She defeated your best archer?"

Banek suddenly grinned. "Our best archer was my sister, Kabli, who had silver-fingered Rani's own eye. Not even a warrior-queen favored by the goddess Vela could have equaled the shot she made that day. Queen Venys pointed to a sparrow in flight, and Kabli waited until it was almost from sight before she loosed her arrow and pierced the bird through its heart. The queen herself said she'd never seen the like."

"Yet the queen bested her?"

"No. Kabli pointed to another sparrow and hardly a moment passed before the queen let her arrow fly—but she didn't hit the bird." Amusement shook through the old man's voice. "Instead she struck the kergen through the eye. Then she smiled and said to us, 'I missed the sparrow. The iron is yours to take.'"

Maddek grinned and Yvenne met his gaze again, her face alight with laughter. The warriors behind them were roaring their own amusement at Banek's expense.

Wearing a broad grin, Kelir asked him, "What then?"

"What was there to do? She bade us to continue our journey—but warned us that if we tarried, she would return and her arrow would not miss again. Then she left us there with a dead kergen and a wagon train too heavy for our horses to pull. So we each took a few ingots and raced for home. I imagine that iron ended up in Syssian furnaces, where it had originally been intended."

"So you were not raiders that season," Yvenne said, still laughing, "but poorly paid escorts for a load of Syssian iron."

"We were," Banek readily agreed. "Though she let us leave with our lives, so perhaps not so poorly paid. A fine woman she was. A fine queen."

Maddek had heard that claim of every Syssian queen. But he had not heard this particular tale.

Neither had the other warriors. "How is it you've never told us this before?" Fassad asked him. "I thought we had heard every raiding story there was to hear."

The amusement bled away from the older man's face, which suddenly wore every one of his years. "That was the last happy arrow my sister drew. While we rode home, the Destroyer's army was crossing Temra's Heart, and at the end of that summer Kabli fell at the battle for Parsa. I was the only warrior in that raiding party to survive his march."

A march that began with the razing of Parsa, the ancient city at the heart of the Burning Plains. Then south—where Rugus fell, followed by Ephorn, Toleh, and Goge before Anumith the Destroyer made his way north again to Syssia. After conquering that city, his devastating campaign crossed the western edge of the Burning Plains toward Blackmoor and the Flaming Mountains of Astal. No one had been able to halt his course of death and destruction, not even the daughters of Krimathe or the warlords of Lith, though the blood of the gods themselves ran through their veins. But it was the Destroyer's ambition that saved those who survived him, because he seemingly had no desire to rule—only to lay waste to everything in his path. As if determined to reduce the entire world to rubble, he continued west across the great ocean and had not been heard from for a generation.

For a long moment, there was no sound but the squelching of mud around the horses' hooves. Then Yvenne said softly, "It is said the Destroyer returns."

"If he does, we will once again see him bleed," was Maddek's vow, and it was echoed by each of his warriors.

A faint smile touched Banek's mouth, his gaze slipping over to meet Yvenne's again. "I was at the Syssian wall that day—when Queen Venys cleaved through his flesh, and when she fell before him. I saw your mother that day, too, and it was as if I were seeing Queen Venys again, for she was just as strong. Every sorcerer and warlord in your mother's path fell before her sword. And she was as a raging storm when she tried to reach the queen's body before the Destroyer reanimated her."

"But was too late," Yvenne murmured. "Yes, she spoke of that day often."

So had Maddek's mother and father, who had also been there—and who had retreated with everyone else when Queen Venys had risen again. They'd all fallen back, not away from the Destroyer, but from the demon who possessed the warrior-queen's body.

In that retreat, the alliance had been formed. For the Destroyer moved on after crushing Syssia, but the demon-queen remained. So every remaining rider from Parsathe and every soldier from the southern realms had come together to defeat her, and it had been her own daughter who finally struck the killing blow.

"She was fierce, your mother." Banek eyed Yvenne speculatively. "She must have been the same age then that you are today."

"Near to it," she replied. "She was six years shy of a queen's age. I am but five years shy."

"Is that why she married Zhalen?" Maddek asked her. "She was too young to take the crown without issue?"

Just as Yvenne was.

"She needed no husband to conceive a child—many Syssian queens never married. Nyset did not. Venys did not. The union with my father was only to strengthen the new alliance." She cast an unreadable glance at Maddek. "She had sight beyond what was seen, but she did not look long enough to see what he truly was. Or perhaps he knew that she would observe him from a distance before offering for his hand, and he wore a false face until they were married."

Gruffly Banek said, "I was sorry to hear of the illness that stole her strength. If not for that, no doubt she would have destroyed him when she realized what he was."

A bitter smile twisted her mouth. "It was not an illness."

Maddek frowned. "That is what has been said."

"Zhalen said many things. He said that he loved her even as he poisoned her wine with a full measure of fellroot."

The same poison that had withered the minister Nayil's limbs—though it had been delivered by a blade, not ingested. Drinking fellroot should have killed her. But perhaps a strong, goddess-favored queen could survive it.

Goddess-favored, but not invincible. "She did not see him do that, either?"

Yvenne shook her head. "Nor did she know that it was he who poisoned her. Not to begin. While she was still fevered and suffering, Zhalen told her there was a conspiracy among the nobles—that they claimed she had been tainted by the same demon who possessed her mother, and had tried to kill her for it. And with that lie, my father purged every strong house that could have stood against him. By the time she discovered the truth . . . she hardly had the strength to hold a sword, let alone lift it. So he locked her in her chamber, visited her in her bed, and got his sons upon her."

"And got you upon her," Maddek bluntly said. "Is being born of her poisoned flesh why you are so much smaller and weaker than Nyset's other heirs?"

Her shoulders lifted in a careless shrug. "My brothers seem unaffected. But I was born almost two full turns too early, so small that my mother said she could hold me in the palm of her hand. I should not have survived. So perhaps that is where all of my goddess-given strength went—it was spent keeping me alive as a babe. And it pleased my father that I was so frail. He believed my weakness and hunger would make me easier to control."

Maddek's bark of laughter drew her gaze to his again. "Your father is truly a fool," he told her. "For I have only known you a short time and know you could never be easily controlled. So you need not worry your husband will make the same mistake."

Her grin matched his, and she held his eyes for a long moment that heated his blood. Slowly her smile faded, though the intensity of her stare did not.

A soft frown puckered the skin between her eyebrows as she continued to study him. "You are much more handsome when you scowl."

He laughed again. "Am I?"

"You are," she said primly. "You should refrain from smiling, especially after we are married."

"That will be no hardship. After we marry, I'll have little reason to smile."

"I will make sure of it. It is so much more pleasant to look upon your face when you are unhappy, I shall endeavor to make your life a misery." She eyed the grin that broadened in response to that. "Already you deliberately displease me." Looking to Kelir, who was shaking with mirth upon his horse, she said, "Remember this moment if ever anyone speaks of how bitterly contentious our marriage is. I only have one small request of my would-be husband—that he does not smile—and immediately he denies me."

"I will remember it, my lady," the warrior choked out.

"As I will," Maddek said dryly.

She gave him such a slyly amused look in response that it seemed to Maddek the worst misery would come not after their marriage, but during these next seven days when he would not have her beneath him, and instead rode across Goge with his cock forged of molten steel.

Her eyebrows arched, head tilted as she regarded him. "*Now* you scowl at me. It pleases me that you are so easily trained. I have heard every good husband ought to be—though perhaps not one who will also be king."

Laughter danced in her pale eyes when his scowl only deepened. But despite the ache in his loins, his mood was still light—and perhaps it was best to let her believe he could be easily led. So he didn't respond but looked forward and said, "We will rest the horses at the head of the ruins."

And rest the woman who would be his bride. For as soon as the moon rose full, she would not find sleep until his seed overfilled her sheath. But there would be no rest for Maddek here.

Until that night came, easy rest would not likely find him again.

CHAPTER 12

MADDEK

At a word from Fassad, his hounds bolted past Maddek's mare. Their agile bodies cut through the ground-clinging mist as they raced for the ruins looming directly ahead. They scrambled up the steep mound of rubble and were lost from sight.

All was quiet except the plodding tread of the horses along the muddied road. The land surrounding the crossroads might have once been cultivated, but the fields lay fallow now, stubbled grasses growing in clumps around scattered boulders and broken stone. In the distance, a small herd of striped-legged antelope grazed near a copse of trees, pronghorn heads raised and alert to the warriors' presence—but the Parsatheans would not be hunting them today.

As the horses were rounding the ruins, the hounds emerged silently from the mist, tongues dangling. Judging by their wolfish grins, they hadn't found any threats within the rubble or the road ahead. Still Maddek didn't call a halt until the path began to curve back toward the river, where he could see both the way forward and the way they'd come. This route was well-traveled, and he didn't expect that Syssian soldiers would catch up to them this day or bandits to be foolish enough to attack a group of Parsatheans, but better to have a view in both directions.

The ground was firmer near the ruins than on the road, yet still soft. Mud sucked at Maddek's boots when he dismounted. Yvenne moved more slowly. She was just swinging her leg over when Maddek caught her waist. Her thick cloak was still damp from the earlier rain, her spine stiffening at his touch—until she looked over her shoulder and saw that it was he. The immediate softening of her body had the opposite effect on his.

Only seven more nights until he knew the softness and heat within her.

Only seven more misery-filled days.

He brought her slight form against his chest and carried her to the nearest slab of stone—a toppled column that lay half embedded in the soft earth, creating a wide ledge that came up to his knees. "You need boots. Your sandals are not well-suited for riding."

"Perhaps not, but muddied toes will not kill me," was her tart reply. "I must tend to my horse."

"I'll bring him to you."

She stood taller than Maddek when he set her upon the ledge—a position he suspected she liked. Her full lips curved as she looked down at him.

"This must be how my mother and her mother felt. It must be a wondrous thing to stand so tall, never having to look up at anyone. Is that how you feel?"

Maddek had never thought of his height as wondrous. He only stood as tall as Temra made him.

But some elevated themselves in other ways. "Did you not look down upon everyone from your tower?"

"No. Zhalen could not risk me being seen. Our windows were shuttered and locked, and we had but cracks to look through." Her shrug could not be as careless as she tried to make it seem, for her voice thickened. "It mattered not. My mother could still see beyond the chamber walls and describe it all to me."

It mattered not. A lie. But not all untruths were on purpose. Maddek would not hold that one against her.

Instead he directed her attention to Kelir, who had ridden toward the river's edge, searching for dangers the hounds might not have scented. "He and Ardyl are in constant competition. When we were younger, she grew taller than he." Taller than Maddek, too. "It was not until he reached his bearded age that his height overtook hers—but he did everything he could to speed it along. Once I found him hanging from a tree by his legs, because he hoped to stretch their length by a span."

Her sallow face alight with laughter, she watched the warrior return across the muddied flat. "Is that why he is always the last to dismount?"

She had noted that? It was true that Kelir sat upon his horse longer than any other, but the height it offered was not the only reason he saw the other warriors settled before he took his own ease. As he was leader of the Dragon, the responsibility for Maddek's security—and now Yvenne's security—lay heavier upon him.

But she was not wrong. "Watch how he rides by her," he said, and when Kelir stopped near Ardyl but did not dismount until the female warrior looked up and saw him sitting so high above her, Maddek glanced back at Yvenne and saw her wearing a grin as broad as his.

"Now she will cut him down with her words," he told her, and though they were not near enough to hear Ardyl's response, the flush that creeped over Kelir's cheeks was easy to read.

So was the querying glance Banek sent in Maddek's direction, for his mare and Yvenne's gelding were still saddled.

"I will fetch your mount," Maddek told her. "You ought to spread out your cloak beneath the sun."

Which was hot and had already dried the ledge she

stood upon, though mist still rose from the sodden ground and from the moss-covered rubble behind her.

Returning with their horses, he saw that she'd done as he'd suggested—and that beneath the cloak her robe was wet, the darkened silk clinging to her slim figure. But he did not think she would remove the robe and lay it out, as several of his warriors had done with their belted linens— as Maddek would have done if the damp and heavy material was not the best leash upon his cock. She'd folded her arms tightly against her chest, hands clamped beneath her chin as if to conceal the way the silk hugged her small breasts.

But it was not out of modesty, Maddek realized as he led her gelding up beside the ledge. Her teeth chattered.

Beneath a blazing sun. Though puffed white clouds drifted in the sky, none shielded Enam's glaring eye. "Are you cold?"

"No." Brow furrowed, she looked uncertainly around, her pale gaze touching upon the ruins before sliding past them to the rushing river.

"Are you fevered?"

Her mouth flattened with irritation. "I did not take ill in the storm. I am not *that* frail."

Even warriors caught chill. He studied her face, the moonstone eyes that were still focused uneasily on the river. "Are you sensitive to magics?"

Her gaze clashed with Maddek's, her face utterly still. "I would not know," she said slowly. "Never have I encountered any."

This would be a place to encounter them. He held out the gelding's reins, and it seemed an enormous effort for her to unlock her arms and close her shivering fingers around the leather lines.

Her palms were blistered, skin cracked and weeping. Maddek's fists clenched against the instinctive need to take the reins back from her, but she would not appreciate it or benefit if he tended to her horse to spare her hands. As with saddle-sore muscles, the only remedy was more riding and calluses.

Instead he moved to his mare's side and said, "There are warriors who feel a chill near Parsa." The ancient city the Destroyer had razed—just as he had razed this bridge and trading village. "Perhaps the same dark magics linger here."

With a grunt, she pulled the saddle from her gelding's back, stumbling under its weight and setting it heavily upon the stone. "Is Parsa still abandoned, as this place is?"

"Yes. It is home to nothing but wraiths." Malignant specters that raised the hairs on the back of any warrior's neck, sensitive to magics or not. As he placed his saddle beside hers, Maddek's gaze swept the fallow fields, the ruins. "The hounds usually sense such things."

In the alliance's march against Stranik's Fang, dogs had often alerted the army to the priests' magics, allowing Toleh's monks to cleanse any befouled areas before the warriors passed through. But Fassad's wolves did not appear uneasy. Instead they were tussling playfully at Fassad's feet as he fed them treats from his store of dried meat.

"Perhaps I did take a slight chill in the rain, then," Yvenne said wryly. "And it seems to be passing."

She no longer shivered, at least. Still, as soon as they were fed, Maddek would ask Fassad to send his hounds over the ruins again.

"Go on," he told his mare, and she immediately trotted to the nearest clump of grass. Not waiting for Yvenne's command, the gelding started after the mare. Yvenne barely managed to strip its bridle free before the fool horse was out of reach.

Her gaze was upon Maddek's face when he glanced back at her. "You hope to get rid of my mount," she said.

"Why do you say that?" Because he'd not said so to her, though he *had* been thinking that they would likely pass through another village before night fell, and it would be best to find her another horse.

"Because you often wear the same expression when you look at me." She glanced away from his sudden frown as

Toric—who had laid out belt, linens, and furs to dry—approached wearing only his sword, boots, and a small loincloth. The warrior offered bread and cheese. Taking a large chunk of both, Yvenne continued, "Danoh told me the gelding has weak pasterns, a short back, a steep shoulder, and shallow lungs."

"He does," Maddek said, tearing his portion from the loaf and sending the young warrior quickly away again with a hard stare. "You must have noticed how rough his gait is. It makes an unpleasant ride—and risks injury to him. With his unsound legs, he's more likely to fall lame. A limping horse is of no use. Better to leave him in a farming village where little is required of him."

Her mouth full, a nod was her only response. Her gaze drifted beyond the ruins again. Even at this distance, the sound of the great river was a rushing roar.

Swallowing, she asked, "Are all Parsathean horses so big and so well-formed?"

Maddek grunted an assent.

"Is it true they are Hanan's descendants?"

"They are not Hanani." An animal with a god's blood running through its veins, a body of great power, and as intelligent as any person. His gaze slipped over his mare's fine lines. "But it is said that a herd of Hanani horses live north of the Flaming Mountains. Perhaps in ancient times, another herd ran the Burning Plains, and the Parsathean horses are their descendants. They are not only bigger and hardier, but also cleverer than other mounts."

"Oh!" she exclaimed softly, then fell quiet.

Maddek looked to her.

Briskly she brushed her hand down the front of her robe, though not a single crumb had escaped her mouth. "I had wondered if the Parsatheans themselves were also Hanan's descendants," she said. "Since you all seem so big and hardy. But . . ."

She trailed off, nibbling the hard white cheese, yet with such a playful arch in her eyebrows that he could not mistake her.

He grinned. "Do you think my warriors are not clever?"

Her pale gaze narrowed pointedly.

"You think *I* am not?"

A laugh shook through her, but she did not confirm or deny.

Nor would Maddek. If his cleverness was compared to his warriors', he would fare well. Compared to Yvenne's, he was not so certain.

But he cared not. A clever wife was not something to lament—and a clever queen was something to celebrate. "Come," he said when her gaze was once more drawn to the rushing waters beyond the ruins. "I will carry you close enough to better see the river."

This time, Yvenne did not protest and insist she cared not if her toes became muddied. Expression eager, she stuffed the remaining cheese into her mouth and leaned forward to wind her linen-wrapped arms around his neck. Maddek swept her from the ledge, letting her form press full-length against his before swinging her legs up to brace his arm beneath her knees. She stiffened, pulling in a quick sharp breath.

Maddek had yet to hear her make a pained noise. But her breath often told him as much as a whimper or a sob.

He gestured ahead. An arrow's flight away, cobblestones formed a path through the surrounding mud and disappeared beneath the mist-shrouded ruins. "We should not go any nearer to the river than that remnant of the old road. You can walk and ease your soreness there without wading through mud."

Tautly she nodded.

All around them, the ground steamed like fresh horse dung on a cold morn. The dank, earthy odor filled his every breath—as did the hint of anise perfume that lingered in her sun-warmed hair.

"The river looked not so wide when we saw it from the Toheli ridge," she said in awe. "I failed to realize it was so broad."

Because when she had crossed the Ageras before, she

was in a curtained carriage—and her brother must have forbidden her to look outside. "It is a mighty river," he agreed.

"Is the Lave so wide?"

The river upon whose bloodstained banks Maddek had spent these past years commanding the alliance army. "At its mouth," he said. "But narrower as it passes through the Farians' territory. An archer could find a target on the opposite side."

Her gaze seemed to measure the distance across the Ageras. "Yet the Boiling Sea is much wider? As is Temra's Heart."

The ocean at the center of the world. "Yes."

"How far would the Boiling Sea stretch?" She looked beyond the Ageras. "To those hills in the far distance?"

"No. It would cover those hills. It would cover everything." Perhaps he could describe the sheer expanse better had she ever seen the Burning Plains. "If we were upon the ridge again, looking out—you would see nothing but water stretching to the horizon. It is like a clear sky, but upon the ground."

Her gaze rose to the white clouds drifting across the blue heavens. After a few long breaths, she said softly, "That is as my mother said. I did not truly believe her."

At the naked wonder in her voice, a strange ache filled his chest. "You will see for yourself when we reach Drahm."

"Yes." A brief smile touched her mouth. All at once her gaze returned to the Ageras, and her tone was somber as she said, "Hanan must have been very lonely."

"Lonely?" The roar of laughter that burst from Maddek couldn't have been drowned by all the water in the river. He halted in his muddied tracks, and felt her arms cling suddenly tighter around his neck as the force of his laughter nearly bent him double.

For she referred to the legend of the Ageras's creation—when the face of the earth had been bare and barren. Then Mother Temra had broken through the vault of the sky and begun reshaping the world with the pounding of her fists.

Other gods had come with her. One of them was her brother Hanan, who arrived after her pounding fists forced the Fallen Mountains to rise from the plains. Hanan had stood atop the jagged peaks, surveying the lifeless land, and had wept with loneliness. In his misery and longing for companionship he had stroked his colossal cock, until his godly seed spurted forth and mixed with his tears, creating the mighty Ageras and overfilling the basin of the Boiling Sea. When Temra's fists struck the earth a final time, life sprouted from the now-fertile ground, watered by his tears and planted by his seed.

Then Hanan, enamored of the new life that had sprung from the earth, had fucked every one of them. Nothing escaped his attentions: not men or women, not reptiles, not insects.

The god had not been lonely then.

Yvenne's arms squeezed tighter as another bout of laughter quaked through him. Maddek struggled for control and slowly found it, yet his steps were not all that steady as he straightened and started forward again.

His bride regarded him with a slight frown. "Do you think his loneliness so amusing?"

Maddek could not even answer for laughing again. Perhaps that *was* answer.

Though with this woman in his arms, he'd never had more sympathy for Hanan's plight. Before her moon night, by his hand Maddek would spill a small river of his own seed.

She studied him a breath longer. "I suppose you have not known loneliness or felt how deeply it can wound."

That was true enough. He had been raised among warriors. Yvenne had shared a tower chamber with her mother . . . a queen who had died three years past.

That realization sobered him enough to say, "I admit that I have never been so lonely that I would fuck my horse—or a fish."

Her lips parted as she stared at him with widened eyes. Slowly her mouth curved. "Or a trap jaw."

Another laugh shook him. "Or a bee."

"I see," she said softly. "When I heard that legend, his loneliness resonated deepest within me. Perhaps because I do not often think of fucking."

Yet she thought of it now, Maddek saw. They finally reached the cobblestones but he did not immediately set her down, for her eyes were afire and burning into his.

Abruptly a new frown pleated her brows. "Why have you not demanded that I ease your need again? I told you that I would willingly take your seed."

That she would take it with her hands or mouth. Gaze dropping to her lips, Maddek stopped his tortured groan behind clenched teeth. For he wanted nothing more now.

But she had also told him something else. "You want me to demand it where my warriors can watch?"

They stood a long distance from his Dragon guard but not so far the warriors couldn't see them.

"No, but—" Her gaze flicked over his shoulder as if to see whether the warriors watched now. "They would turn their backs. So I wonder that you don't."

"Because they are sworn to protect me, but if they are forced to turn their backs, they cannot perform their duty." And Maddek would not ask them to compromise their vows. "So my duty to my warriors is not to interfere with theirs."

Approval softened her tone. "Why do you not demand it of me in the privacy of our furs?"

Which were not truly private, but the courtesy of any camp was to turn away eyes and close ears to the sounds that came from another's furs.

Dryly he said, "You are always asleep."

"You cannot wake me?" Those moonstone eyes dared him to, and a familiar note of challenge rang in her voice.

"This night I will," he said gruffly—and reluctantly set her down, before duty could flee his mind. If he held her much longer, Maddek would not wait until this night. Instead he'd have her on her knees in the mud, her mouth wrapped around his aching shaft.

Feet firmly on the cobblestones, she looked up at him for an endless time before her gaze was drawn to the river again. "It is said that any woman who bathes in the Ageras's waters will be as fertile as Hanan himself, and her children as strong."

"It is also said that any man who bathes in the river will be as virile as that god," Maddek said. "But the only certainty is that the man will be dead."

As if the river itself agreed, the bloated and half-eaten corpse of a mammoth floated past. Nothing was safe upon the riverbanks. The creatures that lurked within the waters could drag even that giant beast to a certain death. Whether swimming or on a boat, anything that ventured into the Ageras never emerged again.

When she had no reply, Maddek told her, "If you fear you will not quickly get with child, do not. After your moon night, I will spend my seed inside you so often that your belly will be swelling before we reach the Burning Plains. I *will* have my vengeance."

"As will I," she said before directing a wry smile at him. "In truth, I was not doubting my fertility. I was thinking of strong children. Though with the mingling of our bloodlines, I ought not worry."

"No." Maddek did not. Even if their children did not possess their foremothers' strength—as she did not—it mattered little. They would be as strong as they needed to be.

Their children.

His heart seemed to still. Not only one. Not just an instrument of vengeance. But a child who would live long after Zhalen was dead and they had taken Syssia's throne—and would be sibling to any others he and Yvenne had. For she was the only woman Maddek would ever lie with again.

Watching her face, he asked, "Will you care for a child?"

"Very much." Her smile softened and her gaze upon the river became unfocused. "I loved my mother, and she loved hers. I also loved your—"

She stopped herself, but it mattered not. She might as

well have spoken his mother's name and claimed to have loved her, too. For there was nothing else that could have followed.

A sly tongue. Speaking that which he had forbidden her to, without actually saying the words.

But perhaps it was just as well that she had done it slyly, because Maddek would take no pleasure in ripping that tongue from her mouth.

After a breath, she continued, "When my younger brother was born, my father took no interest in him, so Tyzen remained with us in our tower for many years. My mother was too weak to properly care for him, so I did." Another quiet moment passed before she said, "I should like very much to be a mother."

To *his* children. And Maddek would be a father.

For days he had thought of nothing but getting a child within her, but had not looked any further ahead. Even though *she* would be his child's mother.

Abruptly he asked, "Are you treacherous?"

A startled blink erased the gentle longing from her expression. Her moonstone gaze rose to his face and she studied him quietly.

Weighing her response carefully.

"Do not lie," he reminded her. "I will not forgive it."

Her mouth flattened into a thin line. "That I know. But it is not a simple answer. If you ask whether I am so treacherous that I would stab my brother in the back—then I am indeed quite treacherous. But if you wonder whether I will betray my people or anyone else to whom I have promised my loyalty, then I am not."

"That is also what you would say if you were treacherous, so that I would not anticipate your betrayal."

She laughed suddenly. "Yes, I would." Tilting her head, she studied his face again, her expression a curious mixture of amusement and gravity. "Why ask me questions if you always doubt my answers?"

Maddek knew not. Better not to speak with her at all, if she was as calculating as he suspected. Only a fool would make the same mistake her brother had—believing that because she was weak, she posed no danger to him. Believing that he could trust her at his back. Yet with every breath he took, Maddek became more and more a fool.

Because he was not thinking only of how he should distrust her, or even of fucking her—he was also enjoying her company and her smiles. These past days, he'd bitten his tongue as his warriors had enjoyed them, because they were not fools, either. Yet none of them looked at her with suspicion. He'd seen her easy conversations with Banek, and frequently heard the old man's rusty laugh join her throaty one. With treats and pettings, she'd befriended Fassad's dogs and, in doing so, befriended the warrior. This morn, after Yvenne asked whether bandits were as common in Goge as in Toleh, Ardyl had returned the jeweled dagger Yvenne used to kill her brother, claiming that on an open road, even warriors were not enough protection. Then Danoh—who usually only opened her mouth to put food into it—had shown her how to strap the weapon to her lower leg, and how best to wield it while mounted. Young Toric could still barely meet her moonstone eyes without blushing, yet seemed to pass each day thinking of new questions to ask of her while they broke their morning fast. Even Kelir had praised her, remarking upon her fortitude, and now was completely caught in her spell, as if she'd known that she could win over Maddek's closest friend by poking fun at Maddek's scowl and his smile.

Did Maddek forget who she was, she might win over him, too.

For despite sharing furs, since the night after she'd taken the half-moon milk, he'd spent almost no time talking with Yvenne—and now he envied every word that had passed between his warriors and her. He wished that her every laugh and smile had been aimed at him, that he'd ridden beside her, that he'd strapped that jeweled dagger to her leg. It was madness.

Yet perhaps . . . not so mad. Or unexpected. He had seen

her cold and shrewd. Likely Yvenne knew exactly what she did.

"Do you deliberately befriend my warriors?"

Sudden bemusement curved her lips, as if she thought his question absurd. "Of course I do."

"You manipulate them? What of the gratitude you spoke of when they rescued you from your marriage to Toleh? Is this how you repay them?"

A soft sigh escaped her and she looked to the river. "Even if I purposely cultivate their friendship and loyalty, it does not mean the loyalty and friendship I offer in return is not genuine."

"Yet you wonder why I doubt?"

She slanted him an irritated glance. "You speak from your lofty height, warrior. For I have not had the luxury of a lifetime spent in their company and forging the same bonds you have. But as my very life depends upon their protection and goodwill—"

"No," he stopped her. "Your life depends on *my* protection and goodwill."

"Then I shall make certain to ease your need very well indeed!" she snapped.

Maddek grinned.

Her burning glare did not cool for a long breath, and then her lips twitched. Brows arching, she ran her gaze the length of his body, lingering upon the ridged muscles of his stomach, which hardened ever more under her perusal. "When you come to the furs tonight and wake me, do you think my purpose will be pleasure or manipulation?"

"I care not what your purpose is," he said honestly. "So long as your mouth is hot upon my cock."

Her gaze dropped lower, teeth pinching her soft bottom lip as she took in the enormity of the erection beneath his linens. Heat and amusement lit her eyes in equal measure when they met Maddek's again. "My body is small, but my heart is still a warrior-queen's. So I shall make a valiant effort to wield your mighty sword."

Maddek could neither stop his laugh nor resist the impulse to touch her again. Palm cupping the side of her slim neck, long fingers wrapping around her nape, he pressed his thumb beneath her jaw and tilted her head back. Her breath stopped, her entire body suddenly frozen, her gaze searching his. Her pulse throbbed frantically in the vulnerable column of her throat. Arousal or fear, he knew not. The last time he had touched her in this way, Maddek had worn silver claws and had intended to spill her blood onto the ground.

Her hot breath shuddered when he swept his thumb across her trembling lips.

"Open," he commanded, and she did.

Without prompting, her wet velvet tongue slicked over the pad of his thumb, tasting his skin. Need clenched upon his body so hard that Maddek thought he might spend there, with nothing but a lick. His heart thundered as if he were in the midst of battle—yet he stood motionless upon the cobblestones.

But perhaps this *was* a battle. Though it could not be properly waged here.

Nor could it be waged now. A familiar chirp reached his ears—Danoh's signal that someone was approaching. Not a warning, simply an alert.

He glanced over his shoulder. Danoh had climbed the mound of ruins for a better vantage and was looking back the way they had come. Other travelers were not unexpected. This route was well-used, and they had passed through a village shortly before the rains had stopped. Anyone who had been waiting out the storm in that village would be coming upon them now.

But so might any bandits who had seen them pass.

"Does someone come?" Yvenne's query was a puff of warm air and a brush of soft lips against his thumb.

Maddek grunted an assent.

"A threat?"

"I expect not." Still, they had lingered here long enough. Maddek's gaze searched the road ahead. Empty all the way to the horizon, with no visible threat from that direction, human or animal. And Yvenne stood a fair distance from the riverbank—almost a full arrow's flight. "You would be safe here if you wish to walk while I ready our horses. Or you can return with me to the road."

"It would be best to walk," she said.

Maddek agreed. They would not stop again until nightfall. "Unless I call for you, do not leave this stone path. Fassad will send his hounds to look after you until I return with your gelding."

She nodded, and with a final slide of his thumb across her mouth, reluctantly Maddek released her. At the head of the ruins, his warriors were all belting on their linens again, even before Maddek signaled across the distance for them to prepare to leave.

After another signal to Fassad, the hounds streaked across the muddied flat. Maddek had only taken ten steps before they passed him, and he looked back to see Yvenne greeting the dogs with a laughing smile, scratching their ears as they jostled each other for her attention.

A sharp whistle from Fassad stopped their playing. Immediately the hounds flanked Yvenne, instead, and her expression was wryly amused when she looked up and caught Maddek's eyes.

She called to him, "They are ordered to protect me! So tell me, Commander—what other reason to pet them, except the pleasure of it?"

"Because Fassad will like you better for it," he said with a grin.

Her scowl pinched her narrow face, and as he continued toward the road her response followed him. "They are called Steel and Bone!"

The dogs' names. Maddek knew them, though he still thought Fassad foolish for naming the wolves. A warrior did not name his sword or his armor, and the wolves also served as tools—but that was likely Yvenne's point. She had learned their names because the dogs were not only tools to her.

As she claimed his warriors were not. And in truth, Maddek believed she enjoyed their company. But that did not mean she valued the warriors at their worth. Many citizens of the southern realms did not. The alliance had set a Parsathean rider's life equal to a few ingots of Tolehi iron or a clutch of swords made from Syssian steel. His people were not so easily replaceable.

At the head of the ruins, Banek had taken a seat on the ledge Yvenne had abandoned. He and Kelir watched Maddek come.

"By your face," Kelir called out, "I see that you still are determined to displease her!"

Because the smile Maddek had worn when he'd left her had not completely disappeared. With a laugh, he shook his head. "Only because she has not yet succeeded in making my life a misery."

"She will have to try harder," a grinning Banek said.

Yes, she would. Much harder. For he enjoyed her company so well, Maddek did not believe their marriage would be a misery.

Which made no sense. A shrewd queen, she might prove to be—but as a wife? She was weak and sickly. She was manipulative and treacherous. Never could she be trusted.

How could that make for a strong marriage? It would be nothing like his mother and father's union, solidly built on love and trust and respect. Nothing like the marriage they had desired for Maddek. Just as she was nothing like the bride he had imagined for himself.

Yet he enjoyed being with her. And still he wanted her. This frail and sly woman.

A woman whose gaze burned as hotly for him as his body did for her.

For she was not always ice. She hadn't been when, in his anger and frustration, Maddek had demanded she ease his need. Then she had responded with challenge burning in her gaze, a heat that hadn't waned when she'd licked his seed from her bloodied fingers, and burned hot again when she'd grabbed his beard and commanded him to never degrade her in front of his warriors.

He had been frustrated since, but not angry—yet still she met his stare with that same challenge. Sometimes hot, sometimes amused. But never balking or backing down.

That must have been why he wanted her so. He was still uncertain whether she was an enemy, so his every warrior's instinct clamored for her defeat and submission. Yet he'd spoken truth earlier: Maddek didn't believe anyone could control her. But she was also a virgin who had spent most of her life isolated within a tower chamber. She had not even known how to stroke his cock and would know less about relations between women and men. Undoubtedly when he took her to his bed, she would challenge him again, but she would not possess the weapons to defeat him.

Maddek suspected that Yvenne had never submitted to anyone. Yet she *would* submit to him. And victory *would* be his.

Until then, he would take his pleasure in her mouth and hands—and her smiles.

"What do you see?" he called up to Danoh.

"Two wagons drawn by oxen, flanked by a dozen Gogean soldiers." Carefully she began to pick her way down the rubble. "They travel at a sloth's pace."

So slow that even Yvenne's gelding would stay well ahead of them. These soldiers would not be a threat—but the fewer people who could report details of their route to any Syssian soldiers in pursuit, the better.

Still a raider at heart, Banek called to Danoh, "What are they guarding in the wagons?"

"Young men and women, it looked like."

"Protecting travelers from bandits?"

She shrugged. As there were no riches to dream of stealing, the older warrior lost interest, his gaze returning to where Yvenne was limping the length of the cobblestone path. Maddek had been keeping an eye on her as well.

Though she still walked slowly and favored her left side, her movements were not as stiff as in previous days.

Already becoming accustomed to the saddle. Maddek collected her mount's bridle and started toward the patch of grass where the gelding was grazing.

At five paces away, the gelding abruptly tossed his head and pivoted on his heels, trotting swiftly away from Maddek and across the road—where he settled down and ripped out another mouthful of grass.

The warriors behind Maddek snorted with laughter. Ardyl called out, "So that nag *can* move swiftly when he wants to!"

So he could. But Maddek had no intention of chasing the fool horse through the mud. Fassad's dogs were currently at Yvenne's heels, so they could not herd the gelding closer, as they usually did reluctant mounts. Fortunately almost any horse could be corralled by its stomach.

He looked to Toric, who was already grabbing a sack of grain—then toward the ruins as there was a clatter of tumbling stone and a foul curse.

At the base of the rubble, Danoh was picking herself up from the ground, her face a storm of irritation.

The warrior was usually as surefooted as a goat. Frowning, Maddek asked, "Are you well?"

"Just muddied my ass. A pig-swived stone twisted beneath my boot, though it felt solid enough when I stepped on it." She angled her arm to look at her elbow, where blood welled from a gash, and swore again. "By Stranik's scaly slit. I'll be riding around with my arm wrapped like a southerner's."

Maddek grinned—then stilled as crimson beads dripped from Danoh's arm and splashed onto the ground. The hairs lifted on the back of his neck.

All fell silent.

Abruptly it was so cold that Maddek's breath was visible as a soft cloud, though the sun was hot upon his shoulders. In the distance, Fassad's wolves howled a warning.

Yvenne.

Maddek's gaze shot across the muddied flat—though he could not clearly see the mud nearer to the river now. Instead the mist had thickened, blanketing the ground in a white fog that rolled steadily toward the cobblestone path. Eddies of gray swirled lazily through the white, as if disturbed by a chill breeze.

Ice rippled down Maddek's spine. That was not a breeze. Something moved within the fog—or was being carried by it toward Yvenne.

"Blood wraiths!" Face lined with horror, Banek lurched up from his seat on the ledge and shouted across the distance. "Run this way, girl! *Run!*"

The fog rolled slowly enough that she could outrace it—but when Yvenne turned to look at the encroaching mist, fear must have paralyzed her, for she moved not at all.

By Temra's fist. A blood wraith's touch was death. *Worse* than death. Heart hammering, Maddek sprinted for his mare.

"To the road, my lady!" Kelir thundered from behind him. *"Run!"*

Fassad's sharp whistle joined the shouts, and either that awoke Yvenne from her terrified stupor or the wolves did. While Steel snapped sharp teeth close at her ankles, Bone snagged her robe in his jaws and hauled back, as if the dog intended to drag her to the road.

She stumbled, nearly fell, then righted herself again. Maddek caught a glimpse of her bloodbare face when she looked toward the road. Relief eased the clutching fear upon his chest.

Now she would run.

But she did not. Instead she looked back toward the fog, as if measuring its speed—then limped quickly toward a broken column that lay half embedded in the mud, not unlike the ledge where she had sat before.

"No, my lady! To the road!" Toric called to her—for the column was high enough that she would be above the mist, but when it overtook the ledge, she would be trapped there.

Unless Maddek reached her first. Shouting *"Fly!"* he

vaulted onto the mare's bare back. Her powerful muscles bunched as she sprang forward, racing headlong toward his bride and the befouled fog. It swept toward her and macabre dread gripped Maddek's heart, for he could see what crawled within the thick mist—the twisted gray visages with gaping sharp-toothed maws, the long grasping claws. The scuttling withered husks were all that remained of the men and women they'd once been before their blood had been corrupted and their souls trapped by perverse magics.

With the wolves at her heels, Yvenne scrambled atop the ledge on hands and knees. Gaining her feet, her frantic gaze clashed with his across the distance before she glanced desperately at the encroaching fog—and when she faced him again, he knew that she'd made the same realization he had.

He would not reach her before the blood wraiths surrounded the ledge. Already the fog was at the far end of the broken column.

"Fassad!" Her shout carried over the pounding of the mare's hooves. "Call them back!"

The dogs. No whistle came—Fassad would not leave her alone.

Her chest heaved, gaze darting wildly behind her. The fog had spread along half the column's length. Both she and the dogs moved to the end nearest the road, where there was still muddied ground visible at its base. Once it was covered, there would be no escape that way.

Maddek held up his fist and Fassad's whistle sounded, short and shrill. The wolves hesitated only a moment before bounding to the ground and racing toward the road.

Never would Maddek forget Yvenne's face in the moment the dogs abandoned her. Her relief, her terror—and the lift of her chin as she met his eyes again. Before the mare had taken three more strides, the fog closed around the base of her column. Gray fingers reached up out of the mist, crawling up the shadowed side of the ledge, then at the sunlit edge shriveling and drawing back from the glare of Enam's yellow eye.

If a cloud shielded that eye, there would be nothing to hold them back.

Maddek looked over his shoulder to where Kelir rode not far behind him, his big body crouched low over his mount's neck.

"Fall back to the road!" Maddek shouted, and for an instant, the warrior seemed as if he would refuse the order. Then Kelir sat upright in his saddle and his horse slowed, veering toward the ruins in a wide curve that would take them back to safety.

His heart like lead, Maddek urged his mare faster even as realization dawned on Yvenne's face. His bride shook her head wildly and shouted something at him, probably that he was a fool, but her voice was drowned out by the pounding of his blood and the thundering of hooves. Without hesitation his mare plunged into the ground-crawling fog, her powerful legs churning the mist. A chorus of unholy screeching seemed to rise from the earth itself, reverberating through mud and stone, the odor of rot thick in the air.

Just before reaching the column he felt the mare's stride falter, then catch pace again. Barely slowing, Maddek swept Yvenne from the ledge with an elbow hooked around her waist, and heard the impact knock away her breath even as she wound her arms desperately around his neck.

Holding her shaking form securely against his chest, Maddek wheeled the mare around. "Fly," he said from a roughened throat, and she did, her great heart carrying them out of the mist and her stride never slowing until they reached the road.

There he drew her to a halt with his voice. His warriors surrounded him and he looked down into Yvenne's blood-bare face. Her trembling arms still clung tightly around his neck, as if she would never let him go.

"Were you touched?" he asked gruffly.

"No." Her voice was a strained whisper, her pale gaze searching his features. "You did not have to come for me. Thank you."

With a stiff nod, he handed her down into Banek's arms and slid from the mare's back. She stood calmly, the only sign of her exertion the faint sheen of sweat glistening on her coat and her flaring nostrils, but when he laid his palm against her shoulder he felt the quivering tension through her heavy muscles. Grimly he examined her legs. Blood seeped from shallow, parallel slashes down their lengths.

"We need to stop the bleeding," Banek said quietly.

Because a few drops of Danoh's blood had been enough to feed the foul magics that had thickened the fog and drawn the wraiths from the ground. They could not know how much faster and stronger the wraiths would be if the mare's blood fed it, too.

"I have more linens in my satchel." Yvenne's moonstone eyes were huge in her thin face. "They could wrap her legs. If you wish, I will fetch them."

Maddek nodded but said, "Toric will fetch your satchel. For I know he will run when told."

She sucked in a sharp breath, but silence was her only response.

For what response could she have? That she had not heard them shouting for her to run? That her legs were too sore from riding? That she had not wanted to muddy her feet?

Maddek had no desire to hear any of her excuses. Neither did his warriors, for they had barely even glanced at her since Maddek had set her down. Instead they regarded his mare, their expressions grave.

Looking away from Yvenne, he addressed Banek again. "How long?"

"Nightfall," the older warrior said.

"Then we continue on to the next village." He paused as Toric returned with Yvenne's embroidered satchel and she began digging through it. Behind them, the fog seemed to have slowed but had not yet dissipated. "Ardyl and Toric, ride to warn the soldiers who travel this way, then catch up to us again."

Immediately the warriors moved toward their horses.

Maddek took the roll of linens Yvenne pulled from her satchel and cast her a hard look. "Ask Fassad to have his hounds round up your gelding."

Swallowing hard, she nodded and limped away, leaving Maddek to tend to the mare. Chest tight, he smoothed his hand down her sleek neck, then crouched beside her bleeding legs.

Softly Kelir said, "Will you saddle her?"

Maddek shook his head. With her great heart, she would carry him to the next village, but he would not ask her to. They'd had their last ride—to save Maddek's bride, who had claimed she would make his life a misery.

Already she was doing a better job of it.

CHAPTER 13

YVENNE

A grim pall hung over the riders as they left the ruins, and it grew heavier as the day wore on. No
longer did Yvenne have a riding companion. Instead she was protected and boxed in. Maddek still took the
lead. Then came Kelir and Banek, with Yvenne behind. A
few paces farther were Fassad and Danoh, and after their
return from warning the soldiers behind them, Ardyl and
Toric brought up the rear.

Maddek's mare was the only lighthearted member of
their party, though her legs were wrapped in bloodstained
linens and her death lay ahead. Maddek did not ride her
now; instead he ran along at her side, and the mare was as
playful as the wolves sometimes were, nickering and butt-
ing her head against his shoulder, prancing and flicking her
tail as if bored by the pace they'd set and challenging him
to a faster race.

The mare's joy and the warriors' silence seemed an un-
bearable weight. A hot leaden lump lodged in Yvenne's
throat, choking into nothing every word she might have

spoken—and blocking the scream of rage building in her chest.

The scream had not started as rage. First it had been mortal terror, when she'd turned to see the blood wraiths writhing in the fog. Although fear still lingered, her skin clammy despite the heat of the sun and the warmth of her cloak, it was her helplessness that had given birth to the anger.

For the warriors had shouted at her to run. But Yvenne could not.

Three years past, her father and older brothers had seen to that.

And *how* she hated them. With every breath and every beat of her heart, she hated them. Hated them and hated relying upon others for her protection. Hated the very silence that choked her, for what could she say to the warriors now?

Her explanation would seem a pitiful excuse, no matter how true.

But Yvenne had never thought to tell the warriors that her knee had been shattered. Her limp and the pain seemed ever-present, so it never occurred to her that they believed saddle soreness was the only reason for her stiffness and hobbling. Unlike the pain of riding, however, her limp would never go away—and although on good days Yvenne could move quickly and smoothly, never would she be able to run again. At such a pace, her leg would buckle after the third or fourth step.

And Banek—who had shown her such kindness and upon whose guidance she had come to rely—had not spoken to her since they had left the ruins. None of the warriors had.

Because she had not run and Maddek's mare would die for it.

If they learned now that she was crippled, what would they do? When Banek had spoken of Queen Venys's moonstone eyes, he'd looked upon Yvenne's eyes with admiration. Would he still after learning the truth? For even if Yvenne ate heartily and learned to ride well, never would she be a warrior-queen. Before her knee had been shattered, every day her mother made Yvenne race back and forth across their tower chamber until her lungs were completely spent. It was the strongest she'd ever been. Yet if she'd attempted then to do what Maddek did now—run beside his mare without once stopping—she'd have collapsed breathless at the side of the road before they'd even passed out of sight of the ruins.

And when Maddek had spoken of the uselessness of a lame horse, she'd believed he already knew about her knee and was simply thoughtless. But perhaps he would leave her at the next village as he would her gelding, so she would not be called upon to do anything more strenuous than her body could tolerate.

If so, they could soon be rid of her. Around them stretched verdant fields of cultivated grain. Ahead lay a village ringed by a stone wall.

It was larger than any of the other settlements they'd passed through. At each village, Yvenne never seemed to see enough—she was fascinated by everything that she'd only known from her mother's descriptions. The clay-walled homes with their thatched roofs were just as her mother had said, but Yvenne had not known the rich scent of plowed earth or baking bread. She had not known the sound of children laughing as they'd run beside the Parsathean horses, or their delighted screams when the warriors teased them with mock growls and bared teeth. She'd never imagined that everyone would come out of their homes and to the edges of their fields to watch the warriors pass, or how even the most welcoming and curious villagers regarded them with wary faces. And her mother had never told her about the fear and hope and disbelief in the gazes of those who met her moonstone eyes.

But upon entering this village, Yvenne's heart was too heavy and her throat too painfully constricted for her to find any joy or muster any interest. The sun had begun its slow slide toward the western horizon, and Maddek's mare no longer had a spring in her step. With her hood up and head down, Yvenne looked no farther ahead than the hind-quarters of Banek's mount until they reached the inn at the center of the settlement.

The stables were at the back of the inn. Yvenne took some comfort in the new routine of caring for her gelding. It mattered not that he had steep shoulders and a short back and unsound legs; still he needed to be fed and watered, and the rhythmic brushing of his coat soothed Yvenne as much as it seemed to soothe him.

But the silence between the warriors did not end. It seemed even heavier within the stables, as if all the words unspoken were trapped between the thick clay walls, a deeper echo of the scream trapped within Yvenne's chest.

So she brushed her gelding and waited for the sound that would break the silence. A thud of steel against bone, or the plunge of a blade through flesh.

Yet the silence broke instead with a rustle of straw beneath leather boots. With Kelir's battle axe in hand, Maddek stood at the entrance to her gelding's stall.

His hardened gaze met hers, his features carved from stone. "Come."

Yvenne did not need to ask where. With halting steps, she followed him to the stable yard, where his mare was tied to a stout post. The horse trembled uncontrollably, eyes reddened and foamy sweat lathering her coat. Her great chest labored with each wheezing breath. A blood wraith's poison would transform a human into a wraith, but animals were corrupted in a different manner—changed into revenants, undead creatures whose only purpose was to consume living flesh.

So she was to witness the mare's death. Perhaps Maddek meant to punish her, but to Yvenne this was a duty willingly performed. The mare's life had been sacrificed for hers. That debt could never be repaid, but Yvenne would never pretend that it wasn't owed.

She owed the mare and she owed Maddek, who had also risked his life for hers. While he'd been racing toward her, she'd seen him make the decision—his mare or his bride.

Yvenne had not truly expected him to choose her.

Nor did she expect Maddek to grip the head of the axe and extend the short handle to her. Yvenne looked blankly at it for a moment before raising her gaze to his in confusion.

"She suffers," he said harshly. "She suffers because she ran, after you refused to. Do not refuse this."

Yvenne wouldn't. She still did not know if Maddek meant to punish her or to teach her a lesson, but this was duty, too—to end the animal's suffering—and it was not a lesson Yvenne needed to learn. Her mother had already taught her well.

She gripped the wooden handle in both hands, then staggered as Maddek released the weapon and the heavy double blade swung toward her legs, dragging her arms straight down.

Barely did she avoid chopping into her own shin. Straining with effort, she managed to heft the blade as high as her waist.

But there, she had to admit defeat. "I have not the strength to swing this."

"Use your dagger, then." Maddek seized the axe from her grip.

Yvenne nodded and bent, unsheathing the jeweled dagger bound to her left leg. The mare snorted as she approached, extending her neck as if searching for a treat—perhaps because Maddek had given her so many since they had left the ruins.

Her throat aching, Yvenne stroked the soft muzzle. Upon this mare, she had flown across a grassy plain. Upon this mare, she'd felt alive for the first time.

Maddek came up beside her, his voice rough as he said, "The longer you wait, the more she suffers."

Yvenne knew. Her fingers tightened upon the dagger's handle. Her gaze slipped over the mare's big eyes, her soft throat.

And she had to admit defeat again. "I cannot do this."

"You killed your brother easily enough."

True. "And I would have made his death more painful if I'd known how. But I have not a warrior's skill. I cannot make this painless for her, and she does not deserve to suffer more than she already is. So I would give you my dagger and ask that you—"

Like a beast unleashed, Maddek sprang with stunning, brutal swiftness. With a mighty heave of his axe, he struck the mare down.

Her blade dangling from fingers gone limp, Yvenne stared at the animal lying on the muddied ground. The horse had not made a sound when the axe had split her skull, and now only her legs twitched feebly, the aftershocks of a body that had not yet realized it was dead.

Axe dripping gore, Maddek said, "Wipe the blood from your face," before striding into the stables.

As if in a dream, she touched her cheek. Maddek's chest and face had been splattered with crimson. So were hers.

Using the long sleeves of her robe, she wiped at her face and slowly returned to the stables. The other warriors had left—or perhaps Maddek had sent them away so that he might have solitude. He was tending to her gelding now, lifting its feet in his big hands to scrape the mud out of its hooves, and without looking up at her, he said, "I will finish here. Go and take your meal."

Not yet. She studied his tense form and felt the silence trapped between the stable walls again, but it was not the same heavy, oppressive quiet that it had been before. Instead it twisted and writhed like the wraiths in the fog.

"You seethe with words unsaid, warrior," she told him.

He gave a short, humorless laugh. "You would not want me to say these."

Yvenne never enjoyed being told what she did and did not want. "I thought Parsatheans never left anything unsaid."

"When it is important." As if to suggest he would never have anything of importance to say to her, his dark gaze raked Yvenne from head to toe before dismissing her, focusing on the muddied hoof again. "But there are also words best left unspoken."

So his mother had once told her. Words that were shameful, or that delivered a wound that could not be healed—or words said in haste and anger.

Or perhaps in grief.

Maddek likely wished he'd left her on that stone ledge and spared his mare. "Do you truly think I will be wounded by what you would say, warrior? Well, then. Let us have it out. If we are to be married, best not to leave words unspoken between us."

Jaw tight, he released the gelding's hoof and straightened. "*If* we are to be married?"

"Are we not?"

They would be. Only if Yvenne was dead would she allow any other outcome.

The way he looked at her, perhaps she *would* be dead. For there was none of the familiar heat in his gaze now as he approached her, only the same lethal fury that had filled his eyes upon their first meeting, when he'd worn his silver claws and held her throat in that deadly grip. He drew close, looking down upon her, and she felt the overwhelming menace of his great size—knew she was meant to feel it.

Would he push her to her knees now? Make her stroke his cock again? Did he not understand yet that she would *never* back down?

Her chin lifted.

His dark gaze dropped to her mouth before meeting her eyes. His voice was a sharp blade as he said, "Every time you need rescue, another life is sacrificed for it. It was your brother's life when you were rescued from your marriage to Toleh, and I cannot regret that. But all of Parsathe lost their queen and king when you needed rescue from your father. You would not run from the wraiths and I lost my mare. So if we are married, I fear what price Parsathe will pay for our new queen's weakness. I wonder how many others will be sacrificed to rescue you."

Rendered mute by the pain tearing through her chest, Yvenne bore each word as if they were blows. Maddek could have slipped a dagger into her stomach and hurt her less. Yet she had asked for it, had she not?

But that was not what she had expected him to say. And he could not know his words cut deeper than any others might have.

It was not only pain, though. For her agony and her anger were always entwined—and her rage had been building through the day.

"They pay for my rescue?" A hard, short laugh burst from her. "And what of your vengeance? Whether I ran was not the only decision made today—you made a decision to sacrifice your horse to save me. Why, except that you need to get a child upon me? Do you think this course you've set does not risk your warriors or your people? By Vela's teeth, you have spoken of your hope that my father and the soldiers from the Syssian outpost will move against you upon the Burning Plains! Do you think you will face him and his soldiers alone?"

"You think my Dragon does not know the risk? Vengeance is not mine alone," he said coldly. "My warriors seek it, too."

"As do I." For she burned with the need to see her father destroyed. Not just for herself, but to free all of Syssia from his tyranny. Yet in doing so, she risked the very people she would help—for she knew not what her father might do to them in his anger. She'd risked her brother Tyzen, who had passed information from the council to her despite the danger of discovery. She'd risked her handmaid Pym, who had sneaked out beneath Bazir's eye to deliver her message to Maddek. "I also knew that I would pay a price for that vengeance. I knew that anyone who assisted me might pay, too. Did you not know? You will be a king. Did you not realize *all* of your people might pay a price for the choices you make? You are a commander who has sent warriors into battle, knowing they might not return. Did you think a quest for vengeance would be any different?"

His brows had drawn low over his eyes, his face thunderous. "I knew what it would be. Every Parsathean warrior would give their life to avenge our queen and king—as would I. What I wonder is if *you* are worth the price we will pay."

"Then do not pay it next time! I thought you would not today. The very first day, you said you would leave me behind if I could not keep up, and that you would not risk yourself or your warriors to help me. But you *did* risk yourself. So either you lie to me or you lie to yourself. But *I* do not lie," she continued fiercely before he could reply. "I do not need a husband; it is *you* who needs *me* to have your vengeance. To have mine, I only need a child—and a warrior's protection and their sword, because my father will not easily relinquish Syssia's throne. That is what I have told you from the beginning. And perhaps you will choose not to save me again. But do not fool yourself, Maddek. You have played your own part in this. It was not only *my* choices that brought your mare to her end."

His powerful body rigid with leashed tension, he stared down at her, his shadowed eyes burning with rage. Her chest heaving as if she'd been running, she did not back down or look away.

A muscle worked in his jaw before he said, "I did make a choice. But I should not have been forced to make it. You asked for my protection and I gave it—and because I am taking you as my bride, my warriors' duty and their protection extends to you. Your duty to them—to me—is to follow the orders that will keep you safe. Today you failed in your duty to me. And though you would be their queen, you failed in your duty to my warriors. If you fail in your duty again and my warriors sacrifice themselves to save you, I will likely kill you myself."

She *had* failed them. Not intentionally. But it had been done.

Throat thick, she nodded. "So I did. I vow I will not fail in my duty again."

His gaze hardened dangerously. "Never make vows you cannot keep."

"I do not." She would not. "I cannot promise to be quick or strong. I will make every effort that I can. But although I wish it otherwise, my body is not a warrior-queen's."

"Or even a warrior's. But it does not need to be. You only need to be strong enough to lie beneath me." His mouth twisted sardonically as his gaze slipped over her form again. "Best you go and eat."

So she would. But there was something left unsaid. "I am sorry that your mare was lost. She seemed a fine mount."

"She was." Maddek turned away. "But even a fine mount is only a tool."

Again, Yvenne could not decide whether he lied to himself or to her. For he obviously cared for the horse as deeply as Fassad cared for his wolves.

But she would not challenge him on this. Not when the mare's death was such a raw wound . . . as was the discovery of his parents' murders. For a full turn, he'd known they were dead, but for only six days had Maddek known the reason why. Only six days had he been seeking vengeance.

That was barely even time to stop bleeding. Surely not time enough to heal. Every sharp emotion must tear open the laceration on his heart.

Yvenne had been seeking vengeance for years, and hers still ripped open more often than she would like.

With a sigh, she made her way outside the stables—where she was not surprised to see Toric and Fassad waiting to escort her to the inn's entrance. Because the warriors would perform their duty. Even if they would still not meet her eyes. Or speak to her.

Feeling as if a blade were pressed against her heart, she followed them inside.

CHAPTER 14

MADDEK

O ne of Maddek's earliest lessons was that a warrior made use of what they had. A warrior did not wish for a sword if they only had a fist, and a warrior did not wish for a horse if they had feet. A warrior did not wish for the sun at night, but saw by the stars and the moonlight. And if there was naught to eat, a warrior did not wish for food; better to go hunting than stay wanting.

Silver-fingered Rani would come soon enough, so a warrior never wasted time wishing for what was not.

But a son did. As Maddek led Yvenne's gelding to the blacksmith's, it seemed that upon his every breath was a wish that his mother or his father walked beside him, offering their sage advice.

For they had taught him so much. How to fight a single enemy, and how to war against legions. How to measure intentions against results, how to administer justice and mercy. How to lead warriors, how to follow his heart, how to stand for his people. How to speak and how to listen. No matter how difficult the problem, his parents' lessons and their solutions seemed so simple.

Yvenne was not.

She was also not as he'd imagined a bride to be. Always he'd pictured a woman chosen for him by his mother and father. They would pick a bride who suited him, a woman who would share the same goals as he, a woman who fit into his life as smoothly as a sword into an oiled sheath.

Yvenne was like gravel between his teeth. A splinter beneath his skin. The steel in his cock.

She was a distraction from a simple purpose: vengeance.

She was a distraction . . . but also a solution. Perhaps that was the true problem. He had complicated that which should be simple. A warrior made use of what he had, and Maddek had Yvenne. The best route to Zhalen was through marriage.

She was but a tool. And between her thighs he would make use of her.

The solution to the rest—that she would be mother to his children, that she would be queen—could come after he felt Zhalen's blood spill over his fingers.

For now, he would focus on his vengeance and that which was *truly* simple: judging a horse's capability.

Maddek left the blacksmith's not wholly satisfied but lighter on gold and better pleased by the selection than he'd been in the previous villages. As he strode toward the inn, he felt the eyes of the Gogeans upon him, but his attention was captured by the soldiers riding through the village gate. The setting sun gleamed dully on their brass helms, but aside from the Gogean crest upon their armor they were indistinguishable from soldiers in any of the other southern realms.

The captain spotted Maddek and urged his horse forward at a canter, then abruptly reined in his mount a few paces away. If a Parsathean warrior had drawn so hard on his horse's mouth, he'd have found himself marching on foot for a tennight.

"Greetings, Commander Maddek!" Despite his heavy hands, the captain sat easy in his saddle. His face was shaven in the manner of Gogean men, chin bare and jaw full-bearded. "I am told that I have you to thank for the warning at the ruins. The wraiths had retreated underground when we passed, but we intended to stop there for our midday rest. I do not know that we'd have escaped so easily."

Maddek inclined his head. "Did you leave warning for others?"

"We did." The man dismounted. His gaze settled on Danoh, who waited ahead near the entrance to the inn, her keen eyes monitoring their exchange and watching for any threat to Maddek.

Few other people glanced in his direction now. It was Danoh who held the attention of almost every other soldier and villager who had reason to be outside—and it seemed many of them had found reason to leave their homes or had business at the inn that night. All of the Parsatheans drew notice. But Danoh's tall, lithe figure—and her bare breasts—seemed to draw more notice than any other.

The captain pulled his gaze from Danoh to address Maddek again. "Do you and your warriors stay at the inn?"

"We do."

"If you have no objection, I will accompany you there. I would ask you how the alliance's army fares at the river."

At the river Lave. Though the Gogeans sent only a single company to fight, this soldier might have friends or kin who served there. With a nod, Maddek continued toward the inn. "They fare well. The savages attack without the numbers or the frequency they once did."

"But the Parsathean army has withdrawn?"

"It has."

The captain gave no response, but his expression conveyed his uneasiness nonetheless.

"There are still alliance soldiers enough to stop the savages," Maddek told him. "Did you ride with the Gogeans?"

"At the Lave?" The man shook his head. "I serve on the queen's guard."

Maddek frowned. "This far north?"

The walled city of Goge—and the queen—lay almost a fortnight's ride south. This captain was far from his ruler's side.

The soldier glanced toward the wagons, within whose beds sat sullen young men and women. "We are recruiting."

And the recruits looked none too pleased by it. Maddek could not conceive of such reluctance, not when they would protect their families and their people. But perhaps he'd been too hasty when he'd spoken to the alliance council and accused the Gogean minister of only raising farmers, not warriors. "They will be trained to serve at the Lave?"

"To serve the queen's guard."

His frown deepened. "In the city? Not at the Gogean border?"

"The southern border is the alliance's concern." But the captain did not appear happy to say so. "Goge must be protected if the savages manage to cross the river."

An entire realm protected by a queen's guard in the city? "What of the people who live between the Lave and Goge?"

For there were many more villages in the Gogean outlands like this one. The citizens who lived in the city were not the ones who cultivated the fields.

Face troubled, the captain shrugged. "Our queen expects them to flee north."

Where they would hide behind the city walls—if they reached the city alive. Disgusted, Maddek shook his head, but there was little else to say except, "The alliance forces at the Lave will hold back the Farians. Never would I have withdrawn if they could not."

Though he didn't appear completely persuaded, the captain nodded. They neared the inn now, and Danoh pushed away from the wall where she'd settled.

A flush tinged the captain's dark cheeks as he looked everywhere but her breasts. "I will perhaps see you within, Commander," he said and, with a nod to Danoh, led his mount around toward the stables.

Danoh made no reply except to nod in return, but when she looked to Maddek, her smirk said much more.

He grinned. The way the southerners wrapped themselves up, it was possible the captain had not seen tits—man's or woman's—since he was a suckling babe. Yet he had not stared at Maddek's bare chest in the same way. Perhaps because the captain had his own male chest to gawk at, but Maddek couldn't truly say. The southerners' ways often made little sense.

The inn's shutters and doors were wide open to let out the heat of the day—or the heat generated by the number of villagers within. When the captain and his soldiers finished tending to their mounts, they would be fortunate to find a seat. It was a lively crowd, though they quieted when Maddek and Danoh made their way between tables to where his warriors had sat down to their meal.

His gaze immediately went to Yvenne. She sat where he would have positioned her—at the center of a long table, with her back to the far wall. Banek, Fassad, and Toric sat across from her, with Kelir and Ardyl at her sides. Protected from every direction.

Protected, and focused on her meal. Her gaze did not lift from her plate, though in every other village they had passed through, it seemed that she could not stop looking, eagerly taking in every detail and questioning Banek about many of them. Here was a crowd of villagers to observe, yet her eyes were downcast and her head bowed, as if she were hiding her face.

Maddek frowned. He had never yet seen her hide from anything—and he had already told her not to fear identification. If her brothers and father were in pursuit, no need to search for a moonstone-eyed woman. The Parsathean warriors she traveled with drew enough attention that every villager along this road could point out their direction.

Kelir's eyes met his and the big warrior shifted along the bench, making room for Maddek beside his bride.

Yvenne's moonstone gaze flicked up then, and by the softening curve of her lips, she was relieved to see him.

Such naked welcome sent heat directly to his loins, and Maddek left no room between them when he took the seat beside her, pressing his hard thigh against her softer one.

On his left, Kelir asked, "Did you find new mounts?"

"I did." Maddek reached for the flagon of mead in front of Yvenne's plate. The drink was half empty, which might account for her subdued manner. Some warriors fell asleep after drinking not much more than this. "Four with Parsathean blood. We collect them from the blacksmith's in the morning."

"We'll pick up our pace, then," Kelir said, and signaled to a barlad with curled hair and bright eyes. "We've not had to pay for a meal or a drink. It is the villagers' gratitude for keeping the Farians across the Lave."

With a humorless laugh, Maddek shook his head. "So it is only the minister Kintus who begrudges every grain of wheat our warriors eat."

Her mouth full, Yvenne abruptly glanced at him again, pale eyes narrowing on his face.

He returned her look evenly. His earlier impression must have been wrong. She did not hide her face. Instead she stared up at him as boldly as ever.

Amused, he drank another swallow of mead and reached for one of the platters of roasted dally bird. Though he held her gaze, he spoke to Banek next. "Did you tell the innkeeper of the blood wraiths?"

"I did," the older man said. "He'll see that the warning is spread."

Her attention shifting to Banek, Yvenne seemed to hesitate before venturing to say, "At the ruins, you recognized that it was not a simple fog. Have you encountered blood wraiths before?"

Without looking at her, Banek replied, "I have."

He didn't continue the story that Maddek had heard a multitude of times. After a long breath, Yvenne bowed her head again, her slim body tense, her throat working.

Maddek's grip tightened on the pewter flagon. He waited.

All of his warriors remained quiet. Letting her feel their censure, because she had not run at the ruins.

It was a warrior's punishment. But she was not a warrior. And she would be their queen.

A better queen than Maddek had known. If they had seen her in the stable yard, they would have known as well—but he had sent them away. She had requested that he not humiliate her in front of his warriors, but Maddek had thought it would be Yvenne who humiliated herself when he asked her to do her duty by his mare. He'd believed she would balk and try to shirk her responsibility.

But she hadn't balked. She had not even hesitated, except to admit her weakness. Then she had done what any good queen would do: delegate the task to the one who could perform it best.

And he *had* been angry with her. Angry enough to speak words that should not be said. He'd also mourned his mare. But he would not waste time wishing that his horse were alive, or that he had a more suitable bride.

What was done was done.

Slowly he set down the flagon. "Many warriors would be paralyzed with fear upon seeing a blood wraith, let alone a fog full of them."

His warriors stopped their eating and looked to his face.

Jaw set, Maddek ripped a leg joint from the roasted bird and continued, "Is that not what you told us, Banek? That half the warriors in your party fell before the wraiths because they were too petrified to run?"

And no one thought ill of those warriors now.

The older man heaved a sigh. "It is."

That was all that needed to be spoken, then. But it was not all Maddek had to say. "She is sensitive to dark magics. She felt a chill and yet I dismissed the warning it held, trusting instead that the dogs would alert us to any danger. Then I foolishly left her alone, far from proper protection—and so blame for the loss of my mare rests on my shoulders."

He felt Yvenne's gaze upon him, yet did not return her

look. Instead he met the eyes of each of his warriors and made certain they understood him.

They did.

She had not run, but Yvenne was not theirs to punish. She was Maddek's. In every way, she was his. If his warriors had an argument with his bride, they had best take it to him—or take it out on him.

Especially as he had failed her, too. She was weak and vulnerable and unprepared to face any threat alone. So if a punishment was to be given, Maddek ought to be the one to receive it.

By sacrificing his mare, he already had. Nothing more needed to be said or done.

Nodding, Kelir said, "Sensing magics is a useful gift."

"For certain we will not stop anywhere she takes chill again," Ardyl agreed.

Tearing meat from bone, Maddek said, "It will be her duty to warn us."

"I will." Her voice held the solemnity of a vow. "Without hesitation."

Banek chuckled. "Hesitate if you are soaked to the bone or unclothed at night," the older warrior told her. "You'll need to learn the difference between a true chill and magic."

"We need not fear a true chill." Maddek eyed her mouth. "I will keep her warm enough."

Her eyebrows shot upward. Around them erupted his warriors' ribald laughter, and a slow grin curved her lips. Holding her gaze, Maddek began his meal, and she only looked away from him when Banek began to tell her of his encounter with the blood wraiths. It was an enthralling tale from the early days of the alliance, one that had taken Banek from the walls of Syssia to the cloud-wrapped mountains of Toleh, where a dark warlord had slaughtered and feasted on the villagers there. Maddek had heard it many times before and barely paid attention now. Instead he watched Yvenne's features as she listened, rapt.

He had thought her as ice when she had killed her brother. He'd thought she felt no emotions at all. But she did, though they were not often worn clearly upon her face. And now he believed that ice had been rage—felt so deep and held so long that it had hardened within her, as steel from a furnace was sharpest after it had been shaped and cooled. For she had wished her brother more pain . . . and she had wished to save a dying horse from feeling any.

That was not ice. That was hatred for one and compassion for the other, and neither emotion sprang from cold ground.

And in truth, whether soaked to the bone or unclothed at night, it was she who would warm him. Even now Maddek could feel the smoldering warmth of her leg through her silk robe and his linens. Against him, she burned as Temra's own molten heart did. A man might catch fire inside her.

Hanan be merciful, for he was ablaze simply sitting at her side.

Throat suddenly parched, Maddek reached for Yvenne's mead and found it empty. He did not have to look far for more. Kelir had taken up a flirtation with one of the barmaids, a generously curved woman with pink in her cheeks. That flush might have come from how busy the crowded room had kept her and the other servers—or from whatever the warrior whispered into her ear.

Maddek lifted the mug, but it was not him that the barmaid's gaze fixed upon. Though Kelir still smiled at her, he and Maddek no longer existed. Instead she stared at Yvenne—as if seeing her moonstone eyes for the first time.

Perhaps it *was* the first time. For Yvenne's gaze had been downcast when Maddek arrived.

"By Vela . . ." The sound of the barmaid's invocation was lost to the room's din, but the shape was clear upon her lips. "You are goddess-touched?"

Yvenne shook her head. "My foremother was."

The barmaid seemed no less impressed that it was her ancestor who had been blessed, but she could not hold

Yvenne's gaze for more than a moment. Eyes averted, she breathlessly said, "Is there anything I might bring you, my lady?"

Her pearlescent gaze flicked to the empty flagon Maddek held. "More mead, perhaps?"

The barmaid scurried off. Maddek bowed his head, shoulders shaking as he laughed. Never had he seen anyone move so quickly.

A mock scowl twisted Kelir's lips. "How humbling it is to know that the prettiest woman in the village can be lured away by a pair of moonstone eyes."

"Not the prettiest," Toric corrected softly, color high and gazing into his drink as if all the treasures of Luren might be found at the bottom of it.

Maddek's laughter deepened. So the young warrior had taken a sweet liking to Yvenne? And she was oblivious. Her gaze had begun flicking around the common room as she tried to determine the woman's identity.

Chuckling, Fassad shook his head. "That is truth. If she were not already claimed, Kelir and Ardyl would be upon her like raptors."

Now Ardyl grinned, cocking a pierced eyebrow and tilting her head as she studied Yvenne's profile, as if looking at her anew—not as Maddek's bride but a potential lover that she and Kelir would share between them. Her confirmation of Fassad's claim lay in the long drink she took.

A contemplative frown appeared on Yvenne's brow. Abruptly she looked across the table at Banek. "You always tell the truth?"

Though any Parsathean might have taken offense at such a question, Banek only nodded. "I do."

"Am I ugly?" she asked.

The older man began to laugh—before suddenly quieting, as if realizing her question was not in jest. "No, my lady," he said. "You are not."

Despite his response, a frown still pleating her brow. "My older brothers said I was, but they often lied and only spoke to hurt me, so . . ." A shrug finished that. "I have never clearly seen my own face—nor did I have many visitors to my tower. Hardly enough to judge beauty."

"Is for the best," Maddek said gruffly. "Such judgments serve no one."

"Perhaps not." Those pale eyes met his. "But I was told you were handsome, and so I think you must be the standard by which I judge. Though it also seems there is beauty in everyone I see. I thought Toric must be speaking of Danoh or Ardyl, for there have been times these past days when I have not been able to look away from them. But I cannot truly judge, for I have stared as often at all of you. And so much that I see seems so beautiful. *That* woman, for example"—she gestured discreetly toward an older woman seated at another table—"has lines beside her mouth and eyes, as if she smiles often. Can you imagine what a happy life she has led that her face is so ready to smile? I look at her and think those lines are the loveliest thing I have ever seen. Or perhaps it is the drops of ale sparkling in that laughing man's beard, do you see him? He looks as if he has not a care."

Maddek grunted. "He looks as if he's had too much to drink."

Her lips pursed and she leveled a withering gaze upon his face, as if to reprimand him for his sour response. "I would like to have not a care. So perhaps *I* ought to drink too much," she said tartly, drawing hearty laughs of agreement from the warriors.

Even Maddek could not find fault in her thinking. With a grin, he said, "When the serving woman returns."

"Do you think that is how the goddess sees us—as you do? As something beautiful?" Toric's face was red as he asked, and reddened further when she met his eyes and gave her somber reply.

"If Vela truly looks through me, I think she must."

Maddek cared little of a goddess's opinion. He should not have cared for Yvenne's, either. Yet he was pleased she thought him handsome.

Foolishness. Appearance was nothing. For all that her

features were pinched and sallow, they were finely drawn, and her eyes arresting. But she was also treacherous—and there was nothing appealing in that.

Yet his cock still stood stiff as an iron pike. That owed nothing to her appearance. It was the bold way she looked at him. It was the heat of her. It was knowing her lips would be wrapped around his shaft this night.

The barmaid returned then, mead sloshing over rims in her haste. She served Yvenne first and plonked another pewter flagon in front of Maddek with as much care as she might serve a dog. Kelir's was delivered in the same haphazard fashion.

As long as the mead didn't spill into his lap, it mattered not. Amused, Maddek drank. The barmaid watched Yvenne's first swallow with the intensity of a mother watching a newborn latch onto her teat.

With foam on her upper lip, Yvenne eased the woman's unspoken concern. "It is refreshing, thank you."

The woman's smile was wide and bright. "Anything else, my lady?"

"I cannot imagine—"

"You will be staying overnight? Your party has secured a private chamber?"

Yvenne's gaze flicked to Maddek. "I believe so."

He nodded. A large private chamber for Yvenne, himself, and his Dragon guard, though a few of the warriors would sleep in the stables. Parsathean horses were too valuable to leave where any bandit might steal them.

"Shall I arrange for a bath in your chambers, then?"

"A bath?" Pleasure lit Yvenne's face.

Her pleasure was outshined by the barmaid's. "We will begin heating the water now. I shall happily attend to you . . . in any way you wish," she finished breathlessly.

Because inns often catered to *all* of their guests' needs. Maddek frowned but before he could respond, Yvenne shook her head. "I am accustomed to looking after myself."

The woman appeared as if she might burst into tears.

Ardyl, who had been quaking with laughter through this

exchange, slid her arm around the barmaid's soft waist and pulled her closer. "Do you wish to attend to someone, you can attend to me."

The woman's devastation seemed eased by Ardyl's interest. Eyebrows arched, Yvenne glanced quickly toward Kelir—perhaps to see how the warrior liked Ardyl flirting with the barmaid he'd singled out for himself—and her brows rose ever higher when she saw Kelir's broad grin.

She looked to Maddek and whispered, "Is this also a competition between them?"

It was. Though not as Yvenne likely imagined. They would not compete for the barmaid's attentions. The competition would come later, after they'd secured those attentions.

And Kelir did not even look at the serving woman now. Instead he focused on Yvenne. "So you think Maddek handsome?"

"I believe it," she said. "But I am no true judge."

"He has a fine brow," Kelir said.

Her lips twitching, her gaze rose as if to appraise it. "Indeed. Placed very neatly above his eyes, where a brow should be."

"Those eyes are also keen. Only half the riders in Parsathe have keener vision than he."

"Commendable. And when he scowls at us, those keen eyes appear quite dark, which I like very much," she mused while Maddek lifted his mug. "And even though he laughs as he drinks, he dribbles no mead down his chin. By his own admission, a beard free of drips is preferable to one that is not."

"He is remarkably adept at drinking and eating," Kelir agreed. "It is thanks to his strong jaw. I have seen him consume a roasted grass rodent in a single bite."

"Is that impressive? How large is a grass rodent?"

Kelir demonstrated with his hands, and Yvenne began giggling.

"To be fair, he ate a young one, and most of it was tail," Kelir added, then lowered his voice as if confiding in her and as if Maddek did not sit between them. "His beard is a foul sight."

Her eyes widened. "Is it?"

"Warriors should be as silver-fingered Rani." Kelir rubbed his own shaved jaw. "Rani has a smooth face. As I do. As we all do—though Danoh and Ardyl have an easier time of it."

Slowly she nodded. "So *you* are the more handsome."

"I am. Unless you think this hideous and repulsive." He traced the scar that raked down the side of his face.

Though her expression didn't alter, Yvenne's leg tensed against Maddek's. "Are scars repulsive?"

"The barmaid thought not," Maddek remarked dryly, and Kelir grinned.

"She did not," he agreed.

Those moonstone eyes met his. "Do *you* think scars are repulsive?"

"No." Maddek set down his mead. "Scars are but stories for a warrior to tell. Just as the smiling lines on that woman's face are."

By the appreciative light that lifted through her expression, Yvenne liked that answer.

Maddek thought she would enjoy something else more. "Ask Kelir to tell you how he earned that scar."

The warrior groaned.

Across the table, a laughing Fassad broke in. "If you do not tell it, we will—and you will fare far worse for it."

Kelir narrowed his eyes at the other warrior. "You were not there to see it happen."

"But we have heard the tale many times over." Fassad gestured to Maddek. "Most often from him."

"You heard the worst telling of it, then." Submitting to the inevitable, however, Kelir turned to Yvenne again. "It was during the campaign against Stranik's Fang. We'd crossed the Lave and ridden south for a full turn when we came upon a great herd of three-horned fanheads."

Beside him, Yvenne sucked in a sharp breath. Her wide

eyes searched Kelir's face before tripping to meet Maddek's, then returning to Kelir again. "Fanheads?"

She sounded almost disbelieving, though they'd seen a family of the heavy reptiles only a day past. She had looked at them wonderingly then—but seemed far more surprised now at their mere mention.

Kelir nodded. "As far as could be seen."

She stared at him, lips parted. "Go on."

"It had been a long day of riding through a narrow canyon." He gestured to Maddek beside him. "I remember not how we came to speak of it—"

"We had been comparing drepa hunts," Maddek supplied. He flicked the four raptor claws threaded on the leather cord around his neck, clicking them together. "Kelir only had two then." And three now. "He thought to make up the difference with the fanhead's snout horn."

"I would have. From it, I'd have carved the finest hilt ever gripped by Parsathean hands." Kelir looked to Yvenne again. "There was a bull, the largest ever have I seen. And I approached it *so* slowly—"

"But it charged," Yvenne broke in, her eyes bright. "And struck you with its two longhorns, tossing you into the air—that was when your cheek was laid open—but you managed to grip its frill and find a seat upon its back. Then it ran, so far and so fast. It took half the night for Maddek and a dozen other warriors to chase you down."

Kelir shot a dismayed glance at Banek. "You told her?"

Brow furrowed, the older warrior shook his head.

"My mother did," Yvenne said, and let go a merry laugh. "Until this moment, I had not known the warrior who'd ridden the fanhead was *you*. Oh, but I remember how she described it all—that the bull was almost twice as tall as you were, and that its frill was as green as new grass."

It *had* been green. Most were not. The three-horned fanheads they'd passed the previous day had red and yellow frills.

Unease squirreling up his spine, Maddek frowned. "Your *mother* told you?"

"We followed the campaign closely from our chamber." Some of the amusement bled from her tone, replaced by melancholy. "She would have given anything to march with the alliance's army. Perhaps even lead it."

But the warrior-queen's body had been wasted by poison—and Maddek's mother had led the army, instead.

"She watched us?" A glance at the other warriors confirmed that they were as unsettled by the thought as Maddek was.

"Yes." Softly biting her bottom lip, Yvenne searched his face before looking to the others. "Not only the army. Everyone."

"Everyone?"

Her gaze returned to his. "The alliance council. Other royal houses. People within villages and cities and outlands."

"Only in the southern realms?"

"Parsathe, too. Sometimes farther. She often looked for the Destroyer, but his magics concealed him from her eyes."

At this moment, Maddek cared not about the Destroyer. "She watched my mother? Envied her?"

Yvenne's pale eyes hardened until they resembled the moonstone they were named after. Tautly she said, "Do *not* suggest that my mother conspired against yours."

He would not. Queen Vyssen had died three years ago, and Yvenne sent the message to his parents in the past year. But in that tower chamber, more than Nyset's heir might have been bred and fostered. "I wonder if it was not your mother who harbored a hatred of mine, for all that she had done and Queen Vyssen could not."

"You think my father did? He hates everyone." But a breath later she understood his meaning. The realization was followed by a bitter and disbelieving laugh. "You think *I* did?"

"Did you?"

"No," she said fiercely. *"No."*

Maddek believed her. But he made no reply, downing the

rest of his mead, trying to wash away the sour doubt that crawled up his throat.

Kelir was frowning at her, too—but in confusion rather than suspicion. "What purpose did she have?"

"To teach me," Yvenne said hotly, as if her fury at Maddek still burned. "So I would know something of the world beyond the chamber walls and be prepared to lead my people."

Maddek believed that, too. From what he had seen, her mother had taught her well. Yvenne had been guided as Maddek's parents had guided him.

"What did she tell you of Goge, then?" Toric asked, though Maddek did not think the young warrior cared much about Goge—only what sort of things her mother's blessed gaze had looked at that he might look at now, too. "Did she tell you of this village?"

"Unless there is some marker, it is difficult to know. I recall no specific mention of the village nearest the bridge ruins." Her gaze slipped around the common room. "It seems much like other Gogean villages she described."

"And how did a warrior-queen describe them?" Maddek tore free another roasted joint from the platter. "Did she see what I do—a land ripe for conquering, because beyond the Gogean city walls there are too few soldiers guarding its roads and borders? Did she see a people reluctant to take up arms, because they must join a queen's guard instead of knowing the pride of defending their own homes? A people who will forever rely upon the alliance to protect them from the Farian savages, and yet whose council minister begrudges every speck of grain the army consumes?"

Nods and low grunts of agreement came from the other warriors. Of course they had observed what Maddek had. Any fine warrior would, and his Dragon were among the finest.

Yet Yvenne did not look upon him as if she thought so. Instead her clear gaze searched his face as if looking for something *more* from him . . . and did not find it.

Quietly she said, "So it is not only me."

Maddek frowned. That was disappointment in her tone, and he disliked the effect it had on him—heaviness within his stomach, tightness in his chest.

"What is not only you?"

For a long breath she gave no answer. Then she said, "Bid your Dragon to leave us alone, for you will not wish them to witness my response."

"Why?" Did she intend to slap him? With a short laugh, Maddek glanced at his warriors and saw the same surprise and amusement there. "They might like to watch."

She merely looked at him. Waiting.

Was this repayment, then? Earlier in the stable, to spare her any humiliation, Maddek had also made certain his warriors would not witness what was done and spoken. "Are they words best left unsaid?"

"No. These words need to be said."

"There is nothing you can say that they cannot hear."

Her answer was firm, her gaze unwavering. "They cannot hear this."

Curiosity warred with irritation. Finally he nodded.

Without argument his warriors rose, each clutching their mead in one hand and their plate in the other as they sought new seats. Among the villagers, there was no hesitation before room was made on their benches and the warriors were welcomed at different tables. Yvenne's gaze followed them, and then she turned to Maddek, who was downing the rest of his drink.

"You are not a king," she said gravely.

A fact well known, as he had not yet been named Ran. And perhaps he would never be, if the Parsatheans choose another to speak for them.

"I am not," Maddek agreed.

"You misunderstand me. Even if you are named Ran when you return to the Burning Plains, you have neither the heart nor the mind of a king. You recognize no strength except that of a sword. You are only a warrior."

So it was not a slap. Instead she ran him through with a judgment as sharp as a blade.

Struggling to draw breath, slowly Maddek set down his drink. He ought not to care for her opinion. But he saw in Yvenne what she did not see in him. She *was* a queen—and she had deemed that he lacked not only a king's title but the character.

Maddek could not even claim with true conviction that she was wrong. For he had thought many times he was only a warrior.

But he also believed he would serve his people well. Yet *she* did not think so? The woman who would be his queen, his bride?

Never had he been eviscerated so efficiently.

Relentlessly she continued. "I thought you resented protecting me because you despise me for my treachery. But now I hear the same disdain when you speak of the Gogeans. Do you always resent those you have promised to help and protect? Do you only offer your sword grudgingly—or do you only resent them when they are not Parsathean?"

Anger welled through the ruptures she had torn in his pride. Maddek had offered his sword in full allegiance to the alliance. That allegiance had not been returned. "It is not I who am reluctant to fulfill my duties to the alliance. The Gogeans rely on Parsathean might to protect them, yet every bushel of grain sent to the Lave must be pried from Kintus's fingers."

Unflinching even in the face of his quiet fury, she simply asked, "How do you feed yourselves on the Burning Plains?"

"We all hunt." As her mother had likely told her, if Queen Vyssen had truly spied upon the alliance. "We all sow the fields and reap the harvest. And when we are threatened, we all fight."

"On the Lave, you did not sow the fields and reap the harvest. You depended upon Gogean grain."

His jaw tightened. An army could not function without food. Was she suggesting they should have grown their own around the camp? "That was the alliance agreement."

"So it was." She reached for her mead and said easily,

"What would happen at home if you could not harvest or hunt enough?"

"All would go hungry."

"Even the children and the elderly?"

"They would be the last." Maddek and every warrior he knew would fill a child's plate before his own.

"Have they gone hungry since the alliance was formed?"

"No."

"The Gogeans have," she said, holding his gaze. "Young, old. Farmers, millers, innkeepers, merchants. All have gone hungry but the queen—and the king before her—and their guard."

Maddek frowned. How could that be? "This is Temra's most fertile land. Never do Gogean crops fail. Always they produce more than their people can eat."

"And the alliance squeezes them for every bushel. Farmers are fined and their children conscripted if they fail to produce their portion, even if giving a full portion will not leave enough for their family or their village. Even if it means that the next year, they will produce even less, because they have not the same number of children to work the fields with them. And those conscripted children are not allowed to return to their villages after serving in the guard, because the queen fears an armed resistance—and she would not train the soldiers who would rise up against her. Yet she cannot reduce the number of her guard, and she cannot loosen her grip upon the farmers, because the alliance makes certain to tell her that the Parsatheans will withdraw from the Lave and her people will all be raped and killed by savages if Goge does not deliver every sack of grain demanded."

"Is this truth?" He searched her face, not truly doubting, but also struggling to believe. "I have fought alongside Gogean soldiers. They never spoke of hunger or the crown's tyranny."

"If you doubt me, speak to the villagers or to the queen's guard." With a subtle gesture, she indicated the Gogean captain who sat with his soldiers at the other end of the room.

"If they *will* speak of it. But do not call it cowardice if they refuse. If forced to decide between indulging a Parsathean warrior's curiosity and protecting their families—considering they might be punished for what they say—speaking might not be their choice."

Perhaps not. Still Maddek would find out more before he left Goge. Because he would fight for and support the alliance, but such tactics could not be tolerated.

In that, Yvenne seemed of the same mind. Little wonder that she cut him down for speaking of the Gogeans in such a manner. He deserved it.

But was she certain all was as she claimed? Her mother had died three years ago.

"You know of this from Queen Vyssen?"

"Yes. But more recently from my younger brother, on the council." Her gaze flickered for a moment. "And I have heard it from others."

Others? While locked in her tower?

Sharply he asked, "Do you speak of my mother?"

Her expression froze, eyes wide and gleaming, her face suddenly bloodbare with a stark fear that gave him no pleasure to see—and then she pressed her lips together, as if to protect her tongue from his ripping fingers, before slowly nodding.

At least she did not lie.

"Do not again," he warned her harshly. "Whether you use a sly tongue to speak of her or say her name aloud, my vow still stands."

Swallowing hard, Yvenne nodded again, and the bloodbare fear faded into something both weary and longing. "May I speak of what was said regarding the alliance?"

Because she was still a queen in heart and mind, and worth listening to. Throat raw, Maddek took a swig and forced it down before he nodded.

"One hope is that burdens within the alliance might be shifted. Ephorn never hungers or thirsts, yet it sends soldiers to the Lave rather than provisions. But if we—Syssia and Parsathe—are united, we will have a stronger voice within the council. With Goge, that would be fully half the alliance who could argue for a better agreement that more evenly weighs contributions, and that does not place so much of the responsibility for the safety of every realm on either the Gogeans or the Parsatheans."

A sensible plan. Yet still his throat burned with a pain the mead could not soothe. "This is your hope or my mother's?"

"Both."

"She never spoke of such hopes to me."

"Perhaps she believed there would be more time. Or perhaps because she was a queen, and you are not yet a king." Her voice was not unkind but still as merciless as a sword. "Perhaps she knew you are but a warrior. A fine warrior, but only a warrior—so when you look at others, you only look for weakness. You look for how to strike them down. That is what a warrior sees."

So he did. A harsh laugh escaped him. "And a king does not see weakness?"

A poor king that would be.

"He does see it." Her warm gaze moved across his face. "But when a king looks at a people—whether his people or not—he also sees their suffering."

Tightly Maddek nodded. He had wished for guidance this day, advice to help untangle the problem of his bride. He had wished for his mother's and his father's simple lessons. Yet instead the lesson came from the woman who twisted him up so fiercely.

Still simple. But much more bitter.

She glanced away from him as the serving woman returned, announcing that her bath was prepared.

Biting her soft bottom lip, Yvenne looked to Maddek. "Do you want me to stay?"

He shook his head. "Have Fassad escort you to the chamber. If you wish for privacy, ask him to stand outside the door. Keep the dogs with you as you bathe."

She watched him a moment more. Sighing, she finally stood, then stumbled when she swung her left leg over the bench and brought her weight down upon it. Maddek caught her waist. She steadied herself with her hands braced against his shoulders, then softly said, "You are already a fine leader, Maddek. And you *will* be Ran." An impish smile curved her mouth. "But just as I will see to making your life a misery, I will also see to your becoming a great king."

A gentle tease that he could not help but respond to—for he was absolutely certain she would do both. With an amused grunt, he told her, "Go on."

Her hands slipped from his shoulders, and as his bride backed away she reminded him, "Wake me."

"I will." Maddek had not forgotten the promise of her mouth.

But that would come later. First he would learn more about the suffering that he'd been too blinded by his sword to see. His gaze fixed across the room, where the captain and his soldiers still feasted, their sullen recruits at a nearby table.

Perhaps they would not speak about hunger or tyranny. But mead always had a way of loosening tongues.

Rising to his feet, Maddek signaled to a barmaid for more drink.

CHAPTER 15

YVENNE

Yvenne could not decide which was more harrowing: seeing the blood wraiths in the fog . . . or facing the stairs that led to the inn's guest chambers.

Her heart raced as the serving maid ascended ahead of her, leading the way. So quickly did the maid climb that she'd reached the upper landing before Yvenne mounted the first step.

Fassad followed her. Perhaps he noticed nothing amiss. Yvenne had been moving awkwardly for days. Her slow ascent while desperately clinging to the railing likely seemed yet another manifestation of her saddle soreness. But it was not her aching muscles or her shattered knee that hindered her, though she had to be careful—stepping up with her right leg and bringing her left even, before stepping up with her right again.

Step, rise. Breathing deep and steady. *Step, rise.* Just as she'd practiced these past three years.

Though for practice in her tower chamber, she'd only been able to build an irregular series of four steps out of footstools and stacks of bedding. This had five times that number of risers, and each one seemed as steep as a mountainside.

A scrabble of claws against wood came from behind her. Yvenne's heart lurched into her throat when Steel and Bone bounded past her legs, upsetting her balance. So fiercely did she grip the railing, it ought have splintered beneath her fingers. Ahead the dogs turned and waited, tongues dangling. Her short gasps echoing the wolves' panting, Yvenne focused on their toothy grins and continued up.

Step, rise.

By the time she reached the landing, cold sweat dampened her brow. Her fingers trembled uncontrollably when she released the railing.

Going down the stairs would be harder. But not until tomorrow must she face that terror.

With a hand upon his sword, Fassad told her to wait with the dogs outside the chamber entrance. She looked curiously through the door as he went inside and began searching the dark corners of the room. It was not a large chamber compared to the one she and her mother had shared in the tower, but it was bigger than many of the other rooms Yvenne had seen since they'd begun traveling. A curtain separated two sleeping areas—one side larger and more open, perhaps intended for the guests' children or servants. Behind the curtain, the tin bathtub sat at the foot of the master's bed, steam rising from the water's surface. Fassad bent to look beneath the bedstead as if searching for thieves who might lie in wait.

At the stone hearth, the maid laid peat on the grate. "It is a warm night," she said to Yvenne, "but your clothing and hair will dry more quickly in front of a hot fire. Shall I help you remove your robe and linens?"

Yvenne had never been bare in front of anyone but her mother, and that rarely. A screen in their tower chamber had served the same function as the curtain did here. "Thank you, no. I can attend to myself."

With a nod, the maid said, "Is there anything more you require?"

"I think this will do." Yvenne opened her satchel to find her coin purse. "What is your name?"

"Sarus, my lady."

"Thank you, Sarus."

Eyes as bright as the gold glinting in her palm, Sarus's gaze darted about the room, as if searching for something else to do. She stilled when that gaze landed on Fassad, and Yvenne did not see the warrior's expression herself, but the maid's hasty exit told her that his face forbade any more delay.

He said a few words to Steel and Bone, who immediately raced inside the chamber and began sniffing the corners.

Digging into her satchel again, Yvenne searched for her soap and silver comb, laying them within reach of the tub. "You do not mind that the wolves stay with me?"

Fassad's reply was an amused rumble. "The true question is whether they mind staying with you, and I think they do not. You spoil them."

So she did. "Do you mind that?"

"No." The tall warrior withdrew to the chamber entrance. "If you need anything, shout. I'll be directly outside."

The door latched behind him. Yvenne wasted no time shedding her soiled robe and stained linens. Never had sinking into heated water felt so fine. A moan of pleasure escaped her, the sound apparently unusual enough that the wolves' ears pricked forward and they drew closer to investigate. Curiously they sniffed the rim of the tub and her cake of soap before thrusting their shaggy muzzles into the water, long tongues lapping.

Laughing, Yvenne pushed at their big heads with dripping hands. "Go and take your rest."

They trotted over to the fire, where they curled up on the wooden floors that had felt so much warmer beneath her feet than the polished stone of her tower chamber. Coarse linens covered a mattress stuffed with straw, and the bedposts were roughly carved. Nothing like the silks and pillows that had adorned the tower. But in truth, there was little difference. Her mother had made certain Yvenne would recognize that. For what was the luxury in the tower but the labor of Syssians? She washed now with soap made by Syssian hands, perfumed with anise grown by Syssian farmers. Her comb was made of Syssian silver, mined and smithed—and when she finished washing her hair, she dunked soiled linens woven by Syssian weavers, then scrubbed a silk robe sewn by Syssian seamstresses.

Her father never understood that. He saw the luxury as his due—not the debt that it truly was. A people's efforts made a realm strong, and a ruler's duty was to dedicate all of her efforts toward protecting her people's safety and freedom.

For freedom was the greatest luxury. Freedom and a full belly.

Now her belly was full of Gogean meat. Wrapping her body in a coarse Gogean cloak, Yvenne hung up her clothing to dry. Warmed by the heat of a Gogean peat fire, she sat on the edge of a Gogean bed, leisurely threading her comb through her hair.

Had she ever been more content? Yvenne could not recall a time. Content in her purpose, though so much remained undone. Content in her choice of husband, who was angry and grieving, yet who still listened when she claimed he was not a king—and who had defended her to his warriors, despite reprimanding her in the stables for failing in her duty to them all. She had not been mistaken when she'd chosen Maddek, though their marriage would never be an easy one. And nothing would ever be settled between them unless he allowed her to speak of his mother.

Perhaps when the grief was not so sharp, when Maddek learned to trust her, he might rescind that vow.

Perhaps.

Sighing, she carefully wrapped the soft perfumed soap in waxed parchment before tucking it away into her satchel. At the bottom lay a heavy velvet pouch containing her gold and jewelry. She wore no jewelry now but would don one item in that pouch after her marriage to Maddek: a silver crest, much like the one he wore upon his thumb.

Ran Ashev had worn the crest that now rested in her

jewelry pouch. Yvenne would place his mother's crest around her own thumb . . . if he ever allowed her to say how she came by it. For just as her fury and pain were all but impossible to separate, so his rage and grief seemed entwined. While still heartstricken by the murder of his parents, if he saw Yvenne wearing Ran Ashev's ring he might cut off her thumb rather than listen to her explanation.

And she did not want to lose more fingers. Or her tongue.

A tap sounded at the door, followed by, "Are you still in the bath? It is Danoh."

Coming to sleep. "I am finished," Yvenne called.

Beyond the request to enter, Danoh did not speak and Yvenne did not expect her to. From her perch on the edge of the bed and behind the thin curtain, she could not clearly see the rest of the room, so it almost seemed as if she were alone. In the quiet, she strapped her jeweled dagger to her calf again, then admired the glint of the hilt's rubies and sapphires against her brown skin. How well she liked the feel of the weapon—especially now, when she had no other protection but her cloak.

She had the wolves and Danoh, of course. But the dagger meant Yvenne could see to her own safety, and she hadn't felt that particular pleasure since Ran Ashev had given her a bow.

Loosing the arrow that killed her eldest brother had been a greater pleasure still.

But that memory was followed by unhappy ones Yvenne had no wish to revisit. Clutching the edges of her cloak tight over her chest, she drew back the curtain. Danoh had tossed her furs onto the floor beside the entrance but had not bedded down yet. Instead she was examining the chamber's corners and checking the shutters—even looking up into the rafters—just as Fassad had done to judge the security of the room. Her gaze slid past Yvenne and the curtain, landing on the dogs.

"Fassad has gone to the stables," Danoh told her.

Instead of remaining outside the door. "Should I send the wolves after him?"

She shrugged. "If you wish. I am protection enough. But if they are not beside your bed, I prefer you keep the curtain open."

Though Maddek would come to the bed—and anyone in the chamber might know how Yvenne saw to his need. Not that a curtain would prevent them from hearing. And not that they had greater privacy in his furs each evening. The only privacy they truly had was the custom of turning away eyes. But it all seemed more intimate within the chamber instead of a camp under the open sky.

Cheeks hot, she said, "I would keep the wolves here."

Danoh grunted, as if the answer did not affect her one way or another. "Do you wish to keep this lamp lit?"

"No."

The warrior extinguished the flame. By the flickering light from the hearth, Yvenne drew the curtains, then wrapped her cloak closely around her body before lying on the bed.

The barrier provided by the curtain looked more uncertain in the dark. Between the panels of fabric, narrow swaths of the chamber were visible. The glow from the fire fell upon the leg of a table, across the wooden floor, and over Danoh's bare foot.

Yvenne closed her eyes. Maddek had said he would wake her when he came to bed. She doubted sleep would come before he did, however. Not with her heart thudding as it was, as if her blood ran slow and thick through her veins. Every breath felt heavy and her skin as hot as if she were still in the bath. Anticipation was a low burn, a warmth that heightened and tightened every time she pictured the way he looked at her with dark eyes full of fire and hunger.

Her heart gave a wild thump as the door latch slid back. Her eyes flew open, her body tense.

Hushed laughter accompanied the shuffling of feet. Abruptly it quieted, followed by whispers and more laughter. A table leg screeched against the floor, as if someone had stumbled into it. Silence fell, then was broken by a woman's muffled giggles.

Sarus, the barmaid—who was between Ardyl and Kelir. In the dark, Yvenne could not be certain whose hands and whose mouth were currently upon the maid's waist and neck, though both warriors seemed determined to put their hands and mouths everywhere.

But she was certain Maddek was not tangled up with them.

She sat up. "Kelir?"

Sudden quiet. Then, "Did we wake you, my lady?"

From her spot by the door, a soft grunt from Danoh sounded like a curse and answer, all in one.

But matters more urgent than her sleep concerned Yvenne. "Who is guarding Maddek?"

Fassad had gone to the stables. Toric and Banek had also planned to sleep there, watching over the horses. If they had already gone to bed, then none of the Dragon was left to protect Maddek.

"He drinks with the Gogean soldiers," Kelir said. "Toric is still with him."

Drinking with the Gogean soldiers. She had suggested to Maddek that he speak with the Gogeans to learn the truth of their situation. It seemed he had followed her advice.

"Thank you." She hesitated before adding, "You may carry on now, if you wish to."

Over Ardyl's muffled snicker, Kelir solemnly replied, "I do wish to, my lady. Thank you."

Eyes closed and determined to ignore the activity on the other side of the curtain, Yvenne lay back again.

Sarus's sharp gasp—as if made in pain—had her eyes flying open again. Were they hurting her? Half afraid of what she might see, Yvenne peered through the slit between the curtain panels and could not at first make out the scene taking place on Kelir's furs. There seemed too many legs and arms and hands. Then the glint of firelight on Ardyl's piercings allowed her to orient limbs and assign them to their owners.

Sarus straddled Kelir's lap, her back to his chest. His big hands cupped her breasts and he kissed the length of her arched neck. Ardyl's face was buried between the barmaid's spread thighs.

Oh. It was not a pained gasp that she'd heard.

Prickles of awareness racing across her skin, Yvenne watched as Sarus bit her lip, her back bowing. Kelir's rough murmur reached her ears, too low to make out the words, but Sarus suddenly gave a breathless laugh and Ardyl lifted her head to grin up at him.

Her heart suddenly full and tight, Yvenne closed stinging eyes. So this was what her mother had spoken of. Queen Vyssen had reassured Yvenne that usually relations between lovers were unlike those between Zhalen and her mother. Always Yvenne had been sent behind the screen when her father came to the queen's bed, and she held hands over her ears as instructed, but still she heard his cruel and mocking voice. Still she heard the slap of skin and thud of flesh. Her mother never cried out. Never. But by the sounds, Yvenne had known Zhalen hurt her.

Still, her mother had told Yvenne not to fear. That they would never choose a husband who was brutal as her father was. That they would never choose a husband who hurt her, but one who could please his partner in bed.

And although Yvenne had believed her mother, she had not known what pleasure truly looked like. Not until this moment, seeing Ardyl and Kelir and Sarus smile and laugh and gasp.

Would Maddek taste her as Ardyl tasted the barmaid?

The moment Yvenne imagined it, an ache centered deep and low inside her. Stifling a groan, she curled forward in the bed, clamping her hands between her thighs.

But Maddek would not be as Ardyl was. Because try as she might, Yvenne could not picture her would-be husband smiling and laughing as he licked her cunt. Instead his expression would be fierce, his dark gaze hot and hungry and intense.

Oh, she would *die* from imagining it. Trapped between her thighs, her fingers were drowning in her need, yet no matter how tightly she squeezed her legs the ache only deepened.

She had felt warmth and pleasure while touching Maddek before. While thinking of him. But *this*.

By Hanan, this need would kill her. And if Maddek felt the same degree, she knew not how he refrained from demanding she ease his arousal every night.

But perhaps he had eased his own—and she did not know how to ease hers. A man had a shaft to grip and stroke. Sarus had Ardyl to lick her. Yvenne had nothing but hot cuntflesh and slippery fingers and a spot that she could not bear to touch, so sensitive it was. The merest brush of her fingertips against that spot made her want to scream. The only relief she found was also agony, for there was pleasure in pressing the heel of her hand hard against her mound—against that spot—but the pressure only increased the need.

Muscles quivering with tension, she looked up again as Sarus's sharp scream sounded—and was quickly muffled by Kelir's lips on hers. The maid's body was bowed in a taut line, her hips thrashing as her frantic hands pulled at Ardyl's braids, as if to drag the warrior's face from between her thighs.

After an endless moment, the maid's body drooped and a grinning Ardyl lifted her head. There was a murmur, and then Kelir broke the kiss and his reply carried to Yvenne's bed.

"You got one from her," he said with a recognizable note of challenge in his tone. "I'll get two, and see her twice as wet."

So that was their competition—seeing who could make the barmaid spend the greatest number of times. Though it seemed a joint effort now, as Ardyl cupped Sarus's face and kissed her, slowly drawing the woman over onto her knees.

His body shadowed, Kelir rose behind her rounded buttocks. Yvenne closed her eyes as there was another sharp cry of pleasure, and Kelir's deeper groan, then sounds that Yvenne had heard before in the tower but they were *nothing* the same, for then Yvenne had trembled with anger and fear and now she shook with desire, her breath shuddering through clenched teeth, her skin afire.

Forever did it seem to last.

Twice was there a lull before another start, with more whispers and hushed laughter and soft cries. Finally all fell quiet on that side of the curtain, as if each had found their release—and never had Yvenne envied three people more, because her body did not find the same ease. Never had she felt so hot, yet she shivered uncontrollably.

At another murmur, her eyes slitted open. Kelir and Ardyl had Sarus's unclothed body tucked between theirs, and the prostrate barmaid already seemed asleep. Kelir's smile was a glint in the firelight as he bent his head to the other warrior's, and despite their rivalry, Yvenne could not mistake the easy affection in their kiss. Both looked utterly pleased, content.

And Yvenne was dying. How she wished to be lying as spent as the barmaid, but Ardyl and Kelir had pleased her with tongue and cock and Yvenne could do neither to herself. She could only clamp her hands between her thighs and pray to Mother Temra for mercy.

Outside the eternal comfort of her arms, that goddess did not often grant it. Nor did she this night.

Instead the goddess sent Maddek to the chamber door, and that was not mercy. At the slide of the latch, her body's yearning increased tenfold, her need weighing upon her so heavily that she seemed incapable of breathing, of moving. In her cloak, she lay upon the bed in a tight ball, facing the curtain with her hands buried between her clenched thighs. Now he would come and wake her. She would take his cock into her mouth and make him spill his seed and then he would lie beside her, as spent as the three who lay entangled on the opposite side of the chamber.

Except she could not truly imagine Maddek so content. Nor could she imagine that easing his need would also ease hers.

And that was not what he did, anyway.

For a long span of breaths he seemed not to move at all. Perhaps letting his eyes adjust to the darkness. Perhaps studying the layout of the chamber.

So quietly did he walk, only the slightest ripple through the curtain as he passed it told Yvenne that he'd finally made his way toward the master bed. Yet he still did not come to her. Instead there was the faint click of ivory as he lay his sheathed sword across the rim of the tub. Then the muffled thunk of his wide leather belt falling to the floor. A soft splash came next, followed by the sloshing of water, and the rainlike pattering of drops against tin.

And Yvenne had not truly known longing until she finally looked at him. The fire smoldered, the soft glow barely touching Maddek's skin as he dunked his red linens into the tub and began to wash, drawing the cloth across the broad planes of his body. Thick muscles were but shadows limned by orange light, and of all the wondrous things she had seen since leaving her tower, none had stolen her breath and filled her with hope as did the sight of Maddek, bare and at ease. Here was the king he would be, not ruled by anger and grief, but strong and calm, and with a faint smile touching his lips when Bone trotted over to investigate his nakedness. Maddek scratched behind the wolf's ears before sending him to lie down again.

Not once had she seen him glance in her direction. Yet as he moved silently toward the hearth to hang up his red linens, she realized her presence must not be far from his thoughts. At the first shadowed glimpse of his arousal, the fierce ache within her seemed to hollow out, as if her body prepared to receive him. To be filled by him.

That could not be tonight. Thighs trembling with tension, she squeezed them tighter. Still a quarter turn remained until her moon night. Then she would take him eagerly and pray he could soothe this burning need inside her.

Her heart tripped to a halt as the bed creaked and sagged beneath his great weight. Unprepared, she might have rolled toward him, but he was already close behind her curled form, lying on his side with his broad chest pressed to her back.

"This chamber is overhot, yet you are wrapped in your cloak." His voice was low and gruff against her ear, his warm breath laden with mead. "Are you cold?"

Burning. Yet he must wonder if she felt dark magics.

"I have no nightclothes to cover me," she explained softly, keeping her voice so quiet that the others in the chamber might hear the sound but would not make out the words spoken.

"Nor do I."

No need to tell her. Never had Yvenne been so aware of anything as she was his nakedness behind her—and of hers within the cloak. An involuntary shiver racked her muscles and she could not stop from drawing tighter, her fingers wedged between her thighs, knees all but touching her chest.

Still he did not roll her over and urge her mouth down to his erection, though she would have eagerly gone, had she been able to uncurl her body.

Instead he told her in the same quiet manner, "I spoke with the Gogeans. Their situation is as you claimed."

Of course it was.

But that seemed not a proper reply. And now she wondered if his talk with the Gogeans was why he did not ask to use her mouth. Mead might relax tongues, but an abundance of mead could relax the body, too. "Are you drunk?"

Amusement shook through him. "I am. In the morning my skull will feel as if a blacksmith uses it for an anvil."

Oh.

When silence was her only response, he shifted behind her, coming up onto his elbow as if to look down at her face. She could not see him at all except as a shadow looming above her.

"I drank, but not enough to soften my steel," he murmured. "Yet you are steel when I expected you to be soft and sleeping. Do you fear what I would ask of you?"

Pleasing him? She had no fear of that. "No."

He seemed to study her, though she could not imagine what he could see in the dark. "When you took the half-moon milk, you held yourself in the same way. What pains you?"

Her cheeks flared hot. "Nothing pains me."

"Speak truth," was his sharp reply.

"I do not lie," she hissed between her teeth. "It is not pain. I saw Kelir and Ardyl with the barmaid and I was . . . inflamed."

Silence followed that confession. Her face grew hotter.

"I should have turned my eyes away," she admitted.

The silence deepened. Against her back, Maddek's body felt more rigid than it had ever been. Was he angry? He had not liked hearing that her mother had watched the alliance army from their tower. Perhaps knowing that Yvenne had watched his warriors seemed an unforgivable breach of privacy.

"It is *not* pain," she repeated, trying to bring her argument back around to the beginning, before he could say she failed in her duty to his Dragon again. "I know not how to ease my need. But it will fade."

Or so she prayed.

Finally he spoke and she could not judge his mood, for although his amusement was unmistakable, each word seemed rougher than before, as if his throat had been scoured with gravel. "How can this not be known? If I were locked in a tower with nothing else to do, my hand would be upon my cock as often as upon my sword."

Yvenne smiled, but the pressure between her legs seemed too demanding and her chest too full to allow a laugh. She barely managed to say, "And if I had neither cock nor sword?"

"A woman only requires a hand." The humor left his voice, leaving only grit. "I will show you how a Parsathean warrior tends to herself."

Her eyes squeezed shut as everything inside her curled tighter. By Hanan's blessed seed, how could a promise of release so abruptly worsen the need?

"Please," she whispered breathlessly. "Show me quickly."

His head lowered, his reply harsh against her ear. "*Quickly* is not how a woman's cunt should be touched."

Yet the hard urgency of his hands belied his words. No time did he waste before gripping the back of her cloak and dragging the coarse material up over the swell of her bottom, baring her skin to the heated air within the chamber.

Her face afire again, Yvenne's gaze darted to the curtains. If the others were awake, they did not look it—no heads were lifted, no eyes were open.

But even if they were, from that direction little of her could be seen. Maddek drew the cloak so high it bunched behind her waist, yet in front the heavy fabric still covered Yvenne to her knees. Only her shins and feet were visible— and only barely. Her legs were but a shadow, the jeweled hilt of the dagger strapped to her calf a mere glint in the darkness.

Then all worry about what lay in front of her fled when Maddek shifted closer. So much taller was he that although their shoulders were aligned, their hips were not. Her bare bottom nestled into his steely abdomen, and his skin seemed so very hot against hers—though not as hot as the hard length prodding the back of her thigh, or the callused fingers that swiftly journeyed over the curve of her ass to delve between her clenched thighs from behind.

Maddek's chest rumbled against her back on a thick groan. "You are drenched in your need."

She was well aware. Her hands were still locked together between her legs, her palms and fingers and inner thighs swimming in her arousal. She trembled as his blunt fingertips glided over the seams of her fingers as if seeking entrance to the sensitive flesh below.

But he did not force her fingers apart. Instead he cupped her hands in the palm of his and murmured, "Do we do this slowly, after all?"

She could not bear that. Shaking her head, Yvenne pulled her elbows back—so very slightly, so that her fingers still covered the apex of her mound. His fingers followed, stopping when she did.

A quiet chuckle sounded behind her. "You hide your sweetest treasure from me?"

It was not treasure, but a burning and aching knot. On a strained whisper, she told him, "That part of me hurts to touch."

"There is pain?"

"Yes."

"Are you certain?"

How could she not be certain? But her irritated reply was lost on a gasp as strong teeth pinched her earlobe. Her entire body stiffened, the knot between her legs throbbing as if that flesh had been pinched, instead.

"Was that pain?" His voice was gravel again, abrasive not just against her ear but scratching lightly over the span of her skin, prickling every nerve.

And that soft bite hadn't hurt. Though the sensation had been acute, with a sharpened edge, it was nothing like the pain Yvenne had known so intimately through so much of her life.

"It was not," she whispered.

"This will be the same." His fingers moved gently against hers. "So much pleasure that you can hardly bear if it continues. So much that you can hardly bear if it ends."

She could hardly bear it now. Still she trembled in an agony of indecision. "You intend to touch me there?"

"Do you fear I will hurt you?"

Yes. And no.

Neither answer was completely truthful. So she had no answer to give.

For a long moment he was quiet, his broad chest rising and falling against her back, his thick fingers gently stroking through the wetness between her legs, as if accustoming her to his touch.

Finally he spoke again. "It matters not. Every Parsathean raider knows how to find a woman's pearl, even when it is kept under guard."

She could not mistake the amusement deepening the quiet rumble of his voice—as if he meant to put her at ease in this way.

Perhaps he would be successful, for she could not think of pain when she was thinking of how absurd such a name was. "A pearl?"

"All Parsatheans know that a woman's clitoris is a hidden treasure." As softly as his voice was rough, his slick fingertips glided back through her saturated folds. "To claim it, first a raider must voyage across this burning ocean."

Still so absurd. Yet she could not laugh, not while pressing her lips together against the moan that threatened to escape with every slow caress through her delicate flesh.

Strong fingers teased her entrance. "Sometimes," he said against her ear, his voice harsher now, his breathing deeper, "a foolish warrior becomes lost exploring the wonders of this cavern. But any Parsathean who vanishes into these depths without resuming his search for the pearl will never claim his prize."

Now Yvenne shook with a laugh, because if she did not laugh she would scream from the hollow ache building within her. Never had she wanted anything more than to feel him exploring those depths, which clenched and tightened as if trying to draw him in.

"Maddek," she gasped.

His sword hand still buried between her legs, he drew her closer, wedging his left arm beneath her head and angling his elbow back to tangle his fingers into her hair, her cheek pillowed upon his biceps—until gentle pressure turned her face upward, as if she were looking over her shoulder. She could not see him. Only feel him, his head bent close to hers, the heat of his breath at the corner of her lips.

His touch roughened, massaging her sultry flesh with long, circling strokes and drawing more wetness from her, as if her cunt were an endless well.

Gruffly he commanded, "Bring your fingers to my mouth so that I can taste your honey upon them."

Just as she had once licked his seed from her fingers.

Need shuddered through her, but hot upon the heels of that memory was another—of the last time Maddek had drawn her fingers into his mouth, suckling away her brother's life-blood, with his desire for Yvenne's death burning like a hot fire in his eyes.

That was not what he burned for now. Yet whether he truly wanted to taste her or to remove the guard of her fingers, she knew not.

At her hesitation, his voice deepened. "I will not hurt you, Yvenne. Though I might make you scream."

As the barmaid had screamed. And now that woman lay satisfied, at ease.

Yvenne wanted the same. So desperately.

Lifting her hands away from that slick, aching knot and raising them to his mouth seemed more effort than even climbing the stairs had been. More exciting than Maddek's iron heat behind her, more terrifying than facing a wraith.

She had not known trust was such a frightening, exhilarating part of herself to give.

Yet the reward was well worth it. Her fingertips brushed his firm lips, and then scalding heat enveloped the remaining fingers of her right hand. His hungry groan melded with her gasp as he drew them deep into his mouth—just as she was supposed to have drawn his cock into her mouth this night.

But that steely length lay against her leg, and Maddek did not seem in a rush to take his own ease when he released her hair to grip her wrists, holding her hands in place for his tongue. His mouth licked as, between her legs, his fingers leisurely stroked. For all his talk of her pearl, though it was unguarded now he did not approach that throbbing knot. Instead he drove her to madness with that unhurried touch, until her body uncurled in her desperation to push back against him, until her breath was coming in great and ragged gasps, until her clitoris ached so fiercely that the agony of need that had filled her as she'd watched Kelir and Ardyl seemed a pale and gentle pleasure in comparison.

Then his hand abandoned her swollen wetness altogether, his slick fingers gripping her upper thigh.

"In this way." Left hand still clamped around her wrists, his mouth was hot against her jaw, each word harsh. "We will both spend."

Hard fingers urged her right leg to lift slightly. With a groan, he pushed his burning length against her, his thick shaft gliding into the slippery channel formed by her cunt and inner thighs. That hot thrust over her aroused flesh was pleasure with teeth, a bite that sharpened when he released her thigh and the weight of her leg trapped him tight against her. He pushed forward until the length of his cock almost brushed across her clitoris. When he stopped short of that aching knot, she clamped her lips to halt a scream of frustration.

But even clamped lips could not muffle the sound she made as his hand slipped forward over her hip and delved beneath her cloak. The moment his deft fingers found her clitoris, agonizing pleasure sheared her nerves and her soft cry broke free.

Immediately she stilled, her gaze darting past the curtain. No movement.

Except Maddek's hand and his cock, which continued stroking her from the front and from behind. Except his mouth, pinching her earlobe again before murmuring harshly, "They know not to look. Scream if you like."

Her reply was a ragged whisper. "I cannot."

Releasing her wrists, his big hand covered her panting mouth. "Then bite me to stay quiet if you must."

Oh, she could not. Would not. But his palm muffled the cries that passed her lips as he set a relentless rhythm, his hardened shaft spearing through the sultry lips of her cunt, his fingers licking like fire over her clitoris, the burn so deep now within her, raging out of control.

Maddek had been right—she could hardly bear this. She had thought release would be sweet, like the cool rain upon her burning face. But if this was a summer storm, it was rolling toward her on dark clouds filled with lightning, each stroke of his fingers a flash that drew her body tighter and tighter, anticipating and fearing the crash that followed. Frantically she gripped the strong wrist pressed tight to her belly, trying to shove his hand away, to find some relief from the ruthless torment of his fingers, but it was as if she tried to move a mountain. Then the storm was upon her, a crack of thunder that split her body asunder, an endless rumbling quake through stiffened muscles, and in its devastating wake she was left breathless, shaking.

And given no time to recover before she was pushed over onto her stomach, Maddek's fingers still stroking her clitoris. He braced his left hand beside her head as his heavy body covered hers, and his demand was growled into her ear. "Again."

She could not possibly. But she lay upon his hand and his fingers commanded more. A scream rose and he no longer muffled her cries, so she sank her teeth into the bedlinen. His heavy shaft thrust through her clenched thighs, that tight channel flooded by the deluge of her release, and the storm was not over, for Maddek was unleashed upon her. Hotter, harder, and this time she did not try to drag his hand away from her clitoris but instead pushed back against him, seeking the same prize he sought with every stroke of his fingers and cock. Then it was abruptly within her grasp and she shuddered again, cries muffled against the bed, his thick groan filling her ears as he stiffened above her.

She had felt the pulse of his cock before, had known the warmth of his seed on her fingers. But against her own swollen and sensitive flesh, the pulse seemed deeper, the seed hotter.

Only a sevennight remained until he spent within her, when she would know that pulse even deeper, when his seed would burn ever hotter.

She yearned for that night. But until then, she would luxuriate in this release. This bedding had been nothing as she'd imagined. Rough, but not brutal as her father had been with her mother. And not what she had witnessed between Kelir and Ardyl and the barmaid. That had been playful and shimmering with mutual affection. This had been more primitive, an eruption of raw need—and had apparently suited Maddek as well as it had Yvenne.

And although there had not been affection, there was some tenderness. As Maddek's heavy weight lifted from her back, he murmured, "You are well?"

Very well. "I am," she whispered.

He left the bed, and her body felt all but boneless as she rolled onto her back. Her cloak fell open in front and was still bunched behind her waist, and the effort to right it seemed to steal all that remained of her strength. From the foot of the bed, the splash of water told her he washed, and she was lazily thinking of doing the same when he returned with a swath of dampened rabbit fur. He lay close beside her, elbow braced and head resting upon his hand as he looked down at her face. Though he could not possibly see through the dark, her cheeks blazed with heat as she quickly washed his seed from between her thighs.

Despite his release, his arousal had not completely subsided. She could feel his heavy length against her leg, could feel the heat of him even through her cloak.

On a whisper she asked him, "Do you still wish me to ease your need with my mouth?"

His low chuckle answered her before he said, "Perhaps tomorrow. Tonight I am well spent."

"As am I." Which filled Yvenne's heart as she had never imagined. As raw and rough as Maddek was, she had not been mistaken in her choice of husband. "I was told that you would see to my pleasure, but I knew not—"

Her words were lost on a strangled breath as hard fingers seized her tongue. Pain tore through her mouth and even before her mind realized what was happening—*Maddek is tearing out my tongue*—her hands flew to his wrists and desperately tried to stop him. She had not been able to stop him before, had not moved that mountain, and so it was not her hands that halted him now.

His fingers stopped just beyond her teeth, the tip of her tongue in a viselike grip. A sobbing breath burst past her open lips. She tried to shake her head, to beg, but the movement seemed to rip at the sides of her tongue, and the only noise she could make was a strangled plea.

"Again you speak sly words." Though it was only a murmur, anger hardened his voice like stone. "Again you speak of my mother."

She could not answer, only attempt to shake her head again. Her eyes watered from the agony of it, but the agony within her was sharper, deeper. She could taste herself upon his fingers, the fingers he had said would not hurt her.

The fingers she had trusted to touch her.

"You will not receive another warning. Do you understand this?"

She'd understood it before. But there was no answer except to nod. He released her tongue and she would have told him then, but her throat was thick with tears and a queen did not cry when there was someone to see. Perhaps he would not see her tears in the dark, but if she spoke he would hear them.

And she could not bear that.

In misery, she turned onto her side, facing away from him, but his next words followed and slipped into her back like a sharpened blade.

"Queen or not, you are but a vessel through which I will take my vengeance. I will plant my seed within you—but if you wish for more, if you wish to be loved, you had best look elsewhere. For I can never open my heart to a woman who took part in the murder of my parents."

That had to be denied, even if it exposed the tears that burned in her throat and her eyes. "I did not," she whispered thickly.

"Perhaps not. But I cannot ever know if it is true. You admit you are treacherous and your sly tongue cannot be trusted. Your sighs and your longing say that you want more than a bedding, but if it is love you seek, look to our children. Look to my people and yours, as you are so adept at securing their loyalty. But do not look to me."

Never had her heart felt so heavy. The weight of it held

back even the tears. Bleakly she replied, "I hear you, warrior."

He made no response as she rose from the bed. Perhaps thinking that she intended to wash more—as if the wound he'd delivered truly bled. Not until she reached the hearth did he ask quietly, "Where do you go?"

Where she was safe. "I will return to your bed upon my moon night. I am only a vessel, so you have no use for me there until then, and I have no wish to lie beside you."

But the wolves would welcome her. With a soft whine, Bone licked her face, and she curled up against him, with Steel a comforting warmth at her back.

Maddek said not another word.

And it mattered not if the wolves felt her crying silently against them. It mattered not if her tears soaked into their fur.

For Maddek was truly a great warrior, finding vulnerabilities Yvenne had not known she possessed. He could even make weapons of her sighs, transform her longing into a blade, and use them to slice through her heart.

A great warrior indeed.

CHAPTER 16

MADDEK

Early did Maddek rise, for that night sleep had not found him. With head pounding, he'd lain upon his cold bed until the gray light of dawn revealed Yvenne's slight form curled up between the two wolves in front of the hearth.

Heavily she slept. Even when he finished dressing and crouched beside her, she did not stir. Her hood was up but failed to conceal her thin face or the reddened skin around her eyes. Her fingers were tangled in Bone's thick fur.

The wolves lifted their heads but he quietly bade them to stay—then gave the same command to Kelir when that warrior disentangled himself from the barmaid. With Ardyl and Danoh at his back, Maddek made his way downstairs, where the travelers and soldiers who had not found rooms were sprawled sleeping over tables and benches.

He looked to Danoh. "See that Yvenne's meal is taken to our chambers." So that she would not have to shove aside a soldier's feet before eating.

With a nod, Danoh went in search of the innkeeper. In silence Ardyl accompanied him to the blacksmith's. If it had been Danoh walking beside him, Maddek would not have wondered at how quiet she remained. But Ardyl's silence was censure, just as his warriors had treated his bride to similar censure the previous eve.

Ardyl's disapproval now was likely in response to his bride's decision to sleep on the floor. His warriors might have heard Yvenne's pleasure, but they could not have heard what prompted her to leave their bed. No doubt they believed she punished Maddek for some insult.

That misconception would not be dispelled by him. Better they believed he deserved her punishment than reveal how she had spoken with a sly tongue—or that he had failed to fulfill his vow.

The last made shame fester within his chest. Only because she had not directly spoken of his mother had he spared her. But he had warned her against speaking with a sly tongue earlier that eve . . . and still gave her another warning rather than follow through.

But if she had spoken directly, Maddek knew not whether he'd have ripped out her tongue—or if he would have become an oathbreaker, the most reviled of all Parsathean warriors.

Never had he imagined his honor would be brought so low.

So Ardyl and the others could believe what they wished. Whatever reason they thought Yvenne had to punish him could not compare to the contemptible weakness exposed in his warrior's heart.

Each leading two horses, he and Ardyl returned to the stables. That the remaining members of his Dragon also refused to speak to him was expected; less expected was Kelir's presence. Maddek had told the warrior to remain with Yvenne. Instead young Toric was missing.

Maddek frowned at his friend, who met his gaze with an anger unconcealed. No doubt he would soon hear what his Dragon believed he had done. "Where is my bride?"

"Still breaking her fast, with Toric at her side. She insisted upon dining in the common room."

Of course she had. There was more to see and more people to watch than in their bedchamber.

But that could not be what had angered his warriors. Maddek waited.

Kelir continued, "I urged her to linger over her meal."

"Why?"

"So that she would not witness your Dragon deliver a much-needed blow."

Torn between amusement and irritation, Maddek began to ready his mount. "Lay it upon me, then. After you tell me what I have done."

"You sent our future queen from your bed and forced her to sleep with the dogs."

Saddle in hand, Maddek stilled. "What do you say?"

"You made her sleep with the dogs." Each word was a sharp bite.

By Stranik's split tongue. Little wonder they had given him their silence. They had not thought she punished him. Instead they believed he'd punished *her*—humiliated her for his warriors and the barmaid to see.

An unworthy king he would truly be then.

Sardonic humor twisted his mouth. "It was her choice to leave my bed."

His warriors stared at him.

Face slack with disbelief, Kelir slowly said, "She chose to lie with the wolves rather than to lie with you?"

An affirmative grunt served as Maddek's response. He settled the saddle onto his mount's back, and the gray gelding shifted uneasily when the warriors' laughter erupted throughout the stables. He would not put Yvenne upon this horse, then. Not if loud noises so easily disturbed him.

And his admission lifted the Dragon's censure. Grinning, Kelir led his own horse alongside Maddek's and began to saddle him.

Full of amusement, the warrior asked, "What did you say to her that she would rather lie with dogs?"

"Only what needed to be said." Though the words had injured her, they had been truth. It was best she built no expectations of love that would never be.

Maddek could not love a woman who might have taken part in the murder of his parents. He could not love a woman he could never trust.

Though he could want her more fiercely than he had ever wanted another.

"Only what needed to be said?" Kelir echoed, eyeing him curiously. "Just as she said to you in secret last eve?"

That Maddek was only a warrior, not a king. His fingers faltered upon the leathers that tied his furs to the saddle. Still her words pierced him through—yet they had carried a lesson he needed to learn.

But he could not truthfully say that his lesson had been for Yvenne. It *was* best that she did not hope to win his heart, but she had also never spoken of such a hope. The marriage she had proposed would allow for vengeance and to strengthen the alliance. Not one word had she uttered about love or companionship. Likely because everything Maddek had said and done already taught her not to hope for them.

She had not asked for his heart last night. She had only asked for release.

It was Maddek who had wanted more. It was he who had drawn her close when he had first come to their bed. It was he who had been so overcome with need that he had rutted upon her like a boar. It was he who had been filled with such tenderness and affection toward her—until her sly words had abruptly reminded him that she could not be trusted.

But he should not have needed the reminder. That he had forgotten even briefly was a betrayal of his queen and king.

He would *not* care for a woman who might have played a part in their murders. It had not been her sighs and longing that prompted his words, however. Instead it was his own heart that needed the lesson.

Feeling Kelir's expectant gaze upon him, he finally responded. "Perhaps they were words best left unsaid."

Humor lifted the other warrior's brows. "She will not need to make your life a misery. You do it too well yourself."

Maddek acknowledged that with a grunt and began readying Yvenne's new mount.

"Best you make peace with her," was Kelir's advice. "If you can."

Yes. *If he could.* Maddek was more accustomed to making war. But now he had to be more than a warrior.

For that, he needed Yvenne.

Which must have been why his chest clenched so tightly when he spotted her approaching the stables, Toric at her side. Yvenne was not the bride he would have chosen. But she was the bride who would make him a king worthy of his people. In his thoughtlessness, he might have jeopardized everything.

Quietly Kelir said, "She came down the stairs on her ass."

"She fell?" His gaze slipped down her cloaked length. Her stiffness had all but disappeared. She only still favored her left leg. Or was her limp from a new injury? Scowling, he looked to Kelir. "Why was there no one to catch her?"

"I was directly behind her, which was how I saw what she did," the warrior replied, his steady gaze on Maddek's bride. "She did not fall. On the first step, she clung so tightly to the rail it was as if she feared she *would* fall. Then she sat on the step and went down in that way. Fassad told me she also had difficulty climbing them last eve—as if she did not trust her left leg to hold her."

As she had stumbled into Maddek when she had put weight upon her left leg while leaving the table. As she had collapsed to the ground when her brother had pulled her from their carriage.

Maddek had seen her weakness. Apparently he had not seen her suffering.

And he knew not what she saw in him now. Her moonstone eyes looked straight through him as he approached,

leading her mount. No emotion registered on her delicate
features as she first regarded him, then her new mare, then
the other warriors and their mounts.

Her gaze lingered on the two horses tethered to Banek's
gelding. "You purchased so many?"

Maddek would have taken more if there had been more
worth buying. "If we traveled with the Parsathean army,
each warrior would have two or three horses, so that we
might saddle another if one tires or falls lame. With these,
we will travel more quickly. We have already lost too much
time."

Nodding, she rubbed the mare's muzzle and softly exchanged breaths with the animal before her gaze began
searching the stable. "Is there a mounting block?"

Because although her riding had improved these past
days, still she could not swing herself into the saddle—and
she would never be so tall as to raise her foot high enough
to reach the stirrup. Instead she needed a ledge or rock to
step upon, or for Maddek to lift her onto the horse's back.

Maddek was here, yet she looked for a block. As if she
could not bear his touch.

Jaw hardening, he clamped his hands around her waist.
Instantly she stiffened, though she did not pull away or argue. Silent she remained as he hefted her astride. With both
hands, she steadied herself on the pommel of her saddle.

He did not immediately give over the reins. "Will you
run today if you must?"

Her soft lips thinned before she answered tightly, "I will
try, warrior."

Warrior. Never had it felt like an insult before. Yet that
was what she had called him almost from the first moment
of their meeting.

Almost. Because the first time she had spoken to him,
she had called him Ran Maddek. How far and how quickly
he had fallen in her estimation.

Perhaps because he asked the wrong questions. "*Can*
you run if you must? Why do you favor your left leg?"

Her pale eyes darted to his face before she deliberately

pulled her gaze away from him, offering the stubborn lift of her chin as an answer.

He liked the look of that answer but it was not the one he sought. Did she fear admitting a weakness? She had never seemed reluctant to speak of hers before. "If I am to protect you, Yvenne, I must know what you can and cannot do."

As he expected, her sense outweighed her stubbornness.

"I cannot run," she snapped. "Three years past, my knee was shattered. It never properly healed."

Shattered while she was locked in a tower room? "How were you hurt?" Tension gripped him. "*Who* hurt you?"

"I prefer not to say. Whenever I reveal anything of myself, warrior, you make weapons from what you learn." A baleful glance was sent his way. "And it matters not. If any Parsathean sacrifices themself coming to my rescue, you have said you will kill me. Best not to attempt any rescue at all."

"I said that if my *warriors* fell. I would risk myself."

This time the glance she shot in his direction was guarded. Wary. As if she did not trust his word.

The muscles at the back of his neck stiffened. To doubt a Parsathean's word was a grave insult. But if Maddek was to make peace, he had to let it pass.

Quietly he said, "When I spoke of warriors sacrificing themselves, I knew nothing of your injury or that you cannot run. I spoke in haste and rage and grief."

Her chin lifted again. "Was it your haste and rage and grief that almost ripped out my tongue?"

That he could not let pass. "You heard my vow and my warning. Yet still you spoke with sly tongue yesterday."

"So I did. Twice."

"Three times."

"Twice." Her sharpened gaze returned to his. "Once at the ruins and once while we ate our meal. I should not have attempted to slip mention of her into our conversations. I regret that I did. But I also told you I would not again."

"Yet you *did* again, in our bed. Unless you will claim it

was my warriors and not my mother who said I would please you there?"

"Why would I make such a claim? I was speaking of *my* mother."

Maddek frowned. "How could she know such a thing?"

On a shaky breath, she looked away from him again to gaze blindly ahead, her jaw set. After a moment she said, "My mother watched you—as she watched every warrior and noble who might eventually make a suitable match for me. She saw you with your lovers and assured me you would see to my pleasure."

Maddek had not taken a lover in years. Not since becoming commander of the alliance army more than eight summers past.

Had Queen Vyssen watched him so long?

In disbelief he searched Yvenne's face. He could not know whether she spoke the truth. But it matched what she had claimed before. Her mother had observed many members of the alliance . . . and after Zhalen had deceived her, surely Queen Vyssen would not let another man deceive her daughter in the same way. What better way to know a man's character than to watch him for years?

Sick shame returned to his chest. He could still feel Yvenne's slick tongue between his fingers. He could still hear her panicked sobbing breaths as she seized his wrist and tried to prevent him from fulfilling his vow.

Had he done so, never would he have known the truth. And he would have not been an oathbreaker. He would have been far worse.

He would not ask for her forgiveness. What he had done should not be forgiven. Instead he offered what poor apology he could.

Throat raw, he told her, "I wronged you. For that, I am sorry."

In either surprise or incredulity, her moonstone eyes darted to his face again. For a long moment she simply looked at him. Finally she said, "Was it your haste and rage and grief again?"

At her measured reply, relief loosened the knot in his chest. "I have been counseled against speaking or making decisions while in the grip of it."

"It was wise counsel."

"Yes." Nayil's counsel often was. Yet Maddek had discarded the Parsathean minister's advice almost immediately upon hearing that Zhalen had a daughter. "In the future, I will better heed it."

"That is also wise," she said softly, though the ironic smile that followed suggested she did not fully believe it.

"You think I will not succeed?"

"Perhaps." Her shrug was lightweight, unlike her gaze upon his face. "In truth, I was thinking of my own poor decision. I cannot blame haste or rage, because my choice of husband was years in the making. But still I regret my choice now."

Regretted *him*, Maddek realized—and the emotion that rose through him was quick and hot, and felt like anger, but fury had never clawed painfully at his chest as this emotion did.

Still it sounded the same as fury, harsh and unyielding, as he demanded, "Could your marriage to any other man better strengthen the alliance?"

Her jaw tightened before she admitted, "No."

"Is there another who would defy the council and destroy your father?"

"No."

"Who will free your people from his tyranny?"

Such a long pause followed, it was as if she desperately tried to think of another name before admitting defeat. "No."

But it mattered not what her answers were. He gripped the pommel of her saddle, covering her hands with his—as his body had covered hers last eve. As he would cover her again on her moon night and every night thereafter.

His gaze held steadily to hers as he said, "Do you believe I would *ever* allow you to choose another?"

"No." A bitter smile curved her lips. "I am your path to vengeance. So let us continue as we are, warrior."

So they would. But not exactly as they had been. He gave to her the reins and mounted his own horse, then signaled to Kelir to take the lead before coming up alongside Yvenne. At a trot they started away from the stables, with Maddek watching her new mount. Thus far her mare seemed placid and steady, suitable for a new rider.

When they reached the road, he spoke again. "Do you still intend to make a king of me?"

A soft laugh preceded her reply. "I will try."

"And I will make a warrior-queen of you." At her sudden frown and searching glance, he continued, "Here is your first lesson: make the best use of what you have. Waste no time with wishes and regrets."

She stared at him for a long moment before a wry smile touched her mouth. "And I have *you*, warrior. Is that what you mean to say?"

"No. I say what I mean: a warrior makes use of what she has."

Her eyebrows arched in challenge. "And I have you."

"Yes." Maddek could not deny that. She had him. It was best that she made use of him. And if the lesson she learned from this was to accept Maddek as her only possible suitor, then he would not unteach her. But there was another he wanted her to learn. "Are you prepared for your second lesson?"

Another laugh was her answer. Blown back by the wind, her hood had fallen away from her braided hair, her cheeks already brightened by the ride.

His gaze fell to her linen-wrapped calf, exposed as the sides of her cloak and robe flapped against her mount's flanks. "It is the same lesson: make use of what you have. And if you are in bed with a warrior who intends to rip out your tongue for a false reason, then use the dagger strapped to your leg to defend yourself."

Sudden and sharp was the grin she turned on him. "I will! Even if the reason is not false."

Maddek did not doubt it—and thought he would be wise

to strip her of weapons before joining her in his furs that night. "Will you give me true reason?"

"I have no wish to lose my tongue." All at once her smile faded, her moonstone gaze solemn. "And a Parsathean warrior who betrays a vow cannot be king—yet that is what I intend to make you. So I will not risk my tongue or your crown again."

Maddek did not doubt that, either. And a warrior wasted no time on regrets but still must admit the wrongs he'd done . . . and it was not the threat to her tongue that had sent her from their bed. When he'd let her go, she had lain beside him still. Only after he'd spoken again had she left. "What I told you afterward, I should not have. Those were words best left unsaid."

Her face shuttered. "Yet you spoke truth, did you not? As Parsatheans always do. Through me, you will have your vengeance. And you intend to give me nothing more than your seed."

Jaw tight, Maddek inclined his head. That was what he intended. A vessel was all Yvenne should be to him.

And he should not need to keep reminding himself of that.

Chin lifting, she looked away from him, casting her gaze down the road ahead. In silence they rode for five long breaths before she spoke again. "It was also true what you said of me. I hoped for more from my marriage and my husband. Yet affection and love are not necessary to our purpose, are they?"

"No," he answered gruffly—more truth. Yet he had to force it from his tongue.

She yearned for more from him. Being certain of what he'd already guessed should not pull at his chest, as if drawing upon some hidden yearning within his own heart.

A short nod was her reply, followed by a sidelong glance. "Will you ever rescind your vow?"

And let her speak of his mother? "If ever I believed you would only speak truth."

"I *would*," she shot back without hesitation. "I have *never* lied to you."

He gave no reply.

Her moonstone gaze searched his face and must have seen the doubt he hadn't voiced. Emphatically she continued. "I *have* spoken with sly tongue twice. But I have never lied to you. I never will."

Such a statement demanded an answer. "Never can I be certain of that."

"You will always doubt my word?"

Maddek believed he would. No matter how he wished otherwise. She would be his bride, his queen, the mother of his children. Of all the words ever spoken, it was *hers* that he most wanted to trust.

But he did not. And he would waste no time wishing.

Grimly he nodded. Her delicate features an unmoving mask, she stared at him with wide and unblinking eyes for many breaths.

Finally she faced forward again, her shoulders straight, her spine stiff. "You no longer need to fear that I want more from you, warrior. I require neither your affection nor your trust. All I require is your seed and your protection."

As it should be. Yet that was another truth he could not voice.

Because even though she no longer wanted more from Maddek, some foolish part of him wanted to give it.

CHAPTER 17

YVENNE

The past few days, Yvenne would have given much for Maddek to ride beside her. So of course on this day, when she would've given much to put distance between them, he never left her side.

Her would-be husband said little as they rode, however, and for that she was thankful. Already he had said enough.

Their route had veered away from the great river, its waters a rippling glint of silver to the north. Blanketed in tall grass, the Gogean plains stretched endlessly before them. Yvenne rode with her chin high and her gaze on the western horizon, fixed at the point where the narrowing road vanished from sight.

After a lifetime spent in her tower, she was no good judge of distance. She could not guess how far away the horizon lay. But surely by the time they reached that meeting of ground and sky, this pain would no longer weigh upon her heart so fiercely. Surely by then, the sharpened rage clawing up her throat would dull and retreat. Surely the icy bitterness that rimed her tongue would warm and sweeten.

Yet although Enam's blinding eye roamed higher through a cloudless sky and Yvenne's mare consumed a long span of road beneath her hooves, the horizon remained ever distant.

And if Maddek knew of her pain or rage, he seemed not at all burdened by them. He rode as tall as ever—and today he wore armor again. Not since leading the ambush upon the Tolehi road had he donned more than his linens, boots, and belt. Now spaulders and vambraces guarded his strong shoulders and arms. No breastplate covered his broad chest, however. Nor did he wear his silver claws or blacken his brow. Prepared for Syssian soldiers to catch up to them, but not yet anticipating a battle.

Remembering the hardened feel of him behind her, it seemed no wonder that he did not armor his chest. His heavy pectorals were already like steel.

She was looking upon those thick muscles when he glanced over. His dark gaze caught hers as surely as his fingers had caught her tongue, and the ravenous fire in his eyes burned as hot as she had burned against him last eve.

His apology for pulling at her tongue had been as sincere as it had been unexpected. But she had trusted his touch once and been hurt by it. Willingly would she lie beneath him on her moon night and every night after—but renewed trust would not come as easily as the flames he stoked within her.

Steadily she returned his look. Her tongue and her mind were her greatest weapons, but they were not as effective as her eyes. Even her father and brothers faltered beneath her moonstone gaze. Now she silently regarded Maddek, wanting him to back down, wishing that he would just once falter, too. But not for a moment did he glance away.

Despite her wish, it spoke *so* well of him that he held her gaze. That he could withstand what so many others could not. That he was not cowed by the goddess Vela looking through her eyes. Such a fine king he would be.

Even if he would never love or respect his queen.

It was she who averted her face then, as the raw ache in her throat built into a stinging burn behind her eyes.

This rage and pain *would* ease, she knew. Perhaps not this day. But Yvenne had spoken truth earlier—to be queen of Syssia and Parsathe, she did not require his affection.

Nor should she give any in return. If Maddek would never believe her word, he deserved no portion of her heart. Which ought to suit them both, as he wanted no portion of it.

But Parsatheans were raiders and thieves, so he'd already stolen some of it, anyway.

By Temra's fist, she would protect what was left—and to do it, she would heed his lessons well. Not only by using her dagger if he threatened her tongue again, but by wasting no time on wishes and regrets.

She would not even regret the pain his words had brought. With them, he'd taught her a more valuable lesson.

He'd taught her how vulnerable her heart was.

It was not the first time she'd been given that lesson. Her mother had before, but Yvenne had not truly learned it then.

Queen Vyssen had told her that love was not something to avoid. For when love was given freely or genuinely returned, everyone it touched was strengthened by it. Yet love could also blind, just as anger and hatred and fear did. It could be wielded as a weapon. It could hurt, when it was rejected or betrayed or lost. It could be confused with lust, or with pleasure, or with gratitude—for it often entwined with other emotions and was not so easily separated from them.

Her mother had tried to teach her how to recognize the difference. She'd served as Yvenne's eyes beyond the tower, had discussed the character of everyone she'd seen, and had warned her of all the ways people might attempt to take advantage of her heart. In that, she'd prepared Yvenne as best she could.

It was not the manipulations of others that had worried Queen Vyssen most, however, because Yvenne's father and older brothers had schooled her well. Instead she feared that Yvenne had been starved for love, just as they'd been often starved for food—and that, once released from their tower, Yvenne would grasp for any affection, no matter how slight, simply to feel full.

But Yvenne had not believed herself in so much danger. All of her life, she'd known love that was strong and unwavering. First her mother's, then her younger brother's—and, for a short time, Ran Ashev's. True, she'd been piercingly lonely following her mother's death, but the memory of Queen Vyssen's love had sustained her then, as had Yvenne's love for her people. Love had strengthened her, just as her mother had claimed it would. Love, and the hope that her father's rule would soon find its end.

And knowing love, Yvenne had never imagined that she would be so hungry for Maddek's heart, or as dazzled by his touch as she was dazzled by the expanse of the sky and the warmth of the sun.

Perhaps that was why her mother had feared so much. Because after knowing love all her life, Yvenne hadn't truly conceived of a future without it—especially not from her chosen husband. Not from the warrior she'd spent so many years admiring from afar.

Yet that future was what she faced now. And Maddek had not only denied all possibility of love between them, he'd also destroyed a hope that was so great a part of her that she'd not even realized how much of her heart it had filled. The emotions churning within her were not just pain and anger . . . but also grief, for the hope her warrior had killed.

This grief *would* pass. When it did, then she would do as he'd suggested, and find the love she longed for with their children and their people. And she would be all the stronger for it.

But that would not be today.

Today, she would begin the painstaking process of disentangling her emotions. For when they stopped at midday, Maddek was at her mount's side before she had even swung her leg over the saddle. He gripped her waist, easing her from the horse's back. Unbidden pleasure flared at his touch, her entire body responding to his proximity—and her heart responding to the care he took with her.

That desire, she would allow to grow. Yvenne would accept no less than pleasure from him in their bed, and arousal *could* be separated from love. She had seen it herself. Ardyl and Kelir had no deep feelings for the barmaid, yet pleasure was had by each of them.

But within Yvenne, desire's roots were entwined with futile hope—and with the sweet emotion that had been nurtured by years of Queen Vyssen telling her what sort of man Maddek was, by the short time his mother had told her the same, and by the even shorter time Yvenne had known him. So she had to let that sweeter emotion wither. She had to starve it. Until only physical arousal remained, and until she never mistook the gentleness in his touch for affection.

Because although Maddek helped her dismount, assistance was not *caring*. He helped her down because her knee might collapse under her weight, and an injury might slow their journey. Because she was a vessel, and of no use to him broken.

Yet even as that knowledge dug painfully into her heart, where the roots of hope were still so deeply embedded, happiness bloomed when Maddek did not immediately set her down. Instead he held her above the ground with his hands clasped around her waist and his eyes locked upon her own. And the warmth that spread through her was not only physical but so sweet again. This love within her was a tenacious weed that kept reaching for Maddek as if he were the sun.

Strong, just as her mother had said. Love—and hope—would not wither in a day. Perhaps not even within a seven-night.

But she had to starve them to the roots. So if his touch nurtured those emotions, then to protect herself it was best that she avoid his touch. At least until her moon night, when she could avoid it no longer.

She could not avoid it now. Stiffly, she waited for Maddek to let her down.

Instead he held her, his gaze level with hers, her feet dangling. Automatically Yvenne gripped his forearms to steady herself. Heated by the sun, the drepa skin covering his vambraces was warm as life, the pebbled texture worn smooth between the scars of battle.

Aside from that small movement, she remained quiet, her body rigid.

Abruptly a frown darkened Maddek's expression. She couldn't imagine what prompted it, until he said, "You no longer soften against me. Have I made you fear my touch?"

No. Trust would not come easy again, yet she feared no physical harm at his hands. But she was already hurt and feared that her future held more pain if she softened.

So there was no simple answer, yet his question was likely simple. He wondered if she was terrified of him. So there was truth in the shake of her head.

That response seemed not to relieve Maddek—or perhaps he assumed that she lied again. His frown deepened into angry frustration. "Your face tells me *nothing*."

Yvenne could not be sorry for that. If she wore her emotions as plainly as the Parsatheans did, what would her face say to him now? That her heart yearned and ached? Should she give him reason to declare again that she could never earn his trust or his love?

She should not. So this time she gave no reply at all.

Eyes narrowing, he studied her for a moment longer, before hissing a breath from between his teeth. "Do you sense dark magics here?"

Irritation burned away the ache. Did he trust *nothing* she said? "I vowed to tell you when I do," she snapped. "And as I have no desire to see thrice-cursed wraiths sucking the blood from my dripping entrails while I scream my last mortal breaths, if I sense anything amiss I *will* let you know."

And Yvenne could read his face easily, but she could make no sense of what it told her now, for Maddek seemed pleased. Not amused, as if finding humor in her answer or laughing at her vehemence, but satisfied by it. Yet what pleasure could he take in her response?

"So my punishment has come to an end?" he softly asked.

What punishment? Utterly confused now, she arched her brows in question—Maddek could surely read *that* upon her face—but instead of giving an answer he gently set her to her feet.

"You will ride the roan mare when we start off again." Wearing a faint smile, he loosened her cinch knot before turning to unsaddle his own horse. "If you must tend to your own needs while they rest, do it quickly. We will not remain here long."

Only long enough for the horses to drink and briefly eat. However, it was not the length of this rest that concerned Yvenne, but the next, when they would stop to make camp.

Slipping her fingers beneath the band of leather he'd loosened, she tugged until the knot came free. "How far until the next village?"

"Two days' hard ride." A soft grunt accompanied his answer, and then he turned again to face her, his great roll of furs propped upon his shoulder and his saddle gripped in his left hand. "Did you hope for another bed at an inn? My furs will be soft enough. Only this time, I would keep you against me the full night."

Then he must have forgotten what she'd told him when she left the bed—that she had no desire to share his until her moon night.

That had been absolute truth. And although she yearned for the pleasure he'd given her, she could not protect her heart if she allowed him so close. Even now, it pounded like the hoofbeats of a galloping steed, as the thought of another night with him raced through her blood.

Yet she had to starve the sweeter emotions that accompanied that fire. Not feed them.

"I hoped not for an inn," she said, reaching up and taking firm hold of her pommel and cantle, "but to purchase my own bedding."

Dragging the saddle from her mount's back took all of her strength—as did bearing its weight without staggering—and so she could not even note Maddek's response until, abruptly, she bore no weight at all. He hauled the seat out of her grip. Then his response was all she could see, for he crowded close. Thick biceps bulged, the sinews of his wrists and hands standing in sharp relief, as if holding her saddle were an effort, yet she knew it was not. Leather creaked under the tightness of his grip, the knuckles of his powerful fingers whitening. His faint smile had vanished. Below dark eyes that flashed hot and feral, volcanic tension pulled the skin across his cheekbones taut.

Yet despite the barely restrained violence within his massive body, still Yvenne did not fear him. Lifting her chin, she met his enraged gaze and silently challenged him to deny her.

He did, his response emerging on a dangerous snarl. "You will sleep in my furs this night. And *every* night."

"And as I said last eve, I will not lie beside you until my moon night."

Perhaps he had not forgotten. Perhaps he had—once again—not believed her word. Now his smoldering gaze scoured her face, as if searching for truth. He must have realized that this was no lie, for the rage in his gaze dimmed. She knew not what to make of the bleak resolve that replaced it, or the softness of his gruff reply.

"Then I will let you sleep alone. But you *will* be in my furs."

That distance would have to be enough, then. She could see no use in arguing further, as purchasing her own bedding today was impossible—and, if they were to be married and serve as queen and king of two territories, surely it would not be the first compromise that she and Maddek made.

They had both made demands. They would both get what they wanted . . . with modifications.

On a sharp nod, she offered her agreement—then looked for more anger but could see none.

Instead he wore that same grim resolve in his firmed mouth and clenched jaw. His dark gaze held hers for another long moment, and then he glanced over her head, to where Banek and Ardyl were caring for the extra horses. "Shall I carry this for you?"

Her heavy saddle. Her throat oddly tight, she shook her head. "I prefer to do as much as I can."

Carefully he gave it back to her, making certain she had a steady grip before releasing the full weight.

"Thank you," she said softly.

An equally soft grunt dismissed her gratitude. He gathered her horse's lead. "I will take them to water. Stay near Ardyl when you piss. You are not yet a warrior-queen."

And able to protect herself. Yvenne knew that very well. Maddek did, too, and he had told her so many times before. But to hear him say it so differently now—not *yet* a warrior-queen—filled her with such pain and hope and confusion.

She bore them along with the saddle's weight across the small clearing—though it was not even properly a clearing, but an area of flattened grasses that formed a thick mat upon the ground. All around them grew stalks taller than Yvenne. When mounted, she could see over their seed-heavy heads. Now she could not, and it was as if a nodding wall of green surrounded them.

A stream burbled across the western edge of the clearing, the water cutting deeply into the soft earth, so that the horses had to be led carefully down its steep banks. Ardyl and Banek had not yet led theirs to drink.

Because they were waiting for her. Ardyl had already singled out the roan, holding it ready to saddle.

Which Yvenne would not be doing alone, she realized the moment she stepped up beside the mare. Though this mount was not as tall as the full-blooded Parsathean horses, it was much taller than her gelding had been—and to lift the seat onto that horse's back, she had always needed a stone or a stump to step upon. There was nothing of the like here.

Lips flattened in irritation, she looked to Ardyl for help.

The warrior grinned as she took the heavy saddle and easily set it into place.

With the strain upon her shoulders and back relieved, Yvenne let out a long breath, then rolled her neck from side to side. As soon as Ardyl stepped aside, she moved forward again, stalks crunching beneath her sandals. Banek had made her practice tying the cinch strap repeatedly during her first days upon the gelding, and she did again under his watchful eye. The process of making the leather knot, walking the horse a few steps, then tightening the cinch again was so familiar now, however, that she need not give it her full attention.

"What do you think happened here, that these grasses are stamped into the ground?"

The older warrior answered, "It was a bed for a family of mirens."

Armored reptiles with hammerlike tails. Yvenne had seen trails broken through the grass where the reptiles had crossed the road but had not yet laid eyes on one. Though they were large animals, they weren't tall and remained concealed within the grass.

Many dangers lurked between the stalks. Which was why Ardyl would accompany Yvenne when she relieved herself.

Because she was not *yet* a warrior-queen. Throat aching, she pulled hard upon the leather.

Beside her, Banek continued, "In the autumn, when the great herds move through, not a blade of grass will be left standing. They strip this plain to the soil."

"And Temra be merciful to anyone traveling upon this road then," Ardyl added with a laugh. "They are more likely to be trampled beneath a fanhead's feet than reach Drahm."

So they would take the road on the northern side of the Ageras instead. Yes. Yvenne knew all of that.

But there was something she didn't know. In a thick voice, she asked, "Are Parsatheans allowed to speak lies if it is in jest?"

The amusement on Ardyl's face vanished into a frown of displeasure. "There is no joke in a lie. It dishonors the speaker and insults the listener."

"Oh." Hope and happiness filled Yvenne's breast, yet the confusion remained. She was not a warrior-queen *yet*. Did Maddek truly mean to make her one, then?

How?

Even Yvenne's mother and younger brother, the two people who believed in her most and loved her best, had never suggested the possibility. In their tower, Queen Vyssen had made her run and exercise her muscles, had shown her how to conceal a knife within her robes, but never had Yvenne's lessons extended beyond that. Given the weakness of Yvenne's body, her mother had often said that her mind was her best weapon. So they had focused on sharpening her brain and her tongue instead of sharpening blades.

Ran Ashev had put a bow into her hands and taught her to use it, true. If she'd ever intended to teach Yvenne more, however, she'd never spoken of it. They'd only spoken of the single arrow that would fly from Yvenne's bow and facilitate Ran Ashev's escape. Yet Yvenne had dreamed of more arrows, and of being free—and using that bow to defend herself and her people. She needed no great strength for that. Only strength enough to draw a bowstring.

Then her father had cut off her fingers and severed any hope she had of using that weapon again.

Maddek knew of her weakness. He knew of her missing fingers. He knew of her shattered knee. Yet still he claimed that a warrior-queen could be made of her?

Even knowing he always spoke truth, she hardly dared believe it.

Perhaps Banek sensed her turmoil, for he was studying her face with concern deepening the lines beside his eyes. "Why do you ask, my lady?"

This newer doubt and pain had too sharp an edge, so she choose the pain that had already dulled. "That first eve, I told you all that I had never ridden a horse. None of you believed me. Yet you did not respond as if you were insulted by a lie. Instead you laughed, as if I had been making fun."

Except for Maddek, whose laughter had been cruel and mocking. Because he had immediately understood that she spoke the truth.

"Ah!" Now Ardyl's face cleared. "If it is something that everyone knows cannot be true, that can be a joke. There is no deception if a truth is well known."

And to a Parsathean, the idea that someone might have never sat upon a horse was unbelievable. It could only be a joke.

So, too, would be making a warrior-queen of Yvenne.

The crushing disappointment within her chest threatened to fold her over, but she hid that pain in the task of untying her wineskin from the saddle.

Behind her, Banek confirmed, "Such it is. If someone were to say your father was a fine king, everyone would know it for a joke."

Yvenne forced herself to answer. "And if the speaker meant it?"

"Then we would know him for a fool," Ardyl replied. "Either way, it is good for a laugh."

Was that why Maddek had said it, then? Had he been trying to humor her? On the heels of his apology, perhaps he had been trying to make amends. For certain, on this day she had not sensed any cruelty in him—and he could not know how making of a joke of it could hurt her so badly. She had joked of it herself at the ruins. Perhaps he'd wished to return to the ease they'd found then, before the blood wraiths had come.

But when he'd given her a warrior's lesson this morn, she *had* thought he might be telling the truth. She'd wanted to believe he was.

Yet making a warrior-queen of her was something no one could believe. Instead, her hope only marked her as a fool.

Well. It would not be the first time. Or likely the last.

Ardyl remained at her side as Banek led the horses to the stream. Standing upon the opposite bank was Maddek, sun gleaming over his dark skin. With a short blade, he scythed through handfuls of tall grass before tossing the fresh stalks to Toric, who cut away the tough, fibrous stem from the tender leaves near the top, which the horses could more easily eat. So quickly they worked that in the time it had taken Yvenne to saddle her roan, they had already harvested enough feed for each horse.

Maddek tucked away his blade. In a single mighty leap that filled Yvenne with both awe and envy, he cleared the stream. Lightly, as if his feet bore feathers instead of his massive weight, he landed upon the near bank in a crouch, the outer length of his red linens flaring wide before settling around his powerful legs.

Left behind to bundle the grasses, Toric waved one of the woody stems in his direction like a mock sword. As Maddek rose, the other warrior called out his name. Then Toric abruptly stopped, tilting the stem straight upward, his eyebrows shooting high. Maddek's hearty laugh rolled across the clearing—a response to something Toric said and Yvenne had not heard, but which prompted both warriors to glance in her direction.

Maddek's gaze caught hers—and she could not read his expression at all, but for the longest breath, that look held her captive. No longer was he laughing when he glanced away.

Yet Yvenne could not stop looking upon him, and she slowly realized that another statement she had taken as truth had likely been a joke.

To Ardyl, she asked, "Is his beard truly a foul sight?"

For surely no one could believe it so. Clean-shaven or no, Maddek must be thought very handsome. No matter who looked upon him.

The woman's peal of laughter was answer enough. But Yvenne wanted more.

"Yet it is also true that warriors should be as silver-fingered Rani, who wears no beard?"

"It is truth. But we must sometimes hope to be more than goddesses are." Drawing her sword, Ardyl added, "You have to piss?"

Yvenne nodded.

"Come then. And mind your feet. The edges of these stalks can slice skin as easily as sharpened steel can," Ardyl said, and led Yvenne into the rustling grass. Almost immediately, they were swallowed from sight of the clearing. The warrior stopped and stomped flat a small circle for Yvenne to squat in.

Turning her back to allow Yvenne privacy, she continued, "Ran Ashev wore her hair unbound when she stood before the tribes."

Maddek's mother. Her dark hair had been braided again when Yvenne had met her. But she dared not ask more—she had promised Maddek not to speak of his mother at all.

"And his father?"

"Cut his braids short. He wore no beard," Ardyl said, and her voice softened, in grief or memory. "Though he did when his own mother died. He was not only a warrior then, not only Ran, but a son." Absently, she brushed her fingertips over the piercings on her brow. "Just as I am a daughter."

The last daughter of a clan that had been slaughtered by the Destroyer. Yvenne had heard that tale their second night upon the road. The piercings were made from the silver rings gathered from the corpses of her family—and Ardyl, then a newborn babe, had been found swaddled within the village's stone granary, where someone who'd loved her had hidden her away.

Yvenne used the water in the wineskin to wash while Ardyl took her place, then offered the other woman the same when she finished.

"So it is not a foul sight."

"No." Ardyl dried her hands on her linens. "When I look upon his beard, I see that the warrior I have proudly followed for much of my life now hopes to become something more. A warrior sends his enemies into Temra's arms, and so aspires to be like the goddess Rani. But a Ran must speak for all the tribes, and so aspires to be like the best of *us*."

Not to be the best of his people. But to be like those who were. What mattered was not that Maddek was the finest of them—for one man could never be—but that he would never stop striving toward that goal.

Yvenne could do a better job of helping him. For she had promised to make him a great king. Yet she had put in little effort so far.

And knowing Maddek wore his hope—and his grief—for everyone to see, even when his immediate expression showed neither, made him even more beautiful to her eyes than he had been before. Yvenne could not imagine always being laid so bare. In that, she had not as much courage as he.

But she did not lack a queen's courage, and that drove her across the clearing. Yvenne's roan ate from a small mound of grasses. At the mare's side, Maddek stood with his back to Yvenne, flipping her stirrup up over the seat of her saddle.

No doubt he heard her approach, but he gave no indication. Instead she heard the soothing murmur he directed at the mare as his fingers slipped along the girth.

She stopped at his shoulder and watched as he began to loosen the knot she'd made. "Did I cinch it too tightly?"

That earned her a swift grin, for the day had not yet come when she had cinched it tight *enough*. Always one of the warriors had to adjust the fit.

Then he said, "It is nearly right," and such joy filled her that she was nearly dizzy with it.

Perhaps she would never be a warrior-queen. But she was stronger than she'd been even a full turn ago.

His gaze fell to her wide smile and lingered before he returned his attention to her saddle. "There is bread and cheese on the gray." Maddek tipped his head to indicate the horse he would ride. "Fassad has also found a nest."

Fresh eggs were a fine treat. "Will you have some?" She would feed him from her fingers while he adjusted her saddle, if he liked.

"On the road."

"Then I will, too. For now, there is a lesson owing. You have taught me to make use of what I have, as a warrior does, but I have not returned that favor."

And even if his lesson had been part of a jest, it had been worth learning.

He shot her an amused glance, then lowered the stirrup back into place. Facing her, he crossed his arms over his broad chest. From his towering height, he caught her gaze and silently waited.

Waited for her to make him a king.

She could not think of one thing to say. Her mind raced, collecting all that her mother had ever told her, yet not a single word seemed relevant now.

Because those had been conversations, she realized—not simplified lessons. Conversations built upon conversations that stretched back to Yvenne's earliest years. Her mother had begun teaching Yvenne before she'd ever taken a step.

Now she knew not where to start. But perhaps Maddek knew where he ought to.

"What would you first want to learn?"

He huffed out a soft laugh, but what amused him she couldn't determine. Nor did she ask. Instead she remained quiet as his gaze lifted from hers. He stared out over the tall grasses, as if searching for something in the distance, before looking to her face again.

"We both had parents who taught us valuable lessons from an early age. I cannot think those lessons were so different. Yet you are a queen, and I am only a warrior. What did you learn that I did not?"

How could she answer that? Yvenne struggled to think of what her mother might say—but perhaps that was the difference. Almost everything Yvenne knew was what her mother had told her. But those had not been lessons given. They'd simply been lived.

"Perhaps . . ." She hesitated a moment, remembering the Parsatheans' reaction to how her mother had watched everyone. But Yvenne could not be sorry for it. She and her mother had little else. "Perhaps it is because my mother and I did not only live our own lives. There was the tower, but there were also so many people that we watched—not only royals of other realms or their armies, but Syssians who went about their lives. Every day, my mother would look in on them and describe what they did, what made them laugh or cry, what difficulties they faced. And in that way we added their lives to our own."

Maddek seemed frustrated by that answer. "I have seen others in the same way—I have witnessed their joys and their struggles."

"So until my mother died, perhaps we were the same. Both only witnesses to how others lived. But after she was gone . . ." Yvenne's throat tightened. "No longer could I see outside the tower. And it was as if not only my mother had died but also everyone we'd watched. They did not know me, but I knew them. And so many were lost to me at once."

Maddek grunted softly. "And you were lonely. Not just for your mother but for them."

"So I was. But I *knew* they still lived, so instead of grieving, I would imagine what they did each day—and imagining is much more difficult than watching. I would imagine myself in their place and then have to imagine how they would feel and react. What would bring them joy, what would they fear? What might break their hearts or heal them again? And every time I imagined these things, I felt it, too." She clenched her fist over her chest. "As if I were also living those lives. I have been maid, soldier, farmer, noble, thief, miller, magistrate—and so many others. I have been celebrated and I have failed. I have been cruel and kind, corrupt and just. I know not whether my imaginings were those of a fanciful fool, but I think it not much different than what a Ran aspires to be. He must be like the best of his people. I have already been the best—and worst—of mine."

Thoughtfully he nodded. "And I have only been a warrior."

"And son. And commander. And friend."

"So I have been. But I have not much imagination beyond my own experience."

"That cannot be true. You would not have won so many battles if you did not understand your opponents and imagine what they might do. You have great capability for imagining. It has simply been directed toward a warrior's purpose."

Suddenly lit by amusement, his gaze caught hers. "Of late, new purpose I have had—and many imaginings I have had of you."

Yvenne's cheeks heated even as happy pleasure skipped across her heart. That tenacious weed, reaching for the sun again.

As if her blush were a satisfactory response, Maddek grinned yet made no move toward her. "So I should imagine myself in another's place."

"That might be a fine start," she agreed. "Though not as I did in my tower. No time do you have to lie around and imagine yourself a seamstress. Instead do it as you speak with others or observe them—as you must have done last eve while talking to the Gogean soldiers, and seeing them not as a Parsathean warrior sees them, but as if you were in their place."

"Then this is not truly a new lesson, but one that you taught me last eve. It only requires practice."

"So it does."

"Then I will practice. But for our new lesson . . ." His eyes narrowed as if considering, before he finally said, "Had you but one lesson for the Gogean queen, what would it be?"

That was easy enough. "That my father's tyranny should not be admired or imitated."

His gaze sharpened on hers. "Does she admire it?"

"Five years past, she did." Beside her, the roan twitched a fat fly from her shoulder. Idly Yvenne waved the insect away, then smoothed her palm over the mare's glossy coat. "My mother watched her and her brothers closely—"

"As a possible match for you?" Maddek interrupted.

"For a time. Though Queen Felis married before I even reached a woman's age." It hardly mattered, as Yvenne would not have chosen either Felis or her brothers. The younger was not so objectionable, but the elder brother was. "She and Prince Oren were speaking of unrest in the villages, and of the farmers who refused to send the full portion of their harvest. Felis wished for a queen's guard as strong and as ruthless as my father's guard, so they could silence dissent more easily. Oren suggested that she hire Parsatheans to do it."

Posture abruptly rigid, Maddek growled, "If such a request had been made, we'd have helped the farmers tear apart the palace walls."

"So they realized."

"And *Oren* said this?"

She heard his disbelief but understood he didn't think that she'd spoken false. Instead his disbelief stemmed from his familiarity with the prince. Oren had served two years upon the Lave, leading the company of Gogean soldiers. Maddek had dined and fought alongside the other man.

"He did," Yvenne confirmed.

A muscle worked in his jaw, anger in every taut line of his body, and Yvenne realized she had taught him the wrong thing. Already he knew not to resemble her father in any way. Although it was a lesson the Gogean queen might have benefited from, her people would have benefited more from another. So would Maddek.

"Yet imagine if she had sent her guard to the villages," Yvenne told him, then briefly left his side to untie a bag of feed from his saddle. "And if instead of—"

"Give her no more than a handful."

Surprised by the interruption, she frowned at him. "What?"

"The grain," Maddek said. Arms still crossed, his feet planted, he had not moved except to follow her with his gaze. "At the pace we ride, too much feed will shorten her breath and tighten her gut. They can eat their fill at night."

"Oh." Amused now, Yvenne returned to stand in front of his mountainous form. "It is not for the mare."

"Are you so hungry, then?" There was a teasing glint in his narrowed eyes.

Smiling, she shook her head. "You are easily distracted from your lesson."

He grinned. "I am."

And unapologetic for it. But she was also too easily distracted, too aware of the pounding of her heart when his gaze fell to her lips.

At least if he was watching her mouth, he would not likely note the unsteadiness of her hands as she fumbled with the ties cinching the bag closed.

"I am to imagine that she sent her guard to the villages," Maddek said. Distracted, perhaps, but still paying attention.

"Not to crush them, though." The sack opened and she glanced up to meet his eyes, which were no longer focused on her lips but seemed intent on the whole of her face. "Imagine if she sent them to help the farmers harvest another row. If in the spring she promised to send her guard to plow another field. Or if she had hired the Parsatheans to help instead of slaughter. For you are more than raiders with swords, and none of you is a stranger to the harvest."

Understanding lit his eyes. "That is truth."

"So here is your lesson, Maddek of Parsathe." Holding the sack open between them, she urged, "Reach in with one hand and bring out as much as you can."

He did so.

And even knowing the size of his hands, she had misjudged the amount of grain he might hold cupped in his palm. He drew out such a great heap that the weight of the bag between them was halved.

Gripping the edge of the sack tighter, Yvenne also reached in and buried her hand deep in the cool, shifting grain. When she drew back, seeds slipped over the stumps of her missing fingers, yet still her cupped palm held a fine heap.

"Whether you rule or lead," she said softly, "with your

people it is always better to keep an open hand. For even in sour times, with an open hand you will be able to carry them all—and their loyalty will remain with you. But the moment you tighten your grip, no matter how strong or weak you are"—slowly she formed a fist, Maddek copied her motion, and grain spilled like a waterfall into the sack—"they will begin slipping through your fingers."

With seeds raining from his powerful hand, Maddek asked quietly, "Is this what your father has done?"

"It is." She clenched her fist as tight as her strength allowed, then opened her fingers to show him the small number of grains that remained in her palm. "He clings to his power and squeezes those still loyal to him, and now there are hardly any left." Abruptly she frowned as Maddek also unrolled his fist. "What have you done to your fingers?"

"It is nothing."

Amusement filled his reply. And perhaps it was a joking lie, or perhaps he believed it was truth, but Yvenne could not. She caught his hand and held him still for a closer examination. Multiple bloodied slashes crossed his fingers and palm, as if he'd repeatedly gripped a knife by the blade.

But not a blade, she realized. Gently she drew her fingertips down the strong lengths of his fingers, brushing away the grains that stuck to the shallow wounds. "This is from the grass you cut to feed the horses?"

Maddek grunted.

Sudden and hot tension gripped her body. That sound had been confirmation—and more. She could not always decipher his grunted replies . . . but his arousal, she could, for her own rose quickly to meet it.

So quickly. In a single breath, concern for his injury dropped away and so many imaginings replaced it. Of sucking his fingers into her mouth, of watching his need burn until he begged her to do the same to his cock. Of urging his hand down between her thighs, where she was slick and aching, so that he might ease her need as he had the night before.

But that would not disentangle her heart from his.

Even as Maddek curled his fingers over hers, as if to catch her hand and drag her closer, Yvenne slipped out of his grasp, stepping back and beyond his reach.

Agitated, her body trapped in a hectic rush of pulsing blood and prickling skin, she folded her arms over her chest and tried to hold her rioting emotions within her breast. Yet despite that effort—or because of it—her voice emerged in a strained whisper. "This lesson is done."

Maddek would teach her another. His fiery gaze and the primal stillness of his body promised it without words.

But he would not teach her now. For he only gave a sharp nod and said, "Then prepare to ride."

He strode away, his arousal still etched in harsh lines upon his face and his erection jutting behind his red linens, though every warrior must see him and know what it meant. Nothing did he conceal or repress.

If Maddek felt any affection for her, if there was any hope of love or trust, anything beyond lust—he would not likely conceal that either.

And she saw nothing of the sort. But it mattered not.

Hers would surely wither soon.

CHAPTER 18

MADDEK

Maddek's bride was truly a southerner, for she loved to build walls. He had not attempted to breach the wall of silence she'd erected that morning—her punishment was one he'd well deserved. Yet several walls remained even after she'd begun speaking to him again, and Maddek was truly a Parsathean, for he could not resist the challenge they presented. Not a moment passed that he did not imagine ways to climb over them, or break through them, or dig beneath them.

For there was little else to do on this journey, and her walls filled him with hot frustration. Yet Maddek would not need to breach them at all, if he could lure her out. First the wall that she intended to put between their beds until her moon night. That one required patience, because she claimed not to fear him, yet he could not mistake the way she'd stiffened and pulled away from his hands. She no longer punished him for pulling at her tongue, and he'd seen how his touch still heated her blood, yet he'd foolishly damaged the one easy bond they'd forged between them—a bond forged by mutual desire. The repair there was his alone to make and it would take time.

Yet now there was another bond: she would teach him to be a king and he would teach her to be a warrior. So when they took to the road again, and she put up yet another wall that was made of short responses, tight smiles, and averted eyes, Maddek had bait that Yvenne could not resist.

"Another lesson," he said to her. "Before any Parsathean becomes a warrior, first she must learn to hunt. If you ever wish to become a warrior-queen, you must look with a hunter's eyes."

Those moonstone eyes were not a hunter's yet and gazed at him full of wariness and doubt. He saw none of the joy of that morning's lesson before she nodded.

"How does a hunter see, then?"

As Maddek did. He showed to her the mounds of earth that told him of the giant rodents burrowed beneath them. The quivering stalks in the fields that said long-toothed cats slinked between them. The large and shallow depressions in the mud where heavy reptiles bedded down for the night. Every marking in the soil, every broken stem or twitch of a leaf, every disturbance that was not created by the wind or the rain, they all told him of creatures that might be hunted—or that might be hunting them.

Her eyes brightened all the while as she began looking anew. As the sun dipped toward the west, it was no longer Maddek pointing to what she should see, but Yvenne noting each marking and asking him what he made of them.

Until she was not always asking, but seeing for herself. "That trail there," she said, indicating a swath through the long grasses. "It is as wide as the trail made by mirens, but those stalks are flattened and these are cut short, as if by a scythe."

Maddek grunted his approval. "Well seen."

Pleasure flushed her cheeks. "But it could not be a scythe, could it? What else could do that?"

He could name many creatures, but only one of that size. "A giant millipede—which also tells us there is likely a stream nearby. They are usually near water, or areas where the ground remains moist."

"A millipede?" Eagerly she glanced at the path. "I've heard they are tasty."

Maddek grinned. His bride had claimed he only saw a person's weaknesses, and he thought it fair to say that Yvenne's stomach was her greatest one. "We will hunt a millipede only after you have had more practice."

She shot him a curious look. "Are they a danger to us? I thought they only ate vegetation."

"They do. But they are not defenseless. Jaws that slice through grass can slice through flesh. And some millipedes emit a foul musk that burns the skin," he told her, frowning as for the first time since their lesson had begun, Yvenne glanced distractedly behind them.

She faced forward again as Kelir called out, "I would not object to millipede this night, if she would observe the hunt instead of joining it."

All of the warriors had been invested in her lesson this day, though they had not interrupted Maddek's teaching. Now she looked to Maddek hopefully, clearly wanting to watch them hunt, before her brow furrowed and she turned again.

"What is it?" Maddek asked, suddenly caring nothing of hunts and millipedes. "A chill?"

"Not a chill. I . . ." Her uneasy gaze searched the road behind them. "I know not what it is. As if . . . something comes."

He held up a fist and the others immediately halted, falling silent and listening. Maddek heard nothing but what he expected to hear. He looked to Fassad, who was studying his wolves.

The other warrior shook his head. The dogs sensed nothing. Yet they had not at the ruins, either. His bride was more sensitive to magics than they.

"How near, my lady?" Banek asked her softly.

Unneeded apology filled her reply. "I am no good judge of distance. But it does not *feel* close. Only . . . coming."

"Then we will put more distance between us," Maddek said grimly. For he had ignored Yvenne's instinct once. Never would he again.

They rode hard until nightfall, when Yvenne said she could no longer feel the presence behind them. Maddek knew not if that meant they had merely outpaced it or if it no longer followed—and it mattered little either way. No more easy nights could be had. Even if the magic Yvenne had sensed was no threat, if her brother's soldiers had taken this southern route along the river, they might soon be.

When they came across a copse near a stream, Maddek called a halt. The trees provided better shelter than the long grasses did and could be climbed for a better vantage—and the monkeys that chattered and screeched overhead suggested that whatever stalked their party had not yet befouled this spot.

While the others made camp, he and Kelir rode a wide perimeter, searching for any threat. Beyond a long-toothed cat, which the wolves would alert them to if it approached the copse, there was little.

Still Maddek knew Kelir was as unsettled as he. Yvenne's vague unease was something they'd both heard from others before, during the campaign against Stranik's Fang, when dark priests used their foul magic from afar. If so, they had much to be worried about. Yet he would not assume that was what she sensed. It might have been like the wraiths at the ruins—dangerous, yet well behind them now. And if dark magic stalked them, they would face that threat when it came.

He saw the same remembrance upon Banek's and Ardyl's faces when he returned to camp, as well as the same determination not to make early assumptions. And he saw that a hunt had been completed, after all. A small millipede roasted over the fire. Brought down by Toric, he quickly learned, when Yvenne happily recounted that young warrior's victory, and that he'd shown her how to pester the millipede from a distance until it rolled into a ball, then safely pierce the creature's segmented carapace with a spear.

The jealousy that roared through Maddek then was fierce and fanged and as foul as the magic that stalked them. He knew Toric had taken a sweet liking to his bride, yet never would the warrior act upon it. Maddek believed that Yvenne never would, either. Her ambitions were too great and she would not risk their marriage with an idle flirtation.

And Maddek himself had encouraged her to seek affection from anyone but him. She'd befriended all of his warriors. He should not resent Toric hunting a millipede for her, or Ardyl receiving her smile, or Banek sharing in her laugh.

Yet he did resent them all. Furiously.

Wordlessly he left again to care for his horse, hating the unworthy emotion burning in his chest. Hating the frustration that put it there. Because with him, Yvenne built walls. And as far as he could see, she had raised none between herself and his Dragon.

It should matter not at all what she did. Such turmoil should not be raging within him. She was but a vessel. A tool for his vengeance.

And he was a thrice-cursed fool, to feel such resentment and jealousy and fury. None served him well.

But his Dragon guard did. And Yvenne did, too. From nearly the moment they'd met, she'd guided him toward becoming a better king. Now she might serve as warning against a danger that none of their eyes could see.

A piercing shriek sounded as he returned to camp, yet the shrill noise—and Yvenne's startled scream in response—only made him grin. That horrible shrieking signaled that their dinner was ready, as steam whistled from the millipede's carapace. His warriors' laughter greeted him at the fire, and they each screamed in turn to match Yvenne's. She sat giggling, facing the flames with her saddle bracing her back, as the others did.

Dropping his saddle onto the ground, Maddek took his

place beside her. She glanced at him, the warmth of the fire reflecting in her pale eyes, but when she spoke it was directed to Toric, apparently in response to one of the endless questions he always had for her during their meals.

"You have seen the Tower of the Moon in Ephorn?" she asked him, and the young warrior nodded. "It is much the same."

"What is the same?" Maddek accepted the bowl of water Fassad passed to him, then quickly tore off a few of the millipede's spiky legs and dropped them in.

"She is telling us of Syssia," Toric said.

Eagerly she watched the legs hiss in the water before looking to Maddek. "Have you been?"

"Only through the outlands. Never to the queen's city."

"Only I have been," Banek said. "The Syssian tower resembles the Ephorn tower in appearance, but the Syssian is much larger."

"Because we knew the tale of Ran Bantik stealing the pearl from the Moon tower," Yvenne said, grinning. "My foremother would not risk the same, so she built hers much taller."

"Do you also keep your treasures at the top?" the old raider asked.

Yvenne shook her head. "It is the chamber where I was imprisoned. Where my mother and I were."

Maddek's mother, too, but he would not spoil the mood by saying so. He only poked at the legs, though the way they floated told him they had not yet cooled enough to eat.

It was Kelir who said what Maddek probably should have. "So there *was* treasure at the top."

Then Maddek was glad he'd not said it, because Kelir's comment might have pleased a barmaid, but it only brought a frown to Yvenne's face. "I am not Syssia's treasure. Her people are."

Maddek grinned as he realized how fully she'd misunderstood Kelir's meaning. "When we speak of Ran Bantik stealing the pearl, sometimes that pearl refers to the king's daughter, whom he also stole from that tower."

"Oh." A blush colored her cheeks as if she recalled what else Maddek had called a pearl, yet amusement danced in her eyes. "So he scaled the walls to have her?"

"And stole her away to the Burning Plains." As Maddek intended to do with his own bride. Yet there the similarity ended—as Yvenne must have realized, as well. For although she smiled faintly, the amusement in her eyes dimmed.

"He must have loved her very much to attempt such a dangerous feat."

"The legends say nothing of love," Maddek told her, and plucked a leg from the water. "Only that after Ran Bantik saw her beauty, he could not resist it."

Kelir laughed. "And if all that remains of her in legend is a pearl, I daresay it wasn't the beauty of her face that Ran Bantik could not resist."

A pearl was not all that remained of Ran Bantik's queen. Her blood ran just as strong through Maddek's line as the thief-king's did. Yet he did not need to explain that to Yvenne. Her own line celebrated warrior-queens whose lovers were rarely even acknowledged in their legends. So he only said to Yvenne, "The story of the pearl is but good for feasts and song. Ran Bantik's true legacy was in uniting the tribes."

"And defeating the Scourge." Her hungry gaze was locked on the millipede's leg as Maddek snapped off the pointed tip and gave it to her. "I've heard that tale, though not how he united them. Only that he did."

She mimicked Maddek when he demonstrated how to suck out the sweet, buttery jelly, her full lips wrapping around the broken tip. Her cheeks hollowed and her gaze widened with delight; then bliss closed her eyes as she sucked fiercely on the leg.

Hanan be merciful. The ravenous, pleasured sounds she made could stiffen a corpse. In full arousal Maddek stared at her, dimly aware of Ardyl's snort and playful shove at Toric, who also stared, and of Kelir muffling his laughter by burying his face in his hands. Yvenne was oblivious to them all.

Until beside her, Danoh said, "Ran Bantik, the thief-king, was born squalling upon Temra's altar."

Yvenne's eyes flew open—less likely because of the warrior's words but because of their rarity. Then Banek, who sat at Danoh's other side, spoke next and Yvenne's attention followed.

"Unburned the plains were, yet fires of war divided the thirteen tribes," the old warrior recited.

Then came Toric, his cheeks hot and gaze averted. "The embattled clans allowed silver-fingered Rani no rest."

"Countless riders she took," Ardyl said next, "eyes spitting lightning, spilling tears of rain."

"She carried them upon her dragon into Temra's waiting arms," Kelir said.

Fassad continued. "Over the Astal Mountains she flew—but one night was unseated."

It had come Maddek's turn, and Yvenne's enraptured gaze moved to his face. He snapped off another leg tip and gave it to her, speaking the words he'd known longer than any others. "From the sky she plunged, for the flaming peaks had erupted the Scourge."

Danoh started the round again. "Spitting fire, the demon consumed flesh of dragon and riders."

"The Scourge then turned ravenous fiery eyes to the un-burned plains."

"With tears steaming, Rani sped to warn the northern tribes and clans."

"Countless warriors fell before the demon, breaking their blades on obsidian skin."

"Her dragon lost, Rani could not fly the newly fallen into Temra's arms."

"She implored the embattled tribes to unite against the demon Scourge."

Maddek recited gravely, "Or the plains would become a realm of blood and ashes."

Eyes wide after that dire warning, Yvenne eagerly looked to Danoh, who continued, "Hearing her, he who was not yet thief-king looked weeping upon the burning plains."

"Of thirteen tribes, only seven remained—and a grieving Bantik the last of his."

"With torn heart, he called upon the clans to unite, but they listened not to his voice."

"Too many years the tribes had warred, too many warriors had been lost to battle."

"Too many lies had been spoken," Kelir said softly. "Too many oaths had been broken."

"So the seven tribes only united in fleeing west before the demon Scourge."

"There, upon Temra's sacred altar"—as that goddess had, Maddek pounded his fist into the ground—"Ran Bantik vowed to always speak truth."

"From the tribes he asked warriors to come and speak for their clans."

"They also vowed to speak truth, never to break an oath or use sly tongue."

"Each clan listened to their own warriors and trusted the words spoken."

"They in turn each listened to Bantik, he who was not yet thief-king."

"To the glass fields he led them, and the demon's fire turned night into day."

"Seven tribes united, the warriors flew into battle, as one with their mounts."

Keeping rhythm with the recitation, Yvenne's gaze moved to Maddek's face. As it always did, passion and triumph filled his chest as he spoke the next verse. "And the Scourge fell before Bantik and the riders of the Burning Plains."

"As the demon lay dying, the tribes spoke as one, and Ran Bantik he became."

"Rani touched Ran Bantik with her quick and cunning, and a thief-king he became."

"Then splitting open the stomach of the Scourge, she reclaimed her swift dragon."

"Carrying the countless dead, silver-fingered Rani finally flew them into Temra's arms."

"And from Temra's scorched skin grew the firebloom, as red as blood spilled, as red as fire burns."

"To remind the tribes never to be divided, only to ride united, and only to speak truth," Fassad said in solemn voice.

Sucking on yet another leg, though more quietly now, Yvenne looked to Maddek, who had counted the remaining verses and filled his mouth with jelly. With a frown she pulled the leg from between her pursed lips. "You broke the rhythm!"

He grinned at her as the others laughed. "It is done."

"Done? It cannot be. No mention was even made of how Rani rebreathed life into her dragon! Or how the six other tribes chose the warriors who became Ran Bantik's first Dragon guard!"

"It was but the opening song," Maddek admitted. "The full legend of the Scourge requires three days to tell."

That only slightly mollified his bride. "Then at least say how Ran Bantik destroyed the demon."

Maddek's grin widened, because he knew of no one who did not ask the same after first hearing the tale. "By uniting the tribes."

"Yes, but . . . was it with sword? Spear? A baleful stare?" She bestowed her own upon him.

"By uniting the tribes," Maddek repeated, more gravely this time. "The method matters not at all, because the Scourge could not have been slain if the riders had not stood together as one."

Heavily she sighed. Then her eyes narrowed. "So Parsatheans know full well the value of an alliance."

"We do. As we know it is only strong if allies all speak true and keep their vows."

And those in the Great Alliance did not. But unlike this morning, Yvenne made no earnest claim that she would not lie to him and never had. Instead her face shuttered and she looked away from him.

Maddek's jaw clenched. Another wall she put up between them. But this one she seemed to think was of *his* making. He'd been unforgivably wrong last night in their bed when he'd snatched her tongue. Now he believed she'd spoken truth then. He'd also accepted her claim that she hadn't conspired to murder his parents. But was he supposed to forget other times she'd spoken with a sly tongue or her insistence that his mother approved of her as his bride? Was he to believe that while his mother had been imprisoned and interrogated and raped and beheaded, she'd given Yvenne her son to wed?

He could not. So that wall would stand.

To the others she asked, "The tribes spoke as one voice to name Ran Bantik king. What if they do not speak as one voice to name Maddek? Are there others who might be named?"

Others she believed might be a better king—or a better suitor? Foul jealousy speared him again. Silently he tore away the white meat from within the millipede's steaming carapace.

The warriors looked to Maddek, deferring the answer to him, but when he gave none, it was Ardyl who spoke. "Each tribe can put forth a candidate. But they will only name Maddek."

"Because he is of Ran Bantik's line?"

"No." Irritatedly Maddek answered her now. "My father was not of Ran Bantik's line and yet he was named Ran before he married my mother, and then she was also named. Our Ran are not chosen by blood but by who has proven capable of leading—as I have upon the banks of the Lave."

She looked to him then with sharp amusement. "But were you not named commander of the Parsathean army because you were the son of two Ran?"

"Perhaps my mother looked to me first for that reason." And because his parents had made certain he would learn the lessons a Ran needed to know. "But she would not have looked to me at all if I hadn't proven myself in the campaign against Stranik's Fang—and if the other riders did not agree, they would have spoken out against me."

Banek nodded. "We would have. Whether leading warriors or all of the tribes, he must have the support of the people."

"But surely the tribes are not always in agreement? What if some dissent?"

"As two did when we joined the Great Alliance?" Banek asked. "Our queen and king heard and considered what they had to say. That is also the Ran's duty and his respect for the people—to listen, for he knows they will only come to him speaking truth."

Her expression tightened. "Listening to someone's words shows respect?"

The older warrior nodded.

"What if he has heard them and still there is disagreement?"

"Then he must speak his own truth and attempt to persuade them—as Ran Ashev and Ran Marek persuaded the tribes when the alliance was created."

"And if they aren't persuaded?"

Banek shrugged. "They might challenge him, if the matter is one of importance. If it is a lesser matter, they might give him their silence so all will know that he does not speak for them."

"Give him their silence? If a Ran speaks for all, that must be a great insult."

"Not insult. Punishment. It is the Ran's honor to hear his people and to speak for them. If he cannot, it makes him not the leader he aspires to be, one who serves all."

Her face softened. "That is also what my mother said—that a Syssian queen must serve all. But if a Parsathean king cannot, what must be done then?"

"He must think carefully over what was said," Maddek said to her, because this lesson had been taught to him many times. "He might also consult others and seek their wisdom and counsel. Or sometimes he must simply wait until they speak to him again."

"Sometimes he must wait a full morning," Kelir said, grinning.

Yvenne blinked. "Only a morning? Parsathean disagreements are resolved so quickly?"

"He refers to this morning's punishments," Maddek told her.

She looked to the other warriors, wide-eyed. "You punished him?"

Kelir snorted. "Not as well as we thought. Ours was nothing to yours!"

Full-on laughter from all greeted that statement, yet Yvenne only looked at them with bafflement.

"Mine?"

"A full morning!" Ardyl choked out, tears in her eyes as she laughed. "Riding beside him with not a word spoken!"

Realization filled her gaze as it swept to Maddek. "You thought I punished you?" At his nod, her eyebrows arched. "I would not punish you with silence. If you anger me, I will tell you so."

As he ought to have realized. He'd assumed her silence was punishment because that was what he knew, as a Parsathean. Yet he should have remembered how quiet she'd been when his warriors had punished her at the table last eve, and how very lonely she'd appeared before he'd joined her. He ought to have recalled what she'd said before of how agonizing loneliness was. And he should have thought of how he'd yet to hear her make a sound of discomfort, though many times on this journey she'd been in pain.

Her silence did not mean punishment. It meant she was hurt. All this morning she had been.

Maddek did not believe it was her shattered knee that had pained her. Often it must have, yet she'd still spoken to him. "So what reason for your silence?"

A careless shrug lifted her shoulders, yet his question stole the light from her eyes. "I only wished to be left to my own thoughts."

Thoughts of what hurt her, no doubt. But also thoughts she clearly had no wish to share. Maddek could allow her that, as there was much he did not wish to share, either.

Such as the hot jealousy within him, or the clenching of his chest whenever he recalled Yvenne saying she regretted her choice of husband.

"I imagine a queen has many clever thoughts to occupy her," Toric said, blushing more deeply with every word.

"More clever thoughts than the king she will marry," Kelir observed, earning a grunt of agreement from Maddek and a laugh from the others. "So your bride will have long silences like Danoh's."

The mention roused the quiet warrior. Frowning, Danoh looked up from her plate. "I do not wish to be left to my thoughts. I hold my tongue out of habit."

Kelir appeared chagrined for teasing her. With a nod, he stuffed his mouth full. The others looked everywhere but at Danoh, except for Yvenne, who waited for more explanation.

When none came forth, she asked for it. "Habit . . . because you hunt so often?"

Danoh shook her head. "The habit of not saying words best left unspoken."

Yvenne's curiosity sharpened. "Do you often want to?"

"When I was a girl, quite often. Now the desire is gone but the habit is left."

"Until we see your mother again," Ardyl said dryly. "Then the desire will likely return."

Danoh's grin flashed. "Screaming at her is only habit, too. Once, I believed it would make her hear me. But she only hears my father . . . and that will never change."

With a heavy sigh, Banek shook his head. Uncertainty pinched Yvenne's mouth as she glanced from him to Danoh, clearly wondering what she meant by that but also clearly sensing that tender ground was being tread upon.

Danoh caught that uncertain glance. "My father was one of the Destroyer's warlords."

And the Destroyer's armies violated all they defeated. Yet it was the female warriors who'd had to bear more than the pain and humiliation of their rape.

"I see." Sympathy and understanding warmed Yvenne's

response. "We cannot always choose our fathers—or heal our mothers."

A slight smile curved Danoh's mouth. "No, we cannot," she agreed. "And something in my mother was injured more deeply than in others. Most warriors took the half-moon milk afterward. There were some who wanted a child and cared not how it came to be. My mother . . . she would not take the half-moon milk but neither did she want me. So I spent many years wondering why give birth to me if only to hate me and beat me? And I was angry for it."

"It was a disgrace," Banek muttered. "Both what she did to you and how long it took others in your clan to see."

"I was almost a hunter's age before I was taken from her," she said to Yvenne. "But in those early years, after the Destroyer, many were blinded by grief and pain. How many were lost? How many violated? It must have been difficult to see through that to one young girl."

"You are more forgiving than you should be," the old warrior told her. "You were right to be angry."

"And angry I was." Danoh shrugged. "Until she told me that she gave birth to me because the only way she could make my father pay for what he did to her was by making his child pay."

Anger tightened Maddek's jaw. "Such words should never be spoken."

"I'm glad they were spoken," Danoh replied with an unexpected laugh. "I wanted her to be a mother as yours was. And yours. And yours." She looked to Kelir and then Toric. "But after she told me that, I knew she would never, and I stopped wishing for what could not be."

As every warrior should. Still Maddek shook his head, because it should not have been so.

"I feel no anger toward her now," she continued. "I pity her. My mother is a warrior through and through—and she makes use of what she has. But the Destroyer's warlord did not leave her much."

"He did not," Banek agreed softly.

"So that is the story of my mother," Danoh said as she

turned again to Yvenne. "And *your* mother killed the warlord who was my father. So I ask Banek for more tales of her than of any other—and I would rather hear new songs of Queen Vyssen fighting the Destroyer's armies than another of Ran Bantik."

"If there are songs about my mother, I know none of them. And I hope Banek will share them with me one day."

"That I will, my lady. Now?"

"Perhaps another night, as those songs will only be new to me. Not to Danoh." Yvenne looked to the warrior beside her. "My favorite tale about my mother is not likely one you've heard, as it happened after the alliance was formed, after she slew the demon-queen, after she was imprisoned in the tower. The poison weakened her body, and she was weakened further after giving birth to Lazen. Still, whenever my father tried to visit her bed to get more sons upon her, she tried to kill him. So he had her tied down before his visits to the tower."

"By your father's personal guards?" The same who'd helped rape Maddek's mother.

Yvenne nodded.

"We will kill them all," he vowed softly.

A pleased smile curved her full mouth before she returned her attention to Danoh. "When Aezil was born, my mother bled an ocean of blood—and for many days afterward, she did not open her eyes. Even after she awakened, however, it was as if her mind was no longer there. She had to be fed and cleaned and dressed as a babe, and she never spoke or moved from her bed. Still my father tied her, for he feared it was a deception.

"When Bazir was born, she made no sound, but lay in silent labor until he emerged screaming from between her legs. When Cezan was born, it was the same. Her body labored but she made no sound of pain. Still my father had her tied. But one night, either the guards who secured the knots were careless, or the knots loosened while he rutted. And in the moment when my father spent his seed, when he was most unguarded, my mother grabbed hold of his hair and with her teeth ripped out his throat."

Maddek gave an approving grunt and saw his enjoyment in this tale reflected on every other warrior's expression—and Yvenne's too. Her face was alight as she continued.

"She failed to kill him. But he bears a horrid scar. Through three winters and two births, she lay in bed, made no sounds, gave no indication that anything still remained of her mind. Yet every night, she secretly moved about the tower to keep up what little strength was left after the poisoning." Yvenne sighed. "She claimed it was her speed that failed her. She meant to tear his jugular yet she was too slow, so he pulled his head back just enough to save himself, and her weakened arms could not drag him back down to finish him."

"It is still a legendary feat," Danoh said in awe. "Such patience she had."

Yvenne nodded. "She told me his blood was the sweetest she'd ever tasted. His blood and his fear." She paused to suck the jelly from another leg. "He did not visit her bed again for some time, but he did not need to. I was conceived that night."

A product of endless patience and cunning deception, with her mother bathed in her father's blood. Maddek thought that beginning fit his bride very well. "If ever you are silent longer than a morning, should I fear that you intend to kill me?"

She laughed at him. "My mother taught me better than that. I would give you no warning at all."

He grinned.

"You jest, my lady," Ardyl said from the other side of the fire, "but I believe you also speak absolute truth."

So did Maddek.

When Yvenne left camp to piss, Maddek sent both Danoh and Ardyl with her. Whether magic followed them or Rugusian soldiers did, greater precautions he would take with her every movement.

He unrolled his furs to make her bed. Only Yvenne would sleep a full night that night and every night following. For the others, a half night's sleep would be had, with at least three warriors on watch at every moment. But Maddek suspected he would sleep even fewer hours than that.

Much he had learned about his bride this day. Yet still she hid much behind her walls.

When she returned to camp, her limp was more pronounced as it often was after a hard day's ride, yet the remainder of her saddle stiffness appeared to have gone. She looked to his face as she approached her bed. Little could he read in hers.

Hot frustration poured through his veins again. He strove not to let it command his tongue as he narrowed his eyes upon her and asked in teasing tone, "Do you lie in wait as your mother did?"

The comparison to her mother pleased her, he saw, though confusion wrinkled her brow. "How do you mean?"

"Silently. Not once have I heard you make a sound of pain." His warriors loved to groan, even over a splinter.

Especially over a splinter. When a wound was worse, hardly any complaint would come at all. But Yvenne was not a warrior yet.

A faint smile touched her mouth, yet her eyes remained solemn. "A queen does not cry when there is someone to witness her tears."

He frowned. No shame could be had in crying. "Why?"

"Whatever pain a queen suffers, her people suffer worse. And the role of comfort should not fall upon their shoulders, but hers."

Far different from the Parsathean role. A Ran spoke for all, so he also spoke for their grief, sometimes only with his tears. "What if it is not to weep in pain, but to scream in pain?"

"It is the same," she said. "A queen's pain is nothing to what her people know."

"Even when your knee was shattered, you were silent?" Maddek did not think he could have been.

"I was." A shadow passed over her face. "Also to deny their satisfaction."

"Whose?" Though he suspected. Only her brothers and father did she know.

Her silence answered him now. Was she hurt again? Or silent for another reason? It could not be about Maddek's mother. The injury was too old. Three years, she'd said. The same number of years Queen Vyssen had been dead.

"Why will you not tell me what happened? What do you conceal?"

Her eyes hardened. "If you believe I have something to hide, will you trust that what I reveal is truth? You will not. So I cannot see what purpose there would be in telling you when you doubt all that I say. I will gain nothing, yet you will gain another weapon to use against me—one that wounds me deeper than any other."

He could make no sense of her. Not of her words and not when she turned from him and began to limp away.

Maddek caught her arm. "Where do you go?"

She spoke low enough that the others would not hear but firmly enough that he could not mistake her. "There is but one bed and I will not share yours."

Maddek had not forgotten. She would deny his place at her side until her moon night. So this bed he'd made for her alone.

Though he'd hoped she would change her mind. "There will be no wolves to warm you this night. They must watch over the camp."

Her chin lifted. "I will be warm enough by the fire."

In her heavy cloak, perhaps she would. Unlike the previous eve, when she'd worn nothing beneath it, now she was also wrapped in her linens and covered by a silk robe. As they neared the Boiling Sea, the spring nights became ever more humid and mild. But if one of them must keep warm by the fire, it would not be his bride.

"The furs are for your use," he told her. "I am on watch as well."

She turned back toward him, but it was only partial acceptance. "You will need a bed half the night through. Wake me, and I will take my turn at watch while you sleep."

"Last eve, you asked me to wake you for another reason."

She went still, her gaze locked on his. "To ease your need?"

Which was suddenly hard upon him. With blood pounding, he snagged the braid at the base of her neck and tugged her closer. She came easily, lips parted, eyes widened. Arousal roughened his voice. "Last eve, you would have taken me into your mouth."

With a lift of her chin, she said, "So I would now, if you demand it."

If he demanded it. Not if he asked, because she would refuse. But if he demanded, she would comply. And Maddek could not tell if the fire burning in her moonstone gaze was challenge or desire.

All that he could read clearly from her face was that Yvenne would ease his need if he told her to. She would go to her knees, even if the shattered joint pained her, and not make a sound but for the hiss of her breath.

So a decision must be made. He could tighten his fist in her hair and guide her down, and know the hot ecstasy of her mouth upon his cock.

Or he could open his hand.

Releasing her braid, he cupped her jaw in his palm, rubbed his thumb over the fullness of her bottom lip. "That is not what I would ask of you this eve. Instead I would ease *your* need."

It was a lure to bring her out from behind her walls—a lure that would give him as much pleasure as it did her. But although temptation shone through her gaze, she shook her head. "You have shown me how to ease my own."

"Not with your fingers. With my mouth upon your cunt." No mistaking the emotion that flared through her eyes now. Pure hunger he saw, as fiery as his own. "Beneath our furs, I would taste your lips and every span of your skin until honey dripped between your thighs. Then I would feast upon the sweetness of you far into the night."

Her breath stopped and she squeezed her eyes shut. With that moonstone gaze shielded, he could better see her face. The flush upon her cheeks. The moistness of her lips.

He could see the effort it took her to pull away from him.

"On my moon night," she whispered, her face averted, her body tense. "I will be better prepared for you then."

Prepared to meet the lust that raged through him? Maddek did not think she could be. With a soft laugh, he let her go.

"Then take your sleep while you can," he told her. "You will need it."

CHAPTER 19

YVENNE

The stars still shone brightly overhead when Yvenne opened her eyes, uncertain what had awakened her until she heard it again. A soft snort, as the horses sometimes made, but this was near her head and accompanied by shuffling and grunting.

Maddek's low voice came from just as nearby, but at her other side. "It is only a louth."

Rooting in the soil with the short tusks alongside its beak. An odd-looking creature it was, the size of a boar but with its squat body low to the ground, four legs splayed like a newt's, and with smooth, reptilian skin.

She turned away from the louth to study Maddek, who sat beside her bed. It was closer to morning than she'd thought; the stars above were bright but they faded to the east. Almost dawn, yet he still seemed to be on watch. At the center of the camp, the fire burned low, flames glinting off the knife he used. So different he looked by firelight, the soft glow making his features seem more harsh, all hardened planes and angles with deep and dark shadows. Yet still so handsome to her eyes.

For a long breath she watched him, trying to fathom what he was doing—and trying not to recall how many times she'd silently eased her need in these furs the previous night, her mind filled with his roughened voice telling her that he would feast upon her cunt. Then falling asleep lonely, wishing she'd invited him into their bed.

Even now she longed to invite him in, to know the pleasure he promised. But pleasure was not all she longed for, and the soft pain beneath her breast reminded her that she was supposed to be disentangling her emotions.

But there was no purpose served by lingering in the furs. She would only wish for what she could not have. Still, there were others sleeping, so her voice was a soft whisper as she sat up and asked, "What is that you are scraping?"

"A stave for a bow." His reply was as quiet as hers.

Fascinated, she watched him. His mother had once made a similar stave with wood painstakingly carved from the frame of Yvenne's bed, yet Ran Ashev had possessed no blade to do it with. Only a bone comb sharpened against the tower walls.

Maddek finished with the knife and collected a twisted length of cord. Bending the bow, he quickly strung it. He examined the weapon, then tested it by drawing the string.

Finally he nodded, as if satisfied. "It is too green but will serve to strengthen your arm."

Confusion filled her. "My arm?"

A soft grunt was his answer and he held the weapon out to her.

Yvenne took it, her heart pounding sickly. In her left hand, she gripped the bow. With the fingers remaining on her right hand, she plucked the string, loving the memory of wielding this weapon. But she could no longer.

"I can barely draw the string." She showed him how difficult it was. "And I cannot do it at all while also trying to notch an arrow."

Maddek watched her struggle with the bowstring before meeting her eyes with a dark, even gaze. "Use your other hand."

"But that is not—" *What your mother taught me.* Yvenne bit off those unintended words before they could be spoken.

He must have known but she saw no anger in his expression. Only patience. "You are not the first to lose fingers—or even a full hand. And most warriors have one arm stronger than the other. But a warrior-queen should learn to use both equally well. So you will."

A warrior-queen. She'd believed Maddek meant it as a joke. Yet now he gave her a bow and claimed she would use it.

Throat suddenly thick and aching, she grasped the stave in her right hand. It was awkward, for she could not firmly grip the wood with only two frail fingers and a thumb, and the bow wobbled in her grip when she tried to draw the string. Her left hand and arm were untrained and weak.

Yet Maddek had given her this to strengthen them. So that she might one day wield a bow and arrow again.

A queen did not cry when there was someone to see. Yet never had Yvenne struggled so hard against tears. Her chest was achingly full and her vision blurred when Maddek came nearer, adjusting her fingers around the bow.

"By wrapping leather here, I can make a grip that will conform to your remaining fingers and give you a stable hold," he said quietly, reinforcing her grip now by curling his fingers over hers. "Try to draw."

She did and could barely pull the string.

Maddek grunted. Despite her poor showing, that response sounded to her like approval—or perhaps *barely* was better than he expected. "Build your strength by pulling on the string as you ride. In time, you'll need a vambrace to protect your forearm, but you are not drawing hard enough to bother with it now. Best to tie your sleeves out of the way, though—and you must practice."

"I will," she vowed, her voice a thick rasp. She felt Maddek's gaze upon her but could not look at him.

His big hand tightened over hers. "Do you sense the same threat you did last eve?"

Yvenne shook her head.

Maddek seemed unsurprised by that answer. "I will finish the grip while you break your fast and make ready to ride," he said gruffly.

Silently she nodded, then moved in haste away from him, her heart painfully swollen within her chest. She was supposed to be disentangling her emotions, separating lust from love. She was supposed to let all her hope wither.

Her would-be husband did not make it easy.

CHAPTER 20

YVENNE

Also not easy was drawing a bow while riding a horse. Yvenne didn't rely on the reins for balance, yet they seemed to offer some small measure of control over her mount, so letting go of the reins sent Yvenne's heart to racing. Then pulling on the bowstring shifted her weight in the saddle, making her instinctively grip more tightly with her legs, and she had not yet broken the habit. Every moment she expected the animal to bolt forward, sending her tumbling over the mare's rump.

One day she would gallop along and shoot her arrows without fear. But that was not this day. Instead she practiced every time they slowed the horses to a walk.

Beside her, Maddek observed, "Soon your shoulders will feel as your ass did the first day in the saddle."

She knew they would. Just as her shoulders and arms had ached in the days following Ran Ashev's first lessons. And those lessons had culminated in the death of her oldest brother. Now she dreamed these practices would culminate in an arrow through her father's neck—a dream that had seemed impossible until this very morning, when Maddek had given her this bow, as if her missing fingers had changed nothing at all.

Grinning happily, Yvenne replied, "I have not a care."

She knew not when Maddek's grin had become more handsome than his scowl, yet she could hardly look away from him. But with effort, she did, focusing on the road ahead.

Maddek brought her attention back round by asking, "What occupies your thoughts this morn?"

Because she had been nearly as silent as yesterday, when he'd believed she punished him. "Staying in the saddle," said she, for they had pushed harder upon the road and she was not yet confident enough to focus on anything but riding when they struck a faster pace. But it was only a partial truth. "And thinking that as much as my mother described to me of the world outside our tower room, I cannot truly understand many things until I have experienced or seen them for myself."

"Such as?"

Such as longing and desire. Or the stairs. Yet all of those answers made her heart constrict, so instead she gestured to the southwest, where a herd of humpbacked reptiles with long necks were walking north in single file. "I thought a whiptail would be larger than a mammoth."

"They are. It is only the distance that makes them appear smaller," Maddek said, and pointed to a nearby cluster of palms. "As we ride closer, you will see they stand taller than those trees."

She looked again in amazement. Since she had left her tower, Yvenne's eager eyes had taken in everything that had only been described to her before. She had looked and looked and looked, desperate to see it all for herself. Yet until Maddek rode beside her, she hadn't realized how much she'd been blind to or how often she'd misunderstood what lay before her, because she didn't know *how* to see.

Yesterday he'd begun teaching her to see as a hunter saw. She had not believed then that he truly meant to make a warrior-queen of her, but it had been another lesson she'd been glad to learn.

And now it was not a joke, but truth. Remembrance sent a thrill of pleasure coursing through her. "If I had an arrow, what could I shoot today for our supper?"

As the other warriors did. They often loosed arrows from their saddles and rode over to sweep up their kill without dismounting.

"A pheasant," he replied. "Or a marmot."

"A marmot?" She looked to him in surprise. Except for the millipede the previous eve, always the other warriors took small game. "Something so big?"

"You are thinking of the hooded marmot from the Ephorn forest. These are the size of a dally bird."

"You've seen sign of them today?"

He nodded. "I'll show you if we pass it again. They're easiest found near streams."

And they had passed many streams. Though still surrounded by tall grasses, the ground was softer here, the soil wetter. Over the constant hum of insects came the frequent chirps and trills from birds and lizards. She focused on a nearby rustling and aimed her arrowless bow before drawing the string. The muscles in her shoulders and arms burned fiercely and her fingertips were raw from a morning of practice, yet she ignored the pain. This she would do again and again until it no longer hurt.

Maddek never warned her when he threw the rock to flush out a target. Now the stone crashed through the grass, followed by a squawk and flap of wings. A pheasant burst out of the grasses and Yvenne loosed her string. There was not yet a satisfying *pting* when she released her imagined arrow, yet she grinned happily again, for she was certain her aim had been true and the bird would have been an evening stew.

"When I have quicker eyes and a stronger arm, I'll kill suppers for us all," she told Maddek. "I will be the greatest hunter with bow and arrow you have ever seen."

His grin matched hers. "It will serve Toric and Danoh well to have new competition."

Because those two warriors were the best archers among the Dragon. Yvenne could never hope to be as strong as they, but their skill was not all in strength. "I shall ask them for lessons, too."

"You learn faster than your current tutor did," said Ardyl dryly as she came up beside Yvenne's mount at a trot. "You are only a day into your lessons, but you already boast as mightily as Maddek did when he reached his bearded age and claimed he would be the greatest hunter the Burning Plains had ever seen."

She was being teased, Yvenne realized with a rush of dizzying pleasure. Teased as the warriors often teased Maddek. Though Ardyl had not spared him in this, either.

Yvenne hoped Ardyl might ride alongside her and continue that teasing, but she joined the two warriors ahead. Banek and Kelir had ridden in front of Maddek and Yvenne all morning. Now Ardyl didn't seem intent on talking to either but simply riding with them. And they all seemed bunched into a smaller party, without as much distance between their horses.

She glanced back and saw that Fassad and Toric were nearly on her mount's hindquarters, with Danoh not far behind.

Immediately Maddek asked, "Do you sense foul magics again?"

"I only noticed that we ride closer together now." And Yvenne had learned that the warriors did nothing without reason. "For what purpose? Do you expect that it still follows us?"

Whatever *it* had been. That uneasy, watchful touch at the back of her neck. But if the threat was behind, Yvenne realized, then Ardyl would not have moved to the front.

"I know not if it does," Maddek said. "This is another danger."

Tension gripped the back of her neck. "Are there bandits ahead?"

"Linen thieves." Which sounded to Yvenne like bandits, until he added, "You might call them uzzads."

A flightless predatory bird. Fascinated, Yvenne searched for them and spotted the head of one sticking up over the tall grasses—and saw why the Parsatheans had named them linen thieves. The red wattle around its beak and neck appeared as if a warrior's red linens hung from its mouth.

"I had not thought them so big." If the grasses ahead grew as high as they did here, it meant the animal stood even taller than Maddek upon his horse. "I only see one. Are there more?"

"One more. A female. Except for when they nest, linen thieves hunt alone."

"So they are not like drepa?" The large feathered lizards that roamed the Burning Plains in packs. Yvenne's mother had described them very similarly, though drepa used their raptor claws to tear out the innards of their prey, while uzzads bashed in skulls with their heavy beaks.

"I would rather face a pack of drepa than a nesting linen thief," Maddek said grimly. "A group such as ours has little to fear from a single bird. It will chase easier prey. But a pair protecting their young will defend their territory."

A territory that the road traveled straight through. Yvenne's heart beat a faster pace. "What do we do?"

"Prepare to ride hard."

So she would need both hands. Yvenne slung her bow across her back. "Are linen thieves quick?"

Maddek nodded. "Faster than a horse at a sprint. When we reach the edge of their territory, the dogs will draw them away from the road. Then we'll race through."

Already her palms were clammy. Yvenne dried them on her robes before grasping her reins. "Where is the edge of their territory?"

"We will know."

By the stench, apparently. The light breeze stirring the grasses brought the stomach-churning scent of rotting flesh to Yvenne's nose. More animals entered the linen thieves' territory than the nesting birds could eat, and their bodies marked the boundary the linen thieves defended. The Parsatheans drew to a halt when the first carcass appeared on the road ahead, covered by a swarm of black flies. In a cloud, the flies lifted and settled again, revealing the grisly remains of a horse. Near to it was what appeared to be a miren, lying upon its armored back with its belly battered open.

But it was not only animals that the linen thieves had killed. Silently Maddek gestured to another fly-swarmed carcass that might have been man or woman. "That is why we have seen no bandits."

"That one almost made it through," Kelir added. "No doubt we'll come across what is left of his friends and their horses on the road ahead. So mind the footing. Being tossed from a saddle after a mount slips in a bandit's guts is a good tale for around a fire but will be not so merry here."

Mind the footing? Nervousness crept up Yvenne's spine. She had planned to simply hold on and let her horse follow the others. Yet she would need to guide her mount?

A loud hiss sent another shiver racing up her spine. The linen thief stepped into the road, neck extended and waving from side to side. It flapped wings that were too small for its huge body, as if trying to make itself seem larger—but it did not need to be larger. Already it looked terrifyingly big. Yvenne's roan pranced uneasily, and she patted her shoulder, trying to soothe the mare though her own hands were shaking and the hairs lifted at the back of her neck.

But . . . that was not because of the linen thief. That was something else.

Something close.

"Maddek," she said urgently.

He glanced at her just as Bone and Steel began growling. Neither wolf faced the linen thief but had turned east, facing the direction from which they'd come.

Ahead, Kelir had not taken his eyes from the giant bird. "What is it?"

Nothing on the road behind them. Yet Maddek had taught her how to watch the grasses to see the direction an animal moved and to guess at its size. Even with the breeze disturbing the stalks, she detected movement heading in their direction. *Many* movements heading in their direction. Some approaching very quickly.

But the warriors were not only looking for dangers in the grass. Danoh pointed into the sky. "Redfoot eagle," she called out.

That announcement flew through the Dragon like an arrow. As one they spun to face the linen thief, horses snorting and pawing, as if preparing to sprint forward.

"The nesting female?" Kelir asked, voice tense.

"We cannot wait," Maddek told him, reaching for the bronze shield hanging from the back of his saddle. "As soon as the male chases the wolves from the road, fly."

"What is coming?" Fear made Yvenne's voice high and thready, though she was not even certain what she feared. The linen thief, yes. But not nearly as much as the unknown things behind them. "What threat is the eagle?"

"It is Aezil."

Her second brother? Yvenne tried to make sense of Maddek's answer, then bit back a surprised cry when he reached over and snagged her waist, lifting her from the saddle. In the next moment she was settled in front of him. He threw a command at Toric to lead her horse.

A word from Fassad sent the wolves racing down the road. The linen thief ruffled its feathers and hissed its warning as they swiftly closed the distance.

"Hold tight," Maddek said, and she felt his steely tension as they watched Bone and Steel.

As soon as the linen thief gave chase, there would be no talking. "What do you mean, it is Aezil?"

"Redfoot eagles nest only in the Fallen Mountains." In her brother's territory of Rugus. "Likely your brother controls the eagle and sees through its eyes—as Stranik's priests once did. To cast their spells from afar, they needed to see what their magics would touch. So they sent birds as familiars."

And those priests had sacrificed children to their god for that power. Using sight beyond what was seen, but gained through evil means.

Rage and horror erupted like bile in her throat, nearly choking her. "You think Aezil did the same?"

"To locate our route." Anger hardened his voice. "Now he uses his foul magic to make revenants."

Also as Stranik's priests had done, reanimating dead animals and sending the ravenous creatures to attack the alliance army. With a shudder, Yvenne pictured the multiple trails that signaled movement through the grass. "How many revenants come?"

"Only a dozen."

The answer filled her with terror. *"Only?"*

He added grimly, "If your brother continues to use his magics, there will soon be more."

Because the linen thieves' territory would be littered with carcasses—likely far more than had fallen along the road that they could see. And those, the warriors were making certain could not get up again. Toric, Ardyl, and Banek swiftly moved among the fallen animals, sweeping low in their saddles to stab through the rotting skulls and necks, sending up swarms of buzzing flies.

"Dragon at the Ran's sides!" Kelir said sharply, and the other warriors fell in beside and behind Maddek's horse.

From farther behind them came a crashing through the grasses, a wet snarling that grew louder. Days upon the road had taught Yvenne that almost nothing made loud noise. Predators crept toward their prey; the prey avoided notice of predators if they could. Ahead, though the wolves feinted toward the linen thief's legs before darting away, the huge bird seemed not to notice them at all anymore, beaded eyes focused ahead, head lifted high.

With a loud honk, the linen thief whirled and dodged into the grass, the red wattle waving like a flag as the bird raced through the tall stalks.

Beneath her, the horse's muscles bunched. Maddek's hard chest pressed against her back and she leaned forward, gripping the saddle tight as the Parsatheans surged forward as one.

This was not the first time they had raced together in this

way. Yet before, wonder had filled Yvenne, exhilaration. Now only fear clutched her throat and pounded through her veins as she desperately clung to the pommel. Other warriors pressed in around them—the Dragon's protection a shield of their own horses and bodies. Wind whipped tears from her eyes. She didn't dare shift her weight and glance behind, probably couldn't have seen anything past Maddek anyway. Only what was forward and directly to the side. She looked over as Danoh turned in her saddle to loose an arrow behind. An unholy screech answered as if the arrow had found its mark, but Yvenne could not imagine what creature might make such a terrible noise. Even the blood wraiths had not sounded so viscerally ravenous.

The linen thieves bolted out of the grass and onto the road ahead of Kelir. A scream of warning ripped from Yvenne, but the birds were not bent on attack. Balls of fluff were tucked beneath their small wings as they sprinted ahead down the road. Carrying their young away instead of trying to fight the revenants coming from behind—and that was more terrifying than anything else, that the predators even the Parsatheans had feared were fleeing the foul creatures.

Though he was directly behind her, Maddek had to shout over the thunder of her heart and the hooves. "Does Aezil want you dead?"

She shook her head. Her brother didn't . . . or so she'd believed. As a bride and Nyset's heir, she was more valuable to them alive. But if Aezil had sent these revenants after them, Yvenne couldn't be so certain.

Her answer seemed to change the tension in Maddek's form behind her. He didn't shout again, yet must have communicated a command to the others because Kelir held up his fist in acknowledgment.

That order was apparently to find a defensible location. They splashed across a wide stream and Kelir came to a halt. All the warriors suddenly seemed in purposeful motion, the horses snorting and prancing in wide circles. Relief filled Yvenne when she saw Steel and Bone at Fassad's heels.

Swiftly Kelir dismounted. "Put your bride on mine."

Yvenne knew not what he meant, but she found herself placed atop Kelir's horse a moment later.

"Stay mounted," Maddek told her, though he and most of the other warriors were abandoning their saddles as well. "This gelding won't bolt while we fight—but if we are overwhelmed, ride at speed until you find a village."

Yvenne could do nothing except nod, her breath coming in heaving rushes. Her own horse and the others Maddek had bought were untrusted to remain steady while the revenants attacked, and only Toric and Danoh were mounted now. Yvenne was sitting amid the riderless horses, the Parsathean mounts on either side of her, the newer ones tied together in a snorting, nervous line.

Ahead, the warriors formed an arc across the road—preparing to fight any revenants who crossed the stream. The creatures would be exposed while fording the waters, so there could be no unexpected attacks from the grasses around them.

"Aezil will not risk his sister," Maddek told them. "So he will fly the eagle in close to better control the revenants. We hold here until Danoh and Toric take Aezil's eyes."

By shooting the eagle from the sky. Still panting from that desperate ride, Yvenne watched the trails through the grass, counting more than a dozen now, some faster than others. Most warriors were not mounted to see. She had opened her mouth to call out a warning when Fassad gave it instead—alerted by the wolves, she realized.

The creature that burst through the grasses on the opposite side of the stream had once been a linen thief but was now a shambling horror within a loose rotting skin covered in ragged feathers. It darted into the stream, hissing wetly from a gristly throat, slowed by the knee-deep water.

"Fassad!" Maddek said.

The warrior's arrow pierced its skull with a fleshy thunk. Another revenant erupted from the grasses—a louth. The same sort of creature that had rooted harmlessly near Yvenne's head that morning, diseased and flying toward them on its splayed feet. This time Banek's arrow felled it while crossing the stream.

"He is raising more corpses from nearby," Kelir said grimly. "Even a revenant louth is not fast enough to have caught up to us."

And could not have been one of creatures that had been behind them at the edge of the linen thieves' territory.

The eagle soared nearer, and Yvenne watched with held breath as first Danoh and then Toric loosed arrows. Danoh's sharp curse followed when they both missed—though not by much. Yvenne's heart thundered as they tried again before the eagle circled north, away from the stream.

More revenants approached, and she bit her tongue to stop from calling out the warning, knowing it wasn't needed and might be a distraction. Each of the warriors faced where the wolves indicated . . . but no revenant burst through.

"It stopped at the edge of the grasses," Yvenne called out. She saw the uneasy glance Kelir and Maddek shared then. "What is it?"

"Your brother has realized that we will defeat the revenants easily if they cross one at a time." It was Banek who answered her. "So he will gather them there until he can make them attack in great numbers."

"He is no experienced sorcerer," Kelir said, with a glance at Yvenne. "Is he?"

"I do not believe so. I never felt this magic when he lived in the citadel in Syssia—and he only took Rugus's throne a few seasons past."

"Then he will not find it easy to hold the revenants here and reanimate more *and* chase our archers." Maddek looked to Toric and Danoh. "Ride."

Both warriors looked pleased by that command. Together they charged north through the grasses and Yvenne followed their progress as it abruptly shifted east—across the stream again.

The eagle made two tighter circles above a rock covered by a swarm of birds before angling east. At first Toric and

Danoh seemed to be heading in the wrong direction, not toward the eagle at all, until Yvenne realized they were cutting across the wide circle Aezil's familiar was making.

"How many, Yvenne?"

Maddek's voice brought her gaze swinging back to the grasses across the stream. She was the only one with a view over the tall stalks now. "I think . . . eight or nine wait."

Grimly he nodded. "That is my count. They are not quiet in their approach."

"At least a dozen more are coming." Approaching from the wide expanse of grasses, the trails they made far apart yet clearly converging in this direction. Nervously her gaze shot back to Toric and Danoh, who rode not far from some of the revenants' trails, but the creatures seemed not at all interested in the riders galloping through the grasses. She didn't know if her brother hadn't noticed the Parsathean archers or if he simply couldn't split his focus in that way.

"Tell us when they strike the eagle down," Maddek said.

Because the revenants across the stream would not be held back by her brother then, and would attack their party. That fight could not be avoided, but hopefully the eagle would be struck down before more revenants arrived. They'd passed so many corpses on that race through the linen thief's territory. A sorcerer could not raise dead humans without a demon's assistance, but there'd been fallen animals aplenty for her brother to reanimate—and those were only upon the road.

With a sharp whistle and command, Fassad sent the wolves to Yvenne's side. Not only to guard her, she knew. The wolves and the horses might only be tools, but they were too useful to risk—and putting any of the animals in a battle with revenants guaranteed their death. A bite or scratch from a revenant was poison to a human, but to a living animal, the revenant's poison would change them into the same.

Palms clammy with cold sweat, her brother's foul magic breathing down the back of her neck, she looked out over the grasses again. Toric and Danoh seemed almost directly below the eagle. With awe, she saw that they did not even slow from a full gallop as they took aim. It seemed the arrows' flight was as swift as the pounding of her heart, released at one beat—and on the next beat, Toric's shaft pierced the eagle's breast.

"It is killed!" she cried.

Even as the eagle tumbled from the sky, the ravenous growls from the stream burst into terrifying howls.

She didn't recognize the animal that leapt the stream without slowing. An antelope, perhaps, its hide hanging in sheets from withered bones, head lowered and antlers jutting like spikes. Grunting, Maddek blocked the spikes with his shield and jammed his sword up through the creature's snapping jaw. With a double-armed swing of his axe, Kelir split the skull of a charging bison. At the edge of the stream, Ardyl spun her glaive in an upward slash that beheaded a cowled lizard, then scrambled back as the big animal fell, viscous black blood spurting from the long, writhing neck.

Banek felled a yellow-horned laybeast, sword impaling its soft underjaw. Yvenne drew in breath to cry warning as another bison charged across the stream at him, but with shield at his chest, Fassad rammed into the beast as it reached the bank, knocking it off-stride. The warrior stabbed through its rolling eye with a short sword while the wolves snarled and whined by the legs of Yvenne's mount, bodies quivering with the need to rush forward and help.

With the same helpless frustration Yvenne watched the battle, until movement north caught her attention. The nesting crows were winging upward in raucous flight. And the rock they'd settled upon . . . had not been a rock.

This creature she recognized, though she'd only seen one before at a distance. Maddek had said whiptails were as tall as trees. And though this one was still a sprint away, it stood taller than any tree Yvenne had seen. Its *legs* were like trees, and the neck and tail each longer than the span of its giant humpbacked body.

Terror in her heart, she looked to Maddek. In the moment after he struck down another revenant, when it was not so dangerous to distract him, she shouted, "Maddek! To the north!"

She saw him glance in that direction, his face covered in gore, before he raised his shield against another revenant that crossed the stream. The warriors slowly began falling back toward the horses, the defensive arc they made across the road smaller and tighter. On the other side of the stream, Danoh and Toric galloped toward the whiptail. Their arrows pierced the hide but were only like the stings of bees to the enormous reptile.

And the trails through the grasses were not all converging now. One crept slowly toward the mounted Parsatheans.

"Toric!" Yvenne screamed the warning. *"Behind you!"*

The young warrior had but a moment to turn, shield in front of his chest, when the creature leapt at him. A long-toothed cat, only recently dead, its yellow fur still spotted instead of rotting away in clumps. The revenant slammed into the shield, knocking Toric from his saddle. Yvenne heard Danoh's faint cry, and then the warrior surged from her horse with axe in hand. The thrashing of the grasses was all Yvenne could see then.

A deafening roar clutched at her heart. The whiptail. It had not been looking in their direction. But Yvenne's scream had drawn its attention.

Not even in her nightmares could she have imagined such a creature. Not even the trap jaw had been so big—beside the whiptail, even that great predator would have been as a wolf next to a mammoth.

No fangs or claws the whiptail revenant had, yet the foul magic that reanimated the decaying brain within its small head and moved its mountain of rotting meat cared nothing about the original purpose of its host—and teeth that stripped leaves from giant palms could tear frail human flesh from bones.

The ground itself shook when the whiptail took a step, then another, faster with each earthquaking stride. Its huge belly had split, bloodied entrails spilling out and dragging along the ground. Through torn skin and gaping wounds, the whiptail rained gore as it came.

Other revenants were still coming, too. Not all at once, as the first burst had been, but still so many the warriors could not turn away from the stream for more than a moment. They could not run. Unlike horses, the revenants would not slow or tire.

"Ran Maddek!" Kelir shouted, grunting as he slammed his axe into the skull of a louth. "Take your bride! We will hold them."

Perhaps the small revenants could be held, but that whiptail could not be. It would be like a mouse trying to hold back a horse. Kelir's axe might chop through the meat of those treelike legs, but it could not crack the solid bones at their centers. Even a mounted Parsathean with a glaive could not swing the blade high enough to reach that snakelike neck. The warriors would die—and Maddek would never leave them. Only a perfectly placed arrow into the brain might fell that monster, yet both Danoh and Toric were unseated, battling the long-toothed cat, at no angle to strike the whiptail's small head.

Maddek's fiery gaze shot to Yvenne. "Ride!"

The rage of helplessness clutched at her chest. She looked to the charging whiptail. Had she only more than a day's practice, she'd have had the strength to kill it.

But . . . she *did* have strength. She had chosen him for that reason.

Urgent purpose gripped her heart. Kelir's bow and quiver was strapped to the cantle of his saddle. Untying the weapon, she slid from the tall horse, careful to land on her right leg. She hobbled as fast as she could toward Maddek, notching the arrow in the string.

Maddek shoved a revenant from the end of his sword and glanced over his shoulder. She knew not what to make of his expression when he saw her coming, carrying Kelir's bow and the arrow. It seemed molten and icy at once, full of anger and fear.

A hoarse, short laugh broke from him and he turned

back toward the stream. "Now is not the time for practice, my warrior-queen. It is time to ride away."

"Help me and I will kill it!"

He whirled on her, eyes on fire. With steely arm he snatched her against his side, tucked between his body and his shield. "Banek!" he roared. "Take my bride and—"

"Maddek!" She reached up and jerked at his beard, slick with the blackened blood of revenants. "*I am Nyset's heir.* The goddess Vela looks through my eyes. She will guide my aim. But I need your strength."

His head snapped down, his dark gaze searching hers. Only a breath passed before he was suddenly behind her, all around her. His left hand gripped the bow beneath her grip, his fingers closed over her fingers, and it was as if his hands were hers when they pulled the bowstring together.

The creak of the wooden bow as it bent was the sweetest of music. She recalled Banek's tale of Queen Venys, the stolen iron, and a beast felled with one arrow. The whiptail was many times larger than any kergen but surely had the same vulnerability.

"The eye?" she asked, because Yvenne believed it would be the same but could not be certain. Yet Maddek always saw every weakness.

"The eye," he replied.

The whiptail thundered toward them, quaking the ground. She only had to look at her target and knew the aim was true, and as if her fingers were Maddek's, he released as she did. The vibrating *pting* of the string filled her heart with such happiness that the slash of pain across her forearm was nothing. Never had an arrow's flight seemed so swift and true. With held breath, she watched it streak upward before plunging into the whiptail's infested eye.

For a long moment, she feared it might have been only another bee sting to the great beast. Another step the monster took, then another, and then suddenly it pitched forward. Almost slowly it seemed to fall, an endless beat before the impact of the enormous body shook the ground beneath her feet and blew through the grasses like a putrid gale storm, bending the stalks in a wave along the stream.

Sheer silence reigned for a moment. Silence from the warriors, from the revenants, even the buzzing of the insects quieted.

Then another wet growl sounded, and Maddek shifted his grip on the bow. "You used the wrong arm," he told her.

And indeed she had, notching the arrow and using the grip most familiar to her, though her fingers were missing. But now he switched their grips, his right hand holding the bow beneath hers and supporting her missing fingers, his left hand assisting hers in notching the arrow on the string.

"The eye again," he said when a miren revenant began fording the stream.

It mattered not that the target was smaller and guarded by armored spikes above the eye. Again Maddek's fingers released when Yvenne's did, and her arrow found its mark. The miren dropped dead halfway across the stream, submerged in the bloodied waters with the bodies of other revenants.

A whoop sounded from Kelir, and breathless laughter from the other warriors, and her own joy almost burst her heart.

"The next is a horse," Maddek said. "The eyes are at the side of its head and not the front."

"How can you tell what it is?" Yvenne could see nothing coming, could only hear it crash through the tall stalks.

"The rhythm of its steps," he told her, and she could hear it now, too—a pattern that had become so familiar during this journey. "We are directly in front, so it will turn its head to better see us. Let loose the arrow then."

She did, and the charging beast plunged to the ground. Immediately she turned toward the sound of more hooves pounding through the grasses.

This time Maddek halted her aim. "That is Danoh and Toric."

Both riding, Yvenne was relieved to see. But behind her, Maddek stiffened.

"Were you bit?"

A bloody gash on Toric's leg was already reddened and swollen. The young warrior nodded, though he was grinning as he held up a spotted pelt. "Though I have a new fur to wear."

Danoh stared at the fallen whiptail with furrowed brow, and then she eyed Yvenne with Maddek behind her, their hands still ready on her bow. Any question she might have had was answered when another revenant burst from the grasses and together they loosed a bow that pierced its eye.

Laughing, Ardyl dipped the blade of her glaive into the stream to wash the steel clean. "Maddek's bride was not boasting! With practice, she *will* be the finest hunter with bow and arrow we have ever seen."

From her perch atop the horse, Danoh looked out over the grasses. "That is the last one—or at least the last one near enough to see."

A maelstrom of conflicting emotions filled Yvenne. Sorry there were not more to kill and exhilarated by what she and Maddek had done and glad the danger was over— then utterly surprised when Maddek's massive arms suddenly wrapped around her, and she felt the press of his face into her hair.

Holding her so close, so tight. As if she were more to him than a vessel.

Then his voice sounded low and harsh in her ear, hot with anger. "You vowed to follow orders that would keep you safe, yet you disobeyed."

Hurt speared through her. "I vowed I would not fail in my duty toward you and your Dragon. Killing the whiptail kept us all safe."

"Your duty is not to protect us."

With aching heart she argued, "It is a queen's duty to protect—"

"You are not their queen yet, but only my bride. When you have strength of your own, you may kill all the whiptails you like. Otherwise you will stay on the horse."

Abruptly he let her go, then lifted her astride Kelir's

gelding again. His face was grim as he looked to Toric. "There will be more coming. We must find a more defensible camp. Can you ride hard now?"

The young warrior nodded.

But he would not for long. Not with the revenant's poison within him.

Maddek turned to Kelir. "Do we have any of Nemek's potions with us?"

Made by that god's blessed healers, and which might draw out the poison to prevent the dangerous fever. The scarred warrior shook his head. His gore-painted face a mask of tension, Maddek glanced up at Yvenne. She knew what he silently asked.

Throat tight, she said, "I have none, either." And warriors did not wish for what they did not have.

But this time, they all did.

CHAPTER 21

YVENNE

They had ridden quickly that morning, but it was nothing compared to the pace they set for the remainder of the day. Three times, revenants caught up to the riders. The creatures were no longer under her brother's control but were still fixated on the humans as prey, their scent easy to trail on the road—and unlike the horses, the revenants never needed to slow or to rest.

By sunset, the tall grasses had given way to green marshlands studded with groves of giant ferns. Ahead lay the scattered remains of Hanan's colossal statue that had once straddled the banks of the Ageras river. Exhaustion stole any amazement or wonder that Yvenne might have mustered at the sight of the gargantuan head half buried in the earth, its sculpted eyelashes so lifelike that the breeze stirring through them gave the appearance of the god stirring to wakefulness.

It was full dark before Maddek called a halt beside the statue's head—because they could ride no farther. A flushed and fevered Toric was swaying in his saddle. As

Maddek helped Yvenne down, they saw the young warrior slide unbalanced from his mount, caught at the last moment by Banek.

Pushing aside her fatigue, Yvenne told Maddek, "If you tend to my horse, I will tend to Toric."

She knew not why his jaw tightened and his expression darkened, and she had little care. Nor did she care to hear any answer from him but agreement.

"If someone else looks after him, there will be one less warrior to stand watch tonight, though both revenants and soldiers might be behind us," she pointed out. "And I am no stranger to caring for someone weakened by poison."

That dark gaze searched her face for a moment before he gave a short nod. "You may."

She would have, anyway. Just as she would continue shooting arrows into the eyes of monsters, with or without the approval of her would-be husband.

But although her throat ached when Maddek led away Kelir's horse without leaving her the warrior's bow, it was not the moment to wage that battle. The bite on Toric's leg was inflamed, the edges of the ragged wound swollen. While the others set up camp in the marble shelter formed by the statue's cheek and nose, she and Banek helped the young warrior to his furs.

His fevered face reddened more when she settled beside him and opened the small pot of salve Banek had given her. "You ought not, my lady. Take your meal and rest."

"After you have taken yours." Gently she smeared the medicine over the wound, glad to see that despite the swelling and the heat, no pus seeped out.

Still, it must have been tender. Instead of asking his usual questions, Toric sat with gritted teeth until she finished. As she put the salve aside, his gaze briefly touched her eyes.

"Do you sense him now?"

Her brother. "Not since the eagle fell . . . by *your* arrow," she added, her voice warm with praise.

He blushed so fiercely his cheeks looked aflame. His gaze met hers before he averted his eyes again, and his voice was low as he confessed, "I never thought to see such things—wraiths and revenants. Those horrors only belonged to tales. Even the Scourge is nothing now but a pile of black glass and stone."

"Such creatures were but tales for me, too," she said softly. And her father and brothers the only monsters.

"*They* have seen them, in the march across the Lave against Stranik's Fang." A lift of his chin indicated Maddek and Kelir, who were returning to the fire with the skinned and gutted makings of dinner. "And old Banek here."

"So I have," was the warrior's reply.

"But I never met any such creatures upon the Lave. There were only animals that might kill us, but that is no different from home—excepting the Farians, who might also kill us. Why do they want to?"

"The savages?"

Toric nodded. "Did your mother watch them?"

"Many of my foremothers did. But I do not think they ever made sense of the Farians' ways."

"The Tolehi monks believe that they view us as demons and that is why they are desperate to kill us." He looked to Banek when the warrior grunted dismissively. "You do not agree?"

"I know not how their savage minds think. But I have faced a demon—and my only thought was of killing it. Not also of raping and eating it."

Toric grimaced. "Or of wearing human teeth and skin."

"No?" Banek's quiet, rusty laugh sounded. "What do we do to drepa but make armor of their skin and wear their claws to boast of our hunts? Why did you take the fur from the long-toothed cat?"

With widening eyes, Toric said in realization, "*We* are the animals to them."

The old warrior shrugged. "We cannot know for certain. But many savages I have seen crossing the Lave seem to me like young Parsatheans on their first drepa hunt."

So that they might prove themselves as warriors. To Yvenne, that seemed as sensible an explanation as any.

"And what would you rather face, Toric?" Yvenne asked. "A drepa or a Farian?"

"A drepa. They will only tear you apart and devour you." Sudden pride swelled in Toric's voice, but the slurring of his words told her that the fever had him well in hold. "And I have singly killed more drepa than any other in my tribe."

The lift of his chin directed Yvenne's gaze to his neck, where a dozen raptor claws decorated a leather lace. She glanced at Kelir with a sly grin.

"You are from the same tribe, Kelir, are you not?" And he only wore three claws.

Kelir made a disgruntled noise, but his amused look told Yvenne that her teasing was well met. "At Toric's age, I'd already seen two years of fighting against Stranik's Fang— and there are few drepa south of the Burning Plains. When one is home longer, one can collect more claws."

Perhaps, but the number of claws Toric wore seemed no less impressive to Yvenne—especially as the young warrior could not be many years past his bearded age. "How long were you with the alliance's army upon the Lave?"

"Only three seasons."

So after King Latan was assassinated the previous summer and Maddek was sent to reassume command, Toric must have traveled south with him.

"Three seasons only, yet you must have proved yourself well, because you already serve in the Dragon guard," she said. "Whoever appointed you to this task believed you would not falter when faced with revenants and wraiths."

His fever-glazed eyes brightened. "Someone must have told Enox of my bravery atop the Scourge."

"Oh? What is that story?"

"When the warriors in our tribe reached our hunter's age, we dared each other to stay a full night atop the ruins of the Scourge. I was the only one who remained until morning. The others were terrified by howls and screams. But I knew it must be the wind."

Crouching near the fire, Maddek bowed his head, shoulders silently shaking.

Kelir wore a broad grin. "The wind?"

"I recall a similar storm when we made our attempt to prove our bravery." Ardyl joined them, dumping her furs onto the ground and sinking down, cross-legged. "But it was only a mudbrain who hoped to best Maddek and me."

The narrowed stare Ardyl leveled at the scarred warrior told Yvenne who that mudbrain was. "Kelir?"

"He might have won, too, if we'd abandoned him to the Scourge. Instead we went in loyal search of our friend—and in the canyon made when silver-fingered Rani split the demon open, we found him howling and moaning, so that noise echoed through the whole cursed place."

Yvenne laughed but Toric shook his head, struggling to sit up as if to physically deny what Ardyl had suggested.

"It could not have been Kelir. He was at the Lave."

Ardyl gave him a pitying look. "What of Seri?"

"She was home, but she could not—" Toric broke off, his frown deepening. "She is not even a hunter's age! And was then still in her milk teeth."

"Take your ease, warrior," Maddek said softly, but with unmistakable command.

His breathing deep and ragged, as if merely sitting up had been a terrible effort, Toric nodded and eased back onto his furs.

Yvenne raised a skin of water to his dry lips. "Seri?"

"Kelir's sister," supplied Ardyl as Toric sipped. "Who is younger than half her brother's age but already twice the warrior."

Kelir made no objection to that description, only nodded.

But although Toric had eased back, again he shook his head. "A pack of drepa have taken up a nest in the eye of the Scourge. She ought not have gone near those ruins alone."

Kelir's grin slipped. "I will speak to her."

Ardyl scoffed. "Will she listen?"

"I will speak to her," Maddek said, and Ardyl did not scoff at that.

Instead it was Banek who spoke next, his brow furrowed and his words precise, as if each one were carefully weighed and measured. "There has been a cold clutch upon my heart since I saw the whiptail rise. I thought it merely worry, as more revenants still pursue us. Yet young Toric has made me think on the horrors I have seen—and realize that I have not seen power enough to raise a whiptail from the dead since the Destroyer's time."

Yvenne cast him a confused glance. "Did not the priests of Stranik's Fang do the same?"

"In method, it was the same—using a bird as a familiar and creating revenants from afar. Yet never any revenant of that size. Usually those are raised by demons, not magic."

Banek looked to Maddek and Kelir as if for confirmation. Both men wore a slight frown. "Nothing that large," Kelir agreed slowly. "So perhaps it was not Aezil who sent them. Surely it would take an experienced sorcerer to raise such an animal."

Banek shook his head. "Never would an experienced sorcerer allow himself to be flanked by Toric and Danoh, or brought down as easily as this one was. He had no great control or awareness."

Dread clutched Yvenne's throat. "You think it was a demon, then?"

"No," the old warrior said. "What demon would send a bird to see for him? More likely, this is a sorcerer of great power but little practice."

Maddek's gaze touched Yvenne's face. "Then perhaps Aezil's bloodline gives his magics greater power."

"Perhaps," she agreed, her heart full of unease. If true, Aezil was a greater threat than her father. "He cannot be allowed much more opportunity to practice."

A wry smile twisted Maddek's lips. "The alliance council will not approve of you killing the king of another realm."

"The alliance's sole purpose is to defend against the Destroyer and those like him. If that is what my brother is becoming, then my arrow will soon put out his remaining eye."

Maddek's smile became a scowl. "I am your strength. So I will do it for you."

"Only if your aim is better and faster than mine," she

retorted. "Because by the time I see my brother again, I'll have had plenty of opportunity to strengthen my arm."

His expression darkened further. Yet if Maddek meant to deny her, he did not before her view of him was blocked by Fassad crouching to examine Toric's leg.

"You will see home again," was the warrior's pronouncement.

Yvenne could not determine whether such a statement was truth or hope—and thought they might need more time to reach that home than planned. She looked to Maddek again and found him watching her with a brooding stare.

"If it was Aezil who attacked us today," she said to him, "then he must know we are headed to Drahm and intend to sail north on the Boiling Sea. Should we not change course?"

His eyes narrowed. "To where?"

Anywhere that her father could not so easily intercept them. No doubt news of their route was winging its way to Zhalen now. He could send a full army to the outpost on the Burning Plains by the time their ship reached the northern shore.

Which was what Maddek had hoped for. His vengeance could take but two routes: killing her father after marrying Yvenne and helping her claim the Syssian throne, or killing her father in response to an attack within Parsathean territory.

And her father's army *would* ride north. Unlike Maddek, Zhalen had no alternatives. He would lose Syssia if he did not recapture Yvenne. So he would take any risk, even one as foolish as attacking Parsathe—or one that angered the alliance council.

But if Maddek killed her father near the outpost, he need not marry Yvenne, and need not help her beyond that point. And she would be left with her father dead, but her brothers still a threat . . . and with no protection or assistance.

She needed him to marry her and have reason to help secure her throne—even if his only reason was to secure the Syssian throne for their children. "South," she said. "We should seek protection from the Gogean queen."

His upper lip curled into a sneer. "The selfsame queen who wished to be more like your father?"

"Because she wished to quiet dissent stirred by hungry farmers. But we would go to her with the promise of cooperation between Syssia, Parsathe, and Goge that would alter the balance within the alliance council and ease the burden upon her people. She would have every reason to protect us—and if our marriage is witnessed by the Gogean queen, my father has no hope of challenging our union before the alliance council. Then I only need give birth to claim my throne."

His expression hardened. "You would have us cower behind Gogean walls until that day?"

Seeking protection was not cowering, but she knew it useless to tell him so. "Better than killed by the soldiers from the outpost."

"It is your father who will die there." Abruptly he stood. "We continue north."

Her chest was painfully tight as she watched him stalk away. So they would continue north, toward the vengeance Maddek preferred.

A vengeance where she was unneeded, except as bait for her father.

With a heavy grunt, Kelir got to his feet and signaled to Danoh. "We will follow him and take first watch."

Snorting, Ardyl rolled out her furs. "While you are behind him, try to pluck the thorn from his ass."

Kelir nodded, his gaze flicking to Yvenne. She knew not what he saw upon her face that prompted him to say, "You might think him in a foul and angry mood, but it is only that his youngest warrior is fevered and his bride is in danger."

No. Maddek had been in this foul mood since the whiptail, when she had saved them from danger. Yet there was nothing to do but nod. Perhaps it truly was worry for Toric.

But it certainly was not care for her.

CHAPTER 22

MADDEK

A bright egg moon shone down upon green marshes teeming with herds. Armorbacks snorted and squatted over dirt-mounded nests. Shaggy bison calves kicked their heels and danced between the column-like legs of dappled trumpeters. At the deep, resounding call from one of those great beasts, hundreds more raised long elegant necks, their plumed heads turning as one.

Atop the remains of a giant marble foot, Maddek looked in the same direction. If any more revenants lived, they would soon catch up to the warriors. But it was not a revenant that alarmed the trumpeters. Instead a sabenar slinked toward the herds. Though reptilian-skinned and several times larger than a long-toothed cat, in movement it more resembled that animal than other reptiles—and its saber-like fangs resembled the cat's, as well.

"The bison calf," Kelir predicted from beside him.

This was a game they'd often played as boys—watching the predators of the Burning Plains and making wagers over which animal would be targeted. But this night Kelir only played it to keep himself awake.

Though weighed by fatigue, Maddek doubted sleep would come for him. But it was not the dangers outside the camp that occupied his mind. His gaze turned toward Yvenne again. Hanan's mountainous head was buried almost to the eyes, and they had made camp in the corner of cheek and nose. The foot where he and Kelir kept watch was a longer distance away, but it offered the best vantage in all directions. They did not want to notice a revenant coming when it was already almost upon them. Ardyl, Fassad, and Banek slept now but would awaken at any noise, and Danoh and Kelir had both eyes on their surroundings and could keep watch over the sleeping warriors . . . and over Yvenne and Toric. One stricken by fever, and the other who had cared for him through first watch.

A small fire still burned. By its soft light, he watched his bride bathe Toric's face with cool water. The warrior moved restlessly under her ministrations, muttering in a feverish delirium.

It was she whom Maddek wanted to keep in sight now, for when she was not, it seemed as if a revenant's poison filled his own chest. As it had ever since he'd yanked his sword from a revenant's gut and turned to see her coming toward him with Kelir's bow and arrow instead of fleeing the magic-fouled whiptail.

She had promised to make his life a misery. He still believed she would. But in that moment, he'd realized his life would also be a greater misery if Yvenne wasn't in it.

A misery with her or without her. Of the two miseries, he would choose what she offered. Yet that choice had almost been taken from him today.

It was not the first time she'd been in danger. Yet when the blood wraiths had surrounded her, Maddek's fear then had been nothing compared to today's. He meant to make her a warrior-queen, but only so she could protect herself if necessary. Not so that she could race toward battle.

His next lesson to her would be that sometimes a warrior's best option was to run away.

With a grunt, Kelir made wordless comment on Maddek's distraction and how much of this night he'd spent looking toward the camp instead of watching for threats coming from outside it.

Then his friend said gruffly, "Do not look at your bride tending to Toric and think a fool's thoughts."

No need to ask what thoughts those would be—suspicion and jealousy. Maddek did not suspect either Toric or Yvenne, yet he could not truthfully deny shameful jealousy. Because Yvenne tended to the young warrior with warmth and without walls. She did not so easily touch Maddek.

But he could only agree. "Such thoughts would be a fool's."

"So do not think them. He has taken sweet liking to her, but it will pass as soon as another pretty woman shows him interest. And her eyes are only for you."

That was truth. At no one else did she ever look at with her gaze full of heat and hunger, except for Maddek—and a millipede's leg.

Kelir eyed him speculatively. "Were they also a fool's words? There must be a reason she slept with the wolves and then refused to share your furs last eve."

Maddek wished the words he'd said had been mere jealousy. Instead he'd almost torn out her tongue. He'd told her not to look to him for affection, though it was Maddek who'd needed that reminder. Not she.

But he could not undo what was done. "The next time she allows me to share her bed, I will put my tongue to better use than saying what is best left unsaid."

Both pity and laughter filled the other warrior's reply. "It is but five days until the full moon."

When Maddek would have her again. And between now and then, she would build stronger walls between them.

Suddenly frowning, Kelir leaned forward. "What's got them up?"

At the camp, Fassad and Banek were no longer sleeping

but had risen from their beds. As Maddek watched, Banek nudged Ardyl with his foot, but she only rolled over and burrowed deeper into her furs.

No threat, then. Maddek glanced at the moon. Still high, so it was too early to change watch.

Banek started in their direction. The older warrior gave a signal that all was well, yet Maddek did not wait for him to reach them. He scaled his way down Hanan's marble foot with Kelir close behind.

"Has Toric worsened?" Maddek asked as they met.

"He is no better or worse than he was," Banek said. "But his restless mutterings mean there is no sleep found in the camp—and if I am to be awake, better I make use of myself on watch. Fassad has decided the same."

Kelir nodded and said, "Better mutterings than silence."

So it was. In the campaign against Stranik's Fang, they had seen warriors as strong and as young as Toric succumb to the fever, and always it was preceded by burning still-ness. Toric was in danger, but not terrible danger. Most strong warriors who died from the fever were not bitten on a limb as he'd been, but nearer their heart or head.

Yet someone as frail as Yvenne . . . that fever killed most, no matter where the bite was. Perhaps she might have been spared death, just as her goddess-touched mother had survived a different poison that ought to have killed her. But Yvenne's body had never been as strong as that warrior-queen's.

It would have taken but one scratch. One bite. Yet she'd run toward danger instead of away.

She was well, but still Maddek's chest ached. His bride had said he was adept at finding weaknesses. He could not ignore that she was becoming his. For he focused on a problem he didn't face instead of the one he did.

"Will he have strength to ride tomorrow?" It mattered not if Toric could sit a horse after they reached Drahm and the ship that would carry them across the Boiling Sea. But it was still several days' ride to that city.

Banek shook his head. "Perhaps the next."

A full day lost—and with Syssian or Rugusian soldiers not far behind, if they'd taken the southern river road.

"I can stay with him while you ride ahead," Banek suggested.

"No." They were all stronger together. Even with Toric weakened. And if the soldiers had taken the northern road and reached Drahm before they did, better not to enter that city with fewer warriors at his side. "If they are on this road, this position is the most defensible."

Kelir's mouth twitched in amusement. "And you have a bride who can place an arrow through any approaching soldier's eye."

So she could. But not alone. And Maddek would not expose her to the soldiers, yet if an attack came, he would also be a fool not to use such a gift.

Nor would she let him leave it unused. By Temra's fist, her stubbornness meant that if he denied her, she would only seek strength elsewhere.

That poisonous ache in his chest deepened.

He felt Kelir's gaze upon him now before the other warrior said, "Are you in need of counsel, Ran Maddek?"

Though the warrior's tone was light, it wasn't all jest. Counsel and consultation was one of the Dragon's duties. And whatever Maddek's friend saw upon his face must have said he was in need of it.

But it was not counsel he needed. There was no help for what afflicted him.

"Not counsel. A promise." But not from Kelir, though it was best that the warrior witnessed it. Maddek looked to Banek. Maddek's guards did not have to obey him. But if the older warrior made that vow now, it would be near the same. "You serve as one of my Dragon guards—but foremost you will serve as my bride's. And if she will not run from a threat we cannot defeat, you will take her away from it."

Banek looked to Kelir. Maddek had no doubt the old man wanted to accept, yet this would be a decision made between the warriors, for it might mean Banek would abandon the Dragon—and Maddek—in a time of need.

The lightness had vanished from his friend's expression. Kelir misliked the request, but he also saw the reason for it.

And he also knew Maddek's own frustration at not having realized it sooner. "We saw what she was—every time she sensed foul magics, or when she looked at us with her moonstone eyes and we could not hold her gaze. She told us a goddess sees through her. We *knew*." His mouth twisted in bitter humor. "Yet even the barmaid understood better than we, and that only on a glance."

Just as so many things had been described to Yvenne, but she'd not truly understood until seeing them for herself. Kelir and Maddek had been similarly blinded, believing they knew what she was but having no true understanding of what they saw. Yet not every warrior had labored under the same misconceptions.

"Banek knew," Maddek said to him. "He'd seen it before."

In Yvenne's mother and in her mother's mother. But the old man shook his head. "I saw the goddess within her. But I was blind to more, because I also saw that she was not the warrior her mother was. And after the ruins, when she failed to run . . . I didn't see how brave she was. I did not see that until today."

Maddek had seen her courage. He'd seen it from the moment her brother had pulled her from the carriage, when she'd boldly lifted her chin and looked straight through him. Like a fool, he'd simply dismissed that courage. But now she was his weakness, and he could not let his weakness leave her vulnerable. "Will you protect her? Zhalen will never let her be. None of that family will."

And Maddek had new reason to kill them all. Yvenne had claimed she was more valuable as a bride than a corpse, but he'd not fully understood what she meant. Even after recognizing how valuable she was as a queen. Her daughters would have legitimate claim to the Syssian throne, yet even that was not all her worth. For her daughters would also carry a goddess's magic within her. And Zhalen and her brothers could not control Yvenne . . . but a young and powerful girl, without the influence of a queen like Yvenne's mother? Perhaps they could. Perhaps the only reason it had not already been done to Yvenne was because of her frailty and weakness. If she'd been as strong as her mother had once been, Zhalen would have raised her as he did his sons. Now if Yvenne had a daughter, Zhalen would take the baby, kill the mother, then mold the child in the same image as he molded his sons. They hungered for power too much to ever relinquish a claim over her.

Little wonder Zhalen meant to marry her to the Tolehi king. Not only would her father have new claim to that throne, but the Tolehi king would not have fought when Zhalen took Yvenne's female issue.

"Until her father and her brothers are dead, she will never be safe," Banek agreed, then added solemnly, "If Nyset's line ends or is corrupted by Zhalen . . . that would be a great loss not only to Syssia but to all who call themselves her allies. So I swear it. My first duty will be to Yvenne."

Though Maddek was relieved by the vow, the ache in his chest didn't vanish. *A great loss.* But not just losing Nyset's line. Losing Yvenne herself would be a loss. And Yvenne's children would be a gain for the Parsatheans. *Maddek's* children.

Kelir's eyes narrowed. "And we can do the same to you."

Maddek grunted. He knew not what the other man meant.

"If you do not run from a threat we cannot defeat, we will make you go."

The warrior looked smug, as if he'd won an argument Maddek hadn't begun. But perhaps it only meant the argument had not been with him. This might have been discussed among the other members of the Dragon. Perhaps as soon as he had begun this quest for vengeance, they had argued about whether to save Maddek from himself if his rage and grief overwhelmed his sense.

He knew for certain his warriors must have questioned his sense when Banek asked, "Why do we not change course now that Zhalen must know our route north? They would not expect us to flee south to the Lave."

"Or to seek help from the Gogean queen," Kelir put in dryly.

As Yvenne had suggested. That his warriors listened to her so well pleased Maddek—though he misliked the thought of hiding in Goge, it had been a sensible alternative, and his warriors had seen that, too. Also sensible was Banek's suggestion to flee past the city of Goge to the river Lave. It was a territory they knew well and where they would find allies among the army who would stand with Maddek and a goddess-touched Syssian queen against her brother and her father. But Yvenne had been intended for Toleh's king, and Maddek knew not if the Tolehi captain who commanded the army now would stand against his uncle. There were Syssian soldiers who would surely be loyal to Yvenne, just as those were upon the ambush road. Yet they were small in number.

And his lesson to Yvenne would not be a false one. Sometimes a warrior's best option was to run. They needed more numbers and they needed a defensible position—and allies whose loyalties were not in conflict.

They would find all in the north. Within the Burning Plains, Yvenne would have an entire Parsathean army to protect her, and no need to rely on her bow.

"Zhalen cannot know our route yet. If it was Aezil who sent that eagle, her brother knows—but he is in Rugus. By the time word reaches Zhalen of our route, we will be halfway across the Boiling Sea. We will see the firebloom before Zhalen's army reaches the outpost. And if he brings soldiers out of Syssia with him, all of Parsathe will soon know it."

Because such movement would be seen and an alarm sent out to all corners of the Burning Plains—but the alarm would not need to travel far, for many of the clans were already gathering near Kilren so they might choose their new Ran.

Kelir nodded. "So we are in a race."

"A race we cannot win if we leave this road," Maddek said. So they might have to face the soldiers from Ephorn—

but it would not be an army that pursued them. The soldiers would have been sent to seek Yvenne and a small party of Parsatheans. They would be mounted for speed and their numbers few, because Syssia and Rugus kept few mounted soldiers in Ephorn. But even if the council added the alliance's guard to their number, Maddek expected no more than a battalion.

"So we'd best pray to Enam for swift winds upon the Boiling Sea," Banek added, though the tension had eased from his face.

"Do not pray too well, or Enam might send a storm. Better to pray to Nemek, to cool a fever and suck out poison," Kelir said, looking toward the camp.

Maddek had no intention of praying to either god. It seemed like wishing for what was not. What he had instead was a bride who soothed Toric's fevered brow.

Though Fassad had taken over that task now. As Maddek and Kelir approached the camp, Yvenne no longer sat beside the poisoned warrior but had settled onto her furs, the green stave she used to strengthen her arm across her lap. She was tying back the flowing sleeves of her robe—as if she intended to practice more before she slept. Her pale gaze caught Maddek's as he collected Banek's furs for himself, and then she looked at him questioningly when he held out his hand to help her up.

"Come," he said. "We will make our beds in a quieter location. And discard that stave."

Even with a goddess's sight and aim, no arrow would fly true from that weapon.

She remained seated, gripping the bow tighter. "But I need to—"

"Use Ardyl's, instead," he told her. Ardyl's bow was too long for Yvenne's arm but was the shortest they had—and if his bride needed the weapon for more than practice, it would be Maddek's arm that pulled the string. The bow would not be too long then. "She prefers her glaive, anyway."

A grunt of agreement came from the warrior's furs.

The happiness that lit Yvenne's face was as bright as it had been that morning, when Maddek had first given her the stave, and almost as bright as after they had felled the whiptail. The constriction within Maddek's chest tightened at the sight, but it was not the same poisonous pain that festered. This he knew not what it was, but the answering heaviness in his loins was clear enough.

Then his arousal was forgotten as she reached for the bow Kelir had fetched from Ardyl's belongings. Yvenne's blood darkened the linen wrappings formerly hidden by her sleeves.

Kelir froze at the sight. Maddek did not. Dropping to a crouch beside her, he snagged her wrist and gently turned it. A stripe of dried blood crossed the inside of her forearm. His gut clenched sickly as he realized what the injury was—and that it was likely not the only one.

"Show to me your other arm."

Her brow furrowed, as if she puzzled over their reaction, and she showed him. The same stripe, but with more blood—from three distinct slashes, Maddek knew, instead of just one. The first from the strike of the bowstring when they'd felled the whiptail. The others after he'd told her to take the bow in her opposite hand and they'd felled three more revenants.

Shame was like anger, hot and thick in his chest and throat. For it had been his strength behind the pull of that string. The first arrow they'd loosed, the one that had killed the whiptail, he could not have undone. But if he'd known the first had hurt her, never would he have continued.

He battled his own tongue until the words of shame would not erupt like rage. Still they were harsh and hot. "Why did you not tell me the bowstring had done this?"

Because it must have hurt. It must have been a streak of agony, as if she'd been slashed by a blade or lashed with a whip.

Still she looked at him in bafflement—and a slight wariness, as if choosing her words very carefully. "It is but the cost of mastery."

Choosing them carefully . . . because she must have first heard them from his mother. Yvenne had changed the words—his mother would have called it the price of practice—but now Maddek recalled the scars he'd seen on her forearm. This was not the first time she'd bled from a bowstring. And clearly his bride thought she must bleed until she mastered the skill.

Perhaps in the tower, that had been true. Here it was not.

He glanced up at Kelir. "She will need an archer's brace."

"It will be ready by morning," the warrior said.

"A guard for her fingers, too," Maddek told him, for the fingertips she used to draw the bowstring were blistered and raw. He'd known they would be tender until calluses formed, for that was the price of practice. But he'd not known when he'd given her the stave how relentlessly she would use it. And he did not believe she would ease up her practice now, simply because of blisters and blood.

"As a queen, you do not cry when you are in pain, and I will not ask you to," Maddek said to her in a low voice. "But if you wish to be a warrior, you *must* tell us when you have been wounded. A warrior has the duty and the honor of tending to a fellow warrior's injuries, just as you have tended to Toric. Do not deny us the honor of tending to you."

Her moonstone gaze searched his features before she looked to the others. Kelir and Fassad gazed back at her with solemn faces. Even Ardyl sat up in her furs now, regarding Yvenne with a grave expression. He could well imagine what they felt now—shame similar to his, if not as deep for being the cause of her injury. For she had saved all their lives that day . . . and then had gone about untended and bleeding for the rest of it.

"I will not deny you," she promised softly, then louder again so they all heard. "I will tell you of it next time."

Maddek would rather there not be a next time, but her response would serve for this night. "I will tend to her," he told the others, though they knew it would be he who did.

She made no protest when he scooped her up, furs and all, only pausing long enough for Kelir to give her Ardyl's bow and a quiver of arrows. No more practicing would Maddek allow before she had protection for her fingers and arm, but if threat came during the night, better she have the weapon within reach.

Carrying her, he started off toward the statue's hand, which lay southwest of the head. With Yvenne cradled in his arms, the poisonous ache in his chest began to ease. Another ache started lower, but that he would ignore until her injuries were seen to.

Then he would ignore it no longer. He had not successfully lured Yvenne outside her walls. But although she was becoming his weakness, her desire made her vulnerable to him in return. So he would steal his way over those walls, again and again, until she finally invited him in.

He felt her gaze upon his face for the first steps. When they passed beyond the statue's ear, she made a soft exclamation of wonder. She had been too focused on Toric to make much note of their surroundings when they'd arrived. So although she'd widened her eyes at the size of the head and foot, she had seen none of the statue that lay behind those enormous ruins because they had blocked her view.

Now the moonlight gleamed over the white marble, rendering it as pale and as bright as her moonstone eyes were in sunlight. Parts of the ancient sculpture had been buried by time, such as an arm mostly covered by an earthen hill. Other parts were completely bare, like the foot Maddek had kept watch upon.

"This, too, was described to me, but I never imagined . . ." She trailed off, her face awestruck.

Maddek hadn't imagined the statue properly, either—and he still could not imagine it. Not truly. Hanan's legendary statue had once stood beside the mighty Ageras, which the god had created with his tears and his seed. But the toe Maddek had climbed was three times his own height, so he could hardly fathom how tall the statue in entirety must have been. The Tower of the Moon in Ephorn could have served as the ankle and calf and still barely reached the knee—yet Maddek didn't think that city's tower would endure through the ages as this statue had. For the sculpture had broken and fallen apart, but the marble hadn't crumbled. It was buried in places, yet no weeds grew from cracks in the stone. The surface hadn't pitted and weathered, though the statue had been already in pieces when Ran Bantik had united the tribes, and the river on whose banks it once stood now flowed farther north, barely visible in the distance. Only the river road they traveled on was as ancient.

"I had not known they built a tower, too," she said now, her voice wondering and her chin tipped back as she gazed up at a shining column of marble. "Is the base uncovered? Can it be entered?"

Maddek grinned. "That is not a tower. That is Hanan's pride."

The god's colossal cock—and perhaps more colossal than Maddek knew, for the lower part of the shaft was buried, too. Yet what jutted above the ground was nearly as long as the statue's leg must have been.

After a moment of stunned silence, a giggle shook through her slight form. "Even in ruins, he is upright."

Because Hanan was always erect. "At least we need not fear that it would soften and crush us."

"Surely he will never wilt," she agreed, and eyed the tip speculatively. "Do you think it ever erupts?"

Maddek could not speak again until they had reached the hand, and he had to stop laughing long enough to climb the fingers while carrying her. There she drew another awestruck breath, as she saw what Maddek had spotted from his perch atop the foot. A pool filled the statue's palm, the glow of the marble through the clear water seeming as if the moon itself were trapped within its depths.

"We must remove our shoes," she whispered reverently.

As if they entered a temple—and Maddek could not disagree. He set his bride on her feet and she placed her bow and quiver aside before bending at the waist, reaching for the ribbons of her sandals.

Reaching with her blistered fingers.

Maddek dumped the furs and knelt before her, catching her wrists. "I will tend to you, Yvenne."

Her eyes met his. The slightest hesitation passed over her features before she nodded and straightened again. Allowing him this warrior's honor.

Though it was not only honor, but pleasure, too. Her feet were small and soft and filthy from the hard travel that she'd withstood better than ever he would have believed at the beginning of this journey. Her silk robes hung to her ankles, the hem as dirty as her feet. He had but a glimpse of the linens wrapping her legs from ankles to thighs as he unlaced her sandals. Mindful of her shattered knee, he bade her to step out, offering support when she had to shift her weight onto that leg. As soon as her feet were bared, he began untying the leather strips that secured his own boots, watching as she drifted to the water's edge and gingerly poked her toes in.

Her pleasured sigh hardened his cock to stone, but it was the smile she turned toward him that bled away the last of the festering poison in his chest. "It is warm!"

"Then we will make good use of it tonight." As they would the furs he unrolled, layering them into a soft bed over hard marble. "When the others discover this pool is here, every moment tomorrow that they are not on watch will be spent bathing."

Her smile widened for a brief moment before furrowing into confusion. "We will be here tomorrow?"

"Toric cannot ride yet." Maddek joined her, fingers working at the fastening of his belt. "We could make a bedsling of his furs for his mare to pull, as we often do with injured warriors. But if there are revenants or soldiers behind us and the horses must run—"

"Better instead to wait where we have an advantage of position."

Nodding, he tossed aside his belt and linens and stepped naked into the water. Her bold gaze ran from his shoulders to thighs, though he read the query in the arch of her eyebrows.

"I cannot tend to your wounds without first washing away the revenants' blood." Which he had wiped away as best he could after the battle at the stream but still was dried in the creases of his knuckles, beneath his fingernails, and in faint streaks across his skin. Did that foul blood infect her wounds, she might soon be muttering in feverish delirium next to Toric.

Backing into deeper waters, he watched her eyes measure the hot steel length of his erection, saw the hungry pinch of her teeth into her plump bottom lip, and thought that he might lure her, after all.

After he tended to her wounds.

Though the pool was warm as a bath, Maddek didn't linger. Instead he turned and swam to the deepest point, where he submerged himself, scrubbing at his hair and skin.

Yvenne's gaze was alight with wonder when he broke the surface again. "I have never seen swimming before. It was as if you were a bird, but underwater. How did you not sink?"

He grinned, swiping the water from his dripping face. "It is also the same as a bird, but I flap arms and legs instead of wings."

"Is that how a fish swims, too?"

"They have no arms and legs. More akin to . . . a snake." For he knew she'd watched a constrictor undulating through the grass, as fascinated then as she was now. "Have you never seen a fish?"

She shook her head. "Though I've heard they are tasty."

A laugh rumbled through him. Almost every animal she encountered, her foremost interest was whether they were good eating. "I think not as tasty as roasted dally bird or millipede jelly, but you will soon judge for yourself. We'll likely eat fish for every meal when we sail the Boiling Sea."

"Did you often eat it while upon the river Lave?"

"More often than I liked," he admitted. But upon the Boiling Sea, Maddek thought he would take his pleasure not in the food itself, but in watching Yvenne enjoy hers. It would not be such a torment when she groaned and closed her eyes in bliss, because her moon night would be past and he could ease his hunger when hers was sated.

As he would this night. His erection had subsided while he bathed, but his shaft was still a heavy, hot weight as he walked back to the shallows. Standing ankle-deep at the edge of the pool, Yvenne watched him come, her gaze slipping downward as he rose out of the water and more of his body was revealed. When the waterline dropped below his loins, there her focus remained until he was almost upon her.

Rarely did she hide from Maddek's eyes, and this time was no different. She tilted her head back. Though he could not read her expression, this near to her Maddek saw more evidence of their journey in the shadows below her eyes. The two braids that ran back from her temples had begun to unravel and fray. Her skin had darkened in these past days, but he was not certain how much of it was dust and how much from the sun.

"Let me tend to your right arm," he said quietly.

Her tongue moistened her bottom lip in a hesitant gesture before she lifted her hand between them. She had tied her loose sleeves back behind her elbow, yet her forearm was still wrapped in her bloodstained linens.

Maddek gently took her wrist and untied the ribbon that secured the wrappings. A quiver moved through her still form. He glanced at her face but her eyes were on his fingers slowly unwinding the linen, revealing soft skin yet untouched by the sun. Her breath moved quick and shallow through her parted lips.

He had become more acquainted with her breaths and their meanings. These were not of pain. Yet they were not of arousal, either. Instead they seemed nervous and uncertain.

"If the blood has dried to the linen, the wound might

open again when I remove it," he said to her softly. "But I will be slow and gentle."

A shrug lifted her shoulders. "Better to be quick and over with."

That response suggested that any coming pain concerned her not at all. Yet her tension seemed greater with every unwinding, and another reason for her nervousness occurred to him. Maddek had known she preferred to cover her skin as many southerners did. In the bed at the inn, she'd kept her front concealed with her cloak even as he'd rutted on her from behind. In all this time, he'd seen her feet and her face and her hands . . . and nothing else.

Yet he could hardly think her modest or shy. Her mind was not. Her words were not. Her gaze was not.

But perhaps in this one aspect, she was. "Have you ever bared your arm to anyone before?"

She trembled and this time did not meet his eyes. A blush darkened her cheeks. "My mother has seen me," was her reply before she added under a breath, "when I was a babe."

And since then only Maddek had laid eyes upon her skin. Only he had seen the delicate tracery of veins at her inner wrist, the faint blue streaming up the length of her forearm to feed her wounds. The bloodied fabric stuck to the first slash, and as he peeled it away from the scab her breath changed, sucked in more deeply through flared nostrils and hissing out through her teeth. Despite her suggestion, Maddek did not go quickly, because that would tear open the wound more. Silent he remained until each of the slashes had been uncovered and her breathing lost its pained hiss.

The wounds bled only a little, small drops welling where the scabs had torn, but no redness or swelling surrounded them.

Satisfied that they would heal again quickly, Maddek blotted the drops with her linens. "Leave these uncovered so they will dry. In the morning, before you wrap your arm, use the salve beneath the linens so the weave will not stick to the wound."

She nodded, and then her blush deepened as he reached beneath her silk sleeve, where another tie secured the linens at her shoulder. Yet she didn't protest as he stripped the wrappings from her arm and dropped them into the water.

He looked down at her, but this time she did not tilt her chin up to meet his eyes. Her cheeks blazed as she stood before him with her head bowed, naked from wrist to elbow.

Yet he was naked from head to foot. Never had she averted her eyes from him or any of the other Parsatheans, and his warriors shared not a modest bone among them.

He could make no sense of it, but he trusted that Yvenne could make sense of anything. Untying the ribbon at her left wrist, he asked, "Why do southerners wrap themselves up even during the summer?"

Her gaze darted up to his face, her brow furrowed. "I have not—I . . ." Abruptly she blinked and her eyes unfocused as if she searched her memory for an answer. Slowly her full lips curved and she met his gaze boldly again. "It is so Parsathean raiders will not be tempted by our beauty and steal us away."

Maddek grunted. She teased him, yet he also thought many southerners likely believed it. "That is what you've heard?"

"Only through my mother." Her attention dropped to her arm. Not avoiding his gaze now, but because he had reached the wound. Her breathing tightened again as he began to peel the linen away from the scab. "And it was not what my mother said to me, but what she saw a weaver say to her son."

As they lived lives outside their tower. "Warning children to cover themselves or they would be stolen away to the Burning Plains?"

A faint hiss and nod was her reply.

"In Goge and Toleh," he told her quietly, "they warn their children that if they do not cover themselves, the Farians will rape and eat them."

She made no response, yet he felt her solemn gaze now upon his face.

He peeled away the last of the linen. This slash was deeper, the torn edges of the scab bleeding more. Bunching the linens, he held them against the wound and waited for the new blood to stop welling.

"It is a fool's warning." He met her eyes. "The Farians will rape and eat their children whether they are covered or not."

"And the Parsatheans?"

"They would rape and eat us, too," he said, and her lips twitched with amusement, but only until she seemed to remember that the Farians *had* done so, and that Maddek knew too many Parsatheans—and southerners—savaged by the Farians during his time upon the Lave. But he had not meant to turn the mood sour. It was her laughter he'd sought. "Our most celebrated legend is of Ran Bantik stealing a king's daughter from a tower after seeing her beauty. So perhaps there is some truth in the reason for the coverings. But southerners are fools if they believe it would have made any difference."

"It makes little sense," she agreed softly. "If bare skin were the temptation, the raiders need never leave the Burning Plains."

So Maddek had once thought, too. Yet now bare skin from wrist to elbow was changing that view. "That is why they sought treasure, instead."

Treasure—or merely excitement and challenge, and seeking treasure brought those, too.

"Yet it was not only treasure they raided," she countered. "And Ran Bantik was not the only one who stole a wife. Many other men and women have been taken in Parsathean raids."

"So they were," he agreed, and checked the wound beneath the bunched linens. Still bleeding, but barely.

"Which means something else must have tempted those raiders. Because Parsatheans do not rape or keep slaves— or so my mother told me."

"She told you true." Though persuasion was its own challenge and excitement. And this time when he reached beneath her silk sleeve to unfasten the linens at her shoulder, he heard no nervousness in her breath, and the color in her cheeks no longer seemed of embarrassment. "Perhaps the very coverings the southerners believed protected them is what tempted those raiders, instead."

She arched a skeptical brow. "So instead of stealing silk robes and linen wrappings, they stole the person?"

Maddek would have liked to steal her clothing away, yet he suspected the arousal that flushed her skin now would retreat into nervousness again.

"No," he told her, and his own need roughened his voice, yet his fingers were light as they skimmed over the silk covering her shoulder. Her bare skin shivered beneath his fingertips when he reached the side of her neck and traced a slow path to the hollow of her throat. "I imagine those raiders could make no sense of these coverings. They would wonder what purpose could they have, except to hide treasures beneath? So they would look for an answer."

"That makes no sense, either. As soon as they looked, they must have known there was nothing beneath that is different from what Parsatheans have."

"Then why conceal it?" His fingers slid downward and teased a circle around the tip of her right breast, where her stiffened nipple was pebbled beneath the fine silk. Her breath stopped, her widened gaze locked on his, her lips parted. "Perhaps this is a ruby."

A laugh shook her again, then cut off on a gasp when he swept his thumb across that aroused peak.

"It feels as hard as a ruby," Maddek told her gruffly. And he was steel.

"Ardyl wears covering," she pointed out, each word emerging on a soft panting breath. "Does she also conceal rubies?"

"That band stops her tits from bouncing as she rides or runs." With both hands now, Maddek cupped her small breasts through the silk. "You do not need such support, so you must be covering treasures."

"You all wear belts and red linens. Do you also hide

treasures beneath? Treasures *other* than a pearl." Her blush returned fiercely yet she did not retreat, her voice bold and her eyes sparkling with challenge. "The women have reason to cover, then, but men do not."

"That is not why female warriors cover. There is no need to conceal a pearl with clothing, for a woman's body already conceals it." In his mind swelled the memory of Yvenne, slick and hot beneath his touch, and the sweetness of her honey that he'd licked from her fingers. "I told you that foolish men could not find it."

He could see by the stuttering of her breath that she recalled precisely when he'd said so, yet his bride would not be thwarted. "Then what reason do warriors cover? Why do male warriors conceal their pride?"

He concealed nothing. She had only to glance down to see the force of his need and the strength of his pride. Whereas he'd had to learn to read her very breath and the depth of her blushes.

"Our coverings are not to hide anything. Instead they serve a useful purpose," Maddek said before adding wryly, "As you will discover if ever you ride without them."

"You wear them even when you aren't on a horse."

"Because we are always prepared to ride."

She appeared outraged by his answer—because she had no counter to it, he realized. Her face was flushed with arousal but also enjoyment, her soft tits a slight weight in his hands that rose and fell with every heaving breath.

His bride had taken pleasure in arguing with him. As had he. Though Maddek suspected that in this sparring match, he only prevailed because he'd kept her well distracted. No doubt had this conversation taken place at a campfire instead of with his hands teasing her, she'd have easily destroyed him.

But Maddek had not lived this long by allowing an opponent time to recover. "Then we shall see who is right," he told her, and tugged back the left side of her robe, revealing her small breast and pointed nipple.

For the barest moment her shyness returned—then disappeared with another outraged gasp when Maddek declared, "I am victorious."

"Victorious? You have just proved yourself wrong!"

"It is hard and reddened, and gleams as a polished gem does," he observed. "So I have found a ruby."

"It does not gleam!"

Only because he'd kept his need leashed. No more.

Gripping her narrow waist, he hefted her up until the tip of her breast was against his lips. She gave a startled cry, abruptly silenced with the back of her hand covering her open mouth. With widened eyes, she stared down at him.

Fierce hunger raged through his blood. Her scent filled him, the sharpness of her anise soap and the smoke of the fire she'd sat beside while tending to Toric. Holding that astonished gaze, he swirled his tongue around her hardened nipple before sucking the taut peak into the heat of his mouth.

Her fingers curled into her palm, her breath coming in smothered gasps. Each one stoked his arousal hotter. Harder he drew upon the engorged bud, watching her eyelashes flutter closed. Her head tipped back and the expression that pinched her face Maddek might have mistaken for pain if she hadn't muffled a moan against her hand. But never would Yvenne make a sound if she was hurt. Only in pleasure.

Soon he would hear her moans and cries and screams.

His cock was molten stone when his mouth released her. Gravel roughened his voice. "Does it gleam now?"

His bride seemed dazed as her eyes opened and she looked down at her nipple, reddened and glistening. No answer she gave but her ragged heaving breaths.

"You are enflamed." Slowly Maddek lowered her, holding her gaze as she steadied upon her feet. Voice raw with hunger, he said, "Lie upon the furs and I will tend to your cunt."

"It is not—I am not—" Each panting attempt at denial ended before she could finish what they both knew for a lie. Swallowing hard, she moistened her lips and tried again. "I can ease my own need."

"With blistered fingers?" He caught her chin between thumb and forefinger when she would have turned her blushing face away. "Allow me to tend to you, Yvenne."

Longing flared through her expression before her eyes closed, as if in pain. "It is not . . . necessary. But you should ease your need upon me—and fill my sheath with your seed."

A harsh laugh broke from him. Maddek wanted nothing more. Yet he could not.

"You ask me to court Vela's wrath?"

"I do not." Steadily her eyes met his again. "Instead I suggest the method of my foremothers, because my moon night is five days away, but I might be fertile now. If I am, a full turn will pass before I ripen again. And if ever there was a place to seek Hanan's blessing, surely this is it."

In the shadow of Hanan's cock and in the palm of his hand. She was not wrong. Yet Maddek still knew not what she meant.

His thumb slipped over her bottom lip. Despite the steadiness of her gaze, that small caress made her soft flesh quiver. Yvenne was not as unaffected as she would have him believe. "What did your foremothers do?"

"Nyset's daughter, Queen Byil, wanted children but wanted no bedpartner. Many years later, Queen Virym refused to take anyone to bed but her wife. Yet both queens had sons and daughters." Now she faltered slightly. "Because they . . . filled their sheaths with Syssian seed."

Wryly Maddek pointed out, "I have no Syssian seed."

Though he was forming some idea of how it might be done. Before a moon night, the goddess Vela only forbade the penetration of a cock into forward and backward passages. But she did not forbid the pleasure of hands and mouths.

"It was only Syssian seed because the queens invited every Syssian male to come and spend into a vessel until it was filled to the brim. That is why the queens of my line are also called the Daughters of Syssia. Many, many men answered those calls, and all their seed was intermixed in the vessel—so they are all my forefathers. And I know not how Byil filled her sheath, but Virym's wife used . . ." She gestured toward Hanan's marble cock. "Though I suspect theirs was not so big."

"I suspect not," he agreed with a quick and hearty grin. Not even the legendary warrior-queens of Syssia could wield a sword of that size.

In response to his amusement, her lips curved beneath his thumb. "For each, seasons of trying passed before the seed took root. Here, it is I who will be the vessel"—her sudden, quick inhalation sounded like a breath drawn in agony before she continued—"but if Hanan blesses us, the sooner I will be with child, the sooner we can claim my throne . . . and the sooner you will kill my father and avenge your parents."

Her father would be dead long before any child was born. Maddek would kill Zhalen upon the Burning Plains when he came for Yvenne. And if her father cowered in fear behind Syssian walls, Maddek would ride south and kill him after Yvenne was safely among the Parsatheans.

Yet that response stuck in his throat, trapped by shame. *Avenge your parents*, she'd said, offering a reminder that Maddek shouldn't have needed to hear. Because his parents—his queen and king—were dead. And from the moment Maddek had met Yvenne, he'd thought of little else but spilling his seed within her. Yet always those thoughts had been in pursuit of avenging their murders. On this day, however, not a thought he'd given to his parents. Instead he'd only thought of killing Zhalen so that Yvenne would be safe. Instead he'd only thought of his need and the poisonous ache in his chest and the walls she'd built between them.

Yet Yvenne had not forgotten their purpose. Because she was a queen. And she taught him a much-needed lesson now, without any effort.

A king's cock should not rule his heart or his head. Just as Yvenne did not allow her cunt to rule hers.

Maddek would have liked it if she did, for then she would be easier to lure. No lure was needed now, though.

The invitation was given. She had told him to ease his need upon her.

So Maddek would.

"Lie upon the furs," said he in soft command.

Her breath trembled across his thumb, her eyes searching his before she nodded into his hand and turned toward the bed. Her easy compliance should have pleased him, not lodged like a sharp stone in his chest. It mattered not that she would lie with him now in cold royal purpose instead of the hot desire he'd wanted.

The queen's purpose was cold. But Yvenne was not. And he would make her burn before this night was through. He would demand her surrender.

And when she did, he would tear apart the walls that stood between them.

In anticipation he stroked his length, watching her ease down onto her right knee before stretching out on the furs—on her stomach, as if she expected him to rut upon her from behind again. But that was not how he would ease his need this time.

"On your back, Yvenne."

The skirt of her blue robe twisted around her legs when she rolled over, cheeks flushed and her dark curls in a tangle beneath her head. Reaching down, she wrestled with the constricting silk, and then her movements froze when her curious gaze locked onto the slow pumping of his hand.

Huskily she asked, "Should I take you into my mouth?"

Always hungry, his bride. But if she sucked him, Maddek could not trust himself to pull away. "That is not the part of you I should fill with my seed." Amusement curved her lips before nervousness returned upon his next command. "Part your thighs and give me a clear path to your sheath."

She'd looked so boldly and eagerly upon his erection, yet turned her head in pained embarrassment now. Her legs she barely spread, widening her ankles to the width of her slender hips. With clumsy hands she tugged at her breechcloth. When she tossed the intimate covering away and jerked open the sides of her skirt to fall outside her linen-wrapped legs, Maddek knew her cunt was bare, yet nothing could he see in the shadowed valley between her thighs.

It mattered not. All that she'd exposed was the smooth swaths of skin at the tops of her thighs and a glimpse of dark curls, yet never had his cock been so hard.

Blushing face averted, she lay quivering. Sudden tenderness infiltrated his hot arousal. Unlike the affection he'd felt toward her at the inn, however, Maddek made no attempt to shove it away. He'd been foolishly blind to her courage before. Now he could not mistake her bravery. Knowing that she would have to lay herself bare to him, still Yvenne had chosen this route. As a queen, she was all unyielding purpose. But the woman was sweetly vulnerable.

And that vulnerability offered yet another opening in her walls for Maddek to slip through.

Closer he came. Her breasts rose and fell in rapid rhythm, nipples stiffened beneath blue silk. Her fingers fisted in the furs beside her hips, as if she knew not what to do with her hands—or as if to hold herself in place when he crouched at her trembling feet.

"In this way." He pitched his voice low to soothe her nerves but could not prevent raw arousal from roughening the words. Her body shook again as he gripped her thighs just above her knees, the heat of her skin a furnace through the linen wrappings. "With room enough for me to lie between them."

Her eyelids squeezed tightly closed but she gave no resistance when his hands urged her slender legs farther apart, not merely wider but higher. Maddek listened to her breaths for any indication that the bending of her knee pained her. Only his bride's shyness did he hear in those shuddering pants—and only her arousal did he see in the glistening wetness revealed before him. With his bride bared to his gaze, brutal lust surged through his turgid flesh, the urge to cover her body with his. Against the rutting length of his cock, she would be slick and hot.

With iron restraint, Maddek only knelt between her splayed thighs. Gruffly he told her, "A mere glimpse of your honeyed cunt draws my seed."

Eyes flying open, she glanced down. His engorged shaft stood as erect as Hanan's, a drop of seed decorating the broad crown.

With his forefinger, he collected the drop. "When I spend, we will fill your sheath in this way."

Not at all did she breathe now, as Maddek cupped her sultry mound and slipped his finger between her silken folds. He found her entrance, the opening small and delicate, and his gaze strayed not from her flushed face and widening eyes as he pressed inward.

So tight she was. He should have used his smallest finger for this first breaching. Though wet, her inner muscles resisted when Maddek stretched her with the thickness of his second knuckle. She gave no sound of pain but gasped and shifted away from his penetration, her thighs tensing.

Instantly he stopped. "Do you hurt?"

Lips pressed in a flat line, she shook her head.

But unused to the intrusion. And discomfited, for although she was enflamed, embarrassment still gripped her body and her sheath hadn't yet softened.

There was sweet remedy for that. Urging her legs wider, Maddek lowered his body to the furs, wedging his hands beneath her bare bottom to fill his palms with her soft cheeks. Her color still high, Yvenne rose onto her elbows to look down at him.

Her brow furrowed as if she tried to fathom why her thighs cradled his shoulders rather than his hips. Breathlessly she asked, "What do you do?"

"What you told me to do."

With barely any effort, he lifted her closer to his mouth, his breath sifting through her moistened curls. Realization flared bright in her wide eyes.

"I told you *not* to tend to my need—"

"And to ease my own upon you." Anticipation thickened

his voice as her heady feminine scent filled his next inhalation. "That is what I intend. Unless you will deny me now?"

If not for the fiery yearning he saw battle with her shyness and uncertainty, Maddek would have denied himself. If he'd seen fear, there could be no pleasure for either of them. Yet she wanted as he did.

Confusion joined the war of emotions upon her face. "How can this ease yours?"

"Because my hunger does not only reside in my cock." Trapped between his abdomen and the furs, his shaft ached and throbbed, yet the primitive urge to rut upon her was a mere spark against the raging need to make her come against his tongue. "And ever since you let me lick the honey from your fingers, I have been starved for another taste of your sweet cunt."

Her soft lips parted. Her breathing deepened, desire and longing emerging as victor in the battle upon her face—though now joined by curiosity and disbelief.

"Is it sweet?" Her hand slid over her silk-covered belly, fingertips gliding over her gleaming arousal before she brought them to her mouth.

Savage need clenched hard upon Maddek's body. His cock spilled precious drops of seed into the furs that he should have spilled into her sheath, yet nothing could have moved him now as he watched Yvenne lick her fingers.

"It has not much flavor at all." Her frown pleated her eyebrows. "And is nothing like honey."

"It is to me." Each word was an iron link in a chain drawn taut by agonizing restraint. "So let me eat my fill and ease this need."

Finally she nodded her consent, sucking a fingertip between her pursed lips, as if trying once more to taste the appeal.

Unleashed, Maddek buried his face in her cunt, groaning at the first long lick he took. Sweetness was knowing that the honey coating his tongue came of her need for him—though as he swiped a broad trail up the length of her cleft, Yvenne seemed to watch him in bafflement rather

than pleasure. She tensed and trembled but only slightly, as
if affected more by the newness than the sensation.

Another long, slow lick over the lips of her cunt, then
another. Her tension began to ease, her gaze locked upon
his mouth. Her hectic flush returned, her arousal deepening
again, yet it seemed more in response to watching Maddek
taste her than what he did to her flesh.

Until he stroked his tongue over her clit.

A shudder ripped through her body, followed by a
sharply indrawn breath that was abruptly silenced by the
hand she used to cover her mouth. This time the slow drag
of his tongue the length of her slit drew forth a muffled
moan and the restless shifting of her hips, noises and movements that became more urgent as he continued his leisurely feast, teasing her clitoris at the end of each lick
before returning to her entrance for another deep taste of
the sweet nectar he drew from her well.

Soon both hands she used to muffle her cries. The brace
of her elbows collapsed and she fell back onto the furs. Her
ass rocked in the cradle of his hands, her hips twisting frantically.

Tightening his grip, Maddek halted her writhing and
sucked hard upon her clit. Her thighs snapped closed
around his head and her back arched, her slim body racked
by a violent quake.

Even with her thighs clamped over his ears and her
mouth covered by her hands, he heard what his bride
screamed as she came. His name. Almost never did she say
it. Only *warrior*.

On her moon night, Maddek would pin her hands down
so that he heard her every gasp and moan and scream. So
that she cried aloud his name with every hard thrust of his
cock.

Now it was her legs that he pinned to the furs when her
orgasm released her from its devastating grip. Her thighs he
pressed apart again, holding her open while she lay boneless
and quivering and panting. So wet she was, her cunt flooded
with her hot release, and his hunger not yet sated. She

flinched now at the brush of his tongue against her clit, so he backed away from it, kissing her slick inner thighs and licking between her sultry lips. This time when he eased a blunt finger inside her, her narrow passage accepted him more readily. The tight clasp of her inner walls stiffened his erection to excruciating hardness as he imagined her cunt clutching his throbbing length in that scorching embrace.

Five nights he must wait for that. Yet he need not wait for more of her sweetness. After a few tentative rocks of her hips, as if she tested the thickness and length of his finger within her, Yvenne's restless movements renewed. Shallowly she fucked herself against his hand, her muffled moans sharpened by a pleading note until he bent his head to her cunt again.

All teasing was done. More even than her honey, he craved her helpless surrender, her eager response. With a choked scream against her fist, she gave both to him, until the inner convulsions of her sheath snapped the chain of his restraint.

Red lust swam through his vision as Maddek surged over her, cock arrowing to her cunt. The broad crown slicked through her passion-drenched cleft and lodged against her virgin entrance, and all his strength it took then to remain rigidly still, though his instincts roared for him to plunge deep, then roared louder when Yvenne's ragged whisper filled the air between them.

His name again. Unmuffled, for she buried her fingers in his hair and arched her hips to receive his seed. At that naked invitation, uncontrollable pressure boiled at the base of his shaft and erupted with a single rough stroke of his hand.

Grunting, he came in thick pulses, a brutal release that stole his strength. He was utterly drained when he collapsed onto his side next to her—and utterly satisfied that she was in the same state, her skin gleaming with sweat, her body languid and legs still splayed, as if she had not the power to cover herself now.

Better that way, for they were not done. And by her own suggestion, she was in his bed. Now he would keep her there.

"You will share my furs again each night." He slipped his hand between her thighs, where his release pooled at her entrance. A soft, shuddering sigh left her as he pushed his longest finger into her sheath, carrying the seed deeper. "For I intend to fill you with my spend whenever we are not upon the road."

She gave no argument. Only a solemn nod, her moonstone gaze locked on his. Seeing through him. *Into* him. The eyes that had seen a warrior, not a king. Yet this night he had been Maddek.

Withdrawing his hand, tenderly he gathered her close, pillowed her head on his shoulder. Faint anise perfume filled his senses as he buried his face in her hair.

"Sleep now," he said. "For my cock will rise with the sun, and then I will ease my need upon you again."

"It will not rise again until dawn? Perhaps Hanan has forsaken us, then." Unexpectedly her fingers curled around his softened shaft, which instantly began to swell beneath her touch. Her voice was full of satisfaction when she said, "Or perhaps not."

He grinned even as fierce possession ripped through his heart. What a treasure she was, a queen and a woman full of purpose and heat. And this night he had made her surrender.

"If that god blesses us, the child you carry will not be Syssia's daughter," Maddek told her, voice roughened by his own purpose. "It will be *mine*."

As Yvenne was.

She lifted heavy-lidded eyes to meet his. Like her arrows, that moonstone gaze seemed to pierce straight into Maddek and fell him with a single look.

"Ours," she replied softly, and that he would accept for now, though it seemed not enough. Though it seemed there was more from her that he needed to have, because his chest had been a poisonous open wound at the thought of *not* having her.

Yet that ache was gone now. Because she lay so close. Because soon she would be safe. And then his vengeance would be had.

All was as it should be.

CHAPTER 23

YVENNE

Though finding passage on a boat that could also stable six Parsathean horses would be difficult, none of the warriors were willing to leave their mounts behind. The horses Maddek had purchased, however, were sold in a village that lay a half day's ride from Drahm.

They started out that morning with four fewer mounts and with Yvenne once again sharing a saddle with Maddek. They rode Toric's horse while that young warrior—still weakened but no longer feverish—shared Ardyl's mount.

Anticipation hummed through Yvenne's veins. For not only would they soon reach the Boiling Sea, this was also the morning of her moon night, and her nerves were alive with excitement. Such pleasure had Maddek shown her these past nights, that the day ahead seemed more endless than the combined length of all of those that preceded it.

Despite the long night that faced her and the little rest she'd had of late, Yvenne had no thought of finding sleep. Yet lulled by the warmth of the morning sun, by the broad support of Maddek's chest, and by the smooth rocking of the horse's gait, sleep found her.

"Yvenne. Look ahead."

The low rumble of Maddek's voice stirred her from slumber. They were still mounted, though he'd brought the horse to a halt. The sun was brighter now, hotter and almost directly overhead—and so she had to blink several times before realizing what he'd awakened her to see.

They were at the top of a ridge, with the road continuing down an incline ahead. But Yvenne saw nothing of the land the road passed through, only where it ended, and the shining turquoise that stretched out to the horizon.

Never had she imagined anything as wondrous as the sea. She knew not what to call the emotion that clutched at her throat, but it filled her chest as well.

Maddek said softly, "It is a fine sight, is it not?"

Her throat tight, Yvenne's nod was her only response. When Maddek had described the sea to her before, he'd described it well—like the sky, but upon the ground—yet still the sheer expanse of it left her reeling and breathless. No matter how far north or south or west she looked, there was only the water. And he'd not spoken of the color, which she had seen before in dyed silks but never had those silks held such depth and warmth. And he'd not mentioned how the sun sparkled over the water as if diamonds were scattered across the surface. And he'd not said that the waves rolled and crashed and frothed like lace.

He'd not told her that Mother Temra dressed herself so beautifully.

He did not tell her so now, either, and Yvenne felt his attention shift behind them, to where unfamiliar voices were in conversation with Kelir. Once beyond the ruins of Hanan's statue, they'd more frequently passed villages and settlements—and encountered more travelers, many of whom had recently come from Drahm. Every one they met, the warriors asked for news of Syssian soldiers on the northern road. Thus far, no one had heard any such rumors.

Entranced by the sight ahead, she didn't turn to see who

spoke to Kelir now—but she did listen when the warrior rode up beside Maddek to report.

"A salt merchant," Kelir said. "He has heard and seen nothing of soldiers . . . and he has spent the past three days trading near the northern gate."

That pulled Yvenne's gaze from the sea. Any soldiers who rode into Drahm on the northern road would have to enter the city through that gate—and such an event would be almost as remarkable as a group of Parsatheans. So what the merchant knew was not just rumor. "Then they have not reached the city?"

If soldiers were coming at all. But Yvenne felt certain they must be—as did the Parsatheans.

"Not before this morning, at least." The warrior looked to Maddek. "He also gave me the name of a bargeship captain who can leave under quiet sail. Everyone will see us pass through the city, but if the soldiers know not which boat we are upon, they will waste time searching—either on the docks or on the sea."

"Then prepare to ride," said Maddek.

Because the other warriors were not mounted, Yvenne saw. When Maddek had stopped to allow her a view of the sea and for Kelir to speak with the merchant, they'd taken the opportunity for a short rest.

She returned her gaze to the water while they readied their horses, leaning back into Maddek's hard chest.

The arm around her waist tightened. "Is it as you thought?"

"No," said she. "It is far more."

"More than I thought, too," he admitted. "A few times I have seen the northern shore that is the boundary of the Burning Plains. But the water there is not so jewel-like."

"That must be why the Parsatheans never raided the sea, or stole an ocean—nearer your home, the water is not a gleaming turquoise gem. So you knew not what Temra concealed beneath her robes."

His deep laugh rumbled against her back. "Mother Temra conceals nothing. She flaunts her beauties, knowing they are too massive for any thief to carry back home. So only a fool would try to steal this gem—and likely drown in the attempt." His big hand slipped down over Yvenne's belly, to where her thighs were spread open over the saddle. "And I am well satisfied by the small rubies and pearl that my raids have uncovered, though the wetness here also threatens to drown me."

His long fingers lightly caressed her silk-covered mound, and fire curled through Yvenne at that subtle touch. Not so subtle was his opposite hand fisting in her hair, angling her head and his hot mouth open at the side of her neck, sucking and licking at her skin, as if in sheer hunger for the taste of her.

Only a moment it lasted, yet she was breathless and enflamed when he drew her head back against his shoulder and flattened his hand over her stomach again.

Because his warriors approached, she realized—and Maddek never eased his need upon her where they could see. Not during the long day at Hanan's statue, not in the long nights that followed. There could be no mistaking what he did to her, emerging naked from beneath their furs with his skin dripping with sweat and with his lips reddened and wet. Yet he always allowed her to remain concealed, even from himself, with only her nipples and cunt ever exposed to his mouth and hands.

Now nipples and cunt were still covered, yet fiercely aching when Kelir rode up alongside them. The warrior seemed not to notice that Yvenne was flushed and panting, or that behind her Maddek's chest fell on harsh, heavy breaths, and her body hid the steel rise of her would-be husband's erection.

Well satisfied, he was—and so was Yvenne. When Maddek eased his need upon her, he always saw to her pleasure, too. And she was glad of it, though it meant abandoning hope of disentangling her emotions and protecting her heart.

But that had been the price paid. When she'd told him to fill her with his seed, Yvenne had known the danger. Maddek had said that he would never give his heart to her, though everything he did demanded that she give him hers.

Or perhaps he made no demands. Perhaps she simply couldn't help herself.

Yet she could help her people. And two routes to vengeance lay ahead. Maddek preferred one and she preferred the other. Her father would die either way, but only one route would not leave her stranded alone on the Burning Plains, without strength enough to take her throne. She'd made the choice that might weigh the scales in her favor—and in Syssia's favor. So she could not regret sharing Maddek's furs again, though her heart was well and truly entangled now, torn between sweetness and pain.

But Maddek was not torn. He was not entangled.

Well satisfied he truly seemed, and not only in their bed. And why would he not be? Her father would soon be within his reach, and Yvenne was in the role Maddek intended for her: a vessel for his seed and a tool for his vengeance.

If tender he sometimes seemed, and attentive to her needs . . . she dared not mistake that for affection. She dared not hope it meant that he was becoming entangled, too. He was a warrior who made use of what he had, and he also attended to the horses he rode and the weapons he used. But never did he kiss her, and his vow still closed his ears to her truth, and he trusted not a word she spoke.

It seemed none of her pleasures could ever simply be pleasures; always her heart was torn. A ragged and bloodied ache accompanied her every joy.

Still. It *was* pleasure. More than she could have imagined. And Maddek was a fine companion . . . especially when he was well satisfied. Both her mother and his mother had described to her a man of deep passions and quick laughter, and more of that Maddek she'd seen in these past days. Not the warrior ruled by anger and grief.

So perhaps Yvenne would never have his heart. But if this was to be her marriage and her future, she would be well satisfied, too.

Kelir gestured ahead. "There is Drahm."

Again Yvenne tore her gaze from the sea. Plains and marshes were two days behind them, and they rode upon a ridge overlooking the Ageras. That broad river no longer meandered to the Boiling Sea but flowed swiftly through a wide, deep channel carved out of stone. She only had to follow that silver path to find Drahm straddling the mouth of the Ageras. Even from this distance, clearly visible was the massive bridge that spanned the river.

A bridge that legend claimed was built by the gods—or perhaps by the same sculptors who'd built Hanan's statue.

"Should we tell them Farians can swim and paddle?" Kelir said, his voice amused.

Maddek gave a short laugh in response.

Yvenne didn't understand. "Why?"

"Never have I seen a city with half a wall," Kelir replied and Yvenne saw what he meant—Drahm's wall only reached the edge of the Boiling Sea, and the city itself was a half circle in shape. "We have spent ten years fighting Farians who have crossed a river by swimming and on rafts. If that wall is meant to protect Drahm from savages, they'd best build one along the water, too."

"It is much like the constricting clothes they use to protect them from Farians," Maddek said. "They know the wall cannot truly protect them. But it still offers some false comfort against their fear."

"*False* comfort?" She agreed that a robe offered no protection against savages, but walls were not made of thin silk. "Why is it false?"

"Because walls are no true defense. They can always be defeated."

Many times these past days, they had debated such subjects—and the Dragon often joined in, usually giving support to Yvenne. Always it had been entertaining. Sometimes arousing, for sparring with Maddek fired her blood. Yet now the smugness she detected in his reply was like steel scraping over the edge of her teeth.

"You wear armor," she snapped over her shoulder. "What are walls but armor for a city?"

Kelir laughed. "She makes a good point."

Maddek grunted his disagreement. "Armor constrains and confines. So Parsatheans only wear armor when under close threat or riding into battle."

"And Drahm is always under threat," said Yvenne. "As is all of Goge."

"Not close threat. Even upon the Lave, we did not always wear armor in camp."

"You do not even wear full armor now." None of the Parsatheans did. Only guards for their shoulders and arms. Not the silver claws or the breastplate worn against opponents they believed were a true threat—because they believed they would not encounter any upon the road. So far, they had been right. Only the whiptail had been a greater threat than they'd anticipated, and against that monster a breastplate would have made no difference. "What if you underestimate your opponent? What if the soldiers who pursue us are more skilled than you expect?"

"Then we will surely not underestimate them again." At Maddek's dry response, the others laughed in agreement. Yvenne could not.

"Perhaps one arrogant warrior can risk his life that way, but would you risk a city? It is not so easy to remove walls as it is a breastplate, and Drahm is not filled with experienced warriors who can easily defend themselves against a surprise attack and survive. Perhaps walls are not perfect armor, but they can slow an enemy. And do not tell me Parsatheans have no use for walls," she added hotly, "for the stone walls of a granary are what saved Ardyl's life when the Destroyer slaughtered her clan."

From behind them, Ardyl said cheerfully, "That is truth!"

Her would-be husband paid that agreement no heed. "And when the Destroyer's army was gone, should she have forever remained in that granary for fear of his return? What life would that be?" he asked, but gave no time to answer. "You are speechless at the sight of this sea. Yet the people living in that city will rarely glimpse the beauty that surrounds them because they've imprisoned themselves within those stone walls. They are all trapped inside a tower, Yvenne, but by their own choice."

On a sharp breath, she stiffened against him. Was that how he saw Syssia and her people? Imprisoned within a city, living lives devoid of beauty?

But she had no response to offer. For under her father's rule, it was not completely an untruth.

At her silence, Maddek gathered her hair into his hand again, but not to expose her neck and taste her skin. Instead he tilted her head back, as if to give himself a better angle to look down at her expression, and she felt his gaze upon the side of her face.

She could not return his look. Not when he might see how his words had speared her through.

It was Kelir who answered him, gazing thoughtfully at the city ahead. "That is not the same as your bride's tower, for the people in Drahm can freely move through the gates. More like . . . they always wear armor, in constant vigilance and expectation of a threat. Yet only when that threat approaches do they fully armor themselves and close the gates."

That was more like Syssia, too. Throat aching, Yvenne nodded.

His eyes still upon her, Maddek said gruffly, "Just as we guard our hearts when we face a worthy opponent."

Kelir grunted an agreement.

Maddek released her hair and pulled her back closer against his chest, as if willing her rigid spine to soften again.

She could not, though he'd agreed with Kelir's assessment. Some nameless hurt still twisted within her chest. But she knew not what it was and could only say tightly, "You say walls are false comfort and fear. But you know what it is to feel helpless. You have seen warriors injured and know there is nothing you can do to stop Rani from coming for them. Yet still you try to halt the bleeding, do you not?"

Voice suddenly grave, he said, "Many times I have done so."

"Because you *must* do something. You must *try*. Perhaps walls will not stop Farians from coming or stop a Destroyer, but at least it is something that can be done. And so they feel not as helpless—which is the most terrible of all feelings."

Kelir nodded solemnly. "That it is."

"It truly is. There is *nothing* I hate more." Her chest hitched, and the rest burst from her in a rush. "And *never* have I felt constricted in my robes and linens."

"No?" Maddek prompted quietly against her hair. "Are they comfortable, then?"

"They are. But even if they were not, it would please me to wear them, because they are made by Syssians. I am proud to wear them. Nowhere else are silks so fine and colors so bright—and I decorate myself in the accomplishments of my people. Just as Parsatheans decorate themselves with their pride, wearing drepa claws and red linens. Even when you are not in battle, you declare to the world that you are warriors who are always ready to ride."

"That is truth," he agreed softly. "It is much the same."

Mollified, she finally eased back against him. "And my robes are not intended as armor against savages or raiders. But that does not mean they serve no use or give no protection. On this journey, I've been stung and bitten by fewer insects than every one of you—and have spent less time scratching my ass."

This time laughter shook through his reply. "That is also truth."

CHAPTER 24

YVENNE

I f she weren't to be the queen of Syssia, Yvenne would have liked to be the queen of Drahm. So much there was to see. So much there was to smell. So much there was to eat.

Just beyond the gate, mongers selling their wares from stalls and carts filled a market square. The mouthwatering scent of cooking meats set her stomach to rumbling and Maddek to laughing before he tossed a coin to a fishmonger.

All the food was on skewers, it seemed, which made eating atop a horse so very easy—and every bite was seasoned with salt, as if prepared for a midwinter feast instead of sold in the street. As they continued on toward the bridge, Yvenne happily devoured a skewer of bloodfish, followed by a skewer of octopus. Maddek had quickly finished his own skewer of fatty boar, so she shared with him a charred tentacle, reaching back over her shoulder and feeding him some of the tastiest, crispiest bits.

The air was humid and thick with the scent of the sea and the perfume of the sunfruit trees that shaded the cobblestone avenue. Everywhere, there were Gogeans—walking and riding and driving carts and leading animals—and she watched them all, yet there was also only Maddek, taking each bite she offered. Licking away the salt. Sucking lightly at her fingertips.

So hard and hot he was behind her. How desperately she wanted him inside her.

Almost dizzy she felt, acutely aware of all that surrounded her yet hardly recalling any of the journey from the gate to the river. Then the avenue opened to the bridge, and sheer amazement sat Yvenne up straight in the saddle as she stared ahead, skewer forgotten in her hand.

The Destroyer had dropped a similar bridge upon a village. Yet the bridge was so wide, if any of the villages they'd seen had been dropped upon it, still there would have been ample room to pass by on either side. And it was so long that *every* village they'd passed could have been lined up, walled edge to walled edge, and still not reached across to the northern side.

Drahm had not built villages upon the bridge. Instead another city seemed to live upon it. The bustling market square near the southern gate was but a mewling infant to the market they passed through now, a labyrinth divided into districts of common wares. Nearest were the livestock pens—and after the stench reached Yvenne, her tentacle seemed not so appealing.

Everywhere before, the Parsatheans had been given wide berth by other travelers. Now there was no berth to give as they made their way through the maze of stalls and carts. Singly they rode through the narrow alleys, often with people walking so close they pressed up against the horse's side and bumped into Yvenne's legs. Once she and Maddek were brought to a complete halt, their mount crowded against a nearby kergen pen as a wagon creaked by in the opposite direction, the wooden bed filled with a leathery egg bigger than the ox that hauled it. Steadily they made their way to the west edge of the bridge—to escape the odor that the sea breeze carried in, Yvenne assumed, until they reached an alley where a few dozen horses waited.

Yvenne threw a disbelieving glance over her shoulder. "You sold four mounts just this morning!"

"I only want to look," Maddek said, his dark gaze already assessing the animals.

So too were the other warriors, and only look they did—for a very long time, especially when they came across a yearling that appeared to Yvenne no different than her short-backed gelding Maddek had been eager to be rid of. Yet both Kelir and Danoh dismounted for closer examination while the horse preened and pranced under their attention. When they eventually continued on through the market, it was hard to judge who looked more sorry—the Parsatheans or the horsemonger.

Until she heard Danoh's curse. By the time Yvenne looked back, the warrior had already turned around and was riding into the crowd. It was not long before she reappeared, leading the yearling behind her mount.

Though that morning the warriors had all made much of how difficult it would be to find a bargeship to carry the horses, not a word did the other Parsatheans say now. Instead they looked on with approval for Danoh and admiration for the horse.

It proved to be the first of many purchases, though the remainder were supplies for the voyage north. Jute sacks bulging with dimpled sunfruit, baskets filled with nuts and dried berries, stacks of salted meats wrapped in broadleaves. The ship would have basic provisions, Maddek told her, but they hoped to sail in haste. So they could not spend days procuring more but must buy what they needed now.

Those needs included a bow and quiver of arrows better suited to the length of Yvenne's arm. When Maddek bought those for her, so pleased was Yvenne that when they finally rode out of the market and had a sudden view of the river widening into the sea, she did not even remark upon how very wrong he'd been to claim that everyone behind Drahm's walls denied themselves of beauty.

She did, however, send a pointed glance to Kelir, who laughed and did a fine job of poking at Maddek in her stead.

Nearing the center of the bridge, the alleys became avenues again and the crowds thinned, the buildings not so densely packed together. Until abruptly there were no avenues at all, but a square that stretched the broad expanse of the bridge from east to west—and at its heart stood a temple sculpted from moonstone.

Yvenne stared at it with widened eyes, the clutch of emotion upon her throat so hard and fierce that she only managed a whisper. "Is that Vela's temple?"

"It looks to be," Maddek replied evenly—as if he were not at all affected by the sight of the pearlescent temple carved from a single colossal block. The ancient builders had sculpted the stone walls to such thinness that any light shone through it, whether sun or moon or merely candles lit within, so that the stone always seemed to glow.

Toric's voice sounded as awed as Yvenne's. "I have only seen newer temples made of marble in Ephorn and Goge. How does this one still stand?"

"Because Anumith and his warlords never came to this city," said Kelir.

And the Destroyer had razed every temple except for those belonging to the sun god, Enam—the god whom he'd claimed had escaped the sun's fiery prison and now lived within him, lending the Destroyer all of his great powers.

"My father never rebuilt any of Vela's temples in Syssia," Yvenne said softly. "After my mother claimed her throne, she began to. Then she was poisoned and my father forbade the building of any temples, for he said they might enrage the Destroyer and draw his wrath down upon Syssia again. So only the temple to Enam is left."

"There are no temples at all on the Burning Plains," Maddek said. "Before or after the Destroyer."

"Not even in Parsa?" That great city had once formed the heart of Parsathe.

"Not even in Parsa." It was Banek who answered—the

only warrior old enough to have seen that city before it, too, had been razed. "There is only Temra's Altar."

Which Yvenne recalled from their song of Ran Bantik, for the thief-king had stood upon it while imploring the tribes to unite against the Scourge. "Is her altar near the glass fields?"

In the territory where the demon had been defeated. The tribe that included Kelir and Toric's clan—and the clan of Maddek's father—resided there.

"It is," Maddek confirmed with amusement deepening his voice.

Why was that so humorous? Yvenne glanced away from the temple's shining dome, but her attention was arrested by a man standing upon a platform a few paces away from the temple's base.

A naked man.

Nor was he the only one. Entranced by Vela's temple, Yvenne hadn't taken much notice of the people milling about the square. Yet now she saw that several dozen men and women wore only the sheerest of robes or nothing at all—and many seemed to be on display. Other men and women approached them, as if the nudes were vendors in a stall . . . or perhaps they were the wares. For some who approached simply examined their bare forms, much in the way the Parsatheans had examined the yearling horse.

"What is happening?" Her chest had tightened. "Will those people be sold?"

Surely not. *Surely* not. Vela had forbidden such practices, just as she'd forbidden rape. Yvenne was not so naive as to believe no one defied that goddess's laws. Yet *never* would she have thought anyone might defy those laws at the door of the goddess's own temple.

"Not sold," Maddek told her. "Hired. They provide service to those with no partner but who wish to have their moon night."

"Oh." Yvenne breathed more easily. "They are Vela's consorts."

"They are."

Yet there were not nearly as many consorts as there were others—mostly young men and women, Yvenne realized now, and most a few years younger than she. Between all of them seemed an air of laughter and celebration. Perhaps some of it nerves . . . but mostly anticipation.

"All of these people have their moon night tonight?"

As she would. An event of such momentous importance— as a step toward claiming her throne, as a step toward defeating her father. Yet she did not take this step alone. Perhaps the reasons weren't the same, but all across this city—across all the western realms—women and men would shed a drop of blood in offering to Vela.

The realization filled her with wondrous emotion. Never had she been part of something in this way. Oh, if only this were Syssia. She could have shared in this celebration with her own people.

Yet this was wondrous, too. Never had she looked upon a crowd and felt what they all felt. Because when Maddek touched her, her throne and her vengeance were far from her head. Instead she was filled with excitement, with desire, with anticipation.

As they were.

"Likely not all here are virgins," Maddek said, and his voice had roughened in the way that abraded her skin in the most delicious manner. As if he was also thinking of the night ahead with desire and anticipation. "But many are."

"And they make their offering to Vela *here*?"

"Some will. Nearer sunset, there is usually music and dancing, and not all make it to a bed. But many are here to visit the temple and seek a blessing from Vela's priestesses."

Seeking such a blessing wasn't necessary. And they had little time to waste.

Yet her heart yearned for one. "Should I seek one, too?"

"Do you wish to?"

"I do."

"Then we will join the line outside the temple."

Never had Yvenne stood in a queue before. She thought waiting in line with seven Parsatheans was a new experi-

ence for the Gogeans, too. Maddek's guard drew many
looks—as did Fassad's wolves. Rarely did the other virgins
seem to register Yvenne's presence in the Parsatheans' tall
and muscular midst, but the vendors who took advantage of
the captive audience outside the temple missed no opportunity to hawk their wares. Soon she had another skewered
fish, and was licking salty juices from her fingers when a
cockmonger making her way down the line spotted her.

Quickly the gray-haired woman glanced at each of the
warriors, pausing speculatively on Toric. She looked back
to Yvenne the barest moment before averting her gaze.
"You must be the virgin?"

Eyes wide, Yvenne nodded. The woman's pushcart held
an array of phalluses and potion pots and a multitude of
leather straps whose purpose she could not imagine.

"Do you wish to have a night filled with pleasure?"

"I *do*," Yvenne said eagerly. By the way all of the Parsatheans seemed to push in closer, not only Yvenne was
interested in what pleasures the woman had to offer.

"Which is your partner?"

With her skewer, Yvenne gestured to Maddek.

The cockmonger pursed her thin lips, giving Yvenne's
would-be husband a doubtful glance. She waved her hand
above the display of phalluses. "And which of these is similar to his size?"

Maddek grunted. "It matters not. She needs no cock but
mine."

Yvenne gave him an irritated glance. No other lover
would she take, but that did not mean she would never have
to see to her own pleasure. "That one is," she said, pointing
to a midsized ivory shaft. Standing beside her, Kelir
choked, and she heard muffled snorts from the other warriors behind her.

Eyes narrowing, Maddek said softly, "I will have to give
you a closer look."

Why? She was not mistaken. "How do I make it swell?"
she asked the cockmonger.

"These do not swell."

Oh. Yvenne eyed the selection again. "None of these are his full size."

"As I feared. You are very small to his very large." Sympathy warmed the woman's voice and her gaze touched Yvenne's before averting again. She selected a small clay jar from her cart and held it nestled in her palm. "Not always is such a fit easy, especially if you are not well prepared. But I have a potion that oils your sheath—and it has a pleasant fragrance and flavor."

Maddek grunted again. "She will be well prepared."

The cockmonger gave him a knowing look. "What of the back passage?"

Dryly he said, "Even with oil, she will never be prepared for that."

That was likely truth. He'd one time introduced his smallest finger to that part of her while feasting from her cunt. After her initial embarrassment and discomfort had passed, it had been quite pleasurable—and it had been quite enough.

"It prepares the back passage?" With keen interest, Kelir came closer. "What is the perfume?"

"There is a variety. This is the rose."

"We'd best purchase three or four pots, if we are to spend a full turn aboard a bargeship with little else to do," Ardyl said as the cockmonger opened the lid for Kelir to sniff. "And there might be a sailor who captures our eye. Do you have half-moon milk and sleeping draught?"

The woman nodded, her face alight with anticipation as she switched her attentions from Yvenne to the Parsatheans more likely to buy her wares. Then her face was simply alight, as if the moon shone directly upon her instead of the sun, and a sudden hush fell around the square.

Heart leaping into her throat, Yvenne glanced to the temple—which glowed white, as if brightly lit from within. The presence that she always felt at the back of her mind had vanished, yet she sensed no absence. Instead it was as if the presence had simply moved outside her mind and swallowed the temple ahead.

Chest swollen with emotion, she stepped in that direction.

Her breath jolted from her lungs when Maddek abruptly snagged his arm around her waist, dragging her protectively against his side. His sword was drawn, his jaw hard, his gaze not moving from the shining temple.

"It is only Vela," she told him, but he spoke at the same moment, giving orders to the others—who were also armed. As if that might make any difference.

"Prepare to ride," he commanded tightly, and began backing with Yvenne toward the horses.

"It is only Vela," she said again, but it was lost as Kelir called out a warning.

"Maddek!" Disbelief filled the warrior's alert. "Look to our mounts."

"And the wolves," Fassad said, his voice not alarmed but awed.

For they were all in a similar stance—down on left fore-knee, heads lowered. As if bowing. Yvenne had never seen the Parsathean mounts balk at anything the warriors asked of them, yet when Danoh urged one horse to its feet, the animal refused to move.

The glow through the moonstone walls faded. In a wave expanding outward from the temple's entrance, the crowd erupted in disbelieving cries and threw themselves to the ground, some on knees and others prostrating. The cock-monger joined them, gasping and pressing her forehead to the cobblestones. Within moments, no one in front of Yvenne stood upright, giving her a view of the veiled figure in black robes who had emerged from the temple.

One of Vela's priestesses—yet it was not the priestess who gazed back in their direction. Her brown skin glowed as if made of moonstone, shining so brightly that her face was clearly visible through the black veil. The orbs of her eyes seemed filled with silver moonlight.

Ardyl's back and shoulders blocked her view again as the warriors formed a king's guard around Maddek.

Kelir shot over his shoulder, "What say you, Banek? Is it demon? A wraith?"

This time Yvenne would be heard. "It—is—*Vela*."

Sharply she tugged on Maddek's beard for each word. He tore his gaze from the figure ahead to meet hers, brows lowered, eyes dark. Sudden tense silence fell over the warriors.

"The goddess? You are certain?" Kelir asked, disbelieving.

"I am."

"Then we had best follow the horses' lead," Maddek said grimly.

As one—and with reluctant grunts—the warriors sank onto their left knees, laying weapons at their sides. Steadying herself with a hand on Maddek's shoulder, Yvenne began to lower herself but was dragged down to sit on his thickly muscled thigh.

"Bowed head is enough. If it is Vela, she will know you mean no disrespect," Maddek growled softly when Yvenne pushed against him. "And if she demands that you kneel on your shattered joint, she will earn that disrespect."

Yvenne would bear the pain. Yet she would not argue with him now. The goddess took a step in their direction.

The next moment Vela stood in front of Kelir. Startled by the quick movement, the warrior flinched and went utterly still. Maddek's muscles became steel. As did Ardyl's, Yvenne saw, as each of the warriors battled their instinctive response to defend against attack.

"And so I face the head of the Dragon." The goddess's voice held the ring of cold steel against stone. "But you do not bow that head to me?"

Kneeling before her, the big warrior trembled, yet there was no wavering in his reply. "A Dragon with bowed head cannot see threat coming, and would fail in his duty to protect his Ran."

"You believe I am a danger to him?"

"I know not your intention. That is why I keep eyes up and watch."

"And if I threatened your Ran, you would raise your axe against me?"

"I would, my lady, as is my duty." His scarred face was bloodbare as he spoke that truth. "Forgive me."

"Forgive what? Your loyalty and your courage serve you well, Kelir."

"Thank you, merciful lady."

"So, too, the Dragon's claw is loyal and courageous—and has blood that burns like fire." On silent steps, she glided past Ardyl, her glowing fingers drifting lightly over the warrior's braided hair. "Ardyl, the last of your clan, whose memory you carry upon your face. Always you have feared that letting yourself fully belong to those who raised you and loved you would mean your own family would vanish from memory. But even as you belong to those you love, so they belong to you—and through the family you build, your clan will be renewed."

A choked sob came from that warrior, who only nodded beneath the goddess's touch. Vela moved on, into the circle of the Dragon guard's protection, toward Fassad.

"And the Dragon's fangs." Though the veil Yvenne saw the curve of pale lips and shining teeth, the sickle moon of a smile. Down on her heels she sank, the billowing of her robes bringing icy wind to Yvenne's face, yet there was warmth in the goddess's voice as she scratched Steel's ears, then Bone's ruff. "I have always favored wolves."

"Yes, my lady," the warrior replied, his voice thick. "I have, too."

"As they favor you, Fassad," she said. "Had they been mistreated, I would feed you to them."

"Had I mistreated them, I would cut off chunks of my own flesh for you to give them."

Smiling, she touched his cheek and rose again. The seat of Maddek's thigh shifted as he pivoted, keeping the goddess in view as she glided around behind them, where Danoh knelt with bowed head.

"And here is the Dragon's tail, which holds deadly sting." With a finger beneath the warrior's chin, Vela raised Danoh's gaze to meet hers. "Born of cursed rape, as were my children, Justice and Law. Even from pain, sometimes beauty emerges. Your rage is beauty. Your courage is beauty.

Your compassion is beauty. Perhaps your mother will never have heart to see it, but all who know you do."

A queen did not cry where there was someone to see her tears. Yet Yvenne's vision blurred then, and the goddess was but a shining star as she continued on. Swiping her eyes, Yvenne watched her stop in front of a silently weeping Banek.

"Banek, my beloved, who serves as the Dragon's golden scales, as armor and shield," she said quietly. "You have never worn the red cloak or quested for me, but so faithful you have been—and you have received so little for it. What would you ask of me?"

The old warrior's reply was thick. "Only to never again see anyone suffer at the Destroyer's hands."

Amusement swept through Vela's cold voice like a summer wind. "You ask me to blind you?"

A rusty laugh shook from him. "No, my lady. Is it too much?"

"Only too much to accomplish alone. But I will do all that I can to grant that request, warrior. I vow to you."

"You do me great honor, my lady."

"No." Sadness filled the denial. "It is you who has honored me these many years. Serve well as the Dragon's armor, Faithful One—and be shield to his bride."

"That is my vow to you."

Her hand cupped his tearstained cheek for a moment before she turned away. Shaking and trembling, Toric watched her approach, his face lifted in helpless wonder.

She stopped before him. "My brother's poison resides within you."

Vela's brother—Stranik, the serpent god. Yvenne had not truly needed confirmation that her own brother had called upon Stranik to give him power. Yet now that confirmation made her throat close and her chest burn, for it meant Aezil had used blood sacrifice to gain those foul magics.

"I am still healing, my lady," he said, in a voice uncertain whether he should be sorry for not being well or to boast that he was recovering.

"Your injury is," she agreed, then lowered her veiled lips to his. Yvenne could not see if there was a kiss through the silk, only heard Vela's murmur. "You are the Dragon's wings. Tell me, how far will they take you?"

"Never far from my duty, my lady," was his passionate reply. "I swear it."

"Do not make vows you cannot keep, young warrior." She sighed against his lips, and Toric's breath frosted against hers. "You will fly so far that you will no longer be yourself when you return."

Confusion furrowed his brow. "Who will I be?"

"Still the Dragon's wings, perhaps. Or perhaps also the head and the claws, the teeth and sting, and the scales."

"And the burning heart?"

Vela laughed. "Do you wish to have it all? Or will you let another be the heart?"

"What is best?"

"If I tell you the answer now," she said in a voice still ringing with her laughter, "then you would learn nothing from your quest."

"My mother did not stick my hand in a fire to teach me it would burn. Instead she told me it was hot, and I learned well enough."

"That is how a child learns, young Toric." All amusement bled from her voice. "Do you want to be a child or a man?"

His face flamed red. "A man."

"Then be at ease. Already you learn quickly. And you are not the only one taking lessons." Straightening, she faced Maddek and Yvenne. "So grudgingly kneels the warrior who is not yet a king."

Maddek's hardened jaw unclenched. "My bride will forge me into one."

"A king is not forged as a sword is, from fire and steel. That is a warrior's way of seeing."

"I am a warrior still," Maddek admitted gruffly.

"So you are . . . and also more. A warrior who is already the burning heart of a Dragon." Her gaze shifted to Yvenne.

"And you are a queen who does not yet sit on a throne—except for the throne this warrior provides for you now, made of his own flesh and blood and bone."

Upon Maddek's thigh. "Would you have me kneel, my lady?"

She held out her hand. "I would have you rise, daughter."

Her fingers were icy and hard as stone when Yvenne took them, but the goddess did not help Yvenne to her feet. Instead Maddek slipped his arm beneath her knees and stood, his forearm braced against her back as he held her in a seat made of his embrace. Still serving as her throne of his flesh and blood—and rising with her, though the goddess had not instructed him to.

For the first time since the goddess had appeared, fear slipped into Yvenne's veins. Vela was merciful and generous but could be vain and cruel—and she had little patience for the arrogance of men.

Yet his arrogance had also lifted Yvenne, so she knew not how the goddess would respond to it.

That sickle moon smile curved Vela's lips again, but there was a sharper edge to it. "This is the one you've chosen, daughter?"

"He is."

"You are brave or foolish."

"I prefer brave."

"As you will need to be." Her gaze held Yvenne's so easily. "I have a task for you."

Unease clutched her chest. "A quest?"

Which she would accept, because those who quested for Vela received great reward—such as power to defeat sorcerers or strength enough to free a people. Yet those quests also took them on a journey from all they knew.

"Nothing so easy as a quest," the goddess said, and Yvenne's chest clutched ever tighter. Nothing so *easy*? Everyone who quested for Vela faced pain and doubt at the edge of their enduring. "And I would not see you so lonely again."

"She would not be alone." Maddek's grip had tightened on her. "What is the task?"

Such coldness filled Vela's gaze that Yvenne's heart seemed as ice. "Do not speak to me unbidden, warrior. As you would take the tongue of my chosen for speaking what you do not wish to hear, so I would take yours—and I know not how you will be Ran and speak for all of your people if I do."

His jaw became as stone but his burning eyes asked the same question.

Vela turned an exasperated gaze on Yvenne. "If you wished to lie beneath a man and be used as a vessel, you could have married your father's choice."

Toleh's selfish lech of a king. Who would never have helped her secure her throne or have intention of killing her father.

"This is not the same." As Vela must know, for through Yvenne's eyes the goddess had seen all that had been done and spoken between her and Maddek. So now the goddess only poked at her would-be husband. Perhaps testing him. Yvenne was unsure of the purpose. "And he also sees to my pleasure."

"Because his warrior's heart perceives you as a walled city to be conquered. When you open to him, when you writhe in his arms, he believes you are defeated."

All of this Yvenne already suspected, by the way he'd been so content of late. Ever since the night by Hanan's pool. Secure in his role and purpose, and comfortable in it—and the warrior's role was the one he best knew.

Yet Maddek responded as if these were secret battle plans revealed. Tighter and tighter he held her.

"Your mother advised you against him. Will you not seek one of her chosen suitors, instead? You would not have to journey far. One resides in this city."

Maddek said not a word, but such hot denial was in his face and in the growl rumbling from his chest, not a word was needed.

"Though I value my mother's wisdom and counsel, I have chosen Maddek," Yvenne told the goddess, though her response was for the warrior who held her. "I have filled my sheath with his seed."

"So I have seen," said Vela wryly. "Many times."

And so she knew Yvenne's purpose. "Have we been blessed by Hanan?"

"Not as yet," the goddess replied, and pain stabbed through Yvenne's chest.

She had hoped. Oh, she had hoped that in the palm of the god's hand, Maddek's seed would take root. That by the time they reached the Burning Plains, they might be certain she was with child.

"You shed no tears, though I know your heart aches," Vela said softly, cupping Yvenne's cheeks in cold iron hands. "But understand, my daughter—if you choose him, you will know much greater suffering than this."

Maddek stiffened against Yvenne.

Dread seized Yvenne's heart. *Suffering.* "How?"

"At your father's hand."

A fierce volcanic sound erupted from Maddek. As if denial exploded within him and stopped at his lips yet still burst through his eyes and his skin and the tightness of his grip. With bared teeth, he took a step back from the goddess, as if distance would be an escape from the fate Vela had seen.

Yet Yvenne knew there would be no escape. "And if I choose another suitor?"

Her shining gaze on Maddek's face, Vela said, "You will not know so much pain."

"What of my people?" Her own pain mattered less than theirs.

"What of them?"

"Will they be freed? Will my father die? Will choosing another suitor make both outcomes more likely?" Yvenne was not a goddess, but she already knew the answer to that. She had already told Maddek the answer to it.

"It is not certain that *this* warrior will prevail."

"But is it more likely?"

"Even my eyes cannot see everything," Vela said with a narrowing gaze.

Twice the goddess had evaded the answer of what was more likely. Which was answer enough.

"Then I will choose the suffering," Yvenne said with quiet resolve, but Maddek shook his head. Pain slipped through her heart again. "You think I should choose another suitor?"

Savagery flared anew in his eyes. On a snarl, he unclenched his jaw as if to speak. Yvenne clapped her hand over his opening mouth.

"Vela will not be merciful, warrior," she hissed. "And I am fond of your tongue."

His gaze shot to hers, his features a dark mask of fury and frustration.

"I still hear him well enough," the goddess said. "He vows to protect you."

He would try, Yvenne knew, and that knowing lifted her heart. Because when facing inevitability, trying was the most one might hope for. "I have allied myself with you so that we might kill my father and take my throne," she told him. "Perhaps then you did not trust my word, but with Vela as my witness, I vow that I will never look to another ally and deny your vengeance. Do you hear me, Maddek of Parsathe, son of Ran Marek, rider of the Burning Plains? Do you trust that vow?"

Though his jaw clenched again so hard that she knew not how his teeth didn't shatter, he gave a short nod.

She looked to Vela. "What task would you ask of me?"

"To destroy the Destroyer," said she.

Yvenne's breath stopped. In disbelief she glanced at Maddek to see his response. All fury had left his face. He stared at Vela, and his expression was one Yvenne recognized. It was the same one he'd worn at the stream with dozens of revenants approaching. She'd seen no fear in him then as he'd commanded his warriors to form a defense. Only fierce determination.

The same fierce determination that filled her, too. "So he *is* returning?"

"He is already returned," Vela said. "His army has landed on the sunset shore."

With a full continent between that shore and the western realms. So there was time to prepare. So little time. But more than none. "Five years it took for his army to march that distance."

"So it will again."

Only five years. Her breaths came fast and shallow. "How do I destroy him? With my arrow?"

"You may try that. In the endless ages that I have lived, I have seen gods felled by less. But the task I require of you is in forming a strong alliance to stand against him."

Blindly Yvenne found Maddek's hand and curled her fingers around his. "We will. Already we hope to purge my father's and brother's corruption, and to strengthen—"

"Not the alliance of Parsathe and the five realms, daughter. That will serve as the heart, but it is a heart already formed. You are imagining a puddle; I task you with an ocean."

The bottom dropped out of her stomach. "You ask me to unite the western realms?"

Vela nodded. "That might be strength enough to stand against him."

Might. Yvenne could hardly catch her breath. "With five years to prepare."

"With no years to prepare. The Destroyer and his army are five years distant. But already his poison is here. It has never truly left. Instead that poison festers and waits—foul seeds planted a generation past so that he can reap the harvest on his return. And it is poison designed to weaken any attempt to stand against him."

A poison that festers and waits . . . and weakens an alliance. Sour bile shot up Yvenne's throat. "My father?"

Nothing did Vela say. Perhaps for the same reason she'd given Toric no easy answer. Some must be discovered, not told.

But Yvenne thought this journey had already given them part of the answer. "And my father has in turn corrupted my brother. Now Aezil courts Stranik's dark power—"

"No," said Vela. "You think of the wrong brother."

Which one? All but the youngest, Tyzen, had been influenced by her father. But Lazen was dead. So was Cezan. If not Aezil, that only left one other, Bazir—who had a clever tongue but was also selfish and indolent. Yvenne could imagine of her brother many evil things. But all of those cruelties would bring him pleasure, and courting a god's power required sacrifice and pain. Never could she imagine Bazir stabbing out his own eye to gain sight beyond what was seen or castrating himself to gain immortality beyond a bloodline of children.

Perhaps Bazir was even more clever than she'd believed, though, hiding a dark purpose behind his indolent mask. And now he sat on the alliance council. What better place to weaken them all?

"Not Bazir," Vela said, as if hearing Yvenne's thoughts. "The wrong brother is not yours, but mine. It was Enam's power that raised those revenants, and whose poison I sense within the young warrior."

Horror gripped her throat. "Aezil courts the sun god? As the Destroyer did?"

No answer again did Vela give. Yet again their journey gave answer enough.

Aezil had raised a whiptail. They had known such a feat required more power than a priest of Stranik's Fang had. Yet they'd assumed her brother's blessed bloodline had strengthened him.

Yet he courted Enam. And meant to assist the Destroyer.

"I accept your task," Yvenne said, her voice as raw as her heart. She'd already meant to see her father and brother dead. She'd known they were monsters among men. She'd not known *this*.

Turning his hand, Maddek interlaced his fingers with hers. A gentle squeeze gave a silent promise of support. But of course he would support her in this. Of all people, the Parsatheans knew that to defeat a monster, they must stand together.

Vela glanced at their linked hands, then crooked a finger at Maddek. "Bend your head nearer to mine, warrior, so you may better hear what I have to tell you."

Something the goddess wanted no one else to hear. Vela

leaned near enough that, as she spoke, every breath passing through her veil was a cold breeze over Yvenne's cheeks. But not a whisper of sound came to her ears.

Maddek began to shake his head, as if in denial. Then he became absolutely still, body rigid with tension. A few more words from Vela wound that tension so tight that his great form quaked with the force of it, sinews and tendons taut as steel, clenched muscles of his jaw twitching.

He lifted his head as Vela drew back, and Yvenne knew not what she saw in his face then. Fury seemed not hot enough. Determination seemed not iron enough. Denial seemed not arrogant enough.

Only clear was his rejection of everything the goddess had said.

Again Yvenne slapped her palm over his mouth. Yet this time she was not so certain he meant to speak. The way his volcanic stare burned as he looked at Vela, she thought the goddess must be hearing every word he did not utter.

"You had best continue your lessons, then," said Vela now, with light amusement. In a sweep of billowing black robes and frigid air, the goddess bent to retrieve a small clay pot from the ground—the jar the cockmonger had dropped when she'd prostrated herself. Opening the lid, Vela stirred the milky oil with her shining finger, then breathed in the scent before closing it again.

To Maddek, she held out the jar. "And you will likely have need of this."

His mouth flattened and a dull flush climbed his cheeks. Sick tension gripped Yvenne's heart, for even she recognized the insult the goddess gave.

But Maddek was not a fool. And only a fool would refuse a goddess's gift.

He did not let go of Yvenne, but using the arm he braced beneath her legs, he opened the hand that had been gripping her thigh.

Vela placed the jar in his palm. As soon as his fingers curled around it, she looked to Yvenne. "You came to me for a blessing before your moon night, and with these words, a blessing I give to you: you are stronger than you know," she said. "Whatever strength you imagine you have, it is as you imagined the sea. You'll find it is so much more than you believed."

Yvenne's throat closed. "Thank you, my lady," she whispered.

The goddess smiled, and her cold stone fingers drifted down Yvenne's cheek. With her voice of icy steel, Vela commanded, "Now look to the northern gate."

The glow vanished from the priestess's skin. Black veil concealed her face. Warm palm cupped Yvenne's cheek. Vela's silent presence again filled the back of her mind.

Immediately she looked to the north. They were not near enough to the edge of the bridge. From the center of the square, the wide Ageras river was in view, but not the city walls or gates.

"To the horses," Maddek commanded.

As one, the warriors rose—as did their mounts. With swift strides, Maddek crossed the distance and lifted Yvenne into the saddle before springing up behind her. He turned the horse north, carefully weaving through the bodies still kneeling and prostrate. The clatter of hooves across cobblestones joined the rising voices of the astonished crowd. Some ran after the Parsatheans, as if also following Vela's instruction to look north—or desperate to see what the goddess wanted them to look for.

Yet Yvenne knew. Even before they reached the edge of the bridge, where the Ageras sparkled below, and peered toward the northern shore. She knew what came.

"It is too far," muttered Kelir, shading his eyes from Enam's glaring sun. "I see the wall but not the gate. Danoh?"

Who had the keenest vision of all the warriors. "I see the gate," she said in hard frustration. "But only the shape."

Not the people who passed through it? "I see a merchant in yellow robes leading a wagon into the city." But not the soldiers Yvenne thought to see, unless they'd already come through the gate and were out of sight behind a building.

She turned her gaze beyond the gates and her heart froze. "Soldiers approach on the northern road."

"How many?" Maddek's voice was grim and unsurprised.

They rode four abreast. She counted the rows. "Two full companies flying the alliance council banner, followed by eight horsemen wearing the seal of the Rugusian royal guard."

Maddek's body stiffened behind her.

"Only two hundred mounted soldiers to retrieve a stolen bride?" Kelir scoffed. "The council must have thought Maddek was alone when he captured you."

His joking lifted Yvenne's heart only slightly. "My brother Bazir rides at their head."

Sudden astonishment arched Kelir's brows but it was Danoh who exclaimed, "You can see *that*?"

They could not? She looked in hope for Tyzen, too, but if her younger brother was among their number, he was not in her view. She returned her gaze to Bazir—and the man who rode beside him.

The shape of his beard marked him as hailing from Toleh. "Does the council minister Gareth have blue eyes and a scar upon his left cheek, and a scorpion sigil on an opal ring?"

"He does," Maddek said.

"Then the Tolehi minister also rides with them." Which might act as a curb on her brother, but only until Bazir found his way around the other minister. So how could she find her way around Bazir? Her mind raced even as Maddek turned to the others.

"Banek, ride at speed with Yvenne to the docks—"

"No," she said. "In Drahm we'll stay, and together we'll stop my brother."

His response was a snarl. "We can purchase two hundred arrows, my bride, but I will not whip your arm to shreds while we fight them."

"We need not fight them at all. And if you attack Bazir and kill him, the alliance council will declare war upon you and Parsathe. You will tear the alliance apart, in the very moment I have been tasked by Vela to strengthen it."

Abruptly he buried his face in her hair. His broad chest heaved against her back. His voice was low and rough against her ear. "I have taught you that a warrior must sometimes run when faced with a threat she cannot defeat. That is what you will do now. But we cannot *all* run. Not if you are to survive. A ship is no easily defensible position. Instead my warriors and I will find one within this city and leave no soldiers alive to pursue you."

"And likely die, too."

"Silver-fingered Rani comes for us all," he said gruffly. "But she will come for more soldiers than Parsatheans this day."

"She will only come for my brother," Yvenne told him, and when she heard his grunting dismissal of that declaration, she sharpened her tongue. "You must stop thinking as a warrior, Maddek, and instead think as a king. But if you will only be a warrior, then I remind you of the first warrior's lesson you taught me: make use of what you have."

Like cold iron he became. Utterly rigid, Maddek held her in a hard and silent embrace. "What do I have?"

"You have *me*, Maddek—Zhalen's daughter, as cunning and as vicious as my brother. But that is not all I am. So if you will not be a king this day, then at least be a warrior who makes use of what he has and follows the lead of a queen."

For a long moment Maddek didn't reply, his body as taut as when Vela had whispered into his ear.

Then he rasped, "What is the queen's command?"

CHAPTER 25

MADDEK

The queen commanded them to seek protection from a Gogean prince and to cower behind palace walls— walls that provided not even comforting defense. Drahm had no fortress or citadel. Instead the prince who governed the city resided in an opulent manse overlooking the sea, and instead of walls the parlors had great open archways that led to balconies and courtyards, with breezes moving freely through every room. Had he been a visitor instead of a warrior who stood in an archway overlooking the wide avenue that led to the palace gates, watching for the approach of two hundred soldiers, Maddek might have reflected that if a man must live behind walls, then an open and airy palace such as this would be an acceptable compromise for a warrior born on the Burning Plains. Instead he only imagined how quickly soldiers might scale the private balconies and invade a visiting queen's rooms.

A foul curse came from inside the parlor behind him. Banek paced in front of one of the few doors they'd yet seen in this palace.

A closed door—with Yvenne on the other side.

"I mislike that she is alone with him," the old warrior said fiercely.

Alone with Cadus, Drahm's governor. A lowly position for the brother of the Gogean queen, yet one of his own choosing, for he had not wanted to shoulder the duties of a prince living within the royal city.

Or so his brother Oren had told Maddek. But when Maddek had said the same to Yvenne, warning her that such a prince would be unlikely to stand firm against Bazir—or the alliance council—she had replied, "Cadus's only fault is that he stands so firm, he breaks before he will bend."

After leaving the bridge, the speed at which they'd raced through Drahm's streets prevented any more discussion. Nor had they opportunity to speak after reaching the palace. Despite their swiftness, news that Vela had appeared and shown favor to a woman with moonstone eyes and a party of Parsathean warriors arrived before they did.

Just as well. Without Vela's favor, Cadus might have doubted Yvenne's claim that she was Nyset's heir. The prince might have looked askance even at Maddek—a Parsathean who claimed to be the commander of the alliance's army, yet who led only six warriors.

Instead Cadus himself had greeted them on the palace steps and agreed to Yvenne's request for an urgent audience with him. That audience had at first taken place in the parlor where the Parsatheans waited now. There only a few more words had passed between Yvenne and Maddek, when she'd quietly asked whether she could make spoken reference to his mother.

He had not cared if she did. She could say whatever she wished.

Yet although she made reference, little detail had she given. Cadus had listened with increasing agitation as Yvenne told him that her father had poisoned her mother, then imprisoned her in the tower. She told him of her own years spent locked in that chamber until she'd sent a letter to the Burning Plains, and that her father had killed Maddek's parents when they'd arrived to judge her worth as a bride. In broad strokes, she recounted how Zhalen had lied to the alliance investigators and that Yvenne had truly been the one to kill her brother Lazen while Ran Ashev made her attempt at escape, how Zhalen had bundled her off to Toleh to be wed, and how she'd sent a message to Maddek that had led to his ambush of her carriage, where she'd killed her brother Cezan—and that she and Maddek had agreed to marry, so they might remove her father from Syssia's throne, but had been forced to travel through Goge to avoid the soldiers in pursuit.

Little the prince had said until she'd finished, and little he'd said after—except to request a private audience with Yvenne.

Maddek could not fault the prince's caution. In the presence of seven Parsathean warriors, a woman in fear of her life might say whatever she'd been instructed to say. In private audience, Cadus could make certain Yvenne was with Maddek by her choice, and offer his protection if she wasn't.

Speaking to her alone was a wise decision. In Cadus's place, he'd have done the same. Yet still it took all of Maddek's control not to tear open that door and see for himself that she was well. To roar at the prince that she needed no protection but his.

"She is alone, but not helpless," Ardyl said—to the pacing Banek, though until Maddek looked at her, he thought it might be directed to him. "She has her dagger."

"And is no stranger to using it," Fassad added with a grin. "As her brother discovered."

Banek waved that away. "We should have given her more lessons with a blade."

So they should have. But a blade would not save her from two hundred soldiers.

With a snarl, Maddek looked through the archway again. Nothing yet.

He turned back to the warriors. Only he and Banek were on their feet. The others lounged around a table laden with fruits and roasted meats. Eating their fill, as Yvenne had told them to—because after her brother arrived, they ought not trust any food or drink that they had not brought themselves.

"When we are settled here," he told Kelir, "secure our passage on a bargeship and take horses and provisions aboard."

His mouth full of pricklefruit, the warrior nodded. Kelir had thrown a multitude of questioning glances at Maddek since leaving the bridge, yet he hadn't questioned Maddek's decision to seek help from the Gogean prince.

And he hadn't known it wasn't Maddek's decision, except in Maddek's decision to follow her lead. Because Yvenne had spoken fiercely to him about being a warrior or a king, yet not so loudly the others could hear. They only knew that after a fiery conversation with her, he'd altered their plans.

They would follow him into a battle or into an opulent palace. But he could see Kelir's relief that another option was still available to them—one that did not depend on the protection of a Gogean prince.

A prince whose character Yvenne knew well. A character that did not match what Oren had described.

There was clear resemblance between Oren and Cadus. Maddek might have known who he was even without introduction. The two princes shared the same brown hair and wiry frame, the same broad nose and narrow face. Yet Cadus had a quiet and thoughtful manner Oren did not. And knowing now how the Gogean queen had once admired Zhalen's methods, Oren's description of his brother as weak might only have meant that Cadus had refused to crush unhappy farmers.

And his only fault was standing so firm he might break rather than bend.

His *only* fault.

"Ran Maddek." Kelir raised an amused voice, watching him with a laughing gaze. "Do you think a fool's thoughts?"

All of his warriors regarded him in the same manner.

Because he was snarling to himself, and all but tearing through the floor as he stalked again to the archway.

Because Yvenne had brought them to the palace of a man that her mother had chosen over Maddek. The palace of a man the goddess Vela had urged her to consider.

Yvenne had vowed she would not seek marriage with another. Maddek trusted that vow. Still poisonous jealousy ate at him. He needed no counsel for that. He knew they were a fool's thoughts.

The warriors were no fools. They'd heard Vela speak of a suitor who lived in this city. It was no great leap to guess that the goddess meant Cadus.

"You heard Yvenne's vow?" he asked them and when they nodded, that was all that needed to be said. "I have no reason for jealousy."

Kelir's eyes narrowed. "What were Vela's words to you?"

Words? They'd not been mere words. They'd been blades the goddess had used to strike through his heart.

In bed and in battle, a warrior is too dependent upon his sword. Until you have the heart of a king, you will never truly have her and you will never truly protect her— and because you lack a king's heart, you will lose her.

Lose her. As he'd lost his parents.

"They are words best left unsaid," he told them hoarsely. And words best left unthought.

He would *not* lose her.

"Ran Maddek." No amusement remained in Kelir's voice now; there was only the head of the Dragon. "Do you need counsel?"

Throat raw, Maddek shook his head.

"Vela only tests you," Banek said, giving counsel anyway. "As the goddess does with those she favors, so they might accomplish all of which they are capable. She prodded at your jealousy and your character, but only because she sees all that you might be. As we do."

Maddek cared not if he was favored by a goddess. "And Yvenne's suffering? Why prod her with a threat of pain?"

Shadows crossed the older warrior's face. "It is not a prod. It is a kindness, so that your bride will be prepared."

"A kindness would be to prevent it."

And if the goddess would not prevent it, Maddek would. Vela had claimed that Maddek could not truly protect her, but he *would*.

He vowed it.

Jaw clenched, he turned to the closed door—which opened before he took a step. Out came Yvenne, wine goblet in hand and a satisfied smile curving her full mouth, Cadus's robed figure at her side. "I will prepare a letter to my sister regarding your hope for a new balance between members of the alliance after you have married the commander and secured your throne. I believe your proposal will be much happily received."

"It is a proposal happily extended." She caught sight of Maddek, and her brows arched. Perhaps in query why he appeared ready to rip apart a palace with his bare hands.

"Commander." The prince approached him, reassurance warming his voice. "You have served the alliance well, and I was very sorry to hear what befell your parents. I thought then the circumstances were strange but trusted the council had resolved all questions. This new account of what occurred is quite troubling."

Troubling? Maddek gritted his teeth.

His father murdered and accused of assaulting a woman, *troubling*. His mother imprisoned and raped and beheaded, *troubling*. Their two Dragons executed and silenced, *troubling*. His heart ripped from his chest and thousands of Parsatheans grieving their queen and king, *troubling*.

Such words were as offensive as sly tongue. Not lies, but truth pale and thin, as if starved of conviction. It was the speech of men who believed that truth had many sides, so they carefully walked in the center, without committing to anything.

"Given such widely different accounts of events, and that your bride believes there will be an attempt to silence the truth, I offer you and your warriors my protection until this matter is resolved by the alliance council."

It would be resolved by Maddek's sword. Still he nodded with gritted teeth, accepting that protection. Even if it only lasted until they left by cover of quiet night and boarded a ship north.

Yvenne came to Maddek's side, her hand curling possessively around his biceps. "I wonder if we might be given quarters separate from the rest of the household and guests?" From beneath her lashes, she cast a shy glance up at Cadus. "For it is my moon night, and Ran Maddek's attentions have so far been quite . . . vigorous. But if we have privacy, he will disturb no one with his bellows and grunts."

"Of course," the prince smoothly replied over the Parsatheans' choked laughter. "We will celebrate the blessed event as we sup together with your brother and Minister Gareth. My attendants will escort you there now, so you may bathe and make ready for their arrival."

Yvenne bowed her head. "I am in your debt, Prince Cadus."

In *his* debt? Only barely did Maddek stop his growl. His bride owed no one.

"The honor of helping you is mine," the prince said. And that was truth, at least.

But Maddek hated that she needed help from anyone but him.

Maddek's jaw didn't unclench until they reached their quarters. There attendants and maids flitted about, preparing Yvenne's bath while Maddek and his warriors took measure of the security of the chambers.

Cadus had honored the request for privacy and separation. Their quarters were not within the palace at all, but were a separate residence called the Queen's Nest. Standing amid terraced gardens overlooking the sea, the structure appeared to Maddek not like a bird's nest, but more like a snail's shell—or the spiral seashells he'd seen in numerous decorations since entering Drahm. Though rounded, their quarters were not built around a central chamber, but in a swirling layout that raised the floor a level with each turn— and the only route to the main bedchamber was through a circling path of parlors and chambers. And although the bedchamber opened to a wide balcony, it was more defensible than he'd anticipated. From the residence, only one door led into the chambers. From outside, soldiers would have to scale steep walls to reach the balcony at the apex of the nest.

It was not secure. But it was as secure as could be had here. As he joined the warriors and his bride on the balcony, Maddek saw his satisfaction mirrored in the other warriors' faces. Yvenne stood at the balustrade, her gaze turned toward the sea. Perhaps watching the ships sailing, for she'd never seen any before this day.

Soon she would be aboard one. "After the soldiers arrive and are settled in the garrison, I will send Danoh and Toric to the docks."

"The soldiers won't arrive," Yvenne said, tilting her face up to the sun, her eyes closed. "Such a large number are forbidden to enter the city without the prince's approval, and Cadus will not give it. Only my brother and Gareth of Toleh will be allowed through with a small personal guard."

Now his surprise and relief was echoed in the other warrior's expressions. "He will refuse the soldiers entry through the gate?"

Yvenne nodded.

"Still we will secure a ship," Maddek said.

She gave him a sideways glance. "You do not trust Cadus's protection?"

"I do not trust your brother."

"As I do not." Turning, she leaned elbows back on the marble balustrade. "This night he will attack us in this nest and claim he saved me from a brutal rape at the hands of Maddek and his Parsathean guard."

The warriors froze, eyes all locked on her face.

"That will not be his first choice. After arriving, he'll make an appeal to the prince, asking Cadus to hand us over to the alliance council so they can conduct a new investigation. That would be simplest for him, as he could kill all of you on the return journey to Ephorn. But Cadus has given a vow of protection and he will not rescind it." She looked to Maddek. "So this is what Bazir will attempt, instead. As it is my moon night, my brother will think you too distracted between my thighs to prepare a proper defense against the Rugusian guard. Then Bazir will tell the council he killed you while defending himself and his sister in a royal house."

Sharp pain knifed through Maddek's chest. "That is what Zhalen claimed that my father did. Made him into a rapist and an oathbreaker."

And suffered no consequences for it. Not yet.

She nodded. "Bazir will claim that you were taking your vengeance against me, since you were forbidden from touching my father or my brothers. It will be easy for him to persuade the council of that view."

All too easy. Because that view had once been truth, though Maddek wouldn't have raped her. Only thrown her skinned corpse over the Syssian wall.

Ardyl frowned. "The prince knows you intend to marry."

"You think Cadus will not be murdered, too, and his death laid at the feet of a vengeful Maddek and his Dragon?" Yvenne asked her. "Bazir will leave no one to tell a different story."

"But we will be prepared for his attack," Kelir said.

"We will. And Maddek would be justified in killing him, too—though there will be fewer questions if it is my arrow that pierces Bazir's eye. For if I kill him, Maddek will not be in defiance of the council's order not to touch Zhalen's sons. They need not know you helped me draw the bowstring."

Sheer bloodthirst sharpened the smile she turned on him then. Cunning. Vicious.

A queen.

"Leave us," he told the warriors bluntly.

So hot and hard he was, Maddek barely trusted himself to touch her. Instead he crowded closer, gripping the balustrade at either side of her cocked elbows. Boldly she held his gaze, head tipping back, never retreating even though the rigid press of his body captured her within the cage of his arms.

"So this is what I made use of this day." Raw need roughened his voice. "A scheming and manipulative queen."

She grinned up at him. "So I am."

More than a queen. "And a warrior, finding a defensible position and planning your attack. You brought us here not for the prince's protection. You brought us here to give us an opportunity to destroy Bazir—but destroy him by using the very rules that he would abuse."

An aroused flush rose beneath her skin as she nodded. "In this palace, he has but three routes to victory. One is by persuading Cadus to turn us over to the alliance council, but Cadus has already offered his protection to us. The second is by overwhelming Cadus's defenses with the force of two hundred soldiers, but it would be near impossible to justify his actions to the council. So only treachery within the house remained."

A harsh laugh shook through him. "My father used to say that wars were not won and lost on battlefields, but in throne rooms. I never truly understood what he meant until this day. You have taught me a king's lesson without even trying."

"Have I?" Her brow creased in a small frown. "I would not have taught you that wars are won in throne rooms. I would say that battles are won in throne rooms, just as they are on battlefields—but they are fought with tongues instead of swords."

War or battle, it was a lesson well learned. And her tongue was so sharp and clever and quick. His gaze fell to her mouth. So desperately he longed for a taste. But never would she tell him if she was hurt, so Maddek only knew by her breaths whether he wanted too hard and took too much.

Hands circling her waist, he lifted her atop the balcony's balustrade. Her fingers clenched on his arms for balance but he would never let her fall from that seat.

Perched on the railing, she was as tall as Maddek, her eyes on level with his. Her linen-wrapped thighs clamped around his sides when he pushed between them. After the ache of denying himself her kiss, no time did he waste taking another taste, pushing aside the front of her robe and revealing her breast.

He should kiss and tease. But with ravenous hunger, he sucked her taut nipple into his mouth. Always he wanted her too hard. Too much. But her gasp was pure pleasure, her soft moan and the arch of her back a plea for more.

That he would give this night. Releasing the engorged bud, he growled against the soft swell of her breast, "And the bed?"

Panting, eyes heavy-lidded, she looked down at him. No reply she made. Because his mouth had erased the thoughts from her head, he realized with smug satisfaction.

He kissed the glistening ruby of her nipple before reminding her of what this lesson had been. "Is the bed also where battles are lost and won? They are fought with swords and tongues."

She came back to herself with amusement curving her lips. Her two-fingered hand cupped his bearded jaw, her thumb caressing the smiling corner of his mouth. "Perhaps it is. Particularly if a warrior views a woman as a fortress, with walls that must be battered down."

His chest tightened. Vela had truthfully revealed what was in his thoughts. Yet Yvenne seemed neither surprised nor angered. So well did she know him.

But it was not only Maddek she knew so well. "How many suitors do you have?"

"Suitors?"

"You knew Cadus would stand firm. All depended on

that. And you knew because your mother watched him. As she watched me."

Coolness slipped into her gaze. "She did."

"How many suitors did she prefer over me?"

"I have no suitors, Maddek." She sharply tugged at the point of his beard, as she did when she believed he didn't listen to her. "My mother watched many people. Some she considered as partners for me. Some she did not. But none knew she observed them, and certainly none courted me as a suitor does."

"Why not choose the ones your mother favored? Why not Cadus, if his only fault is that he stands so firm?"

In hot irritation she shoved at his chest. He moved not a bit.

A fierce snarl curled his lips. "I stand firm, too. Whom did your mother prefer?"

She set her jaw. With a flick of her hand, she closed her robe, covering her breast. Withdrawing from him.

Maddek flicked it open again. "Who?"

Her chest heaved on two sharp, angry breaths. "Why do you ask? Did you not trust the vow I made with Vela as witness?"

"I *do* trust it." Yet jealousy still burned in him, a poisonous blister. Jealousy he resented. Jealousy Yvenne did not deserve. Jealousy that Banek said the goddess deliberately prodded . . . so that he would overcome it. "Vela gave me a lesson to learn. I need to have the heart of a king."

A heart that burned true. Not because it was always afire with foolish jealousy.

She sighed heavily. "That might only mean she wants you to tear my father's heart out."

He would do that, too. "And what manner of heart do *you* want me to have?"

For a long moment she gave no response, only regarded him steadily. "That is not the question a king would ask."

It wasn't. As he well knew. It should not matter what manner of heart she wanted him to have, but what manner of man *he* wanted to be. "What heart will best serve my people?"

Approval lit her gaze. "My mother's first choice was Dagenoh of Toleh."

The captain who had brought Maddek news of his parents and had stepped into command upon the Lave—and who was also son of Gareth, the alliance council's minister, and nephew to Toleh's king.

Truth forced him to respond, "Dagenoh would have been a good choice of a husband and king. A fine warrior he is, clever and fair—and he would have helped you free your people."

"He is *too* fair," said Yvenne. "And like everyone who has studied under Toleh's monks, he favors reason and diplomacy."

Maddek could find no fault with that. "Why not choose him, then?"

"Because he would have tried appealing to my father with that same reason and diplomacy. And while he attempted to find a resolution that avoided bloodshed, my father or brothers would have stabbed him in the back."

That was likely truth, too. "And Cadus?"

"He is a man whose heart longs for justice but whose head is bound to law. He has persuaded himself that if rules are followed, then it is the same as justice. So although he hates the route his sister has taken with Goge, he did not push against her, because he deferred to her position and her rule. Her word is law—but sometimes the only justice is burning rule and law to the ground."

Maddek agreed. Yet now nothing he'd learned made sense. "Why would your mother prefer them, then?"

"Because they both suffer from the same flaw—they rely on diplomacy or law to provide resolutions. But she believed that I could prod them to action."

"I believe you could have, too," said Maddek, and she smiled. "But you preferred a warrior, hot of blood."

"Hot of blood, yes. And hotter of head." Her lip caught

between her teeth before she added, "But I could have found a hot-blooded warrior anywhere. For a time, we watched the wandering king of Blackmoor—until he pissed in one of Vela's offering bowls. You are not *that* hotheaded, even when she insults you."

Or not that foolish. "Why then?"

Her brows arched.

"Why choose me over other warriors?"

"Many reasons," she said, then nothing else for a breath, and he thought she might leave it at that vague response. Until she added, "But I decided during the campaign against Stranik's Fang."

Almost ten years past? "Because you saw me fight?"

"Because I saw when you didn't fight. I saw you hold out your hand."

To the Farians. Instantly Maddek could see them again, as he'd seen them countless times in dreams and nightmares in the years since. The priests had enslaved the savages in dark caves and left them to die in cavernous pits. Maddek had been only a captain in the alliance army then, leading a small group of soldiers to make certain no more priests remained in the caves. Instead they'd found thousands of Farians, half starved and stinking, eating their dead to stay alive.

The Farians were not human, though they shared similarities in shape and expression to the people of the western realms, and the savages spoke their own language made of hoots and clicks. But they were only as similar as humans were to apes—and despite the rapes, never had been born a mix of Farian and human.

He'd heard many different stories of their creation—that ancient human mothers drank silac venom while the children fed at their breasts, that a bat-winged ape had mated with an ice walker and their pale-skinned savagery was the result. Most stories claimed that they'd dwelled in cavernous tunnels within the Fallen Mountains until the god Hanan rocked the world with his fuckings, and then they'd poured forth from those broken caves. Maddek knew not what was true and he cared not. Because he could still see the crying Farian children, the desperation of mothers and fathers—and that they'd had no way to escape the pits.

Until Maddek had reached down and helped them out. Dozens he'd pulled from that pit before his soldiers had found a rope to throw down. And there had been some too weak to climb, so he'd been the first to carry them out.

"My mother described it all to me," said Yvenne quietly now. "And how the Tolehi monk in your group had advised you to leave them to starve, because freeing them meant they would begin attacking the southern realms again."

Which had been truth. Yet he'd given his orders, anyway.

"I have recognized the faces of Farians that I freed that day," he told her now, his voice thick. "Children then. Grown later into savage enemies that I've killed."

"I know you have," she said softly. "But do you regret your orders to free them?"

He shook his head. "I cannot."

A small smile curved her mouth and she cupped his bearded jaw in both hands. "And I do not regret that being the reason I choose you. Had you given me cause to regret that decision in the years following, then perhaps I would have chosen Cadus or Dagenoh. But I have not."

"You did regret it," he reminded her. "The morning after I pulled at your tongue."

"And no longer regretted again by evening." Her eyes were alight with laughter. "Or perhaps I regretted until you put that stave into my hand. Take a lesson from that, Maddek. I am also hot of head—but you only need to give me a weapon and I will forgive you almost anything."

Perhaps it was not a wise lesson to learn, placing a weapon into the hand of a woman angry with him. But if it meant seeing her smile, he was fool enough to shower her in blades. "Is that why your mother disapproved of me, then—because I freed the Farians?"

"No." Her amusement faded. "She called you idealistic and foolish. But she also said you made the hardest decision that can ever be made: doing what is right and good, while knowing how painful the consequences might be. But you did not make someone else take responsibility for those consequences. You were the first volunteer to return to the Lave, and to mount a defense against them."

So Maddek had been. He'd felt no guilt for freeing the savages. He never would. But he'd recognized his role in what followed, and had thought to give the southern realms time to rebuild their own defenses, so they would not need a Parsathean army at their southern borders.

That hope had been as strong as the hope that, when he'd held out his hand, perhaps the Farians would not see them as demons and continue their savage attacks. Neither hope had come to fruition. But hope had not been his reason for freeing them, or his reason for returning to defend the Lave. Both decisions were simply what he felt must be done.

"Why then did she advise you against me?"

She drew a deep breath. "You are certain you want to hear?"

He frowned. "Are they words best left unsaid?"

"I know not. I only know that they are not easy words."

"I will stand firm," he told her, and amusement flashed over her expression before she nodded.

Her hand cupping his jaw again, she said, "It was because you have never lost."

Never lost? That made no sense.

She must have seen his confusion because she tried again. "You have never been defeated. And I do not refer to small competitions with other warriors. You are a fine sport. But you have never suffered true loss or defeat."

That was what her mother had seen? Then Queen Vyssen had not watched carefully. "I have lost warriors under my command, have lost friends—"

"You have," Yvenne agreed softly.

"My parents," he gritted out. "My queen and king, whom I loved with my full heart. Your mother was already dead when your father murdered them, so she could not have seen who I was in response to that. Do *you* think I have not lost anything?"

"I know you have lost those you have loved," she said. "But have you ever been defeated?"

Chest heaving, Maddek searched her face as if he might find answer there. But he could not think of a defeat. Not a significant one. He rasped, "I have not been defeated. That is a fault?"

"It is not."

"Then what reason—"

"You must remember," she told him, combing her fingers along his bearded jaw, "my mother had seen Syssia crushed. She'd seen her beloved mother become a demon that she herself had to slay. She had seen Anumith the Destroyer bring everyone to their knees. And then she was poisoned and betrayed, a warrior-queen born but with her body so weakened she could only watch as my father razed Syssia's noble houses and as he ground our people beneath his heel. And in that time, she watched everyone as they recovered from the Destroyer's march. She believed that was when you truly learned someone's character—after they'd been broken. When they lost someone they'd loved, and everything they'd known was destroyed. When they'd been brought so low, they might never rise again. And when they do rise, then whatever reason they find to keep going, to claw their way up, to crawl to their feet—she believed that reason would reveal who they truly were. She said that she didn't know who *you* truly were."

Jaw clenched, he stared at her. Did Yvenne also not know who he was? But he thought she did. She had seen him in the Farian caves, and had chosen him to wed. She had seen him in the years that followed, as he commanded an army upon the Lave. And she had seen him now, full of grief and rage and vengeance.

His throat was raw as he asked, "Have you known defeat?"

A sad smile touched her mouth. "Over and over again. The only victory I have known so far is that I persuaded you not to kill me, and finally have the opportunity to escape my father and claim my throne. And it is not even a victory yet in full."

"It will be," he vowed thickly. "What made you rise to your feet again?"

"Love for my people. Rage against my father." She paused. "Hope."

All of which Maddek shared with her. "Perhaps I have not known crushing defeat. But I have known difficulty and loss. I have known grief that tore my heart from my chest. If you must judge who I am, use that."

"The vengeance you pursue for your parents?"

He nodded.

"I think you do them honor," said she.

"But I might have done them dishonor." He saw that clearly now. "If I had torn the alliance apart, after they spent so much of their lives building it."

She said nothing, but the tilt of her lips and the thumb she slid across the width of his bottom lip said enough.

And now she had been tasked to strengthen that alliance—and to make it grow. "How far did your mother see? How many realms have you watched?"

"Countless. Some near, some far."

"All the western realms?"

She nodded again.

"That is why Vela chose you, then. Because you know the characters of so many within those realms—as you knew Cadus. You know who will stand firm, who will only speak platitudes. You know who might already be corrupted, who cannot be trusted."

A laugh shook her. "I do not know *all* of that. And those who are corrupted have done well concealing themselves, I think."

Still, her mother had seen so much. Even that Maddek would please her in bed. When Yvenne had first said so the night at the inn, he'd mistaken her intent and almost taken her tongue. Little thought had he given the claim beyond that. He had not believed it of much importance. Yet Yvenne had mentioned his ability to please her again today—had mentioned it to a goddess.

"One reason you gave Vela in defense of your choice was that I saw to your pleasure."

"So you do. I would not take a husband who did not." She bit her lip—not in shyness, he thought, but in hunger. "I like that you see to mine so well, even while you ease your own need."

Ease his need? Not yet had Maddek been able to. It mattered not how many times he tasted her. It mattered not how many times he spilled his seed. His hunger for her had not eased. Instead it consumed him.

"This night I will truly see to your pleasure, Yvenne." He cupped her breast again, lightly pinched her nipple. "But not as I have been."

Her breath shuddered. "No?"

Fisting his hand in her hair, he tilted her head and bent his mouth to her rapidly beating pulse. "So deep inside you I will be."

His name she breathed, a sound of pure need. With a growl of hunger, he tasted the delicate skin of her neck. She trembled in response, her fingers clutching his shoulders, holding him tight.

Not as tightly as her cunt would hold his cock that night. His lips skimmed down her neck. "So long and hard I will have you."

She moaned, arching her back in silent offering, her ruby nipples raised to his mouth.

Against the softness of her small breast he vowed, "So many times I will make you spend."

"Now, Maddek," she pleaded, rocking her hips. "Please."

Only the last could he give her now. Hungrily he sucked her hardened nipple into his mouth. His hand glided up her silky inner thigh, and he groaned when fingers found her already so hot and wet.

Perhaps he did not yet have the heart of a king. But that day, when his bride cried his name and came upon his tongue, he felt like one.

CHAPTER 26

YVENNE

The trek from the Queen's Nest to the prince's chambers carried Yvenne and Maddek through terraced paths, and then along the colonnades that served as open corridors through the palace. Behind them were Danoh and Banek, serving as their guard for the evening.

Riding a horse might have taken them to dinner more quickly than Yvenne's slow walk, but a long bath had loosened her stiff knee and she liked that the distance gave her more opportunity to prepare Maddek.

"Only eat and drink what is prepared in front of you," she said. "Or something that you have seen my brother also eat."

"You think he will poison me, though it might risk you?"

If she ate or drank from Maddek's plate and cup, as lovers often did. Nothing her brother did might surprise Yvenne. But Bazir would not come all this way to kill her. "A sleeping potion would make his plans easier. But what I've told you is good practice at any table."

She felt Maddek's gaze upon her at that. She wondered

if ever he had worried that he would be poisoned as he ate. She thought it was unlikely. Not when so many of his meals were roasted on a fire in front of him.

"Do not touch him or go near him," she said. "He's not likely foolish enough to attack you in front of witnesses, but he might risk a sly poisoned blade."

Maddek grunted dismissively. "Every time he speaks, he uses a poisoned blade."

"I think you underestimate how deeply that blade might cut. He will speak lies framed by truth, so that the picture he paints is more believable."

"I know his sly tongue."

"He will try to provoke you into attacking him in front of witnesses. Do not let him."

"I will not be provoked."

"Tyzen told me how you leapt over the table in the council's chambers."

Maddek grinned. "So I did."

Though she had thrilled to Tyzen's description of Maddek's focused fury and Bazin's scrambling retreat, now worry held her in too tight a grip to return his grin. "He will use your parents to elicit a reaction here, too."

"He might succeed. But I am no brainless warrior, Yvenne, easily bestirred to violence. Leaping over the table was no impulsive attack—I had deliberate intention of killing him. When enraged, *less* impulsive I become."

"And more narrow-sighted." Focused and intransigent, and stubbornly married to his view.

He gave her an unreadable glance. "That is as my mother used to say."

Pain slipped under her breast, followed by anger of her own. Because still he would not rescind his vow or accept that she had never lied to him. Firmly entrenched he was in the first view he'd had of her, a picture colored by his rage and grief, when he'd been so certain he saw the truth of who she was despite never allowing her to speak it.

"That is not sly tongue," she defended hotly. "I have observed it for myself."

"So you have," he said with a wry smile. "And my mother would have called it cockbrained—because a cock only has one eye, and is rigid when enflamed."

She knew he meant to make her laugh, but the lingering anger and pain would not let her. In silence they walked along a colonnade overlooking the sea. Orange and pink stained the sky, mirrored in the waters below. So well she loved this palace. All was open. After many years in her tower, when Yvenne returned to Syssia, she knew not if she could tolerate being always surrounded by walls again.

"What is your new perfume?" Maddek asked suddenly.

"A soap from the bath." Soft and fragrant with coconut oils. "You wore the silks?"

For the prince had gifted them both with clean robes to wear. The turquoise silks she wore now had been sewn in the Gogean style, with tighter sleeves and layered skirts. Maddek also wore the new silks—but wore them as he had his red linens, folded over his belt. Yet she had not expected him to wear them at all.

"For this night," he said.

For her moon night? Or simply because they attended a royal dinner? He had bathed, too, and unbound his braids. His hair hung heavy and wet, as if he wore even more silk loose around his shoulders. In all that luxury, he ought not look as dangerous. Yet he did. He wore no sword or armor, but still an expanse of powerful muscle was on display, and his leisurely stroll seemed as quietly lethal as a long-toothed cat's.

Flushed with heat, she looked forward. They were nearing the prince's chambers, so no time could she waste ogling her would-be husband—and another warning still needed to be given.

She had not wanted to say this to Maddek, for he and the Tolehi minister were friendly and had served together in the march against Stranik's Fang. Yet it must be said. "Do not look to Gareth as an ally."

Maddek's face darkened in a frown. "He is a good man."

"He is. But he has spent at least a tennight with my

brother upon the road. We cannot know what poison Bazir
has told him and how it will influence his view of us."

His firm lips twitched. "As your words have influenced
my views?"

"I have told you nothing but truth."

There his smile died, but he said nothing as they reached
the prince's apartments. She was not surprised that they
were led to the prince's private solar, where they could dine
in a less formal setting than a royal hall. Cadus would stand
firm, but he also liked smooth progression, and he would
hope to ease tensions.

The two Parsathean guards did not enter the solar and
would wait outside that chamber until Yvenne and Maddek
emerged. Already present were Bazir and Gareth.

With heavy heart, she saw that her brother had already
worked not only on Gareth but also on Cadus. So different
was the prince's manner—still polite, yet now wary. He
introduced her to the Tolehi minister, who regarded her in
the same way.

She had thought it would be Maddek whom Bazir would
turn them against. But she should have known. As a disci-
ple of Tolehi reason, Gareth would be more persuaded by
what was seen with his own eyes, and a brother would have
seen a sister more than he would have seen an alliance
commander who had spent the better part of ten years upon
the Lave. Almost any lie Bazir could say about her, however. That she was of unsound mind, prone to fantasy. That
she was bloodthirsty and murderous, fell to fits and rages,
and had been locked away for her own protection. Whatever the affliction of her brain that he chose, Bazir would
claim that her existence had never been acknowledged because a mad queen upon the throne would endanger all of
Syssia and the alliance.

They were led out onto a balcony, where a low table surrounded by plump sofas and cushions waited beneath an
airy tent. The sound of the waves and scent of the sea filled
the air. Breezes fluttered through the transparent curtains.

It was not yet sunset, but the sun was sinking over the

western horizon, painting the sky in brilliant orange. Never had Yvenne seen anything of the like, yet she could not bask in the beauty before her. Not when the danger her brother posed was so near. She would be a fool to take her eyes from him.

Cadus indicated that they settle at the table, which was shaped in a deep crescent that allowed everyone a view of the sea and of each other. The prince sat at the head, facing full west. Maddek took the seat between her and the prince. Gareth and Bazir sank into the cushions at the other side.

She was glad to see the fish brought in and prepared nearby—their meal still flopping as it went beneath the cook's knife and onto the coals. She caught Maddek's eye and grinned.

"You will not leave so hungry now, I think," he said.

She sat opposite Bazir and gave him a thin smile as he sipped from a goblet of wine, looking pleased with himself. As well he might be. "What lies did you tell them, brother?" she asked lightly. "They look at me as if I am a demon incarnate."

There was suddenly such delicate frozen wariness in the prince's and minister's expressions, Yvenne realized she had aimed perfectly without even intending.

And Bazir was clever and persuasive but had not much original thought. In his attack tonight, he likely meant to copy their father's way of discrediting Maddek's father— and now Bazir copied the story that Zhalen had used to destroy every strong house within Syssia.

"Is that the tale you spun to them?" She laughed and addressed the prince and Gareth, who sat nearer to each other. "When asked why he kept his sister imprisoned in the tower, he must have spun the same lie our father did after he poisoned our mother. For our father claimed that after our mother slew the demon who reanimated Queen Venys, the demon then possessed her. But now the story is that *I* am the possessed daughter."

With a heavy sigh, Bazir sank deeper into his cushion, regarding her with a sorrowful stare that he could only hold a moment before averting his eyes and addressing Cadus and Gareth. "I told you that she would use truth to speak lies."

Eating his fish with his fingers, Maddek grunted beside her, a sound of deep laughter—as if amused that her brother gave them the same warning she'd given him.

Bazir's gaze shot to him. Leaning forward, he said in a grave voice, "I have already told the others what happened to our beloved mother. But you have been in Yvenne's presence these many days and under her influence, so it is no surprise that you take her side. You and I have no love for each other, but listen and you will see how she has twisted truth."

"Do not open your ears to him, Maddek. Nothing he says will deserve the respect of your hearing," Yvenne said, and knew the frustration of even that sounding, through her brother's frame, as if she feared that Maddek might see through her deceptions.

Eyes gleaming, Bazir knew it, too. "You do not want him to hear how it was our mother who took the poison herself, so that if the demon inside her gained hold of her, it would never have the strength that her demon-queen mother did? Years she spent battling that evil inside her, locking herself away to keep safe her sons and her people— and my father ruled with her blessing."

"He poisoned her wine with fellroot," Yvenne said flatly. "It was not a demon's evil that kept her trapped in that tower. Instead it was his greed and ambition."

"The corrupt greed of the man who refused reward after he smote the Smiling Giant? The selfish ambition of the man who risked his own life to hold the line at the Fourth Ridge? You would cast such aspersions on an honored warrior?"

"As he ruined the name of Ran Marek with his false accusations," she said, then looked to Maddek, hoping her brother's words were not provoking him to anger.

He seemed to be not even listening. Calmly, he ate his fish.

"That is only partial truth." With an expression of soul-deep pain, Bazir sat back, his gaze returning to Maddek. "Did you never question why a woman born of a legendary line of warrior-queens, each one tall as Rani herself and possessing the strength of ten men, was so weak and small? It is because her own mother recognized what was growing in her womb and took the half-moon milk before it was fully formed. And when the babe emerged with its heart still beating, our mother attempted to strangle her."

Such an unbelievable collection of lies. Such a ridiculous story. Yet that was what made it so believable, too. Not for one moment would anyone suspect that a member of the alliance council would spout such an outlandish tale unless it held truth, for Bazir's own standing would be forever ruined if the story was exposed as false. And if he had simply called her afflicted, her own manner could persuade Cadus and Gareth to her truth. But now her every denial could be read as confirmation through the veil of his lies.

Yet it *must* be denied. "If our mother ever intended to kill me, she would have used her teeth to rip out my throat—as she did to our father as he raped her. What story would you give to his scar?"

He would give no story to it, because he was still continuing his own. "It was my father who saved the weakling demon babe," he said to Maddek, who still calmly ate his fish. Not even tearing it apart, but taking small bites of the delicate flesh. "Fool that he is. But he saw her moonstone eyes, and believed she might be the true heir to the Syssian throne. And he believed that perhaps my mother was mistaken . . . or that the demon still resided in my mother, and through her had meant to strangle the true heir. But my mother was not mistaken, and all that she could do in her weakened, poisoned body was to curb the demon's schemes. And so she did, until her tragic death."

Such hatred filled Yvenne then that she shook with it. Yet her brother did not make the claim she expected him to, a truth wrapped in lies and so painful that she could not even speak to Maddek of that day.

"That was when she sent the message to your mother

and father," Bazir continued with a look of guilt. "And there our lies to the alliance council began, because my father thought if we now revealed that my mother had birthed a daughter with moonstone eyes, our people would be so hungry to see Nyset's heir on the throne that they would not let themselves see her true nature. But your parents saw that nature, Commander. She lured them with a sad tale of abuse and imprisonment, but as soon as my father led them to her, so they might see with their own eyes what she was, they recognized the same demon they'd fought a generation ago. That your father attacked a woman of our household was not a lie; we only hid the truth of who that woman was."

"Ran Marek attacked *no one*," Yvenne said fiercely. "The attack upon him came from our father and his Rugusian guard."

"You note her missing fingers? They were lost when she caught your father's blade—and then turned it upon him."

Now she was Ran Marek's murderer? "That is *not* truth." In fear and agony she turned to Maddek and insisted, "It is *not*."

As if unconcerned by both her brother's claim and Yvenne's denial, Maddek gave no response, except to signal the attendant to bring another fish.

"All that followed might have been prevented had we simply slain my demon sister then . . . but my father still had hope. And he still believed a true daughter might reside in that twisted body." Shame clouded her brother's face. "So he applied to Ran Ashev for help, as she was a warrior-queen in her own right who could stand against a demon as our mother did. Ran Ashev agreed. During the days, she would visit with my sister in the tower, to see if there was anything human in her that might be saved. And there my sister told again her lies of abuse, though she lived in luxury and was given every comfort."

Now Yvenne could not refute him with the truth of what happened, or she would lose her tongue. To Maddek she hissed, "Let me speak of your mother."

He denied her with a shake of his head. Because he believed her already? Or because he did not trust that what she said would be truth?

Pain and frustration closed her throat. Seething, she stared at her brother, made him drop his gaze away from hers.

Yet he continued still. "What story did she give of Ran Ashev's death—that it was an attempted escape? That Yvenne drew the arrow that killed Lazen?" Sadly he shook his head. "In truth, she drove your mother mad with her whispers and lies, turning your warrior mother against my father and brothers. Ran Ashev rampaged through the citadel, and though my father tried to contain her, they were forced to kill her in self-defense. But my father does consider himself responsible for your mother's death, because he was the one who allowed her such close contact with Yvenne through so many turns of the moon."

"This is not truth." She shook with rage. "This is not truth."

"What would you claim is the truth?" he asked her, a smirk in his eyes though he carefully kept that smug smile from his mouth.

Because he was clever and observant, and had seen that she gave no real response to anything regarding Ran Ashev. He might not know the reason, but he knew she would not speak of that queen.

Never had she been so angry and frustrated and helpless. She had thought herself ready to battle her brother's lies. Yet Maddek's vow had shackled her tongue, so she could not use truth to attack or defend. And she knew not what Maddek believed, but she could see that Gareth and Cadus had been well persuaded by him.

Oh, she should not have attempted to defeat her brother here. She should have commanded Maddek to flee with all his warriors to the boat, instead, and taken their chances on the sea.

"And now you are in close contact with her, Commander," Bazir said. "Do you not ask yourself why her skin is hotter than any other—"

"Because I am Nyset's heir! Our bloodline runs hot."

"Or why the weight of her gaze is as terrible as any stone wraith's—"

Without looking up from his plate, Maddek spoke over him. "Why would your father send a demon to marry the Tolehi king?"

Not a breath of hesitation before Bazir's answer came. "He did not send her to marry a king. That was only the story she was given. In truth my father was sending her to the Tolehi monks, who are better equipped to contain a demon such as she."

"You say she needed containment, yet there were no monks in her carriage escort. Only one brother and a handful of soldiers." He took a small bite of fish. "Either your father sent an unfettered demon on a journey through three realms without warning his allies of what passed through their midst, or Yvenne is as she claims: a daughter sent to marry a weak king and to further your father's schemes to control yet another realm within the alliance."

Maddek believed her. Sudden relief burst through her chest, painful and sweet, thickening into a lump in her throat.

"The containment was the story we told her—that she would be married to a king. Her own ambition is what made her compliant."

Maddek choked. "Compliant?" Now he glanced up, shaking with laughter. "If ever Yvenne was compliant for the duration of a journey, *that* is when I would think her possessed by a demon."

Bazir regarded him in sudden dismay. "I feared this. You are completely enslaved."

Another hearty laugh broke from Maddek. "That might be truth. But tell me, was it her compliance that sent the message to me in Ephorn, so I would steal her away—though it meant sacrificing the throne you say she coveted?"

"What ambition is greater—to be queen of Toleh or queen of the Burning Plains? Of course she saw an opportunity and took it." His gaze darted to Gareth, who had been quietly watching. "Forgive me. I do not mean to say that Toleh is the lesser of the two. Only that she could not resist gaining control of the Parsathean army."

"You think the riders would serve as a demon's puppets?" Maddek's amusement hardened, then faded altogether as he turned away from Bazir and addressed the Tolehi minister. "This sly-tongued cur only wishes to conceal the corruption that has festered in Syssia since Zhalen took the throne. Nothing of what Bazir claims happened to my mother and father could he have seen with his own eyes, not while he served on the council in Ephorn. He was but a swaddling babe when Yvenne was born and can be no true witness to the birth he claims was a demon's or the queen's attempt to strangle her. Yet my bride was in Syssia when my parents were murdered. She saw with her own eyes what happened to my mother and father, and so I weigh her truth more heavily than his."

The minister gave a slow nod. "Zhalen gave an account of what he saw with his own eyes, yet now his son claims those were lies told to conceal a demon daughter and heir to the throne. Whatever the truth of your bride's nature, clearly the testimony given in that original investigation was false. So the council will reopen the inquiry into their murders."

"Best the council not waste its time," Maddek replied. "Other matters are of greater concern. Vela told us that the Destroyer returns, and dark sorcery is being used within the realms. With my own eyes, I saw magic used to raise revenants."

Gareth glanced at Yvenne. "You told Prince Cadus that it was your brother Aezil who made these revenants?"

Bazir scoffed. "You cast blame on our brother, though it is you who were there—and it is well known that a demon can also make revenants."

"Only by befouling them with flesh and blood, not with spells cast from afar," Maddek said. "With my own eyes, I saw that Yvenne never had opportunity to befoul the corpses that rose and attacked us. With my own eyes, I saw a Rugusian red-footed eagle flying above us."

And Gareth had also marched against Stranik's Fang, knew how those priests had used their magic to raise revenants exactly as Maddek described.

His face troubled, the Tolehi minister looked from Bazir to Yvenne again. "Are you certain it was Aezil and not another, unknown sorcerer?"

She was certain. But did she have evidence? Not even Vela had spoken a confirmation that her father and brother were serving the Destroyer.

"I have no proof it was Aezil," she admitted.

Her brother gave her a triumphant look. "No proof, because there is no proof to be had. Aezil is no sorcerer."

"With my own eyes, I witnessed the goddess Vela give my bride the task of forming a great alliance to stand against the Destroyer—and to root out the poisonous seeds he left behind. Though we have no evidence that one of those seeds is Aezil, he has lost an eye, and a Rugusian eagle was used as a familiar along the river road at the same time Yvenne's family had reason to be searching for her. Neither of those is proof of his sorcery. But in combination, they give compelling reason to suspect him."

Gareth nodded. "So they do."

"*She* is the poisonous seed left behind," Bazir insisted. "A demon raised by the Destroyer himself. If there was a task given, it was to you, Commander—so that you could continue the legacy of your mother and father, who gave so much to the alliance. It is only Yvenne's influence that warps your view. She is determined to destroy each member of the royal house of Syssia, one by one. Now she twists a task given by a goddess to justify killing another brother."

This time his relentless lies had not as much effect on the others. For instead of renewed doubt, Gareth asked of Maddek, "You were given order not to harm Zhalen's sons, and the Syssian soldiers who returned with Cezan's body claimed it was Nyset's heir who killed him. Was that truth?"

"It was," Yvenne answered proudly, unsheathing the jeweled dagger at her calf and holding it up for them to see.

"Maddek did not touch him. Instead I used Cezan's own blade to pierce his heart from behind."

Anger flashed through Bazir's moonstone gaze like the flash of firelight on the silver blade. "One by one," he said again, each word a hard bite instead of his usual slick tongue. "Until each of us is dead by her hand. What do you say to that, Commander?"

Maddek grunted and turned approving eyes upon her. "I say she has made a good start."

"A good—" Her brother halted, blinked. "You say it was a good *start*?"

Unlike every other emotion he'd shown, the outrage and disbelief in that shrill echo was not faked, and the realization dawning over his face was like a dagger twisting into Yvenne's heart, but despite the agonizing pain it wasn't blood that spilled out. Only rage, rage, rage, swelling up her throat in a howling shriek—but her mother had taught her well.

Never give warning.

Bazir's expression twisted with malicious glee. "Did you not tell him, demon? He knows you murdered Lazen and Cezan. But does your barbarian know that you also killed our—"

Yvenne hurled the dagger with all her strength. No arrow it was, yet still her goddess-gifted aim was true, and the knife flew straight to Bazir's eye.

Her aim was true; the throw was not. Instead of the sharpened point, the jeweled handle thunked into her target. Still, Bazir screamed in pain and slapped a hand over his eye. The dagger clattered to the table. Both Cadus and Gareth lurched to their feet, shock and alarm elongating their faces with mouths gaping open and eyebrows shooting to hairlines. The attendants scrambled, some running to help Bazir and others running to shout for help.

Heart thundering, Yvenne sat back. Bazir was curled over, hand cupped over his eye, and not screaming now but resisting with gritted teeth the Tolehi minister's attempts to examine the wound.

The bridge of his nose bled from a thin cut, where the

misthrown blade had sliced his skin. She had hoped for great spurts of blood. Those few drops were not enough.

Beside her, Maddek calmly took another bite of fish. "Did you not say we shouldn't let him provoke us?"

Her rage was not over. In a low voice she hissed, "Why did you not let me speak of what truly happened? Why did you leave me no defense against his lies?"

"Because a warrior makes use of what she has."

"And you thought this was a good time for a lesson?"

"Battles are won or lost in throne rooms," he said in a measured tone. "And though you have great skill in slinging arrows and sparring with words, never have you taken them to a true battlefield. Now you have. This has been good practice."

"Practice?" Her brother had persuaded good, rational men that she was a demon, that she had murdered Ran Marek and driven Ran Ashev to violent madness. And her brother had twisted and twisted and twisted every truth, as Yvenne had told Maddek that Bazir would, and yet he still forbade her from speaking her own. "This was a true battle and you denied me a sword and shield."

For the barest moment, his gaze touched her face—and that gaze was not calm. Smoldering anger burned in his dark eyes—and she abruptly understood that Bazir's words *had* elicited a response. But Maddek had not let that emotion overrule his actions or his thoughts.

As she had. Nothing Maddek had said to Gareth to persuade him of their truth had been unknown to her. Maddek had chosen an angle of attack that the Tolehi minister would best respond to—by telling Gareth what he'd seen with his own eyes. An angle that Yvenne would have used herself had she not allowed her brother to provoke her. If she had not been so torn by frustration and rage at not being able to speak her truth.

She had thought herself prepared to face her brother, yet she had not been. Perhaps because after so many years spent on the alliance council, Bazir had so much experience in similar battlefields.

It *had* been a valuable lesson. Yet her frustration and
rage and disappointment still filled her chest and throat,
choking her. Because Maddek might have let her speak of
Ran Ashev and *still* she would have learned the lesson. Her
brother would have twisted that, too, but she would have
eventually seen that she'd failed in her attack, and tried
another direction. She'd have stopped sparring with her
brother and focused on Gareth, as Maddek had.

And she was embarrassed. How arrogant and foolish she
seemed, lecturing him on how to respond to her brother and
behave through this dinner.

So badly she wanted to be alone now. So desperately she
wanted to find a private spot and cry until emptied of all
this hot, painful emotion clogging her heart and throat.

Yet she could not. Prince Cadus approached, carrying
her jeweled blade. His expression seemed both abashed and
amused. "My sister once threw a knife at me over dinner,
too. My response was to dump a trencher of stewed boa
over her head. Family has the special ability to lower even
the most reasonable among us to the level of slinging blades
and meats."

Maddek gave an amused grunt. "That is truth."

So many attendants swarmed around Bazir now that
Yvenne could not even see him. She leaned forward, trying
to better catch sight of what damage there was. "Did I put
out his eye?"

In a reassuring voice, Cadus replied, "It will merely be
swollen and bruised."

She sat back with a scowl.

"Did you note his bare lie?" Maddek said, glancing up
at the prince.

"I did." Cadus appeared abashed again. "As did Gareth,
I think."

Yvenne looked at him in amazement. "You think there
was only one lie?"

The prince shook his head, a dull flush on his cheeks.
"Now I do not. But when he arrived and sought an audi-

ence, it seemed fair to give equal weight and consideration to his story that I did to yours."

"Why? If you have bread in one hand and dung in the other, you do not have to give equal consideration of which to eat," Yvenne said, and beside her, Maddek grunted in amused agreement.

"That is truth," the prince admitted. "But he was . . . persuasive. And consistent. Nothing he said contradicted what was known, and he never contradicted himself. Except he claimed Ran Ashev had murdered Lazen in her rampage. But he then told the commander it was you who murdered Lazen, after you angered him by showing the blade that killed Cezan."

That had not been her intention. Yvenne only meant to present evidence of the blade she'd stolen from Cezan. But seeing it—or perhaps seeing how happily Yvenne confessed to stabbing Cezan with it—made even the more experienced Bazir lose his sense in battle, too. "What will you do with him now?"

"That will be a matter for the alliance council to resolve. In the morning, I will tell Gareth to return to Ephorn with him. For even though your brother is a council minister, someone who has attacked the character of a woman under my protection in such a foul manner is no longer welcome. Their purpose in coming was in search of you, who they believed had been abducted and were in danger at the commander's hands; now they have found you under my protection. They can have no reason to remain in my city, and have no standing to compel either you or the commander to return with them."

Bazir would not return to Ephorn or wait for the alliance council to resolve this. What had happened here only made the attack in their chambers more certain—and Bazir more desperate to succeed, because he no longer had the Tolehi minister's ear and would soon lose the legitimizing support of the council.

Unease and uncertainty clutched her heart. She'd

thought herself prepared to face him here . . . and for the Parsatheans to face an attack from his guard. But what if that was also only foolishness and arrogance?

At the other end of the table, her brother climbed to his feet, holding a folded white cloth over his injured eye. Gleeful murder shone through moonstone when his uncovered eye focused on her—but only for a moment, when he was forced to avert his gaze from hers.

Noticing her diverted attention, Cadus glanced behind. He looked down at the dagger in his hand, then to Yvenne, before placing the blade in front of Maddek—as if the prince feared she might attempt to use it again. In deliberate movement, Maddek slid the dagger nearer to Yvenne, the scrape of jewels and silver across the table's marble surface loud and unmistakable.

By Vela's teeth, she was tempted to try. Instead she took another lesson from Maddek and picked a bite of fish from her plate, though she would not be able to choke it down while her stomach roiled.

His face a picture of relief, Cadus stepped back and clapped his hands together lightly in satisfaction. "Ah! Bazir is on his feet, so it seems all is well. I fear the excitement has interrupted plans to celebrate this evening's blessed event, however—and since the sun is nearly set, I believe the lovers must be eager to abandon us."

Not as eager as she had been. Not with the terrible storm of emotions raging inside her now.

With lip curled, Bazir looked upon her as he might look upon a crawling slimeworm. "You are so hungry for your throne, Yvenne, that you will spend your life spreading your thighs beneath that hulking, grunting brute?"

"No." From the corner of her eye, she saw Maddek's fist clench into a white-knuckled grip. The dagger was so near to her hand. She only flaked another bite of fish from her plate. "I suspect that for much of my life, I will not be beneath my grunting brute, but happily spreading my thighs to ride him."

Oh, the satisfaction of seeing Bazir at a loss for a re-

sponse. Not nearly as satisfying as gouts of blood would
have been—or as satisfying as Maddek's fierce grin. Yet
still better than all that had come before.

His hot gaze upon her, Maddek licked his fingers, then
shoved away from the table. Yvenne held out her hand, but
he helped her not to her feet. Instead he gripped her backside in his brutish hands and hauled her up, her face to his
face, and urged her thighs around his waist.

"Then let us wait no longer," he growled.

Riding him already. Yet not straddling his hips, as he'd
sometimes carried her before, so that she might feel the
steel of his arousal between her thighs. Higher now he held
her, and she understood why when he turned away from the
table and said in low voice, "Give me warning if your
brother practices *his* aim."

And throw a knife at Maddek's back. With her arms
wreathing his strong neck, her fingers tangled in his thick
loose hair, she watched over his shoulder. Only after they
passed out of the prince's chambers and Danoh and Banek
fell in behind them did she let go a shuddering breath and
bury her face against his warm throat.

His sword hand slid up her silk-covered spine to gently
cup her nape, the brace of his forearm against her back
holding her against him. "Strong allies we make, you
and I."

That was truth. Though he'd angered her, he'd also seen
that she was faltering and had waded in to help. Just as she'd
frustrated him earlier that day with her decision to seek Cadus's protection, but had also found a solution to stopping her
brother that did not require his warriors to sacrifice themselves fighting two hundred soldiers.

Yet Yvenne feared that any reply might be more sob
than word, so she only nodded against his neck. He smelled
of the same coconut soap that she'd used. Only the faintest
scent of his sweat and horse that she'd become so accustomed to lingered on his skin.

"You learn lessons more quickly than I. And in a cleverer manner, too." A deep breath lifted his chest against

hers. "I should have heeded your caution against underestimating him."

Embarrassment flooded her face. Ashamedly she admitted, "You were more prepared than I was."

"No. Will you not look at me?"

She shook her head against his throat.

His smooth stride hitched. "Are you hurt?"

How to answer that? Did she tell him of the burning in her eyes, the hot lump in her throat, the rage that still felt like a blade in her heart?

She could not. But she could give him partial truth. They had just seen battle, and she'd vowed to reveal a warrior's wounds. "My pride has suffered fatal injury."

His silent laugh rumbled against her and he pressed his face into her hair. "It may seem fatal. But from repeated injuries to my own pride, I know that it quickly recovers— and often swells larger after the healing."

Her lips curved against his neck. Still she did not look up but tightened the embrace of her legs and arms.

"I underestimated him," Maddek said again, voice gruff against her ear. "*Never* did I think a man such as Gareth could be persuaded by your brother's lies. He and Bazir have served on the council many years together. He well knows how sly-tongued the Syssian royals can be. Cadus, too, and I had perceived him as another reasonable man."

"He is," Yvenne whispered thickly.

"I am not so reasonable. This I know. So if I had not already set my cockbrained mind against him, he might have persuaded me, too."

Painfully she said, "It would not be the first time you doubted my motives and intentions."

"It would not." The muscles of his throat worked as if he swallowed gravel. "Better that the only sounds I hear from your brother are screams from his tongueless mouth."

Yvenne nodded in agreement. She would like to hear those, too.

His rough voice continued. "There is no shame in his

provoking you. You are also no impulsive fool. You cleverly persuaded me to marriage even while my claws dug into your throat. But with family, it is not so easy to maintain reason. In that, Cadus spoke true. Every cut is deeper, every pain sharper."

Whether she loved them or hated them. "That is so," she said thickly, and he held her tighter.

Also true was that every wound inflicted on an entangled heart bled more. For Maddek's words had been a soothing balm, yet they also reopened another wound. All this day, she'd been so eager for her moon night, awaiting all the pleasure he'd promised her. But it was more than simple pleasure she wanted from him now, as he held her so tightly and tended to her warrior's wounds after their battle. She yearned for the love and affection that Maddek already warned her that he would never give.

But her would-be husband was a strong ally. And he would ease her need.

She would be content.

In the terraced gardens, she had no view of the moon peeking above the eastern horizon, but Vela's full face always rose with the closing of Enam's eye. Yvenne watched it sink into a fiery sea of red and orange. As the last glare of gold vanished, she turned her face against Maddek's neck again and licked a hot path up his throat.

His groan in response was such satisfaction, as was the possessive grip he took of her bottom again, squeezing her soft flesh with both hands. In full sight of the warriors, never did Maddek expose what he did to her. Yet Danoh and Banek walked behind and she was at his front, so they could not see how he tugged free her breechcloth, leaving her bare beneath her robes, or those brutish hands lifting and lowering so that her swollen wetness rode over the ridged muscles of his stomach. Yvenne panted at his throat, and when licking was not enough she sucked at his skin as he sometimes sucked on hers, with open lips and pressure that pulled at every sensitive part of her. At the first draw of her mouth, he grunted as if in pain, and she did it again and again, until it seemed not like sucking but kisses that she bestowed the length of his neck.

At the spiraling walk that led to their quarters, he stopped the slow ride that rubbed her most intimate flesh against him, and she knew it was because they were nearing the other warriors. She hid her flushed face against his shoulder.

He could not take her to bed now. Though Bazir was still at the prince's dinner, and would likely wait to attack until he believed most of the Parsathean warriors slept, he might send his Rugusian guard ahead.

Yet the bed was where Maddek seemed to be taking her. He passed Kelir with a gruff, "All is ready?"

"It is," the other warrior said.

"Then douse the lamps and send our invitations."

In the dark Maddek carried her past the parlor, then through the vestibule that led to the bedchamber. From beyond the open balcony came the crash of waves. A cool breeze slipped through the chamber and rippled the curtains surrounding the bed.

A bed where another woman waited, her small form covered in sheer robes, her long curling hair unbound. One of Vela's consorts.

Yvenne frowned in confusion. "What is this?"

"A decoy," Maddek said softly, setting her feet to the floor. "Your brother expects to find me distracted between your thighs. If we give the appearance that I am fucking—"

Yvenne's breath hissed out in fury. "You will *not* lie in a bed with another woman." Not even in pretense or for the purpose of killing her brother. She yanked at the point of his beard so he could not mistake her warning, and when his dark gaze dropped to hers she told him fiercely, "If ever you touch another, I will boil the meat from your cockbone with asilor poison before slitting your throat. You will *not*."

"I will not," he agreed with a sudden grin. "Toric is nearest in size and appearance to me."

As the woman was similar in size and appearance to Yvenne. "That he is," she relented, releasing his beard and ignoring the snorts of laughter from the Parsatheans in the

bedchamber with them. And now she understood the reason for the doused lamps. With curtains drawn, the shadowed figures on the bed would appear exactly as Bazir
expected. "So we conceal ourselves in the dark and kill my
brother when he appears?"

"That is what I will do," he said, and gestured behind
her. "But you leave now for the bargeship."

She looked to see Banek holding her cloak and Ardyl
with her satchel in hand. With a catch in her throat, she
turned back to Maddek. "It should be my arrow. You were
forbidden to kill him."

"The council can have no argument with my killing him
if he attacks our bedchamber." As if to block what argument Yvenne might have, he took hold of her shoulders and
made her face him squarely. "I underestimated Bazir once.
I will not again. And I will not risk you."

"Underestimating him is not the reason you send me away
now. You made this decision *before* the dinner." Or the warriors would not have already been prepared to take her.

"I did," he said. "Yet the reason is the same: I will not
risk you. We assume Bazir only has the Rugusian guard
with him. But although two hundred soldiers cannot come
through the gates, perhaps two can. And two more. We
cannot know how many we will face."

"So I will stay and help! Not reduce your numbers by
sending Banek and Ardyl away to a boat."

"Yvenne." The big hands that cupped her cheeks were
gentle, but his voice and his expression were solid, immov-
able granite. "You told me to be a warrior who made use of
a queen. So I did. Now you must be the queen who makes
use of her warrior and the protection he offers."

With a stubborn lift of her chin, she said, "A warrior-
queen needs no protection."

"You are not a warrior-queen yet," he said gruffly. "And
you are not prepared for this battlefield."

Chest heaving with every response she wanted to make
but could not push past the knot of emotion lodged in her
throat, Yvenne stared up at him. No relenting she saw in his

dark gaze. If anything, his resolve seemed to harden with every passing moment, as if he continuously steeled himself against her desperate need to remain.

She knew he spoke truth. And sense. Yet . . . "I wish to stay. I wish to kill him with my arrow."

"You are a warrior wishing for what you will not have." His callused thumbs swept her cheekbones in a soft caress. "I will bring to you his head, instead."

Throat tight, she nodded into his hands. "This time his poisoned blade will not only be his tongue."

"I will be wary."

"But he still has his tongue. Do not allow him to use it. Or believe anything he has to say."

"I will be wary of that, too."

She could ask for no more. Yet still dread filled her. Dread and hurt and helplessness, which was the worst of all. But this was not only a night of battles. And she still had much to look forward to.

"You will keep your promises to me?" Her voice sounded more uncertain than she wished, full of longing for what she could not have. "The three promises you made for this night?"

Renewed heat flared through his eyes. "I will."

Then there was that, at least. He would see to her pleasure in bed. He was still an ally. Yvenne had hoped for more when she had persuaded him to marriage with his claws at her throat, but that was also wishing for what she would not have.

She *would* be content.

CHAPTER 27

MADDEK

From a darkened corner of the bedchamber, Maddek had a clear view of the open balcony and the sea beyond. The full moon hung low in the southwestern sky when, from beside him, Kelir asked quietly, "Do you think your bride was mistaken?"

"No." Many hours they had waited. But Bazir would come. Had Yvenne not already persuaded Maddek, then the sly tongue's face as they'd left the prince's quarters would have convinced him. Her brother meant to steal her back and to kill Maddek—and this would be his best opportunity to do it. "Do you think her possessed by a demon?"

The other warrior's muffled snort of laughter served as response. And it was the only response the accusation deserved . . . yet Maddek could not let it be the only response given.

"If you ever hear rumor that she is—even if spoken in jest—put an end to it. Calling her demon is how her family means to discredit her and prevent her from creating new alliances."

Kelir's nod shifted subtle shadows behind his head. With moonlight shining into the bedchamber through the balcony, they were not as well hidden as before. Still concealed by darkness, but every movement would betray them. "I will tell the others, too."

Maddek grunted quiet approval.

His friend said nothing more for a moment. Then he dryly observed, "Keen vision she has."

At that understatement, a silent laugh worked through Maddek. For indeed she did. Not her foremothers' gift of sight beyond what was seen, but clearly seeing everything within sight.

"Had you no idea?" Kelir asked.

Maddek shook his head. "Nor does Yvenne, I suspect. She assumes everyone has vision such as hers."

For she had always been in her tower, surrounded by walls—no reason would she have to believe her sight better than anyone else's. And in many ways, she had only begun to learn to see. So even what was clear within her sight, she did not always understand what she looked at.

"Her eyes can be put to good use upon the sea. We will know if any other ships are friend or foe. And upon the Burning Plains, we will know who rides in the distance. Is her vision so keen even in the dark?"

Maddek considered that—beginning with the first night, when the trap jaw had attacked their camp. Uncertain she'd seemed then, struggling to see through the shadows. "I think not."

"Still, it is a valuable gift."

"It is," Maddek agreed. As Yvenne herself was.

From the bed came a soft, feminine moan. As they'd prepared for Bazir's attack, young Toric had insisted that the lingering weakness from the revenant's poison would not affect his ability to wield his sword. That he'd well proven this night, for very little that Maddek heard from behind those curtains sounded like pretense.

The moan also drew Kelir's gaze to the bed and a frown to the warrior's face. "Dawn approaches."

And the moon would set as the sun rose. Maddek knew well. "It does."

"Go to your bride. I will finish this for you."

"I have vowed to bring her his head."

"So you will, even if you are not the one to remove it from his neck. I will deliver his head to you in a ribbon-wrapped box and you will place it at her feet."

Then kiss his way up her legs before fully claiming her. So badly Maddek wanted that. For her brother's head was not the only promise he'd made.

He'd also promised to see to her pleasure, so deep inside her. Long and hard, until she came for him again and again.

Yet of the promises he'd made, it was the last Maddek feared most—to not believe anything from Bazir's poisoned tongue.

For Maddek had truly underestimated her brother. Yvenne had accused him of denying her a sword and shield by not allowing her to speak, yet her silence had been Maddek's own shield. Family cut deeper, and the rage he'd known simply listening to Bazir's lies about Yvenne and his parents had been enough. If she had spoken more about his mother, and Bazir had twisted those words again . . . Maddek knew not if the sly-tongued dog would have found a weakness in him.

As it was, he already struggled with doubt. Not in the claims that she was a demon—but from words as yet unspoken. Because Yvenne had stopped them with her knife. But even unspoken, Bazir's intention had been clear. He meant to accuse Yvenne of killing their mother.

And that accusation had found weakness in Maddek. It had wriggled into him as a worm through a crack. He did not believe it—he would not believe it—yet his mind returned to it again and again.

Though it could not be true. Everything she'd said of Queen Vyssen was evidence against it. Yvenne had loved her mother as Maddek had loved his own. But that worm still wriggled in his brain, a sly tongue wriggling behind it.

Better that he never allowed Bazir to speak again. But that was not the plan.

A seabird's warble floated in from outside, joining the song of the waves—Danoh's signal that the soldiers finally approached.

Approached with the intention of killing his warriors and taking his bride.

Many battles Maddek had fought. Many times he'd waited for an enemy's advance, felt the rush through his veins when they finally appeared, his blood thundering and hot.

Never had it been as this. For they intended to kill his warriors and *take his bride*. To return her to Zhalen's prison, where she would know suffering at her father's hands.

This night, Maddek would defy all that the goddess had claimed. Though not yet a king, Maddek would protect her. Then he would have her.

And he would not lose her.

Another warble from Danoh. The soldiers had chosen the spiral entry, making their way up the curving ramp that led to the main entrance of their quarters. Rugusians were mountain men and no stranger to climbing, so Maddek had anticipated their scaling the balcony to the bedchamber. It offered the greatest surprise and allowed them the best vantage prior to attack.

Perhaps because Bazir was no Rugusian and could not climb. By Temra's fist, Maddek prayed that cur was with them and not waiting for a signal that the deed was accomplished.

Swiftly Maddek abandoned the shadows for the position chosen if the attack did not come through the balcony. Kelir followed, feet silent. The soldiers would likely split their numbers after entering the nest—half seeking out the Parsathean guard to kill them, and the remainder attacking the bedchamber through the vestibule. Quick and quiet they would need to be, giving the Parsatheans no opportunity to raise an alarm or to reach for weapons and shields.

The door between the corridor and vestibule was closed, yet the vestibule was open to the bedchamber. No sound could Maddek hear from the corridor. Southerners wore so much metal armor that always they clinked and jingled like a purse of coins. The stealth of these gave indication of experience.

Toric's grunting came louder, faster, creaking the bed-frame. Luring the soldiers in, giving them false belief that their target was well distracted.

Maddek slipped into the vestibule, then sprang against the wall adjacent to the closed door. His fingers caught a marble protrusion made from the carving of a shell. He hauled himself upward, using another carving to climb higher. Into the corner of the vaulted ceiling he wedged himself, hands and feet braced against the adjoining walls. Kelir took position on the other side. Here the moonlight did not reach them. Only the faintest glow spilled into the vestibule below.

The Rugusian soldiers likely expected that any Parsath-eans guarding Maddek and his bride would stand watch in this small chamber. The most danger and uncertainty the soldiers faced here, not knowing how many warriors waited beyond the closed door.

They came as Maddek would have sent his warriors through—in a silent rush of four soldiers, swords at ready, in a sweeping burst that covered each corner of the vesti-bule. Finding it empty, they hurried to the bedchamber door and took new defensive positions at either side of it.

All wore leather armor instead of metal plates. None wore helms, which would have gleamed in the moonlight. A gray-haired man looked to be captain of the others. He'd led the other three into the vestibule and now knelt by the bedchamber door, his gaze scanning that room—and was bold enough to peer past the frame of the door to check whether any Parsatheans stood against the nearest wall.

Sly nudges passed between the other soldiers when To-ric's grunts quickened, as if nearing release. The soldiers stilled to attention again when the captain held up a fist, then splayed his fingers.

Two more soldiers swept silently into the vestibule. Bazir boldly strode in after them, carrying a sword and wearing no armor. Instead he was dressed as if coming from the prince's dinner, though that was long over.

Only the top of Bazir's head was visible, but Maddek could easily picture his enraging smirk. Confident they all must have been that no Parsathean guards waited inside the bedchamber, for the captain allowed Bazir through the door first. Sheathing his sword and arming himself with a crossbow, the captain and three other soldiers flanked him—leaving two in the vestibule to halt any Parsatheans who might come down the corridor.

Maddek found no fault with the Rugusian captain's strategy. Except that he had not looked up.

Lingering by the bedchamber entrance, as if to watch the attack, the two soldiers in the vestibule had not yet taken post by the corridor door. Nor would they ever.

As one, Maddek and Kelir sprang from their hiding places. No weapons did they draw, for they wore them. Silently Maddek landed behind the nearest soldier and with silver claws ripped out the man's throat to the spine. Hot blood spurted over Maddek's fingers and splashed the wall. With his opposite hand, he caught the soldier's sword as it fell from his grip. The soldier convulsed, hands flying to his neck. If any scream he made, it emerged as a bubbling wheeze from his gaping windpipe.

Maddek eased the thrashing body to the floor. Metal armor would have clattered against marble tiles, but the leather armor muffled the soldier's dying throes, and what little noise remained was concealed by Toric's heavy grunts.

So too did his grunts conceal the next attack. Like raptors Maddek and Kelir bolted from the vestibule. The group of soldiers had crossed half the distance to the curtained bed, moving silently in a fanned formation that could better keep watch on the darkened corners of the large chamber. But it was from behind that death came for the two soldiers at either end of the fan.

No attempt did Maddek make at silence now. So near to

the others, not even Toric's grunts could mask the tortured wheeze or the wet thunk of throatflesh that Maddek threw to the floor. No attempt did he make to stop this soldier's sword from clanging against marble. Instead of letting the body fall to the floor, he anchored the dying man against his chest, holding him upright with silver-clawed fingers cradling the soldier's jaw, letting the others have a clear view of what awaited them.

And using the body as a shield against the crossbow leveled at his heart when the captain spun around. Even in the moonlight, he saw the bloodbare tension that paled the captain's face.

"Abandon the sly-tongue," Maddek told him. "I will let you flee by the balcony."

As he spoke, sudden silence came from the bed, leaving the bedchamber filled with the crash of waves and the heaving of breaths. Though Maddek had not expected the Rugusian to possess any honor, he was not sorry when rage and determination chased the terror from the captain's skin. But although flushed and shaking, neither the captain nor the remaining soldier fired his crossbow at Maddek or Kelir, wasting the bolt on the corpses the Parsatheans used as shields. Instead the captain and soldier drew closer together, providing better protection for Bazir.

In the council chambers Bazir had scrambled fearfully away from Maddek's approach. The two guarding him would slow Maddek no more than the table had, yet no fear did he see in the sly-tongue now. Instead there was only familiar arrogance and disdain. That cur's moonstone eyes gleamed with it—one eye partially slitted closed, swollen and bruised.

"If you are here, who then mounts Yvenne in that bed? There is your answer to why we encountered none of his guard, Holern," Bazir said to the captain. "The barbarians have not laid a trap for us. Instead they take turns between my sister's—"

A hoarse scream from deeper within the nest sounded, followed by savage growls as the remaining Rugusian soldiers found the sleeping quarters where Fassad and his wolves waited.

Bazir's head cocked, listening. When silence fell again he said cheerfully, "Perhaps you had it right, Holern."

The captain's jaw clenched but he only told the remaining soldier to keep an eye on the bed, and his own gaze did not move away from Maddek and Kelir. Perhaps hoping for rage to overcome Maddek's sense, too.

That would not happen. It mattered not what Bazir said.

"She killed our mother. Did she tell you that?" the sly-tongue asked, but the words were nothing, no more substantial than a breeze, because Maddek expected them. "How familiar it must have sounded to you—a queen tragically killed in a failed escape attempt. Is that what you told him, Yvenne?" Raising his voice, he called toward the bed. As he continued, true anger seemed to burn away his smirk. "Or did you give to him a false story, so he would not see through your schemes? Perhaps a tale where our father killed her, though his use for our mother was not done? Or perhaps you blamed Lazen or Cezan, because you have made certain they cannot defend themselves against your lies?"

A failed escape attempt. Harder the words blew, a gale wind battering his heart, yet Maddek stood firm against them. "What use would Zhalen still have for your mother?"

That smirk returned. "To get another daughter upon her. The sickly heir she whelped was . . . inadequate."

Kelir's grin flashed through the blood painting his face like a blade through flesh. "Vela does not find her inadequate."

Neither did Maddek.

Bazir gave a dismissive laugh. "You place your trust in a goddess who abandoned us to the Destroyer? Where was Vela when he killed Queen Venys, the only warrior to ever draw his blood? And when he reanimated Syssia's beloved queen as a demon, where was the goddess then? But it was not only Syssia that Vela had forsaken. Not only the nations of this alliance. All of the western realms, she abandoned to his destruction. Yet you truly expect her to assist us now?"

Maddek cared nothing of what the goddess did. Only what he believed Yvenne might accomplish.

Those moonstone eyes sharpened, so shrewd and yet so unlike the cleverness of his sister's. "If you wish to survive the Destroyer's return, do not look to Yvenne. Join with my father and Aezil, and bow to Enam—and you and your people might have a chance."

By serving the Destroyer? By welcoming his rule and more of Enam's corrupt magic?

"I think not," Maddek said.

"So instead you will follow a queen who is sickly and weak? What fool would do such a thing?" Her brother laughed again, and Maddek knew the shame of having thought and said almost exactly the same. To the bed Bazir called again, "You have truly enslaved him! Perhaps you are no demon, Yvenne, but you have proved yourself more persuasive than ever I believed. First you clear a path to a husband by setting a trap for his queen and king, then you convince him to marry their murderer. Are you certain you do not wish me to take her back to Syssia?"

The last was directed to Maddek—as it all had been, he knew. Trying to stoke his rage, to fuel his doubt.

And enraged Maddek was. Impulsive, he was not. Neither were his warriors.

Danoh had fought beside him far longer than she'd been part of his guard. Maddek knew the only delay had been the moonlight, as Danoh found route to the balcony where the shadow she cast would not expose her movements. The moon was low and shone directly into the bedchamber, so she would be forced to find a wide angle of approach. So wide, she was still nowhere in his sight when he heard the *thwap* of her bowstring.

Vela had called her the Dragon's sting. So she was this night, as her arrow pierced the soldier's back, flinging him forward with the impact. A bad angle she must have had on the captain, or she misguessed the direction he would turn in response to the soldier's cry. Her next arrow embedded into the leather armor protecting his shoulder, yet it was enough to make him stumble and lose his steady aim. With a roar, Kelir dropped his corpse shield and hurled his axe. The blade struck the captain's chest with such force that he flew back off his feet and was dead before he landed.

Bazir, they left for Maddek.

Now that sly-tongued cur fell back from Maddek in desperate retreat, holding his sword out before him. This time Maddek would not underestimate him or forget Yvenne's warning about poisoned blades. The body he still carried as shield, and as he passed the fallen captain, he swept up his crossbow.

Bazir's moonstone eyes widened. "You cannot—*Arrrrgh!*"

With a feathered bolt jutting from his right shoulder, the cur scuttled back nearer to the balcony, switching his sword to his left hand. Little practice he seemed to have with that grip, wobbling and weak, slashing wildly. Bazir hit the corpse shield that Maddek carried once, twice, before lunging forward as if intending to run the body through and strike Maddek with the poisoned blade. Maddek shoved the corpse at him as Bazir impaled it. Overbalanced by the weight on his blade, Bazir's grip failed. The weapon slipped from his hand and the cur stumbled.

Maddek caught him by the throat, claws digging in. "Her only return to Syssia will be to claim her throne. Never will your brothers or your father touch her again."

Gasping and struggling, Bazir wheezed desperately, "She will betray you, as she did my mother and yours—"

Stabbing his fingers between those open lips, Maddek ripped out the wriggling worm of a tongue and released him.

Choking, blood pouring from his mouth, Bazir looked at him stunned. Ragged sounds came from his throat. Not screams. As if still trying to speak.

Maddek yanked Bazir's sword from the soldier's corpse and skewered the cur's gut with it.

A quick death it was—quicker than it should have been,

and quicker than Maddek would have liked. No doubt the blade had been poisoned. As Bazir thrashed on the floor, green foam bubbled through the blood coming from his mouth. Then abruptly he stilled, moonstone eyes glazed and unseeing.

"It is done," Maddek announced.

Toric opened the curtain, revealing Vela's consort behind him, and the other two occupants of the bed who had waited through this long night—Gareth and Cadus. Both wore grim expressions, though when the prince's gaze took in the carnage, horror and sickness joined it.

"You heard with your own ears?"

Jaw tight, the Tolehi minister nodded. "Syssia and Rugus will betray the alliance to save their own skins."

"Zhalen. Not Syssia." Nothing Maddek had seen of Yvenne's people suggested that they supported their regent. Only feared him. He knew not if Rugus was the same, but that they would discover when Aezil was dead. Maddek yanked Kelir's axe from the captain's chest. "Carry that knowledge back to the council, but travel with care. If they can, Zhalen and Aezil will have you killed before you reach Ephorn."

"As they will also come for you."

"So they will." So the race to the Burning Plains would resume.

"All of Syssia and Rugus against seven warriors? Come with me, instead, and speak to the council. Let them also hear Nyset's heir."

"I will not risk her."

"Two hundred soldiers will serve as escort—"

"And do you trust that Bazir has not filled their heads with his lies on the journey here? Can you assure me that she will not be set upon by soldiers who believe her a demon? *You* believed it for a time." When that silenced the minister, Maddek turned back to Bazir's corpse. "When you remove this body, beware the poisoned blade."

"Green spittle," Cadus said, carefully lifting the hem of his robes and stepping around pools of blood as he moved closer to examine it. "Silac venom?"

"Odd choice, if it was." That from Vela's consort, who had remained steady through this night. "The venom will kill an opponent, but not quickly."

That was truth. The poison only weakened those it infected, until they fell asleep and woke a brainless beast. "Not so odd if he meant to turn the alliance against me. Weakened, I could have been defeated and he could have taken Yvenne—and after waking, I would have slaughtered everyone in the palace, with no one aware the cause was poison."

And no doubt Bazir would have claimed Maddek killed Yvenne in his rampage, so no one would look for her afterward.

"Will *he* wake?" wondered Cadus, frowning.

Maddek gave answer by chopping off Bazir's head.

CHAPTER 28

MADDEK

Cadus's fastest horses they rode to the docks, with an escort to show them the shortest route. Dawn lightened the eastern sky. Over the western horizon, the full moon blushed pink.

No hired bargeship did they have now. Drahm's prince had offered Yvenne his protection, and as they'd waited for Bazir's attack, he'd first attempted to persuade Maddek to remain in the city. When that failed, Cadus had insisted on the honor of continuing his protection as they sailed north. His own ship he'd offered for their use—an offer Maddek gladly took. For they truly were in a race, and the prince's vessel would cross the water more swiftly.

The change had been made during the night. Instead of a wide bargeship, this ship more resembled a swan, with a great sail furled against the curved mast of the neck. Carrying a jute sack, Maddek strode up the gangway. Ardyl and Banek waited, and the deck was busy with crew—but no Yvenne.

"Where is she?"

"The royal quarters," Ardyl said, pointing to the tail of the boat. "She left to prepare for your arrival after seeing her brother felled."

In surprise, Maddek glanced to the shore. The nest he could see, a pale shell nestled amid the terraced gardens, but he had not thought her sight able to pierce the dark.

Yet it had not been dark, he realized. The full moon had shone into the bedchamber, as if Vela herself had allowed Yvenne to witness her brother's death.

"The horses?"

"Aboard."

"Then tell the captain to set sail." Striding the length of the deck, he looked to the western horizon again. Never had the moon seemed to sink so quickly. Not much time would he have to prepare Yvenne for a fucking—and now Vela's gift of cockmonger's oil seemed not such an insult, but necessary to ease his entry if Maddek had no time to use his mouth and fingers. His cock only needed to breach her cunt before the moon set. Then he would keep his promises to her.

His clawed fingers left crimson marks on the palewood door he slid open, ducking his head as he entered. If not for the low ceiling and creaking of the ship, he might have been in the prince's palace again. No doors or walls divided the space. Silk screens gave privacy to the bed and the bath. The rear of the chamber lay open to a private deck—and beyond that, the sea.

Only a small distance separated the moon and the water.

A steep flight of stairs descended to the recessed floor of the chamber. Skipping the steps, Maddek leapt down and could stand properly without hitting his head. The jute sack dripped blood onto polished wooden planks as he crossed to the bed.

Yet it was from behind the bath screen that Yvenne emerged—long curling locks unbound, and clad only in a robe. No linens wrapped her limbs. Her cheeks were flushed, her hardened nipples pebbled beneath silk, her soft bottom lip trapped between her teeth as she watched his approach.

He reached into the sack. Fingers tangled in matted hair, he set her brother's head upon a table. "It is done."

"I saw," she said huskily, and held out her hand as if to lead him to bed.

He swept her up into his arms instead, carrying her behind the screen. More steep steps led up to the wide dais supporting the bed. He lifted her onto the platform, where she stood taller than he, his face on level with her breasts. "Where is Vela's potion?"

"In my satchel." She caught hold of the spaulders armoring his shoulders before he could go in search of it. "But my sheath needs no oiling."

Because she had come here to prepare herself as soon as she'd seen her brother fall. Maddek assumed that meant to bathe and to undress. Now he drew her fingers into his mouth, gave himself a taste of the sweetness that lingered at their tips.

Her breath shuddered, a sound of hot desire—and soft humor. "Our bed truly will look like a battlefield as you come to me wearing blood and claws and sword." With the two fingers on her right hand, she swiped through the gore painting his chest, and her smile diminished to a sad curve. "Though I must pose no real threat, for you do not shield your heart against me."

What use would such armor serve? Already she had reached in and taken hold of it. "Only a fool would underestimate you, Yvenne," he told her gruffly.

Maddek had been a fool once.

The slightest smile returned, as if she believed he spoke platitudes. "You used a shield against my brother."

"The corpse?" His claws skimmed up the outsides of her thighs, bloodied silver over slippery silk. Her scent reached him, faint coconut and stronger anise, as if she'd applied that Syssian perfume to her throat and breasts before his arrival. "My true shield was your warning to avoid his poisoned blades. Else I might think as he wanted me to, and believe that you betrayed and killed your mother."

She became utterly still. "What do you believe, instead?"

"That you had painful reason," he said gently, hands curving over her hips. A reason that her brother had wrapped in other lies, perhaps. That a demon had possessed her mother's weakened body—or she'd been maddened, as Bazir claimed Ran Ashev had been, and Yvenne killed her mother in defense of her own life. "And no other choice."

Never had her walls erected so swiftly, so visibly. She neither moved nor spoke, yet he could see and hear the barrier she put up between them, in the hardening of her moonstone eyes and the deep slowing of her breaths. A poisonous ache filled his chest. These walls he'd battered down and now they stood again, as if he'd never touched her. As if she'd never invited him in.

Then she yanked on his beard and hissed, "I told you not to believe what he said."

Not even in bed yet, and already the battle was here, with a pointed blade piercing his heart. "You also said he would frame lies with truth, to better persuade me to his view. That view I saw for the lie it was."

"Yet *your* view is still that I killed her?"

"Of everything he said about you, only that held a ring of truth." And was confirmed by her reactions. First in the throwing of her knife and now because she *did not deny it*. Every time he'd suggested she had a part in his own mother's death, Yvenne immediately denied it. Always she'd denied it. Here she only yanked at his beard for listening to Bazir. Hoarsely he asked, "*Did* you kill her during a failed escape?"

For an endless moment, she stared down at him from walls so high he could not read her face. Then she drew a breath that was agony.

As if suffering. Not at her father's hands, but at his.

Sudden dread closed his throat. His fingers tightened on

her hips, but she pulled out of his grip, stepping back with a cold smile curving her lips.

"I think you like that view. It fits so neatly with the one you already have of me." Her chin lifted. "Very well. Let us frame it that way. I *did* kill my mother during a failed escape."

She would not have. He *knew* she would not have.

Yet Maddek also did not believe she was lying. In a raw voice, he said, "I cannot believe—"

"Anything I say. Yes, I know. Because I am the foul, treacherous vessel for your vengeance. And you'd best hurry and make use of me. If you do not fuck my sheath full of your seed now, you will have no opportunity again." Turning her back to him, she bent over the side of the bed and braced her elbows. "You need not even look at my scheming face while you mount me."

By Temra's fist. Sheer frustration gritted his teeth. It should not be like this, without resolution between them. With her walls still so high.

Yet little time they had. The moon's chin rested on the horizon. So he would breach her quickly, then slow until they no longer battled but were allies again.

The low ceiling above the bed would give him no proper room to stand on the dais, so it was on his knees that Maddek settled in behind her small, rounded ass. Her anger with him must have burned away even her shyness. When he swept aside the skirt of her robe, baring her bottom and legs to his gaze for the first time, barely a tremble moved through her breaths.

The only shaking was Maddek's. Need so hot and urgent that he did not trust the steadiness of his clawed fingers against her most delicate skin. With his mouth he tested her readiness, a long deep lick through her glistening cleft that sent Yvenne swaying forward on a gasping moan that she quickly muffled against the bed. Hot and slick his tongue found her, and when he suckled on her clit, her shaking began to match his.

With more time, he'd have made her come in this way

first. Instead he slowly rose from kneeling into a crouch, leaving a hungry trail of openmouthed, biting kisses up over the curve of her ass. The silks tucked into his belt shredded beneath his claws, freeing the steel length of his cock. Anticipation surged down his shaft like the stroke of a tight fist. He reached the edge of her robe and his tongue slicked over the dimple at the base of her spine.

Yvenne flinched, the barest tensing of her muscles.

Maddek frowned down at what had caused that reaction— a faint welt he'd felt beneath his tongue. But it wasn't a welt. A scar slashed across her upper left buttock, not unlike the stripes from the bowstring on her forearm, though thicker. Newly healed, but apparently still sensitive.

"What is this?" Carefully, not touching the scar and mindful of his claws, he traced the skin alongside the stripe with the pad of his thumb.

"The punishment from my father for sending a message to your parents. One you'd likely approve." Each word was bitter and hot, punctuated by her heaving breaths. "Or perhaps you think I deserved worse. Both of you decided to strip me of skin for it, but you'd have flayed me and tossed me over the Syssian wall. My father only used a whip."

Punishment. A mild one from Zhalen, compared to her knee and her fingers. Yet even this single stripe was more than she'd deserved. *Any* punishment was more than she'd deserved. And Maddek recalled saying what vengeance he'd planned for her—but more than his words, her reply.

If you intend to kill me, I only beg that you do it quickly. My life has been a torment. I pray my death will not be.

Too many punishments she'd known. Too much pain. So she'd chosen a husband who would see to her pleasure.

She'd chosen *him*. A man who'd threatened to flay her. And now a man who would give his life to protect her from any more suffering.

Yet he could not protect her from all hurt. And some he would inflict upon her.

Throat raw, Maddek bent over her tense form, guiding his cock to her virgin cunt. "Forgive this pain," he said hoarsely. "It will be but once. Then I will keep my promises to you."

"The promise you made to rip out my lying tongue?" She panted the question, and her back arched as she did, hips tilting up as if to invite him in.

Her walls, crumbling.

"To fuck you long and hard and deep. To make you come over and over again." Voice harsh, he lowered his mouth to her ear, and glided the broad head of his erection through her sultry cleft, up and down, teasing her entrance with each pass. "Do you want me to fuck you, Yvenne?"

"I do," she breathed, a whisper of sheer need.

So Maddek would, but not easily. She was so very wet, dripping with her honey, but her sheath was small and un-softened by his fingers and tongue. Bent over her slender form with one hand braced beside her shoulder, he pushed against her entrance and only shoved her entire body forward, unbalancing her on the bed.

The moon barely peeked above the horizon.

Rearing back, boots planted beside the bed and as upright as he could stand, Maddek grabbed hold of Yvenne's hips to anchor her in place for the brute force of a thrust that half buried his cock in hot, tight cunt. The blinding ecstasy of being inside his bride cleared in an instant when a strangled gasp tore from her lips. Then she went utterly silent, pressing her forehead to the bed.

"Only this time." Chest heaving, Maddek tried to soothe her, sweeping his palms up and down her trembling flanks. "We will wait until you no longer hurt."

Without a word she nodded, the gesture a tumble of upended curls that hid her face from him. Her fingers twisted in the bed coverings, fisting the white linen as if to hold herself in place instead of fleeing from the pain of his possession.

Those twisting fingers dug into his heart. "Is it too much? You are breached, but it was roughly done. We can continue later."

She shook her head, and her shuddering exhalation eased

the piercing worry in his chest. That breath said it was no longer a sharp pain, but one that was fading.

Around his cock, her heated sheath softened and tightened, softened and tightened, her honeyed walls accepting and then resisting his thick penetration. Her body's inner struggle was exquisite pleasure that Maddek bore with gritted teeth. Every instinct roared for him to stroke into her with his full length, hard and deep, and to feel the scorching clasp of her cunt clamp ever tighter around his shaft as he made her come.

His heart thundered with the need to finish this battle in the sweetest way, with Yvenne yielding and surrendering to him. And in that surrender, Maddek would know that he'd protected her, and he'd truly had her, and he would not lose her.

But he waited. The moon vanished into the sea. The ship creaked, faint shouts from the sailors joining the cawing of seabirds, and the swaying of the floor deepened as the sails caught the faint breeze.

Yvenne's breath became as soft as that wind. No longer did her fingers twist, though she had not yet lifted her head. Her back was not so stiff, her slender torso wrapped in thin silk. Such a pretty ass she had, a narrow flare from her waist into small, rounded buttocks. As his splayed fingers anchored her hips in a firm grip, the tips of his claws lightly dimpled skin softer and finer than the silks she wore. His gaze followed the sweet shadowed valley dividing her cheeks, then lower, to where his heavy shaft speared between her delicate folds.

He was only partially inside her sheath, yet her cunt had a stranglehold on his cock. Had a stranglehold on *him*. Inside her, he throbbed and ached, her slightest movements tugging and pulling at his turgid flesh.

With a long indrawn breath Yvenne raised her head, her back arching. "Deeper now."

Command or plea, Maddek knew not. But he would have obeyed, would have given what his bride needed but for the way she rocked back onto him, as if in bold intention of claiming his cock. But for the way the voluptuous grip of her cunt both welcomed and resisted him, so that her claim became like hot suction on the length of his arousal. But for the way she moaned deep in her throat, and when it emerged from her lips that sound of pleasure was his name.

A storm of sensation his bride became, lightning that struck the base of his spine and forked to the root of his erection, then surged along his shaft. His seed boiled up in uncontrollable pulses, spilling into her sheath while Maddek grunted through clenched teeth and fought a war that had already seen his defeat. In denial he tried to stroke deeper, but the honeyed channel that had barely yielded to his stiffened cock utterly resisted his softening flesh.

Moaning again as he thrust futilely against her, Yvenne rolled her hips back. "You need not be so easy with me, warrior. If you are to plant your seed, you must plow deep. And I am eager for more."

So eager. Her cunt was drenched in her need, greedily clutching the heavy thickness still within her.

"More I will give you," he told her. Wearing sharp claws, Maddek could not stroke her clit, but his mouth was all he needed. "Lie upon the bed. I will feast upon your sweetness until I rise again."

On her elbows, she looked back over her shoulder, disbelief clear upon her face. "You already spilled your seed?"

"I did not intend to. But it matters not."

Still she stared at him. "Because you already eased your need upon me?"

"Never will my need for you be eased. So with my mouth I will see to your pleasure until—"

"I will see to my own." Abruptly she pulled forward. His cock slipped from her sheath, his spent member glistening with blood and honey and seed. Flicking the skirt of her robe back into place, Yvenne covered her soft bottom and crawled up onto the bed. "I should have purchased the cockmonger's shaft."

Shame scorched Maddek's face. "When I stiffen again, I will keep my promises to you."

In the center of the bed, she sat and regarded him—her walls high again, with no sign of the arousal that had overcome her defenses, no indication of the need that had invited him in. Yet they were walls more brittle than he'd ever seen, as if built not of moonstone but of shattered glass, glittering in her eyes like tears.

Usually her walls concealed her emotions, yet these did not. So much devastation Maddek saw, and he struggled against the need to reach for her with a comforting hand, knowing she would reject his attempt. His gut churned, sick and heavy with shame and dread. She would not take a husband who did not see to her pleasure. Yet at this moment she clearly did not want him to touch her.

"It has been a long night of battles, Yvenne." And Maddek could not fight his bride or her blade of a tongue now. "Let us take our rest, and then—"

"Battles!" She gave a laugh like nothing he'd ever heard from her, high and wild, and with such pain in it—the sound an animal caught in a trap might make, if it laughed and screamed at once. Or the sound a queen who did not cry might make, for as she laughed tears spilled from her eyes.

"Yvenne?" he asked hoarsely. "Are you crying?"

"No," she said, still laughing but wiping her cheeks. "Though if ever a queen had a reason to cry where someone might see, this would be it. For there is no greater pain than losing one's children."

Her children? Tension gripped the back of his neck. "What do you speak of?"

"I thought to be content. We would have children. I would look to them for love and affection. And they would be strong, because you are." Her laughter slowly faded as she spoke, but her breaths still shuddered through her slim form as if in the aftermath of sobbing. "But now I know that the first time they ride into battle will also be their last—because if they inherit their father's strength, they will only have stamina enough for one thrust of their sword before they falter. Our poor doomed children," she ended on a heavy sigh.

He stared at her in awe. *Such* a sharp tongue she had. If Maddek had not already been gutted by his own shame, she would have eviscerated him.

Instead he leaned nearer and told her with unmistakable resolution, "This is not the battle we will fight on this bed, Yvenne. And after we sleep, you will have no doubt of my stamina."

Her glittering eyes narrowed. He heard the pain that lay at the sharpened edge of her voice as she demanded, "You want to sleep next to a queenkiller?"

"I do." He cared not what had occurred. He only cared that Queen Vyssen's death had hurt her, and that he knew not how to breach the walls she'd erected and soothe her pain.

"But I do not wish to share a bed with someone who views me as you do." Her lips trembled, and she turned away, presenting him with only her frail shoulders and back. "When your cock rises again, you may return to ease your need upon me—but do not bother to wake me for it."

Once more she caught him with that blade of a tongue. Though it was sharp, however, hers was not a poisonous one. She left nothing in him that was not already there. No anger toward her was in him as he said harshly, "I *will* return and keep my promises to you."

"As you say." Her breath hitched. "But go now."

So that she might be alone to cry. Everything in Maddek rebelled at the thought of leaving her in this way. Yet she did not want him here.

With aching chest, he strode to the stairs leading out of the chamber. Yvenne did not cry where there were eyes to see. She also did not cry when there were ears to hear.

Yet Maddek did hear. As if the sob broke from her before he left the chamber because she couldn't contain it anymore—though she tried. That sob she quickly muffled. But still he heard, and the sound was sharper than any word that ever came from her tongue.

As if it wore claws, one quiet sob tore out Maddek's heart. Yet even that ragged and bleeding wound was not as painful as knowing he was the cause, or as painful as not knowing the remedy.

So many promises he'd made and not fulfilled this night. Not only to Yvenne, but to himself. For he might have protected Yvenne from her brother, but he hadn't protected her from himself. And he'd not truly had her.

And now he might have lost her.

MADDEK

Swift wind blew into Maddek's face as he stepped onto the deck. Unfurled, the white sails were at full billow, and the ship skimmed across low, rolling waves.

Laughter and voices coming from quarters near the tail led Maddek to his warriors. A long night they'd also had, and more than a full turn of hard riding since leaving the Lave. Fatigued they must be, yet much had occurred since their last waking, and much to discuss and celebrate. For a tennight they'd spent every moment in expectation of soldiers coming upon them and the battle that would follow, and when Yvenne had told them those soldiers' numbers, each warrior had likely felt Rani coming from behind them. Yet that battle they'd won with little bloodshed and no injuries to their own. And the goddess Vela herself had recognized each, showing favor that must swell the heart and pride of any warrior—even Parsatheans who rarely prayed to any gods.

On his approach, Maddek heard them turning over that favor and examining it, suggesting possible meanings for

Vela's claim that Toric would fly far on a dragon's wings
and no longer be himself on his return. Many meanings
they would likely find, and of none could they be certain.
Except for silent Mother Temra and truthful silver-fingered
Rani, gods were the most sly-tongued of all beings.

The chambers were not sleeping quarters but similar to
the prince's solar, with a table surrounded by low cushions
and sofas, with more scattered about the room. No longer
wearing their armor, the Dragon sprawled around the table
loaded down with fruits and meats and drink.

As Maddek came in, Kelir looked up from cleaning the
blood from his spaulders. The warrior's wet hair hung
heavily around his scarred face, and he wore only a small-
cloth around his waist.

At a glimpse of Maddek's expression, his own became
dismay. "Did you not reach her before moonset?"

"I did. She is no longer a virgin."

With a smirk, Ardyl eyed the shredded silks hanging
from his belt. "You must have been in a rush to get to her.
I trust that blood is not all hers?"

Nor his, though his heart had been torn away. Chest hollow, Maddek shook his head, then looked to Fassad. "Will
you send the wolves to guard her door?"

The warrior tossed them each a bison joint to chew on
and sent them off.

Kelir surged up to his feet, collecting two flagons of
mead. "I will show you where the wash bucket is, because
a bath will only leave you sitting in a bloodied pool. Then
you can return to her."

He could not. Maddek took the mead Kelir pushed into
his hand but did not drink as he walked with the other warrior past the ship's wings. There attendants filled buckets
from the warm sea. Five dousings it took, removing armor
and belt with each bucket tipped over his head, bloodied
water running over the side of the deck and returned to the
waves below. The shredded silks he gave to the attendants,
not caring if ever he saw them again, and received a fine
white robe in return. He tied it around his hips. His red

linens were rolled up with his furs and those were in the chamber with Yvenne.

Where she sobbed, devastated by hurt and disappointment.

As if numb, Maddek returned to the solar, and there Banek gestured to a platter. "Best you take that back to her."

Because his bride was always hungry. "I will not disturb her yet."

Surprise crossed Toric's expression. "Does she already sleep? Such a night it has been, I will not sleep for years."

Maddek shook his head. "She does not yet sleep."

"And you do not return to her?" With a grunt, Kelir threw himself back down to his sofa. "With a woman such as Yvenne in my bed, I would spread her thighs and—"

"Do not speak of her such," Maddek warned him in a dangerous tone.

"And *there* is a bit of fire," his friend laughed, though his eyes were keen on Maddek's face. "The burning heart of our Dragon seemed doused, but I do not think it was the buckets that did it. Do you seek counsel? As Rani breathed into her dragon's heart to reignite its spark, so we will re-spark yours."

Counsel. That was not what he needed. He needed Yvenne.

But he might not have her again.

Throat raw, Maddek told them, "It is not counsel I seek from you all, but help."

"You will have it," Fassad said.

"Vela did not give favor to me, but a warning that if I do not have the heart of a king, I will not be able to protect Yvenne. And that I will lose her. If that occurs . . ." Hard he had to swallow before continuing. "If that occurs, I beg that you protect her."

"So we will," Ardyl said with a slight frown, leaning forward. "Now tell us what demon has possessed you, that you are not raging against Vela's words and denying it will ever happen?"

"I have done that," Maddek said thickly. "Now my bride does not welcome me back to her bed. And I have lost her."

"I do not think you will lose her so easily." Faint amusement lit Banek's eyes. "Sit with us, Ran Maddek."

Maddek did, for he had nowhere else to go.

Fassad asked quietly, "What is it she said?"

"That I have a twisted view of her. That I see her as a queenkiller."

Kelir frowned, his drink halfway to his lips. "You did not believe what that snake-swiving sly-tongue said about Queen Vyssen?"

"I did not," Maddek replied, rubbing his tired eyes. "But Yvenne claims it is true. She killed her mother."

Stunned faces looked back at him. Then slowly shaking heads, as they all denied it—as Maddek had.

"What does Yvenne say occurred?" That from Toric, who seemed in a daze.

"She will not tell me. Instead she builds high walls between us. I have tried to—"

"Conquer her walls? Defeat them?" That was Toric again. "As Vela said you did."

"It is truth. I have battered myself against them, tried to go over them, lured her out and received invitation . . ." His throat closed. No invitation did he have now. "Always she rebuilds them."

"Her walls," Kelir echoed, then looked to Ardyl. "Our friend sees walls, yet she told him what they are to her. 'What are walls but armor for a city?'"

"Or armor for a heart?" she said.

"Or armor over a wound." Fassad tore off a soft chunk of bread. "A borrowfly once tried to carry away one of my brother's pups, and in the fight Steel's shoulder was stung. Not deep, but it became infected—and so painful that he growled and snapped at me if I attempted to touch it. More than any other, that wolf trusts me. Loves me. Yet he could not bear for me to tend to that injury without striking at me with his fangs."

A painful injury as her mother's death must be. Yet it was not only her mother's death. For he'd first seen those walls the morning after he'd pulled at her tongue. The morning after he'd told her not to look to him for affection or love.

The morning after he'd betrayed her trust by telling her that he would not hurt her—and then doing so. She had said he made weapons when she revealed herself to him. He had not understood then. But now he did. They were not walls at all, but protection for her heart. Just as she'd armored her open wounds. And Maddek had been battering his way through to prod them.

Watching Maddek's face, Kelir declared smugly, "So he finally sees."

"What *do* you see?" Danoh asked, frowning at Maddek. "A queenkiller? Someone who is no more than her father's daughter?"

Maddek shook his head.

Banek's eyes narrowed. "You do not still believe she played any part in your mother's death, except to send that letter in hope of escaping Zhalen?"

"I do not." And that was truth, Maddek realized. Full truth. Not just accepting her word but still harboring doubts. No doubts did he have. "But that is the view her brother would have had me believe—that Yvenne had repeated a murder."

"Yet she admitted to it?"

"After I told her what I thought it meant. That only in defense of her own life would she have ever harmed her mother. If Vyssen had been possessed by a demon or gone on a rampage. Blameless Yvenne would be then."

"So she would," Ardyl said. "Yet still you assume she would have done it with deliberation and intent. Did you not suppose she might have been tricked?"

"Tricked?" So clever and careful was she, Maddek had not thought of such a thing. "By Zhalen?"

"Perhaps with a poison," Toric agreed. "If she had fed the queen without knowing it was there, your bride might feel that she'd killed her mother. And we have seen how much care she takes with food and drink when her family is near."

Banek nodded. "That would be a killing with no intention—and an accusation would cut ever deeper for it. Especially if she did not perceive the trick. She would blame herself."

So she would. And that Maddek could also easily perceive . . . now. "An unintentional killing is more likely," he acknowledged. "I did not even see."

Kelir frowned at him. "You are not usually so blind."

"With her, I seem to be."

"As made sense when you first knew her," Banek said. "We were all suspicious. But now how do you see her?"

"As a queen who is clever and vicious and cunning, who would destroy her father and brothers, but who would never betray or abandon anyone she is loyal to or responsible for—including all of her people."

Toric said, "We will be her people."

Maddek nodded. "If I am named Ran, no finer queen could we ask for."

"So you say, but still this view of her you have?" Banek frowned. "Has she ever spoken to you with sly tongue?"

"Twice," he said. "But she will not again. And even when she did, there was no malicious intent."

"Has she lied?"

Maddek struggled with his answer. He did not want them to know that she had. He did not want to say that truth. Because a Parsathean queen should never lie.

Yet truth must be said. "She has."

All expressions darkened. Worry and dismay filled the many glances the warriors exchanged between them, as if weighing each other's reactions before Kelir slowly asked, "What was the lie?"

"That my mother chose her to be my bride."

"But she doesn't wear Ran Ashev's crest," his friend said, frowning. "Has she made mention of it?"

"No." And if his mother had truly approved of her, in that approval Ran Ashev would have told Yvenne what it meant to give that crest. But even if the crest could not be given, if it had been stolen by Zhalen, a message his mother would have given her instead to explain why the crest was absent.

Which meant Yvenne had no knowledge of it. Yet if Ran Ashev had approved of her, she would.

Again, they all struggled. Conflicted as Maddek had been.

"Perhaps Ran Ashev would have approved of her," Ardyl said slowly. "As we have come to do. But to give that approval after Ran Marek was murdered and while she was held imprisoned and raped . . . ?"

So she said what Maddek had thought. As the others did, too.

That troubling knowledge lined Banek's face. "When did she speak this lie?"

"At the very first. As she tried to persuade me to marry her. I told her I knew it for a lie then, so she persuaded me with the promise of killing her father."

Now they were frowning at him. "You knew she'd spoken a lie and yet agreed to marry?"

No excuse had he. "I meant to have my vengeance by any means." And how torn he'd been then at the thought of marrying a lying woman who might have murdered his parents. No longer was he torn. "But my vengeance is only secondary now. Protecting her is the greater purpose."

No censure did he see in them for that—admitting that avenging their queen and king had fallen behind in importance. Such shame he'd felt before, yet none did he feel now. Vengeance was still necessary. Yet that vengeance was not foremost in his heart.

Nor was it foremost for his Dragon. Yet they were not unconflicted—as he was not.

"That lie still disturbs you?" Fassad asked.

"It does," he admitted.

"Because if you take her to wife, you might not be named Ran?"

"No." Painful though it would be, if he must choose between leading Parsathe and Yvenne . . . he would choose Yvenne. "Because it is a lie. And though we have become allies, still she insists on its truth."

"Does the lie make you reconsider your marriage to her?"
Nothing could. He shook his head.

"Are you conflicted because Ran Ashev did not approve
of her?"

"No." That he was certain of. "I would have no other.
Even if her lie means that I am never Ran."

"You say she spoke it at the first?" Banek asked now, his
gaze narrowed thoughtfully. "When you had your claws in
her throat?"

"It was."

Satisfaction filled the older warrior's voice. "And she
spoke it while persuading you to marry her—to save her
own life and in hope of freeing her people?"

Brightening, Toric sat forward. "Even Ran Antyl lied to
save her children."

That was truth. And it was as if a pressure upon Maddek
eased. When spoken against an enemy and to save a life,
lies were justified and forgiven. Yvenne had been an enemy
to him in that moment—and he had been to her. Yet he had
viewed the lie as if it came from an ally.

All of his warriors felt the same ease, he saw. Relief
passed through them like a knot loosening.

"And it was only that one lie?" Kelir pressed.

"It was. Except that she lied again to insist she has always told me the truth."

"But that is likely the same purpose and reason," Ardyl
said. "Though you no longer have claws in her throat, still
she must feel the weight of all the Syssian lives upon her
shoulders. And she is alone among Parsatheans who have
warned her never to lie. Her mother may have watched us,
but Yvenne does not fully understand our ways—she had
to ask Banek whether even a jest must always be true. So
she is still a stranger among us and might believe that admitting to a lie now will destroy every hope she has of
marriage, or of freeing her people. She might believe you
would abandon her for that lie—especially if she knows
that her lie might cause issue when it comes time to vote for
our new Ran."

Such ease and relief filled him. As if her lie had been festering in a wound that was even deeper than he knew. Yet his warriors spoke sense and truth.

"This does give me a different view of her." Gratitude swelled through him . . . and eagerness to return to his bride. Gaining his feet, he scanned the platters of food. Yvenne's favorites were the meats, but many of the fruits and berries would be new to her, and she would enjoy trying them.

"A different view you might have," Danoh said, pulling his gaze from the table. "But you must overcome habit first."

He frowned, not understanding. "Habit?"

"The habit of viewing her as you did. Of responding to her as you did. Even though I better understand my mother, still I always yell at her. Still I am easily angered by her. It is habit. So your view might not so quickly change . . . but you will be better at recognizing how those old habits twist it. And you will have to relearn how to see her."

"So I will," vowed Maddek, filled with fiery purpose.

Kelir grinned. "And so the heart of our Dragon burns again."

Did it? "I know not if that is true," he told them, chest suddenly tight. If he burned, it was only with hope. And if Yvenne would not have him after this, even that hope might be destroyed in an instant. "For she is *my* heart. And when I left her, she was doused in her tears."

Sympathy smoothed the lines of Banek's face. "Then you must also do as silver-fingered Rani did after she pulled her dragon from the belly of the Scourge, and reignite that spark in her. But do not forget how that story goes, Ran Maddek, for at first Rani was so eager for her dragon's return, she blew too hard and the gale of her breath extinguished the faint ember that remained of its heart. Then from her own heart, Rani had to cut a new spark—and it was with endless patience and gentle breath that she rekindled her dragon's from spark to burning flame."

And so Maddek would, too.

CHAPTER 30

YVENNE

Maddek had torn out her brother's tongue.

Feeling as empty as that bloodied mouth, Yvenne carried Bazir's head out to the private deck. Drahm lay far behind them, a shining jewel nestled upon the shore. The previous day, she'd ridden into that city filled with such happiness and anticipation. Little of both remained.

She had never lied to Maddek. But she had lied to herself.

She would be content? She would not be. Instead she was greedy. Only a sevennight past, in the bed at the inn, she would have rejoiced if Maddek had looked at her with such sympathy and warmth, and with the clear belief that she had not conspired to kill her own mother.

But now it was not enough. And she had thought that desperately clinging to the pleasure he promised would overcome the pain of everything else. Yet that had not been enough, either.

She knew he would have kept his promises to fuck her hard and deep and to make her come. Yet when even her breaching had only brought pain and a quick end, something had shattered within her. As if every dream and every hope she'd been hoarding close to her heart from the day she'd chosen Maddek to be her husband had broken apart—and she had broken with it.

What was in her now? Nothing, it seemed. She felt as lonely as she had within her tower. But no more imaginings of other lives and dreams were left. There was only the life she lived.

No hope. Only purpose.

She would lie beneath Maddek when he returned.

She would take her pleasure if she could.

She would build an alliance as tasked.

She would withstand the suffering to come.

It was fortunate Vela had given her blessing, or Yvenne would have not known if she had the strength to do it all.

On a shuddering sigh, she dropped Bazir's head. It splashed into the water and bobbed to the surface, where it spun and rolled through the swirling eddies of the ship's wake. Then with a flash of iridescent scales and thick slithering body, the head was gone.

"A sea bask," Maddek said quietly from behind her.

So he had returned already. But not with cock risen. When she faced him, he wore white silk around his hips and nothing else. No armor, no blood, no claws. His hair was wet and not yet braided. Nothing of his warrior's garb did he wear. Why did he seem no less dangerous, no less strong, no less impervious to any harm?

Even when covered, she felt like an open wound.

Without a word, she strode past him into the chamber. He'd brought food and drink. Two heaping platters sat upon the table. Never had she been less hungry. Behind the bath screen, she poured water into a bowl and washed her brother's blood from her fingers, then Maddek's seed from between her thighs. Bloodied marks he'd left on her, and those she scrubbed away, too.

Would he be gone when she finished? She dared not hope.

Yvenne was done with hope.

From beyond the screen came a heavy sigh, followed by Maddek's roughened voice. "Your father ripped my heart asunder when he murdered my parents."

She stopped, chest aching. Would he now explain why he viewed her with such suspicion? He did not need to.

Tightly she replied, "This I know."

"I thought I would be prepared for their deaths," he continued hoarsely. "Nothing was left unsaid between us. And a warrior knows Rani may come for those we love at any moment. Yet I was not prepared. So my rage and grief ruled everything that I saw. It ruled my view when I looked at you. Perhaps it will taint that view for some time. But I will strive to see you more clearly, Yvenne."

Now he held out a hand to her? When she had resigned herself to nothing? When she had given up all hope?

How could she bear taking the hand he extended if it only meant broken hope and disappointment again?

How could she *not* take it? Was it not the reason she'd chosen him? That hand had come late, perhaps—but it had come.

"What I *do* see is how much you loved Queen Vyssen. I cannot guess what befell her. I only know that you loved her as I loved my own mother. And so your heart must have also been torn asunder when you lost her."

So her heart had been. And it had shattered again, this very dawn. Could she survive if it shattered once more?

Closing her eyes, she prayed to Vela. Yet that goddess had already given her the answer.

You are stronger than you know.

With a shuddering breath, she moved from behind the screen. Though she said nothing, sheer relief eased the tension upon Maddek's face, in the rigid set of his shoulders.

Gaze entreating, he said to her, "Vela has told me that unless I have the heart of a king, I will not truly be able to protect you. And so your lessons I could use."

Vela had said such to him? Yvenne knew not what to

make of that, but she would ponder it later. Now she steadily regarded him. "What lesson do you need?"

"A warrior wastes no time on wishes and regrets but makes use of what he has. But I hope to be a king, not a warrior. What does a king do?"

"Almost the same," she told him quietly. "A king may wish and regret, for he has the power to enact change. But he also makes use of what he has to enact those changes. And he sees more uses in what he has than a warrior does. An axe that might cleave skulls is also a tool to fell trees and build homes for his people."

"Or he sees not just a vessel, but a queen."

Heart aching, she nodded.

"And if he wishes that he had not hurt her with his assumptions?"

She shrugged as if his question were nothing to her, as if it did not send her aching heart tripping and tumbling. "He still must make use of what he has. What is done cannot be undone. But perhaps he can take what is broken and remake something new of it."

His dark gaze searched her face. "Then let me see what I have to make use of."

That was Yvenne. So that he could remake what was broken between them. If she allowed it.

If she wished for it, too.

With trembling fingers, she untied the laces of her robe. Though she wanted to hide her blushing face, instead she proudly lifted her chin as the covering dropped to the floor, standing before him bare as she never had been before.

Now his cock rose. Yet it was as if he were unaware of his own arousal, his gaze smoldering, scorching her skin as it slowly drifted from her hair down to her toes.

"What do you think is my view when I look at you?"

She could well imagine. "My tits are too small to succor a child."

Slowly he nodded. "Perhaps they are. So I should suckle upon them regularly to prepare your nipples for our children's hungry mouths. What more?"

Her eyes narrowed. "My hips are too narrow to birth a giant Parsathean baby."

"It is not your hips that are too narrow," he said, stepping closer, "but your tight sheath. I will have to accustom it to a stretching with my giant Parsathean sword."

She refused to laugh at that. Her lips pressed into a firm line and drew his gaze to her mouth. Perhaps thinking of the lying tongue that lay behind it. "I am small and crippled, and my muscles are weak."

"That is all true," he said softly, and his big hands cupped her face. "Yet I believe that you are much stronger than I ever knew."

Her heart filled with sudden, terrible hope. No response did she make.

His voice deepened. "I would ask more of you than a lesson, Yvenne."

Her brow arched in silent query.

"You must tell me if anything I do causes you pain, for I will not be able to know by your breaths. And if you cannot speak to tell me, then pull at my beard, or stab me with your dagger, or boil the meat from my cock with poison."

"I will," she assured him.

A smile quirked his mouth. Then he lowered his head and softly kissed her.

No sound could she make. No breath could she take. Raider that he was, Maddek had stolen both.

Gently he tasted the corner of her mouth, then the center, then the opposite corner, his lips moving tenderly against hers. Again and again he did this, and so sweet it was. As if with this kiss, he was seeking out all the delicate, shattered pieces within her and smoothing their painful edges.

She knew not how to respond except to cling to his arms, and then she began to tremble when he licked the seam of her lips. His hand cupped her nape and he tipped her head back, slowly coaxing her mouth open, sliding his tongue along the sensitive inner flesh of her bottom lip.

Shivering with sensation, she opened for him, and received the luscious thrust of his tongue—oh, why had he not kissed her before? Why had she not kissed him? Fiercely now she reached up, tangling her fingers in his thick hair and hauling herself closer. So heady was this sensation, not at all like everything that had come before. Not just receiving pleasure but taking it, glorying in the sweetness and the heat. Wanting so much more. So many times he'd sucked her skin and licked her cunt, so many times he'd growled that hungry growl, starting softly and becoming more ravenous with every taste, yet never had it been so all-consuming.

"Maddek," she gasped when he broke the kiss.

He braced his forearm beneath her bare bottom and hefted her up against his chest, until their mouths were on level. His face was a harsh mask of need as he said, "Now we will ride into battle together. Not as enemies, but allies."

On the bed. As answer, greedily she kissed him again. He carried her behind that screen, as he had before, but this was nothing like before. With no rush, Maddek set her upon the dais to stand in front of him, then cupped her breasts and sucked at their taut peaks until Yvenne thought she might scream of pleasure and frustration. Her nipples throbbed, red as rubies when he abandoned them to trail ravenous kisses downward, tongue slicking into her navel before he glanced up, his eyes hot.

"Lie upon the bed, Yvenne, with thighs widespread."

So he would assume the role of commander in this battle. Yet it was an order she could not easily follow, lying upon the bed but not yet exposing herself to him. Discarding the silk around his hips, Maddek climbed up onto the platform, head and shoulders bent beneath the low ceiling, his gaze hungry upon her. Slipping his fingers under her knees, he gently spread her open.

Quivering with anticipation, she eyed the thick length that hung heavily between his muscular thighs. "I do not want to be the horse."

That stopped him. "The horse?"

"As we ride into battle, we become one with our

mounts—and it is as if we fly." She recited the words that
had branded themselves on her heart beneath a moonlit sky,
the very first night she had begun living. "But I do not want
to be the mount."

So beautiful Maddek was when he grinned. Settling his
shoulders between her splayed thighs, he told her, "You
need only be a warrior-queen."

Then she would. "And what will you be?"

"Yours," he said in a raw voice, and bent his head to
feast.

And this, too, he had done before. So many times. Yet
all was different as he devoured her slowly. For this was the
first time that wonder blossomed within her, the exhilarating thought that he might be entangled, too. Maddek had
returned to her. Not just to fuck but to see her anew. To see
her as more than vessel, as more than queen, but as a
woman who might be trusted with a small piece of his
heart.

That wondrous thought was within her as she came
against his tongue, her body quaking and her chest swollen
with sheer emotion. Maddek moved over her shuddering
form, pushing her right leg higher, spreading her open
wider. He kissed her, his mouth still glistening with
her arousal, and still it seemed nothing like honey, but her
blood was—pulsing slow and thick and sweet beneath
her skin.

Into her eyes he looked, holding her gaze as pressure
built at the entrance of her cunt, then abruptly gave way
into a sharp, stretching burn. Yvenne gasped softly, clutching at his shoulders. There was no pain this time. Yet it was
not entirely pleasure, either, for there was so much of him.
More than he'd given her before.

Endlessly his thick cock wedged deeper, until she could
take nothing more. His hips settled fully in the cradle of her
widespread thighs. He kissed her again, a caress of lips
softer than his voice, which was a strained rasp against her
mouth.

"So hot and wet your cunt is." Barely he moved within

her, drawing another gasp as the pressure within her sheath deepened. With a groan, he stilled again. "Such a fierce grip. Only by Hanan's mercy I do not spend again."

"Wait for me," she panted.

"Always I will. We are as one now, Yvenne." A callused palm swept down her right thigh and urged her leg over his back. "So let us ride into battle together."

No urgent battle it was, for he only kissed her. Sweetly, then with breathless heat, stroking between her lips with ravenous licks. Only when she began to move restlessly beneath him did Maddek begin their ride, with a long and slow rocking of his hips.

His full length he pumped into her cunt, and it was lovely to feel him within her, so lovely, but the sweetest pleasure came from his kiss, from his skin beneath her fingertips, from his groans each time he slid deep. Yet the stroking of his cock seemed to pull all those other pleasures into the slick lining of her sheath, dragging in more sensation each time. The flex of muscle beneath her searching fingers became the flex of her cuntflesh around his shaft. His heavy weight above her and his warmth and his nearness heightened the heat and pressure within. The burn of linen against her back and give of the bed, the creaking of the boat, the crash of the waves all seemed to rock with the rhythm of Maddek sliding back and forth inside her.

Then suddenly his pistoning length was not just pulling in pleasure from outside her cunt, but drawing it from her own inner walls, ecstasy doubling with each slow thrust. All she could feel was that incredible fullness, her tightening sheath, and his hot open kiss that moved from her mouth to her throat when she arched helplessly beneath him, lifting her hips and riding his cock.

She cried out his name, seeking the release hovering just beyond her reach. Frantically she clawed at his shoulders.

"Fly, my bride," he urged, his mouth hot on her throat. "Fly with me."

"I am. But I need—" *More.* Her own strangled sob as he fucked suddenly hard and deep choked her plea into silence. Almost enough, it was almost, almost, almost enough. "Please."

His fingers wedged between them, roughly stroking her clit. "Fly, Yvenne." Hoarsely he commanded her with a long, hard thrust. *"Fly!"*

And she did, soaring, clinging to Maddek as he groaned and pushed through the clenching inner muscles of her sheath. As she came down, he sat back and hauled her backside onto his lap, pumping into her harder, deeper.

"Again," he demanded through gritted teeth.

She could not. But it was as if every hard thrust captured the ecstasy that her release had flung free and shoved it deep into her sheath again. His thumb stroked her clit and his cock pounded within her, a harder ride than before, her hands twisting in the linens for anchor and her breasts bouncing with every rough beat. This time the exquisite shudders started deep, where his thick shaft worked into her in that luscious, brutal rhythm, a fluttering of internal muscles before she was launched upward again. With a grunt, Maddek bent over her, still stroking deep until his breath caught hard in her ear. Then his teeth locked on her shoulder and his tortured groan followed her up, up, as his cock pulsed and spilled hot seed.

Together Yvenne crashed with him, winded as if she had been tossed from the sky. Maddek's chest heaved, his dark skin slick with sweat, his softening cock still within her. When he moved, as if to lift his weight off her, she held him tighter.

"I like the feel of you inside me."

A kiss he pressed to her neck. "As do I."

He rolled her instead to their sides, with her thigh draped over his hip. She pillowed her head on his arm.

So quiet they were now. She knew not what lay behind his eyes as he looked down at her. But a better view he had.

Or so she hoped.

In bed with him at the inn, she'd discovered that trust was a difficult and exhilarating part of herself to give. An agonizing part of herself, when that trust was betrayed.

Yet he had held out his hand. She would try to meet him halfway.

"It was the stairs," she whispered.

No response did he make but she felt his gaze sharpen on her face. She couldn't look up, couldn't meet his eyes. Already hers burned, her throat a painful lump, and never would she make it through this telling if she saw . . . any response. Sympathy, pity, blame. Nothing could ease this pain.

"Always, my mother was patient. For years she planned our escape. Mostly we lacked opportunity, for the door to our tower was bolted from outside. But just as the guards one time did not tie her properly when my father visited her bed, she knew one time that door would not be bolted—or we might have help."

"From whom?" he asked quietly.

"The handmaids. After all, a queen does not empty her own chamber pot or carry water for her own bath. So we had maids that were never allowed to leave the citadel, and my father had threatened their families if ever they spoke of us—or spoke *to* us. They only came once per day, and always they were watched by the Rugusian guards while inside the tower chamber. But these were not merely days of watching, but years of days, and the guards were not always careful. A note could be slipped into a maid's pocket, or left where she would find it. And in that way, one day a maid bumped a linen basket against the door latch and it was not locked properly."

"So you escaped."

Emotion like a vise on her heart, Yvenne nodded. Twice she had to swallow before speaking again. "My mother made me exercise so that I would be as strong as I could be, and every day we practiced running with me carrying her as best I could. I knew our exact route. Across the landing, down one hundred spiraling steps, along the north corridor and into the servants' quarters, and from there the service stairs. And she told me what stairs were, described them to me. They would take us down, she said. So I ran at them as fast as I could . . . and it was as if the world dropped out from beneath my feet. We fell and—" Her breath hitched raggedly, again and again. "We fell. More than a hundred steps. Because I didn't understand that I must run on them differently than I would a floor. "

Long fingers slid into her hair, bringing her face to his chest, allowing her to hide. "You had never seen stairs before?"

She shook her head. Dully she said, "Her neck was broken, her body twisted. She had wrapped herself around me and took the worst of the fall. I only bumped my ankle— and have no memory of reaching the bottom. Only of lying on the stone landing, and seeing her lying there beside me. Knowing she was dead. Knowing that she would still want me to escape. Knowing that I had to get up again. But my father and brothers had been alerted by the commotion. And they made certain I would not get up then, and would never run again."

"Bazir was among them?"

"He stomped the hardest upon my knee. He loved our mother . . . in his way."

"I would kill him again for laying her death at your feet." Strong fingers tilted her head back. Dark gaze searched her eyes. Gruffly he said, "You are not to blame, Yvenne."

She laughed because otherwise she would cry. "Do you have a warrior's lesson to give that might teach me how to believe that?"

A wry smile curved his mouth. "If I did, first I would have to learn it myself."

"Do not look to me for that lesson," she told him. "All good kings carry more blame than they should."

"It is fortunate I have broad enough shoulders for it." Bending his head, he pressed a kiss to the point of her shoulder. "And yours look frail, yet mountains they can bear."

Now she would truly weep. With shuddering breath, she pillowed her cheek on his biceps. As if sensing her need to hide again, Maddek said nothing for a long time. She was drifting off to sleep when his stirring awoke her.

In a low rasp he said, "Take your rest, Yvenne. I will return when my cock rises again."

Because Yvenne had told him that she would not sleep beside him. Now she reached out, caught his hand before he left the bed.

"Stay," she said.

And he did.

CHAPTER 31

MADDEK

Hard Maddek must have slept. He knew not when Yvenne left their bed or their quarters. But he heard her return—the slide of the palewood door, then her labored steps down the four steep stairs to the recessed floor.

Then the sound of her climbing the stairs. And descending again. And climbing. And descending.

Practicing, her every breath shuddering and fearful.

Chest tight, he lay in bed—making no sound, because he suspected Yvenne might stop if she knew he listened. She had opened the wound of her mother's death for him to see. Yet still tender she must be. And with her armor gone, easily he might hurt her.

By Temra's fist, he would never batter at her walls again. And he would take more care. He could not bear to see her spark blown out.

Her breaths sounded heavier from exertion than terror when she finished her practice. Directly toward the bed she came then, and Maddek closed his eyes, as if asleep instead of lying with his heart full from listening to Yvenne battle her demons. The stairs to the bed's platform she climbed without much fear, it seemed. Her slight weight he felt upon the mattress—and her soft mouth, just above his knee, then higher and higher. Kissing her way up his thigh.

Instantly he was hard as stone. She chuckled softly and gripped his thickened length.

"You are awake," she said throatily. "Now lie still."

He could not—not if lying on his back meant missing the sight of her mouth upon his cock. Onto his elbows he rose, gaze riveted upon her face, groaning as her tongue traced a scorching path over the crown. Hands fisted in the sheets, he bore the excruciating pleasure of her hunger as she tasted him. So many times he'd imagined this. Yet never had his imaginings been near to the truth.

Eyes hot, she looked up at him. "Every day, I intend to practice my riding upon you. So that when this journey is over, I will not be so saddlesore again."

Hoarsely he told her, "That is a fine idea."

Her full lips curving, she moved back onto the dais, shedding her silk robe. Only her linens wrapped her limbs when she climbed into the bed again. With his gaze, he devoured her, then met her eyes again when she gave a husky admission.

"I like the way you look at me, Maddek."

"I like knowing that I am the only one who has seen you thus." A foolish thing to enjoy. Yet he did.

Her smile widening, she swung her leg over his hips. "Should I ask you to cover, too?"

"I would." For her, he would.

"I do not think I will." Her soft hand clasped his jutting length. "I like knowing that everyone can see your strength, your handsomeness . . . and it is all mine."

His teeth gritted with sheer pleasure as she angled his cock to her cunt. He caught her hips, stopping her. "You are not ready."

"I am." Eyes heavy-lidded, she dragged the head of his cock through the wet lust between her thighs. "Nothing else have I thought of since waking but the memory of you inside me."

So wet she was. Sinking down upon him, drawing him into that scalding embrace. Yet she could not take him all—the difficulty not in her arousal, but her knee as she tried to bend it against the mattress. Discomfort shortened her breath.

"I cannot—" Utter disappointment shattered her expression. "I cannot ride you like this."

"That is not proper riding, anyway." He held on to her and slid to the edge of the bed, feet braced on the dais. When far enough he went, her legs dangled free, just as if she sat upon a mount with no saddle or stirrups.

There Yvenne's weight carried her down the full length of his cock and she gasped. No pain he heard, only pleasure in that sound.

"You're so deep," she breathed.

"Do you want less?"

She shook her head, lip between her teeth. And then she rode in truth, not with legs braced on the bed, but rising through her hips. A deep moan rose up from her chest and her head fell back, the tip of her braid swinging against his thighs. Then she leaned forward and braced herself upon his chest, her gaze locked with his as slowly she rode him.

And no greater pleasure had Maddek ever known than now, buried inside the warm embrace of her cunt. No great height did she rise and fall, so deep he remained, her snug entrance sliding and working the base of his shaft as Yvenne used him for her pleasure. Slowly she increased her speed and he slipped his thumb through her moistened curls to rub her clit.

"Maddek." Again her head fell back, then forward. Her hips began a frantic circle. "Oh, Maddek."

"Fly, Yvenne." Sitting up, he caught her nipple in his mouth, sucking hard. She cried out and buried her fingers in his hair. With thumb still circling her clit, he gripped her ass with his left hand and urged her faster, harder, higher. "Fly."

With a scream through clenched teeth, she did, her inner

muscles clamping hard upon his length, and swiftly he followed her on that flight. Then so sweetly she came down, cupping his face in her hands, her mouth on his for a long, slow kiss.

He was still inside her, yet even closer he wanted to hold her. His hands slid up her bare back, callused palms gliding over skin that was rougher than his.

His heart turned to stone and he stiffened. Her mouth froze upon his.

"Yvenne," he said, his voice shredded. As her back must have been.

She hid her face in his shoulder. Gently, so gently, he drew her with him to the center of the bed, where he laid her on her stomach. On hands and knees he saw that her back was a mass of scars. The punishment for sending the letter to his parents. Always before, her back had been covered, so he'd thought it was just the one slash from a whip—and that one was too much. But Zhalen had ripped her open.

His hand hovered above her skin, not touching but shaking. Never had he known such rage. Yet none did he let rise to his tongue.

"Does it hurt?" Had he unknowingly caused her more pain, touching her or holding her?

"No," she whispered. "It itches, sometimes."

Still healing. From a whipping that might have killed her.

In choked voice, he asked, "How did you survive this?"

"I almost did not." With a shuddering breath, she turned onto her back and looked up at him. "There are two answers. One I cannot say unless you give me leave to speak of it."

Because she would refer to his mother. "Tell me."

"She tended to me. This was how she met me. In bed, the wounds still open, sick with fever and unable to move far. She cared for me—and perhaps this is why she did not doubt me for long, or believe I lured them. Not after she saw what my father did for sending the message. Never would I have harmed her, Maddek."

"This I know." Raggedly his reply came from his shredded throat. "What is the other answer?"

She reached up with her two-fingered hand, traced his bearded jaw. "Your father told you that wars were won in throne rooms. You thought they were won on battlefields. But wars are not won in throne rooms or battlefields—or even the bed."

"Where, then?"

"Here." She flattened her hand over his pounding heart. "If the Destroyer came today, and enslaved us, and made us crawl across the mud to lick his feet—even if I did crawl, still that war he would not have won. In my heart, I would still be fighting. Looking for a way to defeat him. What would you do?"

"The same," he said gruffly.

"So if you fight here, never will you lose. Not until you are dead. But even then, I would fight to my last breath. And I would call that a victory. And if it's the only victory I will ever have . . . it will be enough." She bit her lip. "Do you think that naive?"

"No," Maddek said softly. "I think you are right."

"That is how I survived. You asked before if I have been defeated. I have. You asked before what was there after defeat—and I said there was love for my people, rage against my father, and hope. When I understood that my messenger had been found out and killed, when my father laid my back open—there was almost nothing left. No rage. No hope. All that I had was love and the determination to keep trying . . . because that was all I could do. I was helpless, but it did not mean I had stopped trying. And when your mother came . . . hope returned. And not much time passed before I found my rage again."

When his mother and father had been killed. "That I understand well."

"I know you do." Sadly she looked at him. "Do you think you will ever rescind your vow?"

"Yes," he said, and watched the shadows chase from her eyes. "Though not yet. And you never have to fear that I would pull out your tongue."

"Do you still believe I would lie?"

He shook his head. "But I have the habit of a certain view . . . and of responding in haste and rage. If you ask before speaking of her, then I will be prepared and make certain not to see you with that same view—or respond with words best left unsaid or hurtful. And when that habit is broken, I will not need to check myself, or for you to prepare me for what you would say."

Slowly she nodded, but it was with a sigh that she said, "You have promised to make the attempt and you are. But how long do you think it will be before you see me clearly?"

Maddek wished that he did now. But he would not waste time on wishes; instead he would change what was. He would change what *he* was. "I suspect when I have the heart of a king."

Sudden amusement curved her mouth. "Then I will continue your lessons."

"As I will yours." Bending his head, he softly kissed her smiling lips. "Did you practice the bow today?"

He would wager she had. As she had the stairs. And riding.

She nodded. "Drawing the string. And Kelir helped me find a spot where I might practice without losing my arrows to the sea." Her brow furrowed slightly. "And he said that my vision is not as others' is."

He cupped her face. "It is a gift you have, such perfect sight."

"A gift that apparently requires as much practice as the bow does."

So it did. "Danoh has the keenest eyes to learn from. And she and Toric can best teach you the bow."

"I will ask them for lessons—though perhaps not from Toric. He is sick again."

He frowned. "The poison and fever?"

"The sea and the waves. He has spent all day belowdecks with the horses. He claims their smell soothes his stomach." She bit her lip before saying, "If I become sick, it will likely not be the sea."

But because she was with child. Though Vela had said that she was not yet.

So many times would Maddek have her, soon that would be remedied.

Her moonstone gaze slipped over his face. "Do you still wish to wait until I am with child before we marry?"

Maddek had told her that. That he would not marry her until she was bred. Because she was no use to him barren.

Now he cared not if she was. "We need not wait. But a Parsathean must stand on Temra's altar to marry."

And that was also where he would stand if named Ran. Would that be when he had the heart of a king?

Yvenne deserved no less than a king. So he would learn her lessons well—and give his own in return.

"I have a hunter's lesson for you this day."

Anticipation lit her face. "What lesson?"

Dryly he said, "How to properly throw a knife."

And when she laughed so sweetly against him, he kissed her again.

CHAPTER 32

YVENNE

By the time the ship reached the northern shore of the Boiling Sea, Yvenne could throw her knife and stab the point into her target four times of five. She could loose an arrow with accuracy, if not incredible range. And it was not only on Maddek that she practiced riding. When the horses were brought to the upper deck for exercise, she sat upon their backs. They never moved faster than a walk, but she still learned to loose her arrow from atop a mount.

She could also climb four steps—not smoothly, for her knee would never allow that—but easily and without fear.

And so many wonders she saw, so many sea creatures she'd eaten. From the ship, she'd seen more of her realm than ever before. The great white cliffs that marked the western boundary of Syssia were visible in the distance for the last tennight of their voyage.

Those cliffs ran north and became the river gorge that also marked Parsathe's western boundary. A port city lay near the shore. Not as elegant or as populous as Drahm, yet still bustling with people from the realms north and west of the Burning Plains.

Though there was so much that Yvenne would have liked to stay and see, they could not linger in the city. From almost the moment they disembarked from the swan ship, they heard rumors of soldiers coming from the south— from the direction of the Syssian outpost.

They only remained long enough to collect supplies and horses for the journey east—and to collect more Parsathean riders. Most Parsatheans from this area had already ridden toward Kilren to vote in the gathering for the new Ran, yet those who'd had a farther distance to travel now joined their party. Their numbers swelled to nearly four dozen riders as they left the city, following a well-worn road that would lead them through the rolling hills east of the river.

"Do we ride directly to Kilren?" That from Jakon, a warrior who had returned to Parsathe after serving as a hired sword in the northern realms.

Maddek shook his head. "We ride to meet Enox and the Parsathean army. In the morn, we will separate into two groups—one swift and one slow. I will be in the slow, because my bride may be with child."

"I will ride in the quick," Toric said. In the full turn aboard the ship, his features had sharpened and thinned— and he'd spent most of the journey belowdecks with the horses, for the waves continually made him sick. "I am the Dragon's wings, so make use of me."

Kelir frowned. "Are you recovered enough to ride with speed?"

"Being on a horse stops my stomach from swinging like the sea."

Kelir accepted that with a nod. "Fassad, you ride with him. We will meet in the hollow north of the glass fields— and if for any reason we cannot stay there, your wolves can track us."

The warrior nodded, while Yvenne's heart beat faster. The glass fields—near Temra's altar. Where she might finally marry Maddek.

If he still intended to marry her. For he would have no need to after Zhalen attacked them in Parsathean territory.

But he put no distance between them yet. He rode at her side until they made camp; when they settled around the fire, he sat close to her as the new members of their party spoke of the realms they'd traveled to and of all that they'd seen. And in his furs later, Maddek gave her a long, slow fucking that had her clinging to him long after her shudders faded, her head pillowed on his broad chest.

In the quiet afterward, she said softly, "It is as you wanted, then. Syssian soldiers from the outpost invade the Burning Plains. And so my father declares war upon Parsathe."

His arms tightened around her. "But you will not suffer at his hands."

As if Maddek could prevent it. It was lovely that he would try, yet Yvenne had no hope that she would escape her fate. "Vela has said that I will."

He gave a derisive grunt.

Lifting her head, she peered down at his shadowed face. "Do you think she lies?"

"No. But she does not clearly speak. That is why Parsatheans prefer Temra—she makes no promises except to always be beneath our feet. And Rani, who is always truthful in her purpose and clear. Why would Vela not say how and why you will suffer, so that we might prevent it?"

"I *do* think she speaks plainly," Yvenne said. "She told Toric why she gives no easy answer. She believes that some things must be experienced to be properly learned."

His jaw clenched. "You do not need to suffer to learn anything."

"Then perhaps it is something she cannot prevent, and only prepares me for it."

"Then plainly she should say that."

Yvenne huffed out a quiet laugh. Even though Vela looked through her eyes, Maddek did not hesitate to criticize the goddess. "As plainly as you speak?"

He grunted his own amusement. "Vela knows very well what I think."

So she did. But knowing what the goddess thought in turn was impossible to guess, so Yvenne did not try. For when her mind *did* wander that way, she wondered if the suffering at her father's hands meant something entirely different from what she assumed. Vela had said she would suffer more for choosing Maddek, but perhaps that was only because Maddek had taken a route north to lure her father, and Yvenne might have traveled another direction. They knew not for certain whether Zhalen rode with the soldiers from the outpost. He might still be in Syssia, and Yvenne's suffering at his hands might not come from what he did to her, but from whatever horrors he might visit upon her people.

Yet such wonderings helped no one. If Yvenne tried to imagine all of Vela's possible meanings, and tried to make choices based on what could not be known, she would be paralyzed with indecision. Better to forge ahead as best she could, and meet her fate when it came for her.

She would suffer. But whatever form that suffering took, she would be strong enough to survive it.

So instead of fretting over what could not be known, she held Maddek close, and slept.

CHAPTER 33

MADDEK

When they finally passed through the hills east of the river and crested the ridge overlooking the Burning Plains, Maddek's bride was rendered speechless. Ahead of them stretched endless red blossoms—a riot of fireblooms, their petals so red and numerous that the plains appeared aflame.

His chest tight with emotion, Maddek watched as she urged her mount a short distance up the track, seeking a higher viewpoint. Her face was alight with wonder, much as it had been the first time she'd glimpsed the beauty of the sea. Yet now it was his home that she regarded with the same wonder and astonishment.

Mounted beside Maddek, Kelir asked quietly, "You do not marry her? I thought you would when your feet touched the ground."

Seven days past. Maddek would have wed her then. But for one thing. "She deserves to marry a king."

Especially after she'd put so much work into him.

That amused the other warrior. "And if you are not named Ran?"

"Aezil must die," Maddek said easily. "I will kill him and take the Rugusian throne."

"You would be taking your bride's throne." Kelir laughed. "She is next in line after Aezil."

And would be queen of that realm in truth, then, after they destroyed that sorcerer.

"Toleh, then," Maddek decided.

Kelir grinned. "And would you shave your beard as a Tolehi man does?"

With a bare chin. "I could not. My bride would have nothing to yank when she wants my attention."

"I think she would," Kelir said dryly.

So she would. And did often. Maddek grinned.

Flushed and happy, Yvenne rode back from the ridge that overlooked the plain. "Shall I hunt our suppers?"

As she had every day since they'd been off the ship—for themselves and the dozen other riders who'd remained in their group. "You should."

Her gaze swept the nearby grasses and flowers. "What do I look for here?"

"Many animals are underground, so require a stick instead of an arrow," he told her. "Those aboveground are small, so many times all you will see is the shivering firebloom."

"There." Ardyl pointed.

Yvenne aimed, loosed. Within range, she always hit. Danoh rode over and swept up a grass rodent.

Murmurs came from watching warriors. They had seen that display many times on this journey, yet never did it fail to impress, nor did they grow tired of it.

With a grin, Yvenne looked to Maddek. "I should try for a drepa next, and boast a claw around my neck."

He shook his head. The simple kill was not why their claws had such significance, because drepa were no harder or easier to hunt than any other dangerous animal. Instead the drepa claw boasted either surviving a pack—or being such a stealthy hunter that the pack did not know what happened. "Make certain to count your arrows first."

"What do you mean?"

"Drepa are not like other animals we have hunted. If you injure or kill one, the rest do not flee. The drepa will attack. So be certain that you have enough arrows to fell an entire pack."

"I see." She eyed the claws around his neck. "Did you have to fight off a pack?"

"I did not fight them off. Three of these, I happened upon one and it was surprised as I was." Then he survived as many Parsatheans did. "If you ever have not enough arrows, lie upon the ground as if dead. They will ignore you."

"You have done so?"

Maddek nodded. "Many times."

Her gaze turned to the horizon again. Faint creases formed in her brow. "How far to the Scourge?"

"Four days' ride. You see it?"

"The head and shoulder, I think."

"It is turned on its side." Silver-fingered Rani had done so when she'd split its belly open to retrieve her dragon.

Yvenne straightened slightly. "There are riders coming from that direction."

"How many?"

"Two. A woman and a girl. The girl is even younger than Toric, I think, though she is dressed as a warrior. The woman is perhaps the same age as Banek—and is a warrior. She wears drepa-skin armor and her hair in braids. A ragged crescent scar is on her right shoulder."

Kelir let out a whoop that nearly startled Yvenne out of her saddle. "That is my mother and sister," he told her when she looked at him in surprise. "Toric must have sought her out and told her we are following behind."

They met Kelir not long after with laughter and embraces.

Nami approached Maddek more soberly. Her embrace was tight. She was the leader of the firebloom tribe—a position his own father once had. Many times in his childhood, his family had visited hers. "No words were left unsaid?"

His throat thick, Maddek told her, "There were none."

She patted his arm. "That is the most we can ask for."

He nodded, then introduced her to Yvenne, who had carefully dismounted and joined them. "My bride."

Nami took Yvenne's hands in her own, met her gaze briefly. "I have seen those eyes before. You are Nyset's heir."

"I am."

"And you are to unite us against the Destroyer."

"I will try," Yvenne said.

Maddek asked, "Toric has told you of our journey?"

"I would hear more," Nami said.

"I will tell you as we ride," he promised.

Seri took place beside Yvenne, Maddek noted, with Banek on the other side. When he lifted her into the saddle, Yvenne's attention had already been captured by the girl.

"I have heard that you are a better warrior than even your brother," Yvenne told her.

Kelir's sister grinned. "So I am."

"I am learning to hunt," Yvenne said. "But I am not accustomed to the plains or detecting prey. I need someone to be a guide for my eyes. Will you do me the honor?"

Seri flushed with pleasure. "I will."

A good match they made. A young warrior eager to demonstrate her skills, and a new warrior eager to learn them.

Nami's solemn voice drew Maddek's gaze away from the pair as they rode ahead. "Is it truth that she spoke a lie?"

If Toric had told her that, then no doubt he'd also told Nami the circumstances of it. Yet Maddek knew that when he stood before each tribe's elders, he would have to explain it again and again, and would have to find the words to sway them in Yvenne's favor.

As one of those elders rode beside him now, he might as well begin practicing those words. "She lied to an enemy to save her life and the lives of her people."

Nami huffed out a laugh. "You would take your enemy as a bride?"

"I would have no other. And she is no enemy now but a fierce and clever ally."

Her eyes narrowed. "So you would make a mere ally our queen?"

"She will be one of the finest warrior-queens that Parsathe has ever known, and our marriage will strengthen both of our realms."

"A warrior-queen?" Nami scoffed. "She sits her horse uneasily and a girl teaches her to hunt. She is not the bride your mother would have chosen."

What did that matter now? "Yvenne is stronger than she appears."

Dismissively she said, "Then you are clearly blinded by your love for her."

"No." Other emotions had blinded him. "Love has made me see her more clearly."

Her expression softened. Yet her gaze was still sharp, her inquiry not done. "Then tell me of that strength, and why she would be a fine queen."

So Maddek did.

CHAPTER 34

YVENNE

Yvenne had learned that even her vision could not see everything, for the ever-moving horizon hid the world beyond it. She knew not how far away the horizon was, except that it was more distant when she was on a tower or a ridge. And when she stood upon the ground, ridges and towers could be seen from farther away, as well, even if she could not see what lay at their base.

So when they entered the Parsathean camp, she knew not how far the horizon stretched—yet in every direction, there were warriors and horses, spread out so that there was grazing and room for all.

And not just the Parsathean army, she learned, though not much difference could she see in the camps. For many of the warriors who had gathered in Kilren to name the new Ran had accompanied Enox and the army to the glass fields—with news that even more Parsatheans were coming.

Many slept under the open sky, but studding the landscape were also tents of mammoth hide, bleached pale by the sun. All smelled of horses and grass and cooking fires.

They rode toward the largest tent, where the leaders of each tribe and clan had gathered. Into that tent, Maddek went, along with Nami and Seri, and five members of his Dragon.

Only Banek remained outside—to watch over Yvenne, who had been introduced to many of the tribes' leaders outside but was not allowed admittance into the tent, for she was not Parsathean or yet married to Maddek.

She sat with Banek at a nearby fire, instead, eating roasted meats and speaking with the warriors who joined them, and trying so very hard not to let her frustration at being excluded from the meeting burn hot upon her tongue. So far she had come. So much she'd set in motion with a letter to Parsathe. Now no say did she have. Her future lay in Parsathean hands. And although she tried to tell herself that this was no different than Drahm, when she made use of a warrior and his strength . . . not truly could she persuade herself of it. For that battle against her brother had been truly of steel and blades. Yet this was a throne room, where she should be most useful to her warrior.

Except that it was also a throne room that one day would be his. She had to trust that Maddek could fight this battle. But she'd have rather fought it at his side.

At least there was much to learn outside that tent. The warriors she and Banek spoke with told them that a company of Syssian soldiers had indeed left the outpost and headed north, accompanied by larger numbers of Rugusian soldiers. Zhalen had been identified among them with some certainty, especially after Yvenne mentioned the scar on his neck. Her father's army had come as far north as the Scourge, and not yet farther.

That news turned her gaze south. She could not see the soldiers that her father had brought with him, or the base of the Scourge, yet that giant demon's corpse was in clear sight, only a day's ride distant.

Yet the Scourge was not all that was near. To Banek, she asked, "We must be close to Temra's altar?"

The old warrior's brows pulled together. "Close to it?"

"To where Ran Bantik stood and implored the tribes to unite."

His confusion cleared. "We are near that spot. But Temra's altar is . . ." He made a sweeping gesture. "Everywhere."

"Everywhere?"

"Everywhere." He pounded his fist into the ground. "This is Temra's altar. That is why we build no temples to other gods upon it. All of it is hers."

Her chest hollowed. "Temra's altar is the earth?"

He nodded.

"*All* of the earth? Or just Parsathe?"

"Anywhere there is solid ground."

Which was why Maddek could not marry her at sea. But they had reached solid ground ten days past.

Throat thick, she said, "But it is true that you must be married upon it?"

"That is truth. And it is where a Ran stands when he is named." With a lift of his chin, he indicated the tent where Maddek was.

Surprise burned away her hurt. "Is that what they are doing now—naming him Ran?"

He shook his head. "All must raise their voice. But the leaders of the tribes and the clans will first speak with him, and hear what he has to say—so they may carry it back to their people, who will know whether he is worthy of speaking for all of us."

"What will they ask of him?"

"Many things." Banek stirred the fire, sending up crackling sparks. "Likely they began with grief for Ran Ashev and Ran Marek. Then they would ask the questions that their clans and tribes want to know of a warrior who might be Ran—and of the woman he would make his queen."

"They will ask him about me?"

"So they will."

"And what they know of me might influence whether the Parsatheans name him Ran?"

"It will."

And Maddek might not become king if they did not approve of her? She looked toward the tent in renewed frustration. "I would rather speak for myself."

Banek grinned. "In time, they will call you before them. Our gathering is not set yet. And never have we been pushed to name a Ran even as another army approaches. Likely they will decide to delay the true gathering until that battle is fought—because your father's death will change much."

So it would. She would be more patient, then. As Banek was.

As Banek was with her, especially. "From the day we met, you have been a good friend to me," she told him now. "I am grateful for it."

A smile touched his mouth. "As I am grateful to you. Much have you given me."

"I do not feel as if I have."

"But it is truth." A touch of melancholy came over his face as he stirred the fire again. "All that I loved was lost when the Destroyer came. There were many of us left with emptied hearts. Some filled theirs again with children and family. Others with rage."

As Danoh's mother had. "Or purpose," Yvenne said quietly. As her mother had. As Maddek's parents had.

He nodded. "Mine . . . I did not fill it again. Not with wife or children. I was afraid to lose it all again. I have fought these many years, and I have always done what was needed to be done, whether it was standing against the savages on the Lave or slaying a dark warlord, yet it was merely . . . doing. Because there was nothing else for me."

Sometimes doing was all that was left. And then all that mattered was the manner of fighting and doing. "But you have fought and done it all honorably. Vela herself noted it."

"So I have. And so she did." His voice thickened. "And her favor gladdened my heart. Yet it is what you have set forward that has filled it. Because I do not merely fight. Now, I fight *for* something. And my heart is full as I never thought it would be again."

Throat aching, she asked softly, "Do you think then that you will now have that wife and child?"

His rusty laugh broke out. "No. *This* pleases me. This purpose I have now, serving as armor for my Ran and his bride."

And perhaps he still could not bear to lose so much again. Her heart full, she said nothing for a long moment. "Do you miss the raids?"

He responded with the side-to-side head motion that meant there was no truthful or easy answer to give, and then they both glanced up as Maddek and the Dragon joined them, along with Nami and Seri, and the woman whom Yvenne had been briefly introduced to before he'd disappeared into the tent—Enox, his first captain.

A strange combination of expressions they wore. She saw tension and unease, as if perhaps the gathering had not gone well. Or perhaps it was only the battle ahead and the knowledge that her father's army lay not far south. Maddek's face she could not easily read, though he seemed not tense.

"I would hear this, too," Maddek said, settling down beside her. "All that I have known of raids are legends and songs, and many among our tribes feel as if we are not truly the riders of the Burning Plains if we are not also raiders."

"Was that one of the questions posed to you?"

He gave a quick smile. "It was. But I would hear Banek's answer."

The old warrior's reply began on a heavy sigh. "I would give much to raid again—though when those dreams come to me, it is not the treasures or valuables that I wish to have. It is the nights by the fire with my sister and fellow warriors. It is the laughter we shared, and the excitement of it. Of concealing ourselves so carefully as a caravan would pass, and then my sister farting so loudly that she gave away our hiding spot. What I miss is not the theft. It is what we shared. And is what many warriors still share in the Parsathean army—or here, with the Dragon. I suspect that is why I have always been part of the alliance army. There are many moments that are the same."

"Except the farting is usually Kelir," Ardyl said, though

emotion burned in her eyes—as if she had been deeply affected by Banek's words.

As had Yvenne. For she had shared so many similar joys and excitement and dangers while traveling with them. She looked to Maddek. "And what was your answer?"

"Much the same," he said. "But also that in those legends and songs, a raider's honor was in never stealing from those in need and always taking from those who had plenty. From nobles, from kings. No true harm was ever done, they said—and if any raider took from someone in need, always he made amends."

"That is truth," Banek said.

"But it is not a full truth," Maddek countered quietly. "Allies we have made of Syssia and Rugus, and so we trade now instead of raid them for riches. But in that alliance, other friendships have we made. And we have learned much about their kings and nobles that we once stole from—enough to know that stealing from them harmed those in need. Either because a generous king would have passed on those riches, to feed or clothe his people, or because a greedy king would extract from his people the cost of what was stolen. Always the most needy and vulnerable paid for our raids in some way."

Yvenne's heart had swelled all the more as he spoke. She knew not what the Parsatheans in that tent might have thought of such an answer, yet to her, it was the finest of responses.

And it was not one of the lessons she had given him, though many similar conversations they'd had while sailing north. So perhaps she had been in that tent with him in some way, after all.

But the battle in the throne room was over for now. A far different battle lay ahead. "What was decided regarding my father?"

"We ride south at first light," Enox said.

A full day of travel. And perhaps a day or more of messages sent and demands made. Then if her father did not surrender . . . the fighting would begin.

Throat tight, Yvenne nodded. She had not been fully prepared to face her brother. But much had changed, and so many warrior's lessons she'd had—lessons that had sharpened her mind as well as her bow.

"You will not ride with us," Maddek told her—gently, as if he knew what a blow it would be, and yet still it left her reeling.

"Not ride with you?" What sense did that make? "He brings Syssian soldiers with him. They will listen to me and—"

Maddek shook his head. "We know not what lies he might have told them. Just as your brother tried to paint you as a demon, he might claim that we have forced you to send any message. No doubt he will tell them this is a rescue and to ignore all else until you are securely in his possession again."

Enox nodded. "If your father's sole purpose is to reclaim you, then we must not make it easy by taking you to him."

That was sensible and yet . . . "Those are my people you will be raising swords against," she told Maddek in anguish. "My soldiers you will kill to reach him. Let me try to persuade them to raise their swords against my father, instead."

"I swear to you that I will reach out my hand to them," he vowed gruffly. "The soldier you sent to the council with your brother's corpse—"

"Jeppen."

"You asked him to tell the others that you would return and that your father's rule would end. You told him that you went with me willingly. If that word has spread, then you may have already persuaded them."

Perhaps. Though she knew it was a thin hope. "So I am to stay here?"

"No. This camp will be near to empty—and is the most obvious place for him to search for you after he realizes you are not with us. Instead we will hide you away."

She did not want to be hidden away. But in this, it seemed she had little say, too. Throat thick, she asked, "Where?"

He held out his hand. "I will show you."

CHAPTER 35

YVENNE

They rode west and north, with dread tightening in Yvenne's gut all the way. For tomorrow would see Maddek leaving to fight her father's army, and her own people, and nothing she would know of what happened there until two or three more days had passed.

As the sun was setting, Maddek drew closer to Yvenne's mount. "There it is."

With a lift of his chin he gestured ahead, yet Yvenne saw nothing. Only grass and firebloom, all the way to the horizon.

When she looked to him in confusion, he grinned at her. "We make use of what we have. We have not many stones to build walls, and the dirt crumbles too easily to make good bricks. So this is our defense, instead."

She looked again. "But I see . . . nothing."

"That is what it is. Come." He nudged his mount to a quicker pace and she followed suit. "Keep watching."

Watching nothing . . . until there was something. A slight ridge upon the ground ahead. As they drew nearer, a depression became visible—deep enough to conceal tents dyed to match the grasses.

In astonishment she looked to him. "There was nothing!"

"It is only a trick of the eye. Even from a short distance, there is nothing to see. Only the plain. An enemy either would be lucky or must know where it is to find anyone hidden within a hollow."

So it seemed. Still bemused by the cleverness of that disguise, she rode with him into the small encampment. The Dragon rode behind them, along with two dozen other warriors who would stay secluded here. Hiding her away, so her father could not find her—and so that she would not suffer at his hands.

Yet the goddess almost never spoke clearly. And although Yvenne did not like to dwell on what couldn't be known, she began to wonder if the suffering Zhalen would inflict on her would not be physical pain. For Maddek had seen so well to her protection. An entire army stood between her father and her.

But that distance between Maddek and her father would be erased. And if Maddek did not return from this battle, if Zhalen killed him . . . Yvenne would truly suffer.

She knew not if the same dread filled Maddek. But they had barely finished tending to their horses before he caught her up against his chest, carrying her to a private tent. Inside he kissed her, and it was with frantic need that she kissed him back. One night she had before he would leave, and then so much time would pass. Already those days were agony, and only by touching him could Yvenne seem to hold them back.

Fiercely she returned every caress, and his urgency matched hers. Rough he was, rougher than he'd ever been, his grip tight upon her arms and legs as he held her wrists to plunder her mouth and then devour her cunt, yet she wanted the bruises he might leave. She wanted to still feel his touch within her while he was gone, and Maddek fucked her so hard and so long that he must have wanted the same.

Over and over he had her, kissing until she was breathless, making her scream and scratch and come. On her back, then riding him, then from behind, his grunts harsh in her ear as he branded himself on her, inside her.

Then he held her against him, her scarred back to his strong chest, arms wrapped around her and breathing in her hair. So quiet the tent was, only filled with the sound of their breaths.

She could not bear to sleep. Sleep would only bring him closer to leaving. Into the dark she whispered, "Did you think the tribe leaders would not approve of me?"

For perhaps that was why he'd waited to marry her, though they'd been on Temra's altar. He might not have known whether he would have to choose between his bride and becoming Ran.

"No." His voice was a quiet rumble. "All doubts were settled."

"What doubts were those?" For she wanted very much to know what doubts might rise again in the future.

"About whether any lies were spoken."

Oh. "That might change their vote if I had spoken lies?"

"It would."

Not *might*. But *would*. So it was fortunate, then, that Maddek had accepted that she'd spoken truth about his mother, though his vow still stood while he was changing the habit of his view.

His hand swept up her arm, as if in reassurance. "You have no need to worry. They know that it was justified."

She frowned, turning within his arms so that she might see his face, shadowed though it was. His eyes were closed and his voice had roughened in that lazy, drowsy way he had before drifting to sleep. "What was justified?"

"The lie you spoke. That my mother approved of you as my bride."

He still did not believe her? Yvenne's heart tightened painfully, and she sucked in a sharp breath. His eyes flew open even as she said, "That was no lie."

"Yvenne—"

"It was no lie," she said again, more forcefully. "I have *never* lied to you."

"It matters not." He caught her face in his hands. "My claws were at your throat. You lied to save your life. It was justified."

"Justified? I need no justification. I spoke truth."

Eyes closing, he pressed his forehead to hers. "Do you fear I will abandon you for it? I will never. We are allies. I know all else you have said to me is true."

So sweetly he dug his claws beneath her breast. So gently he tore out her heart.

Throat raw as if filled with bloody wounds, she asked him, "This is what you said to the tribes? That I lied, but it was justified?"

"I did. And they agreed."

"All of them? Did your Dragon say so, too?"

"They did. Of how we had attacked your carriage, seeking vengeance, and how you persuaded me to let you live. And then they spoke in support of you."

"But did no one suggest that I might have spoken true? Did no one suggest that I might come and speak for myself instead of accepting your view of it? Is it so impossible to believe that she might have approved of me?"

"No," he said quietly. "In time, she would have. As they do. As I do."

Yet he still thought her claim had been a lie. Though justified. "So all is well," she said thickly.

"It is." Kissing her softly, he lay back again, drew her close.

Soon he slept. Because all was well.

Yet it was not.

Pressure behind her eyes and in her chest built, hot and aching. When she could bear it no longer, she carefully slipped out of his arms and collected her robe. Barely did she make it outside before her tears began to fall—and then there, too, she had to hold them back. For at the small fire were Kelir, Nami, and Seri sitting together, with Nami holding her daughter close. Everywhere were warriors quietly talking—and others had slipped away as she and Maddek had done.

Because the Parsatheans did not leave anything left unsaid. And before a battle, they took extra care to speak what needed to be spoken.

Yet what had Maddek said to her? That she was still a liar. Even though she insisted over and over again that it was truth. She was a *justified* liar. As if that made a difference when it meant he still did not trust her word. When he had said that never could he love a woman whose word he could not trust.

She had hoped so desperately that he had become entangled. So desperately she had wished for his heart.

Yet nothing had he said of love or affection. Only of being allies. Only of protecting her.

And no longer could she hold back the tears. Through the blurring of her eyes and the dark, she searched for somewhere alone. She found it at the edge of the hollow, where a small stream spilled into a pool that reflected the bright stars above. No moon there was this night; Vela's face was turned away, so even the goddess would not witness these tears.

How long Yvenne cried, she knew not. But these were the marks that this night would leave—the ragged wound of her heart, the raw ache of her throat. Those would last far longer than his touch.

She should never have hoped for so much.

CHAPTER 36

MADDEK

In the bed, Yvenne's face was pale, her eyes raw. As if she had spent part of the night crying.

With a heavy sigh, Maddek crouched beside the bed. He hated to wake her. Yet dawn neared and he already had extra distance to cover before catching up with the army. He ought to have sent her here with Banek and remained at the camp, yet he had needed this night with her.

And it appeared that she'd needed it, too. Hers were not the only tears shed this night, he knew. Many warriors would ride into battle soon, and not all would return. Many would say words that needed to be said, not knowing if opportunity would come again.

For most, it would. Zhalen would not defeat the Parsathean army. The numbers he'd brought to the Burning Plains were but a small fraction of those riding against him. All that Yvenne knew. Yet there would likely be warriors lost, and her soldiers . . . even Maddek was at risk.

Maddek knew not how to ease her fears except by returning.

Softly he kissed her, waking her gently. As always, she came out of sleep with a single blink.

With his hand cradling her cheek, he told her quietly, "We are ready to ride out."

She sat up on a shuddering breath. "Already?"

He kissed her again in answer. Her hands caught his face, her lips trembling against his.

So sweet this was. Sheer emotion he could taste in this kiss. If he could but stay here longer, Maddek would try to draw words from her tongue that matched all that her kiss said.

Yet first he would make certain that she never suffered at her father's hand.

Drawing back, he told her fiercely, "I will bring you his head."

She gave a quivering smile. "Perhaps his heart, too."

"I will bring both upon a pike, so you might shoot your arrows through them." His thumbs brushed down her cheeks. "But your soldiers, I will do all I can to keep them alive—and bring them here, too, as they will rejoice to see you."

"Thank you," she whispered, and he kissed her yet again. From outside came the snort and stamp of waiting horses—and warriors.

Reluctantly he released her. "I will send word as quickly as I can."

On a shuddering breath, she nodded. Never had leaving a tent been so difficult. So difficult that when she called his name, and he turned to find her limping toward him, nothing could have moved him another step away from her.

Her eyes were bright and shadowed both, as if she held back the painful tears that thickened her voice. "Nothing should be left unsaid. Is that truth?"

What had she left to say to him? All that he'd felt on her kiss? So similar it seemed to what burned in his own heart—which was not gentle but fierce, so fierce that he feared that his might blow out her spark if he did not take care.

But if her fire already burned like his . . . then he had not as much to fear. "It is truth."

It was not a fire that burned as she stopped in front of him, though her chin was lifted and her fists clenched. Not since her moon night had she looked so utterly fragile, so ready to shatter.

"Then I need to say . . . you can have your freedom from me."

He could make no sense of that. "What freedom?"

Her chest lifted on a small, agonized breath. "From any obligation you feel to marry me. When you return with my father's head, the agreement we made will be complete. We will have our vengeance. I'll claim my throne, and you can then choose a bride who you believe is more suited to you."

Was this a jest? "You are suited to me."

"You do not truly believe that." It was a ragged whisper. "Because never did you think that I might be speaking the truth. Because you tell me that, *in time*, your mother would have approved of me. Yet we spent three turns of the moon together in my tower, Maddek. More time than I have spent with you. Yet *still* you refuse to believe that it might be truth. You believe so strongly I have lied, that you tell all of Parsathe that I have spoken it. And so after my father is dead . . . I will return to Syssia as a queen, but no longer a bride."

No air seemed to fill his chest. Instead it roared in his ears, and he shook his head, denying what he'd heard. Refusing to believe that he'd heard it. "You will not marry me?"

"No," she said on broken breath. "I will not."

This he could *not* believe. Already she'd spoken a vow. "To Vela, you swore that you would take no other."

"And I will not." Her eyes closed but not before he saw the gleaming there.

"You carry my child," he said. An unfair weapon it was, but a warrior made use of what he had. And he was desperate enough to use anything.

"It is too early to know for certain."

Maddek was certain. "It has been one and a half turns since your moon night and you have not bled."

"I have never regularly bled." Her eyes opened, and the new resolve he saw in them was a blade through his heart. "But even if I am with child, we need not marry. Many Syssian queens do not. And I will not deny your right to her. She will know you as her father and spend her time between our realms. She will be the best of Parsathe and Syssia—and we will still have a strong alliance."

"Marriage will make it stronger."

"But it will also be strong without it. We are both resolved to the same purposes: to strengthen the alliance and to kill my father. He has arrived here, as you hoped he would, so your vengeance is at hand. Whether I am your bride or not, I know you will help me build a new alliance. The only reason I have to marry would be for my own happiness . . . and I have no hope of that."

No happiness in a marriage with him? Gutted, Maddek stared at her. Those were not words from a sharpened tongue, for she sounded dull and hollow, as if her chest were as empty as his.

"Why?" he asked hoarsely.

"Because I did not lie to you!" she burst out. "I have *never* lied to you! If I did not believe your word, how insulted would you be? Do you think that because I am not Parsathean, my heart and honor are not torn apart by your disbelief? And not only did you say this to me when we were alone, you have told all of Parsathe that I am a liar! And you seem not to care that it is your own untruth that you spread, simply because you will not trust my word. Would you tell our children, too? Should I spend the years trying to explain to them why their father does not respect me enough to believe everything I have to say—or even to *listen* to what I have to say? What happiness would I know in such a marriage?"

No words did Maddek value more than hers. And no heart did he have left. Everything she said was of truth, and left a bleeding wound in his chest.

But he would *not* lose her like this. "I listen to you now. When I return, we will speak more of this. You will tell me all of what my mother said and did."

For they had not enough time now. But he would extract a promise from her not to immediately leave.

But she shook her head. "What point is there when you are stubbornly certain of my lie? You promised to look at me from another view, but in this matter you never attempted to—you held on to your belief that it was a lie, and made a vow that prevented me from ever saying what was truth, and so *never* did you try to truly change your view. Everything I say will be seen through that view—which you still think is not true."

"I swear I will not. I rescind that vow. And I believe what you say now." In truth, he did. She did not wear the proof of his mother's crest, but Yvenne's truth he believed. For she cut out her own heart to tell him. He took her face in his hands, felt the hotness of her cheeks that was the flush of unshed tears, saw her eyes close as if his touch were agony. Voice raw with emotion, he said, "You say to me that I should return and choose a bride suited to me and that my mother would have approved—so I will, Yvenne. And she will be you."

"And what then? Will I hope and then be hurt? So many times with you, I have hoped and been hurt and hoped and been hurt again." Her lips trembled and she turned her face against his hand. In a pained whisper she said, "I have so little hope left, Maddek."

Again that dull, dull blade. "I will choose you," he said hoarsely. "And never will I hurt you again. You need only stay, and we will talk, and you will see."

For such a long time she was silent. Hurting. Then she nodded once, and relief filled his chest.

Catching her trembling bottom lip between her teeth, she finally looked up at him. Such faint hope he saw there amid the unshed tears. He wondered if this was what his mother had seen the first time, with Yvenne fevered and her back slashed open, so near to defeat.

Yet it was not her father who had brought her to this point. Again it was Maddek.

So much he would have to make up for. But he could not yet. "I must ride. So much I would say to you, my bride—but I vow this: I will return. I will marry you. And I will see you happy."

A spark more hope returned. On a shuddering breath, she nodded again.

Hard he kissed her mouth—then made himself leave, into the cold morning. His warriors waited, some of them smirking as if assuming what had kept him so late. Nearby stood Seri, arms folded and with a mutinous jut to her chin. Most likely because her mother had forbidden her to join them. Yet judging by the girl's expression—and the repressive look that Kelir sent her—Seri would only wait until they were out of sight before following behind.

"Seri of Firebloom, daughter of Nami and Kalin!" Maddek barked.

She startled, pivoting to face him. When her eyes met his, he told her, "Banek guards my bride, but he is of *my* Dragon, my armor. I would have you be Yvenne's—and to continue her hunting lessons while we are away, as she would have no better teacher."

Her expression softened with surprise, and she only seemed torn for a moment before new purpose settled her features into proud, determined lines. "I will," she vowed.

Nami gave him a grateful look as he reached his horse. Mounting quickly, he swept his gaze to the eastern sky, already bright with the approach of dawn.

"Maddek!"

He reined the horse around to see Yvenne limping toward him, her face still pale and eyes still shadowed, but not in so much pain. She carried a small velvet pouch, and was digging through it—pulling out jewels, strands of gold. As if she meant to bestow a token upon him, as young lovers did.

He would not stay to kiss her rubies, then, but wear them into battle. "What do you have for me?"

"For your vengeance. I made no mention of it before, because I feared you might think it was akin to speaking with sly tongue—or you might believe I'd stolen it, and cut off my thumb." Her voice was wry but laced with real pain as she continued digging through the pouch. "But now that your vow is rescinded, I can give it to you, to wear next to your father's as you cut off Zhalen's head."

His mother's crest. She placed it into Maddek's palm, and for a long moment there was nothing inside him. All this time, she'd had it. And it was his own vow that had made her fearful of showing him—not just the crest, but the seam bent to fit a smaller finger, and a symbol roughly etched beside the dragon of Ran Bantik's tribe. A crescent moon, the sigil of the House of Nyset.

The weight of that small silver ring in his palm seemed to drag Maddek from the horse, for he had no memory of dismounting before he stood before her.

"You cannot give this to me," he rasped, his throat raw. "She has pinched it to fit your thumb."

"You could wear it on your smallest—"

"I could not, Yvenne. Even if it did fit, I would not. This is not the crest of a warrior who has fallen, but one who lives." One who belonged to both Syssia and Parsathe. Not merely a crest offered to show approval, but far more. "This mark adopts you into the dragon tribe. She has made you a daughter of the Burning Plains. Only you can wear this."

He took her hand. His own fingers shook as he slid it over her thumb, and then he brought her hand to his mouth and kissed her crest so fiercely. There was sudden silence from the riders behind him, who saw what Yvenne wore now. Who understood what it meant. She had not lied, she had never lied. Even without this proof, Maddek would have married her and had come to believe her—though almost too late. Now this crest would help combat the lie that *he* had spread about her.

The consequences of that, Maddek would have to face later. Most likely, it would be said that his doubt had been justified. But he cared not what was decided. He would bear anything—because the one consequence that he couldn't bear had already been thwarted.

So close he had come to losing her. So very close. Because of a vow made in grief and rage and haste. But a clear view he had of her now.

And a much clearer view of himself.

CHAPTER 37

MADDEK

T he wolves are uneasy."

Maddek glanced over at the two dogs circling restlessly in front of Fassad's mount, their lips raised in snarls.

"Dogs are always uneasy near the Scourge," Kelir said. "The demon's foul magic lingers here."

"Perhaps," Fassad agreed, staring ahead. "Except I am uneasy, too."

Kelir shot a glance at Maddek. One that said his friend could not truthfully reassure the others, because he was uneasy, too.

As was Maddek.

Much different it was from the constriction in his chest as they'd ridden south the previous day, when Yvenne's hopeless gaze seemed always before him. A constriction that increased whenever the crest was mentioned again, along with idle wondering if she hadn't known what the gift meant, and that was why she'd hidden it for so long.

But she had hidden it for good reason. And had been

right to. For in truth . . . if she had presented that crest to Maddek, he *would* have believed it stolen. At the beginning, he had been stubborn in his certainty that his mother would not have chosen such as her. So even if she'd given him proof, he would have doubted.

That shame had been a festering wound in his chest as they'd ridden south. This unease and prickling tightness over his skin was not the same.

The sun was rising to the east. Facing the Scourge, the Parsatheans were lined up on their mounts—a thousand riders strong, with Maddek and his Dragon at the center. The Syssian soldiers at the Scourge's base would see but a line of riders across the horizon.

It was those soldiers who should be uneasy. They were already in formation, ten by ten, only a hundred in number. These were the soldiers from the Syssian outpost. The bulk of the might Zhalen had brought was in the Rugusian army, three hundred more in number—not in sight, but instead gathered behind the Scourge.

"Do they think to conceal their numbers from us?" Toric asked.

Maddek shook his head. He knew not what the purpose of it was. And that likely added to his unease.

Enox rode up, the faint light catching in the silver beads in her hair. "Our scout reports the same—Rugusians waiting behind, only Syssians ahead."

"Do they have a position on Zhalen?" So that Maddek might kill him.

Enox shook her head. "Not yet."

"It makes no sense." Ardyl spoke what they all thought. "We cannot see them, but whoever is their command can also not see us."

No, they could not. "What of the Scourge? Might they have archers hidden in the ruins?"

"Not that I have yet seen or heard reported from my scouts."

So there were only the Syssian soldiers who posed an immediate threat. "I will ride forward and appeal to Yvenne's soldiers as I promised."

Enox nodded.

An alarm she would give if any new threat appeared. Kelir raised a flag, signaling that they only approached to speak. Trotting forward, Maddek studied the Syssians. No clear leader was there among them. None were mounted. Where would an order come from?

"Movement at the head of the Scourge!" Danoh called.

"Drepa?" Toric asked. "There is a nest in the eye."

"There was a gleam of metal."

From armor or weapon. Yet the Scourge's head was a poor position to take. The ruins were so huge that an archer standing between the eyes might only hit a target as distant as the Scourge's nose, and could be no threat to anyone near the Scourge's belly.

Maddek neared the Syssians, his unease lifting the hairs over his skin. For not only were none of the soldiers mounted, neither were they armed. Instead they only wore heavy armor, their arms strapped with vambraces jutting with spikes. He slowed his horse, the Dragon doing the same.

No soldier would wear such armor. Too easy it would be in battle to stab one's own face or chest—though these were well protected in both face and chest. By the orange torchlight, Maddek could see little within the close-plated helms—only the wetness of drool that stained chins green, as if they'd been eating grass.

Realization gripped his chest. "Fall back!" Spinning his horse about, he shouted again. "Fall back!"

Snarling and roaring came from behind him, a wave of brainless beasts unleashed. With one hundred poisoned soldiers after them, the Dragon raced back to the Parsathean line.

"Silac venom?" Kelir yelled. "But they were held!"

Just as revenants had once been held at a stream, though humans could not be made revenants. And never had Maddek heard of a poisoned beast waiting for anything. So he knew not how it had been done, but it had been.

"It must be Aezil!" Ahead, he could see the Parsatheans

readying for the soldiers' charge, but they still didn't know what came behind them. "Is there a familiar?"

"No birds!" Danoh shouted.

But the sorcerer would need eyes on the soldiers to control them. Realization hit them all at once, but it was Ardyl who yelled it. "He's on the Scourge's head!"

And so too would Maddek be. But not yet.

He galloped along the line. "Fight by two!" he shouted. "Bludgeon to hold, blade to kill! By two, bludgeon and blade!"

For the soldiers were armored so well they would not be easily struck down. But a blunt force might knock them back long enough for a blade to find a mark.

He pulled up alongside Enox. Their horses had outpaced the rampaging soldiers, yet soon they would be upon them. "That is why the Rugusian soldiers are hidden behind," he told her, chest heaving. "So not to draw notice when the beasts are released."

Which also meant whatever control Aezil had over them was not absolute, if he could not make them distinguish between Parsathean and Rugusian.

An angry gleam flashed through her eyes. "Should we draw notice to them?"

By riding around the ruins, with the beasts following. "As you will. The sorcerer must be on the Scourge—and perhaps Zhalen with him. I will take my Dragon with me."

She nodded. "Ride as one."

As silver-fingered Rani did, as death did—though she had already come for the soldiers. Many times in the past day, Maddek had wondered whether Yvenne ought to have accompanied them. She was well protected, yet not having her near was a fear in itself. That he couldn't stop what might harm her.

Yet he was fiercely glad she hadn't seen this—her soldiers, poisoned. Sacrificed and changed into beastly weapons instead of allowing them to fight of their own will. Turned into brainless animals that the Parsatheans would have to put down.

Zhalen must have feared that the soldiers wouldn't be loyal to him.

Leading the charge, Enox raced down the line and a thousand warriors thundered after her. Remaining in place, horses snorting and stamping, Maddek and his Dragon watched the brainless soldiers turn in that direction.

"When we have a clear path—"

The ground shook. His mount snorted, prancing uneasily.

A great boom followed, as if thunder were right upon them. The galloping army transformed from a flying arrow to whirling confusion, like leaves scattered on a stream. A thousand horses screamed in fright, the warriors upon them staring in terror as the ruins in front of them *moved*. The mountain of obsidian shifted and heaved, cracking and shattering, like an old man stretching his bones after a long sleep.

The Scourge was rising.

"Temra be merciful," Toric said, his voice full of horror.

Maddek shook his head. He would not pray for that. That goddess only showed mercy to the dead.

"Fly to the Scourge!" he commanded. "Fly!"

As one, Maddek and his Dragon raced toward the monster that was awakening.

CHAPTER 38

YVENNE

Yvenne's satchel spilled from her hands to the bed as foul, cold, strong magic sliced down the back of her neck.

Gasping, she braced her hands in the furs, her head swimming.

"Yvenne!" Seri hauled open the flap of the tent. "You must come see this!"

Heart pounding, Yvenne followed her outside. It was just after sunrise, but the sun was still low on the horizon, the hollow still in shadow. Only a short time ago, she'd risen from her restless sleep. The rest of the camp was still awakening, fires being stoked, breakfasts cooking. But the warriors had abandoned those fires and breakfasts.

Yvenne looked to the sky, searching for birds. High above, geese arrowed north. No others could she see.

"This way!" Seri grabbed her hand.

As fast as she could make her leg move, Yvenne followed her to the southern edge of the hollow, where Banek stood watching something in the distance. She had been warned not to climb the steep sides of the hollow, or her presence might break the illusion of unbroken plain from outside. Yet all of the warriors stood on the rim, looking southeast.

Where the Scourge was rising.

Sheer dread and horror gripped her throat. The mountainous heap of black rock shifted higher. Like a beast it was, six limbs topped by a horned head. The face resembled a skull, with gaping eye sockets and nasal cavities, the cheeks deep hollows above a jaw full of razored teeth. When the demon had lived within the monster, those cavities were filled with fire and molten rock. But now they were cold and dark.

"It is Aezil," she whispered, staring. "He is doing this."

In pale blue robes, one of his eyes nothing but a puckered scar. The movement of his body faintly echoed the movement of the Scourge, careful and slow. Guards surrounded him, bracing themselves as the head swayed.

"Riders from the east!"

A warrior called out the alert. Yvenne glanced east, squinting against the rising sun that was directly behind the approaching riders.

"What do you see?" Banek asked.

"I cannot . . ." Shielding her face, she tried to see through the glare of Enam's eye. She could make out little. "Red linens at the front. Helms behind. They ride two abreast but I cannot see how many."

"Parsatheans leading southerners?" Banek squinted, too. "Perhaps the alliance council has arrived?"

For they had heard at the camp that Gareth had reached the council and there was word of them coming north. "I cannot be certain."

A choked noise from Seri drew her gaze back to the south, where the Scourge was rising in full. In ruins, it had lain on its side. Her brother had managed to get its legs beneath it, and it rose ever higher.

Tears standing in her eyes, Seri gave a sobbing breath. "My mother and brother are there."

Maddek, too. With her heart a burning lump in her throat, she watched Aezil take a slow step—and the Scourge did the same.

"My lady," Banek said in a low voice. "Wait for me in your tent. Seri, go with her. Make ready your bow and arrow, Yvenne."

"What is it?"

The old man was watching the approach of the riders. "Parsatheans do not gallop in such close formation unless they are on a road."

As she'd learned while crossing these plains. Better to not have dirt clods flung into the face of those riding behind.

Enam glared, so bright at their backs. Eyes watering, she shook her head. "I still cannot see."

"It matters not. We will know soon enough if they are friend or foe," Banek said, and she realized all of the warriors had torn their attention from the Scourge. "Go now."

Heart thundering, Yvenne went.

CHAPTER 39

MADDEK

I wish now that those songs told us how Ran Bantik killed
the Scourge!" Kelir shouted over the thunder of galloping hooves.

Maddek grinned, wind rushing his face as they raced
alongside the enormous ruins. The Scourge was rising, but
a slow and lumbering rise it was. "It matters not!" he yelled
back.

"Because we are united?" Kelir's exasperation came
clearly through his shout.

"Because it is not the Scourge!"

Not a demon. Only a puppet, controlled by the true
monster—Aezil.

Reaching the quaking mountain, Maddek swiftly climbed
onto the second leg, still folded beneath the beast. The horses
could not follow and with a slap to the rump, he sent his away
again. The warriors scrambled after him, wolves nimbly racing up the rough surface of pitted volcanic rock and sharp
obsidian.

Maddek had no time for care as he ran toward the gaping canyon that had once been the Scourge's stomach, until silver-fingered Rani had split it open to retrieve her dragon.

"Into the belly," Maddek called out.

Fassad sent his wolves ahead. "Are we not climbing to the head?"

"There is a better way to reach it," Maddek told him.

Danoh and Fassad exchanged glances—Fassad from the northern Storm tribe, Danoh from the central Fist. Neither had spent any time playing among these ruins as children.

"The throat," he said.

A dark tunnel it was, of slick obsidian. Danoh flared a stick torch and the gleaming sides threw light far up the channel. Together they raced upward.

With heaving breaths, his face dripping sweat, Kelir said, "Beginning tomorrow, I will run beside my mount more often. I am on fire."

"It is not only that," Ardyl said grimly. "The air is hotter."

It was true. The air shimmered with heat.

Toric's face blanched. "Has Aezil reignited the furnace of the heart?"

"In a Scourge that can spit fire?" Fassad said. "And we are headed for the mouth?"

"Faster," Maddek told them, and sprinted up the throat—which was at more of an upward angle now than when they had been younger and the beast was lying on its side. Thighs burning with effort, he climbed the last stretch to the top of the throat and reached back to help his warriors up.

No time did they have to rest. They were in the back of the mouth, and the heat billowing upward from the Scourge's heart was like standing too near a fire.

Maddek ran across the pitted volcanic tongue, where wind whistled through the closed jaw. Aezil had not opened the cavernous mouth, but it was no cage. The huge teeth had gaps that even warriors of Maddek's size could slip through.

He looked out now, bracing himself against the slow

swaying of the head. Below, the Parsathean army had re-grouped against the brainless soldiers. The Scourge was not yet advancing on them, every movement it made ponderous, careful.

He looked to Danoh. "Where was Aezil standing?"

"Between the eyes."

Maddek looked up. Far above, in the ceiling of the mouth, a crevice opened up to the sky above—the nasal cavity, like a vent through the face.

"Perhaps we might climb up the inside of the mouth to reach that, and up to the face," Ardyl said, "but I do not think we want to linger here for long."

Maddek did not think so, either. An orange glow lit the back of the throat. "Kelir, Fassad, and I will climb up the cheek." They rose like cliffs against the flat, broad nose. "Ardyl will lead Toric and Danoh around the back of the head and come down from the horns. We will approach Aezil and any guards he has from two directions."

Ardyl knew these ruins as well as Kelir and he. "It will take us longer."

"We will wait on the cheek."

Nodding, she headed for the teeth. Maddek followed, then the others. The wolves wriggled through, surefootedly making their way along the edge of the jaw and back to the hinge, where Maddek, Kelir, and Fassad would climb the slope of the cheek toward the eye, and Ardyl would lead the others behind.

Wind buffeted the face of the Scourge, whipping at his linens. Still the sorcerer made no swift movements. Likely for the same reason Maddek feared that those swift movements would begin.

Climbing beneath the eye socket, he glanced over at Kelir. "Aezil is afraid of falling off."

The other warrior grunted with amusement. "The whelp didn't think this through."

"Maddek." Fassad's grim voice pulled his gaze farther down. "The teeth."

Molten rock dripped out between the gaps. The heat

from within the mouth had not penetrated the rock they climbed, but the liquid fire steamed the air and fell to the ground, where flames sprang up amid the grasses.

These plains would *not* burn again.

Jaw set with determination, Maddek climbed higher. The bulge of the eye socket hid them from view of the face. A chirp nearby turned Maddek's head. That sound he'd heard from Danoh countless times. Yet this one was not hers.

An infant drepa.

Maddek froze. Seeing the raptor, the other warriors followed suit. No fear did he have of the small reptile—but if that chirp became a squeal, an adult drepa would appear.

It chirped again, turning its angular head back and forth, the thin feathers around its neck waving with the movement. A full set of those thin feathers it would have when it grew. Just as its little claws would become razor-sharp sickles to tear open a gut.

The drepa hopped closer, then hopped away. Into the cavity of the eye socket it disappeared.

The molten stone dripping from the jaw had become a thick stream. The mouth was filling up with the fiery liquid. Steam poured from the vents above.

They had to cross those vents to reach the broad plane of the face. Ardyl could not be in place yet, but no longer could they wait, or they might be cooked while leaping across.

He gestured to Kelir, who nodded. Fassad and the wolves readied.

"I will jump across first. Then follow."

During that jump, they would be exposed to any guards that Aezil might have waiting. So the others would cover while each one crossed.

Drawing his sword, Maddek gave the signal. As one, they surged up over the edge of the cheek, onto the flat plane of the face. He heard the shouts from Aezil's guards as he sprinted a short distance, then made a flying leap through a blistering wave of heat.

He landed, then was pushed forward by an explosive burst of flames through vent.

"Steel!" Fassad shouted from the other side of the curtain of fire.

The wolf had jumped with Maddek. "He is here!" he shouted to the warrior, then met the charge of a Rugusian soldier with his sword. His curved blade was made for slicing through flesh when mounted, and Maddek had no frequent reason to use a sword against an armored man. Yet every armor had weaknesses and joints, and his blade swiftly tasted the soldier's blood and flesh.

He heard Kelir's roar, and then the warrior's axe flew through the flames, slamming into another guard's armored chest. With a snarl, Steel leapt for another, teeth slashing open the softest part of any man. The soldier's screams abruptly ended when he doubled over and the wolf ripped out his throat.

Maddek grabbed up Kelir's axe and raced to meet the next charge. Only a dozen guards. Those were fair enough odds. Snarling, he sliced open a gut, then met the next guard with silver claws through his neck. The heated glass stone beneath his boots grew slick with blood.

The red haze of battle filled his vision. All the guards he seemed to see, knowing as they came close, when they would move past each other to strike. Well trained, they were, but trained they would always be. Against the untamed viciousness of Maddek and the wolf, they fell.

The battle took them nearer the eye, the wolf at Maddek's side when the guards' dwindling numbers made them regroup and, instead of charging as one, join up into concerted attack. Chest heaving, Maddek defended against one sword and narrowly avoided the swing of another. With an upward slash, he split the guard's arm from his body and kicked him back, then charged the next. The Rugusian died swiftly, and Maddek booted aside his head to meet the weakened swing from the guard's remaining hand. Only one left, and Steel was on him.

A pained yelp brought Maddek racing, where the wolf

wrestled wildly with the soldier, teeth clamped on the guard's arm—and both of them dangling over the eye socket. With an angry grunt, Maddek cut off the guard's head and lurched forward to catch the wolf by the ruff before he fell into the drepa's nest.

He hauled back, and a streak of pain crossed his thigh. A crossbow bolt clattered against the stone. Teeth gritted, he dragged the wolf up, pivoting to face Aezil. The one-eyed sorcerer stood at a distance, watching Maddek with a curious gaze, and lowered his crossbow.

Maddek gave him a feral grin. "You have not your sister's aim."

"I have no need of it," Aezil said.

Adjusting his grip on the bloodied handle of his sword, Maddek advanced on him—and staggered on the first step.

Aezil tilted his head. "It's a quick poison."

Silac venom. Already leaching his strength. Grunting, Maddek fell to his knees. He could barely hold his sword.

The sorcerer smiled. "If only my father could see this."

"Zhalen." Maddek had promised Yvenne his head. And heart. He struggled to stand. "Where is he?"

"He has gone to retrieve my wayward sister."

Maddek shook his head in denial. "He will not find her."

"No? You have a spy among your own. We know where you have hidden her."

Maddek's heartbeat pounded in his ears. Again he struggled and his boots slipped in blood. He crashed backward, and this time it was Steel who saved him from tumbling into the eye socket, the wolf clamping his teeth around Maddek's vambrace and pulling him from the edge. From below, he heard the drepa's warning hisses.

"You fight, but you will not win," Aezil told him now, slowly coming closer. The Scourge swayed with each step, the wind whistling past Maddek's face. "My sister thinks to build an alliance against the Destroyer. But when everyone sees the power I have, when they see how I have crushed the Parsathean army, they will unite instead under me."

"Crush the Parsathean army?" Maddek gave a hoarse

laugh, then spit green foam before telling him, "You think this number is all we have? You will need a bigger monster."

"In time." Amusement lit the sorcerer's eye. "Are you still trying to come after me with that sword? A fine weapon you will be against my enemies. Revenants have minds filled with hunger. But the silac venom leaves nothing, and it is so much easier to fill those emptied brains with one thought. To stand. To attack. What thought will I put into your head?"

"To slay you." Difficult it was now to even sit up. "Monster."

"Then lift your sword against me, warrior."

Maddek shook his head. "Vela told me that a warrior relies too much on his sword."

"Did she?" Aezil laughed. "So you will not swing it at me in hope that the goddess will save you in reward for learning a lesson?"

With this poison in him, nothing would save Maddek. "I expect nothing from a goddess. And so I will use my sword one last time."

Grinning, Aezil spread his hands. "If you can make it this far, I will give you one swing."

Maddek was not going anywhere. Rolling over onto his stomach and dragging himself to the edge of the eye socket took all his strength. As did shoving his sword across the slippery obsidian.

He did rely on his sword. So he let it go.

Like an arrow it fell downward, into the drepa nest—and speared one of the raptors in the haunches. A screech tore through the air, echoing from that cavern.

Heaving himself back, Maddek reached for Steel. "Dead!" he commanded gruffly.

Instantly the wolf lay against him. No effort it was for Maddek to remain still as the screeches rose in number. In a rush of clicking claws and racing feet, the reptiles poured out of the nest. Utterly still, Maddek didn't look to see Aezil fleeing, but the jerk of the Scourge's head and the whipping jolt of the rock beneath him joined the sorcerer's screams. Then a harder jolt, as if the mountain suddenly fell again. The flames jetting through the vents abruptly went out.

Longer Maddek waited, as the drepa tore into the body and then carried the pieces back to the nest. Happy chirps from the infants soon followed. Steel whined and moved slightly, licking Maddek's face.

Then Ardyl was rolling him over, tears streaming. She wiped the foam from his mouth. "Don't sleep," she begged him.

Kelir was there, his face a mask of anguish. "Maddek." He took his hand in a crushing grip. "It is done. Enox stopped the poisoned soldiers. And the Rugusians are on the run."

"I am not done," he rasped. So little strength he had, even in his breath. "My bride. Take me to Yvenne."

He saw the look that passed between them. Knew they thought it was impossible. A day's ride it was.

Hoarsely he told them, "There are words left unsaid."

"We will tell her for you," Ardyl vowed on sobbing breaths.

Heart aching, Maddek shook his head. "No one can say these."

Not if they were to mean anything. To hear love from someone else's lips only sounded like a platitude.

"You fool," Kelir snarled at him. "You didn't tell her? You cockbrained fool."

As if in rage, the warrior hauled him up, slung Maddek's arm over his shoulder. Ardyl took the other side.

"Don't sleep," she commanded. "Whatever it takes."

It would take all that was left of his strength. But it mattered not.

Only Yvenne mattered now.

CHAPTER 40

YVENNE

Seri raced ahead, collecting a sword and armor before catching up again with the slower Yvenne, and together they entered her tent.

Forever they seemed to wait. With quiver on her shoulder and bow in hand, Yvenne stood surrounded by walls of mammoth hide, listening for any sounds from outside.

The young warrior stood with her, breaths quick and sharp. "I hate this. I hate not knowing what is happening. I feel so helpless."

As did Yvenne. But she had more experience with it. "We're not helpless. We are waiting for our opportunity to act."

Seri nodded. Some of the tension in her shoulders eased—then stiffened again as a shout sounded. A scream, a howl of rage. The clash of a sword.

Banek slipped into the tent, carrying a bloodied blade. "Come, my lady. We must run—"

The old warrior stopped abruptly, gaze dropping to her knee before rising again. For the longest moment, his eyes held hers, and she agreed with all that he said in that silent look.

He turned to Seri. "You must be a mouse, do you hear? Find three horses, and meet us at the north end, by the pool. Be silent and swift, and if you cannot find three mounts, then one will do."

Face bloodbare, the girl nodded. Banek crossed the tent, his curved blade slashing the hide at the back. "Through here. Quickly."

Seri darted through and vanished. Banek followed. Yvenne slipped through the gash into a swirl of choking smoke, then notched an arrow. The warrior stopped to listen. So many sounds she heard, a confusing clash of shouts and blades.

"Who has come?" she whispered.

The warrior's jaw tightened as if he would not answer. Then, "Zhalen."

Her father. Terror struck her heart. "How did he find us?"

For the riders had been coming straight to the hollow, as if they knew where it was. But no magic had Yvenne felt before this morning. Not since the revenants.

Banek shook his head. He gestured forward, and she crept with him, behind another tent. Figures raced through the smoke. Yvenne readied her bow, but she could not see whether they were friend or foe.

Until two rushed out of the swirling smoke, helms gleaming. Instantly Yvenne loosed her arrow. One soldier fell dead, the other running two steps before realizing his partner had been killed. Then Banek was upon him, slicing open his gut before following through with the neck.

Yvenne readied another arrow. Sour fear climbed steadily up her throat, her mouth watering and stomach clenching. They slipped past another tent, then another, and past the body of a warrior with an arrow through her chest.

A breeze swept through, clearing the smoke in front of them—revealing a dozen soldiers gathered. Yvenne fired, then fired again, and then the smoke concealed the soldiers but she could recall where they stood. Another arrow. The soldiers rushed toward them. With a roar, Banek charged, his blade a striking snake, so fast and deadly. Yvenne loosed another arrow, then screamed as a soldier snagged her from behind. She fought, swinging her elbow, and heard the soldier's grunt.

"Don't kill that one! She's the one we take!"

The shout came from another soldier, but Yvenne would not be killed *or* taken. Reaching down, she snatched her dagger and buried it in the soldier's stomach.

"My lady! More are coming! We have to run!"

She could not run, but Banek could. Dragging her away from the dying soldier's grip, he swept her up against his chest and ran. She clung to the dagger, shaking, before slipping the dripping blade into its sheath. All was chaos as they passed a bloodied warrior standing with his sword, snarling to Banek that he would hold them. Then an arrow caught that warrior's throat and threw him back. Into the smoke they continued, deeper into the hollow, and Banek began to slow.

"To the pool," the old warrior told her, his words a gurgling wheeze. "Seri will be waiting."

"No." In horror she clung to him as he stumbled. "Banek! Banek, my friend. We can make it, I will help you."

Holding her tightly, he sank to his knees. "I am your shield. But you must go on alone now."

No no no. Wrapping her arms around his thick torso, she tried to pull his heavy form with her—and felt the arrows in his back. So many arrows.

Silently screaming through clenched teeth, Yvenne eased him down onto his side. Frantically she tried to see if there was a way to help him, yet there was not. And his breaths were slowing now, the sound of each one shallow and wet.

She cupped his face. "Please, Banek. Stay with me."

His bloodied hand reached up to clasp hers. "Go, my lady."

She would not leave him alone. But so quickly silver-fingered Rani came for him, he was with her one moment and gone the next. Yvenne screamed against his still chest, her pain and rage all as one. Through the smoke she heard the approach of more soldiers, the soft clang and jingle of their armor. She reached back for an arrow—her quiver was gone. Lost when the soldier had grabbed her from behind and Banek had torn her from his grip.

But a warrior made use of what she had. Jaw clenched, she yanked the arrows from Banek's flesh.

With burning heart, she waited until their shadows resolved through the smoke and she killed them, one by one, with the arrows they'd used to kill her friend.

Then no more arrows she had, and there was no one to see her cry. Tears streaming, she kissed Banek's still cheek. Then she did as he'd bidden her, and went.

Pulling her dagger from its sheath, she crept silently forward, gaze searching through the smoke. A soft nicker from ahead lifted her heart.

Then a breeze slipped through the hollow and revealed her father holding a blade to Seri's throat. A dozen soldiers stood behind him.

Zhalen smiled. "A fine morning this is, daughter. And you have a decision to make."

The young warrior lifted her chin as if daring him to slice, defiant tears in her eyes. "Save yourself, my lady."

By running? Or by killing Zhalen? Her grip tightened on the dagger. Four throws out of five, the pointed end of the blade found her target. She might kill him. But he might jerk in a death spasm, killing the girl. If her blade didn't find the mark, for certain Seri would die. And she had not enough knives for all of the soldiers.

But she was not helpless. She would simply wait for her opportunity—and endure whatever suffering was to come. Because she was stronger than she knew.

Far stronger than Zhalen knew, too.

Yvenne tossed her dagger to the ground.

CHAPTER 41

MADDEK

Full dark it was when Kelir slapped Maddek's face, yet barely did he feel it. So numb his cheek was. As if he were drunk. But never had Maddek drunk so much.

"Maddek!" the warrior roared into his face. "Yvenne is gone!"

The numbness vanished. Only pain now, filling his chest as he saw the bodies in the hollow, the burned tents. But Yvenne's tent stood.

Hope only lasted until Ardyl and Kelir dragged him inside. Her satchel was spilled out onto the bed. A breeze blew through a slit in the hide.

"The wolves found her dagger," Fassad said grimly from behind him. "And Banek."

"Seri?" Kelir asked, voice taut.

"Taken with them, I think."

Taken. By Zhalen. And she would suffer.

Maddek roared, strength surging through him, but it only carried him forward to the bed. There he fell to his knees beside it. Foam dripped from his mouth, and he wiped it away, gathering up silk that smelled of anise. Yvenne's wedding raiments. He buried his face in them. His last breath would be of her scent.

Crouching beside him, Ardyl gripped his shoulder. "Vela said—"

"That I would lose her." So he had. "And that she will suffer."

"And she said—"

"That I won't protect her. But I vow I will."

Ardyl gave a sigh. "Maddek . . ."

"Do not kill me when I sleep," he said raggedly, for he felt that darkness closing in now. "Aezil said that he gave the brainless beasts one thought. So I will have one thought—to protect her. Even after the poison takes me."

Brainless he might be, but his heart . . . that would still burn true. And belong always to a queen.

Yvenne.

Holding to the thought of her, he slept.

CHAPTER 42

YVENNE

B ehind her, Yvenne felt Seri shudder herself awake.
"We still ride," Yvenne told her softly, though she
didn't think the young warrior was in any danger of
falling out of the saddle. Unlike Yvenne, Seri seemed as
comfortable sleeping on a horse as riding it.

A shaky little breath and sniffle followed. Though the
girl was taller and bigger than Yvenne, she was not yet a
warrior's age—perhaps only twelve years. Only twice in
these two endless days and nights had the girl cried, but
Yvenne thought it more of exhaustion than fear.

Not yet had they stopped or slept. They'd changed
horses, but her father had driven them hard south—and
nothing had Yvenne or Seri eaten or drank, though her father had made the offer. But Yvenne had given the same
warning to the young warrior as she'd given Maddek before
their dinner in Drahm.

Now the girl's stomach rumbled, loud and hard enough
that Yvenne felt it against her back. Her own gave an an-

swering growl, but the dull cramping below her stomach worried Yvenne more than the empty ache in her belly.

So hard and so far they'd ridden. And they were not yet done, though they might finally have rest tonight.

"We've slowed?" Seri whispered.

Yvenne nodded. "There is the Syssian outpost ahead."

"Will they keep us imprisoned there, do you think?"

She heard the hope in the girl's voice. Because the outpost was only two days' ride distant from where thousands of Parsatheans were camped.

But that was why Yvenne had no hope. "Perhaps a night. Either the soldiers from near the Scourge will already have returned or they will soon join my father here. Then we will travel to Syssia."

For a moment Seri was quiet. Then in a small voice, "What do you think happened at the Scourge?"

Yvenne couldn't guess, and she hadn't seen. Her father had put a cloth over her eyes—to prevent Vela from helping anyone find them, he'd said. But he seemed not worried about it now, for a full day the cloth had been untied.

The girl had seen the Scourge fall. But Yvenne didn't know if that meant the monster had been defeated, or if her brother hadn't been able to maintain such powerful magic . . . or if Aezil had crushed the Parsatheans as intended and had no more use for the ruins.

That her father had removed the blindfold told Yvenne what he believed: the Parsatheans posed not as much threat now. Yet she couldn't accept that. "The warriors likely defeated it."

The girl released a soft, relieved breath. "That is what I hope."

Yvenne only prayed it wasn't a false hope. "If you have opportunity in the outpost to escape, take it." Seri was strong and quick and clever, a warrior through and through. "Do not wait for me or try to rescue me."

"But—"

"Do not," Yvenne said firmly. "I will try to negotiate

your release. Most likely my father will force a promise from me, or ask me to give him something in trade—and I will agree to it. You may hear me speak lies, but it is only to save your life."

Because as long as the girl was here, Yvenne dared not defy him.

"I am your Dragon," the girl whispered thickly. "I will stay with you."

"You will not. Instead memorize all that you can—how many soldiers, how many horses, how fast we ride—and carry that information back home to Maddek. Swear this to me, Seri."

"He will come for you." Absolutely certain she sounded. "And I swear it."

"I may carry his child," Yvenne told her. And for that possibility alone Maddek would come. Perhaps also because he'd vowed to choose her as his bride, and she had been chosen to build a new alliance. Yet she was certain he would come for the child. "That will also be my first lie, when I say that I cannot be pregnant."

The girl nodded, then tensed as the outpost gates opened ahead.

"Be brave," Yvenne told her softly. "Have hope. Let them *think* you are beaten and defeated, if you must. But whatever happens, do not give up."

"I will not," the girl whispered, her voice trembling. "I will not give up."

Neither would Yvenne.

Or perhaps there would be no lie. In a sparse room, Yvenne was given clean robes and linens and a pitcher of water. Faint crimson stained her inner thighs.

With trembling fingers, she washed the blood away. Nothing did it mean. Just because they had ridden hard—so very hard—and she'd eaten nothing for days did not mean she would miscarry. And some women bled a little, even with child.

Or perhaps she had not been with child to begin. Never had her menses been regular.

Yvenne had believed she was pregnant, though. Perhaps it had only been wishful thought . . . yet she'd hoped so much.

Though she would persuade her father that she was not.

She requested rags from a female soldier. If her request reached her father's ears, more likely he would believe her.

Dressed, she was taken past a chamber where Seri sat at a table with Rugusian soldiers. The girl ate hungrily—from a bowl served by the same stew pot from which the soldiers ate, Yvenne saw with relief. The young warrior had listened well.

No Syssian soldiers did Yvenne see, though this outpost contained so many signs of home. Small moonstone carvings decorated the mantel in the chamber where her father waited, and against the wall hung a tapestry depicting Queen Nyset's victory over the twelve-faced Galoghe demon.

Her father appeared haggard, the lines in his broad face deeper than she had ever seen them. Tall and as solid as an ox, always he'd seemed to her so strong—especially in comparison to herself and her poison-weakened mother. Not so much now, and not only because she had Maddek to compare. For so long Zhalen had been a terrifying figure who ruled over her life. But so much more of the world she'd seen since leaving her tower, so many more of the people in it. How small he seemed now.

And as always, the ragged scar on his throat filled her heart with sheer vicious pleasure.

"Sit, Yvenne," he said, pouring wine into her goblet. "We await your brother's return."

The hot, grassy scent of roasted boa on her plate made Yvenne's stomach growl. She sat but made no move to drink or eat, though her tongue was parched and her belly aching.

Only a spoon sat beside her plate. No knife.

Her father appeared in no hurry to eat his own meal.

Sitting back, he regarded her steadily for a moment before averting his gaze . . . though pretending that he wanted to avert it. Idly he stirred his fantail soup, breaking the fat yellow yolk into the cream with the edge of his spoon. "If you truly wish to build an alliance, you should join with us, daughter."

"And bow before the Destroyer? I will not."

"Bow before him?" His brows shot upward. "We intend to stand against him."

Yvenne scoffed.

He smiled thinly. "Little choice will I have. Once, perhaps, I would have bowed before him. It would be the only way to survive him."

"You survived him before."

"Did I? Or after I held the line at the Four Ridges, did he come with the intention of killing me—and only let me live because I vowed to complete a task for him?"

A dull ache constricted in her gut. "What task?"

"He wanted a bride—a woman of the same bloodline that severed his arm. And a virgin, but your mother was not. So I was to get one upon her." He put down his spoon, his gaze critical. "Imagine my panic when she whelped a sickly, weak heir. I was to present *you* to the Destroyer on his return? He would kill me."

"You lie," Yvenne said. "You sent me to Toleh to be married. Did you expect that king to leave me a virgin?"

"That was only after Aezil found his power—and I found a new use for you." He lifted his goblet, looking at her over the rim. "Not all of my children are worthless. You think an alliance between the western realms will stand against the Destroyer? He ripped through us like paper. But if Aezil courts the same power, the same god? Then we will be victorious."

"By being no different than him?"

"The difference is that we will not be crushed. Instead we will do the crushing. That is the only difference that matters, Yvenne, though you are too naive to see it now. One day you will." Her father shrugged. "And if Aezil fails, then perhaps the bride will be the child you carry. I do not think the Destroyer cares how young she is."

Vomit shot up the back of her throat. "I carry no child."

"Do you pretend that barbarian did not rut upon you night and day?"

"No. But his seed has not found root. Even now is my bleeding time. Do you wish to see my rags?"

"Rags that you have bloodied with a prick of your finger?" He gave her an amused look, then glanced to the door when a soldier appeared there, face filthy with travel and sweat. "Captain! You have arrived. Where is my son?"

"Your Highness." Eyes darting nervously to Yvenne, the Rugusian captain came into the room. "Our king is dead."

Yvenne burst out with a laugh. So much for his plan to conquer the Destroyer.

Zhalen cocked his head. "What do you say?"

Face so bloodbare it was gray, the captain repeated, "The king of Rugus is dead. Slain by a barbarian."

Knuckles white, her father demanded, "*Which* barbarian?"

"Their king. Maddek."

Grinning broadly, Yvenne sat back. Her father said nothing more for an endless time.

Then a quiet, "Bring the barbarian girl."

Yvenne's grin vanished. "You will *not* hurt her."

"I will not," her father agreed easily. "Instead I will release her, so she might send a message to Maddek."

"What message?"

"Something that will keep him from coming for you. You'll say that you no longer want to marry him. And you no longer wish to have his child."

Her heart twisted painfully. "He will believe the first. The second will not matter. There is no child. He knows this."

Certainly not a child that her father might make a bride, to save his own skin now that Aezil was dead.

"You do not think he will come for *you*?"

"Maddek has told me that he will never come to my rescue. He will not risk his warriors' lives for mine. And that he would kill me himself if any warriors died while attempting to save me."

As Banek had. Sharp grief closed her throat.

Her father gave a short laugh. "A loving suitor you have, daughter." He lifted his goblet as if in a toast, then downed a long swallow.

When he set it down, Yvenne picked it up and, careful to place her lips where his had been, thirstily drank the wine. It tasted sickly sweet, but she had no care as long as *something* was in her belly.

Her father gave her a bemused look, and then his gaze moved to the door. "Take her to the next chamber."

Seri, looking uncertain and afraid. Yvenne gave her a reassuring smile in the moment before the girl was led away.

She faced her father again. "Have you ink and pen? I will write your message."

"I think not to trust you with a pen," her father said. "The girl will remember what you tell her to say—that he has not the heart of a king, and he couldn't protect you, so you have no more use for him as a husband. And that I am relinquishing Syssia's throne to take Rugus's, so you also have no more use for his child."

Her heart froze. Never could she imagine saying such words to Maddek. They were not at *all* the same as what Zhalen had said before—that she didn't want to marry or have his child. So completely different the messages were, as if designed to rip open Maddek's heart.

How had Zhalen known exactly what to say? The words that should be left unsaid, because they could never be forgiven?

Her father leaned forward. "Or I can send the message with the girl's head."

"No," Yvenne whispered. "I will tell her."

"Good girl. But of course, it will only be part of the message. The rest will be a stain on a sheet."

She frowned at him in confusion.

"He killed two of my sons. Now I will take his." He

reached for the goblet, tipped it as if to see how much remained inside. "Three full doses I put in here."

Doses? Yet he'd also drunk some. What would he put in there that he wouldn't fear his own—

Oh, Vela. *No.*

In desperate horror, Yvenne gagged and gagged. Some of the sickly sweet wine came up, but not enough. Not enough.

Zhalen began eating his soup. "You said you were not pregnant?"

She truly didn't know. But it didn't matter. "If you send this message, with what he believes is his child bloodied in that sheet, he will come and kill us both."

"He will not find it so easy. The walls of Syssia have held back barbarians for ages."

They would not hold back Maddek. Desperately she tried to vomit more, but no more would come. Pain ripped through her, but it wasn't the potion. Not yet. So little hope she'd had. So little. Yet when she'd remembered how Maddek had left her, his fierce kiss, his sweet promise—it had been a tiny hope that she'd so desperately clung to. Yet her father's message would fit every twisted view that her would-be husband had ever had of her, and crush Yvenne's every last hope.

Nothing would she have of Maddek then. Nothing at all.

Voice ragged, she told him, "Do not do this."

"It is done," her father said, and slurped more soup from his spoon. "Take heart, daughter. I have never heard what happens when a man takes the half-moon milk. But I am about to find out. And at least we will be suffering together."

Not enough suffering for him. Too much for Yvenne.

Oh, Vela. She was not strong enough for *this.*

The first cramp ripped through her belly. Then another, tearing open her rage and pain that had been together for so long, tearing open a heart that was already battered and bloodied, tearing a scream from her lungs and throat and soul.

And when she stopped screaming, her hope was gone.

CHAPTER 43

MADDEK

Awakening as a brainless beast whose only thought was of Yvenne felt no different than any other of Maddek's recent awakenings. Except that he still felt weak. And hungry.

"He stirs," Ardyl said in a hushed voice. "Take care. We can't be certain until he speaks."

"Yvenne," he rasped, his mouth and lips so dry that the word felt as if it cracked his tongue. Above him stretched a hide tent. The familiar comfort of piled furs lay beneath him.

"They left the outpost two days past, riding hard for Syssia and surrounded by Rugusian soldiers," Fassad answered.

"Seri?"

Toric told him, "The scout did not see her leave the outpost with the others, but Kelir and Nami have taken warriors to follow."

So would Maddek next. His head swam as he sat up. "Banek?"

Danoh silently shook her head.

Grief gripped his heart. "And at the hollow and the Scourge?"

"Fifty-three warriors lost."

In addition to one hundred Syssian soldiers who would have been loyal to Yvenne. Voice thick, he asked, "How long has it been?"

"You have been sleeping four days."

But he shouldn't have woken at all. "How did I live?"

"I tried to remind you," Ardyl said, crouching beside his furs with a small pot in her hand. "Vela said that you might have need of this. We weren't sure whether to rub it on your cock or into the poisoned wound or make you drink it. So we did all three."

The cockmonger's oil. A potion that the goddess had stirred with her glowing finger, Maddek remembered.

And he remembered what else she'd said. That Yvenne would suffer at Zhalen's hands.

He tossed back the furs and stood. Unsteady and weak, but only because he'd been abed so long. None of the poison's weakness lingered. "Bring to me a horse."

The journey to Syssia would take a full turn of the moon. Too long. Far too long.

"We will ride with you," Ardyl told him. "All is prepared. But you must delay for a moment. There is something that needs doing."

There was nothing that needed doing except going after Yvenne. His linens and belt hung from a nearby hook. By the time Maddek dragged on his boots, he was steadier.

He emerged from the tent into the bright sunlight and with all of Parsathe gathered before him. No longer was he at the hollow, or the camp, but where Ran Bantik had stood when he'd united the tribes. As far as he could see were Parsathean warriors, their voices lifting and lifting into a roar that was his name.

Ran Maddek.

"The vote was cast while you slept." From his left came the familiar voice of Nayil, the council minister who had served as advisor to Maddek's parents—and had tried to serve as a fine advisor to him. The old man's eyes were bright as he came forward on his withered step. "We had already been of one voice. But your felling the Scourge sealed it."

"It was not the Scourge," Maddek said, voice hoarse with emotion. "Merely a sorcerer."

"A monster is a monster," the old warrior said. "Will you lead us? Will you speak for us?"

Heart swelling, he looked out over the gathered warriors. Maddek knew not if he deserved this honor, but he would try to do right by them.

"I will."

The roar of voices lifted again, accompanied by the pounding of feet, the gleam of raised swords.

"We know you intend to ride for your bride, Ran Maddek. We will keep the ceremony and feast for when that is done," Nayil told him. "But first the council would also speak with Parsathe's new Ran."

Maddek nodded, then looked beyond him. The alliance council stood near, lacking only Bazir, whose tongue he'd torn from his mouth and whose head he'd given to Yvenne. He was glad to see Gareth among them, for it meant that there was little explanation to give. They knew what Zhalen was, what Aezil had been.

"I would have a strong alliance," he said to them. "But it cannot stand strong if you coddle corruption such as Zhalen's and Aezil's. The council will say what they wish, and I will listen, but no argument will sway me. I *will* storm the walls of Syssia. I *will* have Zhalen's head. Not for vengeance, but for my bride and for her people."

Pella stepped forward, the gold at her wrists and ankles clinking. "Ran Maddek, we are not here to forbid you from marching against Syssia. Instead we would ask you to lead the alliance army against Zhalen, and to help root out any of Aezil's remaining corruption around the Rugusian throne."

He looked to Rugus's minister, not even in his bearded

age, and the moonstone eyes so much like his sister's that Maddek's need for her crushed his heart. The boy regarded him with a wary gaze, as if facing a drepa—perhaps because Maddek had killed two of his brothers, and next would kill his father.

But not all of the House of Nyset were corrupt. And the boy had given Maddek no reason to view him as such. "Yvenne trusts your word. And so will I. Do you ride with us, Tyzen?"

The boy nodded, surprise and emotion rushing over his face, ending with pride and determination. "I will."

"Then make ready, brother."

For the young man would be his. Now the boy gave him a wry glance. "Yvenne's brother is a dangerous thing to be. It is likely safer to be yours."

Maddek grinned. "So it is."

He turned toward his Dragon, then back as a commotion stirred through the gathered warriors, as three riders sped through the crowd. His heart jolted against his ribs.

It was Seri. The girl was flanked by two scouts, her young face pale with fatigue. She reined in her mount in front of him.

"I have a message from my lady."

And held a bloodied sheet in her lap. With a dull roaring in his ears, Maddek reached up for her, helped her shivering and exhausted to the ground. His hands cupped her face, saw her tearful eyes, and steeled himself.

He had delivered Bazir's head to Yvenne in a bloodied jute sack. Whatever was in that sheet, he would not falter.

"Tell me," he said hoarsely.

"She says she will never marry a man too weak to protect her," she recited, voice breaking. "She said your seed took root but like any weed, she removed it."

Seri pressed the bloody cloth into his hands and understanding ripped through him, tore his heart in two. So hard she had hoped for a child. Not only to claim her throne but because she'd wanted to be a mother—a mother full of love and wisdom, as Queen Vyssen had been to her.

"You are certain?" he asked from a raw throat. "This is hers?"

Tears spilling over, Seri nodded. "I held her hand as she lay on the sheet and screamed."

She had screamed? Maddek's heart bled. Only for the greatest suffering would she ever make a sound. "And then she gave this message to you?"

"She did." Her chin lifted. "But before we reached the outpost, she said that she would lie to save my life. Her father released me so I might deliver this message. And because she told him that you would not come for her, or risk warriors' lives for her. That you would kill her if any warriors were lost in her rescue."

Deeper pain slashed through his heart. Those had not been lies, but truth. Those things he *had* said to her.

Did she know that they were no longer truth? Did she know that he would come for her? Or had those words he'd said long ago destroyed her hope?

So alone she must feel now.

Throat choked by pain and shame and grief, he laid his forehead to Seri's. "You looked after her well, warrior. I see your fatigue. But will you ride with us? You can share a saddle with Toric and take your rest."

"I will, Ran Maddek. But I need not share his saddle. I can sleep on my horse."

A fine warrior already. As they all were. He looked to his Dragon, then to Enox. "You are ready to ride?"

"We are," she said.

"You are commander of that army now," he said, though she had no liking of that alliance title. But he was Ran. No longer commander. "So it will be you who gives the order—"

"Ran Maddek," she broke in. "You misunderstand. It is not only the warriors in the alliance army who are prepared to ride. We are *all* prepared to ride."

The sweep of her arm indicated the gathering, warriors as far as could be seen. Not just the army. All of Parsathe, all the members of the seven tribes, willing to ride with him.

Heart thundering, he stepped forward and roared, "Riders of the Burning Plains! Fly with me, and together we will raze the walls that stand between Parsathe and a daughter of the Dragon tribe, chosen by Vela to unite the western realms against the Destroyer, the woman who will be our queen!"

Thousands of voices shook the vault of the sky in agreement. Maddek turned and looked to his Dragon, who appeared as fiercely eager to ride.

He gathered his claws, his shield, his sword. "Let us go claim my bride."

CHAPTER 44

YVENNE

I f her father would but come out farther into the courtyard, she would kill him.

Four days, Yvenne had been back in her tower chamber. Each day she sat on the windowsill, bow and arrow
across her lap, waiting for Zhalen to come within range.

She knew not how her mother had silently waited years
and years before ripping out his throat. Such patience,
Yvenne would never have.

But she had learned well from her mother. After the outpost, Zhalen had thought her weak and broken, with only
strength enough to hold on as their horses raced south day
after day.

Though he had not been wrong. Not to begin. And Yvenne
wondered now whether her mother's long plan had begun the
same way, truly shattered in body and heart and mind. If
those first days Queen Vyssen had lain in bed, unmoving and
silent, had not been pretense. And if it had been in those shattered and broken moments that she'd decided to continue in
that way, and wait for her opportunity.

For that was what Yvenne had done. Truly broken she'd been. Truly weak, barely able to cling to her horse.

Yet it was not the first time she'd had to. Her journey with Maddek had begun in the same way. And that journey had left her stronger than she'd known. Within days, her only pretense was not sitting up straight in her saddle, instead riding as if she'd never had horses or Maddek as her mount. The pretense was hobbling about as if saddlesore, slow and aching. The pretense was always being tired, when in truth she listened and waited.

She'd not found the opportunity she'd wanted on that ride, but she was not sorry. Because when they'd arrived in Syssia, she'd ridden through the gates of her city, and she'd finally seen her people—and they had seen her. No more could her father hide her, though he claimed now that she'd been savaged by the barbarian king and was recovering in her tower. There the Rugusian guard had carried her again, and again she'd pretended to be weak and unable to climb steps.

That weakness and pretense might be why her father didn't bother to check the tower chamber for weapons.

Because it had not only been her mother and Yvenne who had waited for opportunity. Her people had, too. Word of a queen had reached Syssia before she'd returned, brought in whispers by the soldier Jeppen, and then spreading more loudly after her father and his Rugusian guard had abandoned the city and charged north. And although the guards outside her door now might search the maids as they entered, while Yvenne had been gone, no one stood watch there. So the maids had brought in anything they'd pleased, then hidden it out of easy sight.

And as her father no longer concealed her existence, the tower windows had been unshuttered. So now Yvenne waited. Whether he came through her chamber door or merely walked through the bailey below, she would put an arrow through him.

The sound of the lock lifting on the opposite side of the door had her concealing her bow beneath the cushion of a sofa. Precious few arrows she had, but they were much easier to hide. She lay listlessly in bed when the Rugusian soldier allowed her maids through.

"Your braids have come loose, my lady." Pym tsked softly. "Let us fix them."

Without energy, Yvenne moved to her chair and Pym settled in behind her. Brightly the maid spoke of all the clever preparations her father was making to defend them against any attack from those brute Parsatheans from the north. So safe the maid claimed to feel, knowing that the great king who'd once smote the Smiling Giant would the one who defended the city now—and she was so happy to be living in the citadel, where most of the defenses were being built.

"And how pretty you look now!" the maid chirped, leaning forward to fiddle with a few curls around Yvenne's temples. On a soft breath she whispered, "Jeppen said that all is as you requested."

Yvenne gave a tiny nod, then glanced over as the Rugusian guard made a rough sound in the back of her throat. She no longer watched the maids and Yvenne. Instead she gazed out of the north window.

Another of the maids caught Yvenne's eye, then gave a quick look to the guard, making a little shoving motion with her hands. Asking whether to rush the guard and push her out the window.

No good would it do. Two more guards still waited outside the door. Yvenne shook her head, rose to her feet, and crossed over to the window. Pym joined her.

"That is a strange cloud," the maid said.

"It's not a cloud," Yvenne told her, heart thumping. "It is the dust raised by tens upon tens of thousands of charging horses."

With Maddek riding at their head, black paint on his brow, silver claws on his fingers. So beautiful he was.

And so savagely determined he looked, as if no time at all had passed between receiving her father's message and this moment. As if driven by rage and grief.

As he had been in his very worst views of her.

"Oh," Pym breathed, clapping her hands. "Surely they will kill us all."

No. Maddek was not here for the maids, or her people. Only her father, and the Rugusian guards . . . and if he had believed the message Zhalen had sent, Yvenne.

She looked to the guard. "You should run."

"And tell your father?"

"Or that, too. Tell him that death has come, as silver-fingered Rani does, but it is instead a silver-clawed Ran." Whose gaze had fixed on this tower, though he could not see her from that distance. Chest tight, she watched him come.

Wondering if she dared to hope again.

CHAPTER 45

MADDEK

During every short rest they'd taken on the journey south, Tyzen had described Syssia's defenses. All were strong, and the great shining wall stood even taller and thicker than Ephorn's.

Yet the wall had been broken once, Maddek reminded himself grimly. The Destroyer had crashed his way through it. But although the pounding of hooves in the thundering horde behind Maddek seemed mighty enough to shake the wall down, still it stood. His gaze rose to the ramparts atop the wall, where a metal helm gleamed. Syssian soldiers. Both Yvenne and Tyzen had said that the Rugusians were centered in the citadel and the Syssians had been given orders to guard the outer walls. Maddek would have to go through them—but he had told his warriors not to harm the Syssian soldiers, if they could. For soon their nations would join under Yvenne and Maddek's marriage, and he would not begin that union by killing her people.

Yet there would be fighting. Of that he had no doubt. Her father would lock the gates against the Parsatheans, Maddek would make demands and begin his siege—but there would be no reasoning with Zhalen, he knew. It would come down to bloodshed, and most of the crimson that ran would not be Zhalen's.

And it looked as if Zhalen was about to make demands of his own. Ahead, the gates opened and two mounted soldiers galloped toward them.

To deliver another message? A piece of Yvenne at a time?

Bloodrage rising, Maddek raced to meet the soldiers, Enox and his Dragon at his sides.

"Ran Maddek!" the soldier shouted—and Maddek knew him. The soldier from the ambush, Jeppen. "Our queen says we are to give you any assistance you need! So you have a clear path through the city to the citadel!"

In astonishment, Maddek reined his mare to a halt in front of the soldier, and his mount snorted, prancing in eagerness to race again. "You are giving me a clear path?"

"Against Zhalen's orders but at our queen's command." The soldier regarded him earnestly. "We have not the strength to take the citadel ourselves, or we would. But we will fight beside you!"

Was he to believe this? Or would he ride through the gates into a trap? Maddek glanced at Enox, who shared his suspicion, and at Kelir, who appeared bemused.

"Your bride has a habit of unseating us during our ambushes," Kelir said dryly. "We come to perform legendary feats, and she opens the gates."

It was his bride who would be the legend, Maddek thought. In the ages to come, he would rate but a mere mention in the songs they sang of his warrior-queen.

And did he believe Yvenne could inspire her people to defy their regent like this?

He did. For the Syssians were prepared to love their queen before they'd even met her. Before he'd met Yvenne, Maddek had been prepared to kill her—and now there was nothing Maddek would not do for his bride.

They would do no less.

"All gates?" Maddek asked.

Jeppen nodded.

"Enox," he said to her. "Split our warriors into the directions of the wind. I will take the north. Send your captains to the east and west, and lead the remaining warriors to the southern gate. We will come at the citadel from all sides. Let them know that soldiers who bear the Syssian sigil are our allies."

With a sharp nod, she galloped back to the waiting riders. Maddek gave a signal for the north to follow, and brought Tyzen up to ride beside him, now that they would not be fighting their way through the city. He would not have put the boy at the forefront of a battle.

Instead they seemed at the forefront of a parade as they rode through the gates. A surge of Syssian soldiers came at them from the sides—wielding few weapons, riding fewer horses—and joined their number instead of fighting. The wide avenue leading to the citadel at the center of the city had been cleared, as Jeppen promised, but only of carts and carriages. Syssians lined the street, cries of encouragement spurring them forward, tears streaming down cheeks. And as the soldiers had, many of them joined the riders in their march to the citadel.

When the first Rugusian guards appeared—a pair of mounted soldiers who appeared into the avenue ahead—no chance did Maddek even have to draw his sword. A mob of Syssians rushed in, wielding sticks and pots and cursing as they pulled the screaming guards from their saddles.

A large square stood before the citadel gates—and was already full of Syssians as they reached it, wielding weapons of whatever they could carry. Making use of what they had, as warriors did.

And these would be Maddek's people, too. Such pride he had in them already.

Cheers rose as Maddek appeared, and they made a path for him and his riders, squeezing close together on either side of the square. Yet so many the crowd numbered, there was hardly room for Maddek and his warriors to ride two abreast.

Kelir looked over the scene in astonishment and concern. "What do we do? When the fighting begins, they will be crushed."

"So we give them better weapons," Maddek said, leaning over to offer his shield to an old woman who looked up at him with such hope, tears streaming down the lines on her face. Straightening, he called out, "Syssia! We are here to fight alongside you! Every mounted Parsathean warrior carries an extra blade. Make your way through the streets and back to the avenue to claim your weapons from the riders behind me, and with the warrior whose blade you choose, you will fight together!"

Quickly the square emptied, giving them an easier route to the citadel gates. Only mounted warriors and a few Syssian soldiers filled the square as he advanced.

The citadel was surrounded by a wall, and inside was yet another wall protecting the main keep—and at each corner of that inner wall stood a tower that pierced the sky, with entrance only from the interior courtyard beyond the inner wall. Tyzen had told him which was Yvenne's. The northwest tower, nearest to him now. It stood so tall that Maddek had no angle to see into a window where she might be looking back at him.

Yet so close she was. Only two more walls to breach.

He looked to the citadel's gate, a thick lattice of iron and steel. Through it he could see the inner wall's second gate—not yet closed, as Rugusian soldiers scrambled to their positions. They must have known the riders had come, yet had not anticipated the Syssians letting the enemy in through the city's outer wall.

If the soldiers were not all in position, then they might not be prepared to defend against warriors who would climb this wall. Only a few Rugusians did he see upon the battlements.

He looked to Tyzen. "Where is the gate's lever?"

Tyzen pointed to the stone above the gate, where narrow slits revealed where the gatehouse chamber stood. "It can be reached from—"

A soldier silently fell from the battlements, a feathered shaft jutting through his helm. Then another toppled over, gurgling and clutching at the arrow protruding through his throat at a deep angle. A screech and clang sounded from within the gatehouse.

The gate began to rise.

Two women burst out of the gatehouse entry onto the battlements, carrying heavy chamber pots splashed with blood, racing along atop the wall. An arrow felled a soldier who chased after them.

"Race to the inner gate!" Maddek shouted through a burst of hearty laughter. Again Yvenne had paved the way for them. His horse surged forward, warriors thundering after him. Within that inner courtyard, they would be vulnerable to attack from arrows loosed from within the wall through loopholes, yet most soldiers would take to the battlements, not knowing that their death sat in the northwest tower.

"How many arrows does she have?" he yelled to Jeppen.

"Not many!"

And no doubt, she would save one for Zhalen. So she would not be able to clear the battlements.

"Take the gatehouse!" he shouted to the Syssian as they raced through. Yvenne must have sent more maids to keep that gate from closing quickly, for a woman sat gasping against the inner wall, holding a cloth to her bloodied head, laughing and cheering them forward.

He recognized her. It was the same handmaid Yvenne had sent to Maddek with the message that first lured him.

Then he met the charge from the Rugusian guard and bloodrage took him. His sword was a hungry beast, tearing flesh and slinging blood. A war drum pounded in his heart, accompanied by the clash of steel and Rugusian screams. For they had taken his bride *and she had suffered.* Never would their suffering be enough, the quick death a mercy he hated to give, yet he did, with claws and blade and teeth. With his Dragon behind him, he fought his way to the northwest tower.

Another gatehouse stood at the base of that massive tower—and Zhalen had not hidden within the citadel's keep, as Maddek had assumed. Instead he waited in the shadow of the gatehouse, in front of the open gate, mounted and flanked by his personal guard.

The guards that had raped his mother and tied down Queen Vyssen.

Dripping with the blood of Rugusian soldiers, a grinning Maddek called to him, "It was *you* who smote the Smiling Giant? You look not warrior enough to smite a suckfly! Perhaps you blinded him with the shining armor you wear. For certain that has never seen battle!"

"And you are as arrogant as your parents were, pup!"

So he was. But not as arrogant as Zhalen, standing before an open gate with mounted soldiers who numbered not even a fraction of the warriors Maddek had brought.

And though hate and bloodrage blazed within Maddek, Zhalen's life was not his alone to take, vengeance not only his. Yet no angle did Yvenne have with her father so near to the gatehouse. So Maddek needed to lure him away from the walls.

Luring away from walls had not worked well with Yvenne, but Zhalen was not near the warrior and ruler that she was.

Dismounting, Maddek spread his arms wide, grinning ever wider as he dropped his bloodied blade to the ground. "I have come for my bride! If you wish to keep her, then meet me in warrior's challenge. I vow I will not even use a sword, and never will I break an oath."

"And your warriors will stand by? You think me a fool."

"True!" Maddek laughed, because in his experience, men such as Zhalen could not bear being laughed at. "But they will also vow not to raise a sword against you. Let this grass here be the battlefield where this war is lost or won."

Zhalen looked to the warriors behind him. "I do not hear a vow!"

Maddek could not order them to make a vow. They had to give it. Yet although he could hear the unease as they did, their voices rose as one.

Hefting an axe, Zhalen gave a sudden grin and urged his stallion forward. "Prepare to die, barbarian. You are a fool to think you can take what is mine!"

Maddek's grin became a baring of teeth. "You are a fool to think that locking Yvenne in a tower would *ever* be the same as controlling her."

He knew not where she would place the arrow. Zhalen wore a thicker helm than the soldier on the battlements had, yet even the force of an arrowhead striking it would likely knock him unconscious from his horse. From almost directly above, not much other angle would she have. Perhaps his arm, holding the axe.

Or his leg, bent with his foot braced in the stirrup. A whistling streak, and the arrow embedded feather-deep through the top of his knee, straight down—likely splitting the bone of his calf.

Shattering his knee. As hers had been.

Yvenne did not want her father to have an easy death. And so he wouldn't.

Maddek's warriors surged around him, heading for the Rugusian guards who hadn't yet seen what had struck their king. Zhalen had made no sound, though his face whitened with agonizing pain.

With deadly intent, Maddek started for him.

Eyes widening, fury drawing back his lips, Zhalen began to rein his mount aside—as if to flee.

Then he made another fool's choice and charged Maddek, swinging the axe at his head. Bloodrage volcanic, Maddek dodged the heavy blade and ripped razored claws through the leather girth that secured Zhalen's saddle to his mount.

Overbalanced by the swing of his own axe, Zhalen tumbled from the galloping horse, saddle still between his thighs, landing hard on his shattered leg. The king screamed then, clutching wildly for his fallen axe.

Maddek heaved the murdering dog-king up by his hair. "For the lies you said of my father," he told him, and ripped out his tongue. "For the rape of my mother and Queen Vyssen." His silver claws shredded cock and balls. "And for Yvenne's suffering."

This Maddek would have made last longer. Forever. Yet he had not yet seen his bride, and she mattered more than vengeance ever could.

Still it was slowly, slowly, that Maddek dug his claws beneath the man's ribs, relishing the agony in his rolling eyes and gurgling scream. All went silent and still when he tore out his heart. He used Zhalen's own axe to cut off his head.

Both Maddek carried to the tower, for he'd promised to return to her with these on a pike. Late he was in keeping that promise. Yet it was still kept.

His Dragon had made a path for him through the Rugusian guard and into the tower's opulent royal chambers, then ahead up the stairs. So many stairs. A few guards they caught up to, as if the Rugusians had hoped to use Yvenne as protection, for no mercy would they find from warriors whose queen and king the guards had murdered and tortured and raped and beheaded.

At the top, his Dragon sent more guards into Temra's arms. Maddek stepped over their bloodied corpses as Kelir swung his axe at the heavy lock.

Throat thick with emotion, he bade them, "Wait for me."

In the center of her tower chamber she stood, and nothing he saw of their surroundings. Only Yvenne, staring at him with armor so thick that he could read nothing from her face. So thin she was again, as if starved or afraid to eat, and the sight made his stomach ache.

Yet such joy also filled his heart and his throat, that not a word he could say.

He lifted the pike, showing her the head and heart, before tossing them aside. Because it was done. Vengeance was done.

There was only Yvenne. Maddek started for her.

And she said on a broken whisper, "Please do it quickly."

He stumbled to a halt, agony ripping through his chest, because she had said that before. With his claws at her throat. "You think I would kill you?"

She gave no reply, though her lips trembled.

Silent.

Hurting.

Roaring filled his head. Cavernous pain opened within him. His voice was but a hollow echo of it as he said, "Do you not know I would tear my heart from my chest before I would ever harm you?"

Her moonstone eyes squeezed shut. A short, sobbing breath ripped from her.

In devastation, Maddek sank to his knees. "What have I done, never saying this to you?" he said hoarsely. "Never telling you these words that I should have said over and over again. What have I done, that you do not know how I would ride across the world just to lay my gaze upon your face? That I would crawl there on the mere hope of knowing your touch again? What have I done, that as I kneel here, you still do not know that with my full heart, I love you?"

Tears spilled down her cheeks and she buried her face in her hands. Sobs racked her small frame. So alone she seemed.

Never again. Rising, Maddek went to her, removing his bloodied claws before slipping his hands into her hair, gently urging her to look at him. "You are a queen, but you do not have to hide your tears from me. You say it is not the role of your people to comfort you—that is a duty that I will claim. Do you think I cannot see the walls you've built to protect yourself? Do you think I cannot see the scars you conceal or how many more are within you? My only prayer is that your wounded heart will one day heal enough to love me in return. If only a little. And trust that I would give up my life before hurting you. You are my heart, Yvenne, and my strength—and certainly my brains."

A laugh shook through her sobs. Finally she looked up at him, moonstone eyes gleaming with unshed tears. "To have you after all of this, I would have to love you more than a little."

Hope filled him. Throat aching, he agreed softly, "After

all that I have done, you would have to love me very much. So will you have me, Yvenne?"

In answer, she wrapped her arm around his neck, urged him down for a kiss. He lifted her instead, brought her to his mouth, where her lips still trembled against his. Her breaths shuddered as he softly tasted her again, and he knew the sweetness of her love for him.

She drew back, her eyes searching his face, her hands cupping his jaw. "You shaved your beard."

"Because no longer will you need to tug on it when you want me to listen," he told her. "Always I will listen to you. Always I will hear your words."

Her eyes shimmered with tears again as she smiled.

Gruffly he added, "And because it is custom to have a shaved jaw when I marry."

Happy were these tears now, he saw. She kissed him hard, then again. "I will still make your life a misery," she said between kisses.

The sweetest misery it would be. Cradling her against his chest, Maddek carried her to a door that would never imprison her again. "Then let us begin."

CHAPTER 46

YVENNE

I n the great courtyard still stained with her father's
blood, with bare feet on Temra's altar, Yvenne married
Maddek with all of Parsathe and Syssia looking on.
Then celebration began, with Yvenne opening the luxuries
of the citadel to all, but there were such great numbers that
the feasting and singing spilled beyond the city walls.

With her brother and the Dragon, she reunited in private
that evening around a table—and not one thing upon it did
she fear would be poisoned. When Kelir's sister joined
them, Yvenne kissed Seri for her bravery, making the girl
flush with embarrassed pleasure.

So happy Yvenne already was, so happy Maddek had
made her—and this only their first day married. Her cheeks
ached from smiling and laughing.

Yet not all was happy news. Toric seemed distracted
throughout much of the evening, until finally he said, "I
must leave the western realms."

All other conversation around the table fell silent, and
Yvenne sighed. Well she'd known this might be coming.

Vela had said the Dragon's wings would fly a great distance. And given all that her father had known—but shouldn't have—she'd guessed what had happened. Because Vela had also said Toric still had the revenant's poison in him.

"Aezil is dead," she told him. "No longer can he see through your eyes."

Maddek looked from Toric to Yvenne, realization dawning. "That was how Zhalen knew to find the hollow?"

Jaw clenched against rage and grief and shame, Toric nodded. "I didn't realize he was there," he admitted in a thick voice, and touched the back of his head. "I thought the odd feel was lingering sickness and fever. But I showed him the way to our queen."

"It is no fault of yours," Maddek firmly said. "You need not go anywhere."

"But it wasn't only Aezil." Fists clenched, Toric looked at them all with renewed determination. "Vela said it was her brother's poison. Enam. And that god is still here. I still feel him. So perhaps the Destroyer can see through me, too. And he will see all that our queen does to build the alliance against him."

"We cannot know that he could," Yvenne said quietly, heart hurting for him. So fascinated he'd been by the knowledge that Vela was always looking through her eyes, and the gifts it brought. Yet now a god looked through Toric's eyes and the knowledge only brought him pain.

"We cannot know that he couldn't." Throat working, Toric said, "I will visit the Tolehi monks first. Perhaps they know how to remove Enam's poison from within me. Or blind him, so he cannot see through me. And if not, I will search for answers elsewhere. But I will *not* remain here and risk everything you try to build. After you have defeated the Destroyer . . . then I can return."

Yvenne looked to the others, saw the need to persuade him to stay on the warriors' faces—yet no words to do it with. And so there was only pain and frustration and loss.

Except from young Seri, who scraped meat from bone

with her teeth as she told him, "You have to return. You are the greatest warrior in our tribe, so obviously you are the only warrior I would ever deign to marry."

Toric choked on a laugh. "Perhaps I will return for that, then."

The girl grinned at him, and lightness returned to the other warriors' faces. But still, it was pleasure and pain, as a wedding feast became a goodbye feast, as well.

When it was full dark, Maddek carried her up the steps that led to the top of Syssia's great wall. Cradled against his chest, she told him softly, "I can climb these better now."

"So you can. But not once this night will I let you out of my arms."

Nor would she let go of him. High they climbed, because Yvenne had not known where else to go. To claim her husband within the citadel seemed to show preference for Syssia. To claim him in the Parsathean camps outside the wall seemed to show preference for them. But in this way, they could be both.

The great wall was wide enough for horses to ride its length six abreast, and so their furs they easily spread between the battlements. Yet not immediately did they lie upon them, for this was a view such as neither Yvenne nor Maddek had ever had. All of the city they could see, as celebrations carried into the night. Many warriors still remained within the walls, though not all, because even a city such as hers had not enough grasslands to feed tens of thousands of horses. So across the rolling green fields outside the wall, many horses grazed amid the camps—joined by many Syssians, especially those who had shared blades with Parsathean warriors that day.

So full her heart was as she looked—then lifted her gaze farther east. "Enox rides to Rugus next?"

"She does," Maddek said softly behind her, kissing the length of her neck.

"I am next in line to the throne," she told him. "But I do not want to take that crown. So I know not what to do."

Her husband's strong arms came around her, pulling her back against his chest. "I have a suggestion."

"I will take any."

"Your brother imprisoned Commander Iova. Free her, and allow her to act as regent until the people of Rugus choose their own queen or king."

"As Parsathe does?"

He nodded against her hair.

Perhaps a difficult change to make. Or perhaps easier than she knew. "That is a fine suggestion. Should I do the same for Syssia?"

He laughed. "What would be the purpose? They would have no other but Nyset's heir."

"Perhaps not, but they would *choose*." She sighed. "Though I could not make that change, even if I wanted to. I am not truly a queen yet. And will not be until I reach a queen's age or until . . . until . . ."

Her breath hitched, and so tightly he held her then.

Blindly she stared out over the wall. "I was *so* careful, Maddek. Drinking only what he drank. And . . . still." So terribly her chest ached. "But I was already bleeding, so he may have only hastened the inevitable after the battle at the hollow and that long ride. Or I was never pregnant to begin. Yet I still . . . Why did I not guess what he had done? I should have been more careful, protected her from him."

His voice was thick against her ear. "You did all that you could."

"It was not enough."

"And many times since I found you gone, I have said the same. I did not protect you, and because you fell into Zhalen's hands, you suffered this. If you will blame yourself, my wife, you must blame me first."

"I will not," she said. Maddek had done all that he could to protect her. Nothing better could he have done.

"Blame Toric, then."

She knew his purpose and yet still the thought could not be borne. "I will not."

"Banek?"

Her throat knotted painfully. She shook her head.

"Then blame Aezil," he said softly.

She nodded.

"And your father."

She drew a deep, cleansing breath. "Yes."

"Then that blame is where it belongs."

"And where is yours?" she asked dryly. For she knew he still carried it on his shoulders.

His rumbling laugh said it was true. "I would add Vela. Though that is more difficult."

"Because she saved you, too?" She had heard of what the potion had done.

"Even that is difficult. I am grateful, but also angry she did nothing for your soldiers. But that is a futile anger, because what do I know of gods? I know not what they can and cannot do. So I save my blame and anger for Aezil and Zhalen, who poisoned them and used them."

"Yes," she agreed.

"But she also spoke truth. I did not protect you. I never truly had you. Then I lost you. And I would have died without saying that I loved you. Utterly defeated I was then, Yvenne—and so I discovered what sort of man I am."

Eyes burning, she whispered, "What sort is that?"

"A man who will never give up fighting for those I love. Even unto death, I had every intention of coming back to protect you. But it is not only you. I love my people, too. And today, I learned to love yours. Never will I give up on them. So I am a man with the heart of a king."

So he was. Tears slipping down her cheeks, she whispered, "You think you never truly had me?"

"I know I did not, for if I had, you would have never doubted whether I would come for you. Not for a moment would you think I might hurt you." Maddek turned her to face him, cupping her tearstained cheeks in his big hands. "I know not what challenges and dangers we will face as we complete Vela's task, but I know this: from all that I have learned, never will I look at you again without a clear view. And you will always know that I'll come for you. Do you have any doubts?"

"Not one."

"So it matters not what will come at us as we build this alliance against the Destroyer. No matter what lies we are told, no matter what occurs—after all we have been through, there is nothing now that could tear us asunder."

Nothing at all. With happy tears, she told him, "So much I love you."

His dark eyes flared hot, and he lifted her against him. "Then ride with me, my warrior-queen. Into battle we will fly."

So gladly she kissed him. And this battle they fought in the same manner as they would every battle to come.

As one.

EPILOGUE

Maddek found Yvenne atop the Syssian wall. Not since their wedding night two years past had they been up here, yet it was not those sweet memories she was reliving, he knew.

With arms wrapped around herself, she watched a group riding north, away from the city. So many people they loved were among that party—her brother Tyzen, who would try to persuade the rulers of northern realms to join their alliance. Kelir and Ardyl had also gone with him as her brother's primary guard. And Seri, who would have followed them even if she had been forbidden to—so the young warrior had been given permission instead.

Maddek circled his arms around her waist, pulled her back to his chest. "You have prepared them well."

As she had so many others sent out to the many realms. So hard she'd worked in the past years, first rebuilding the alliance nearer to home, seeking those who were willing to go with the message that they would all need to stand together, to ask the realms what was needed, and to promise that when the time came, all would converge and ride against the Destroyer. To those groups, she had told them everything she knew about the people they would encounter on their journeys, the queens and kings they must persuade—all that her mother had told her.

"So hard this is," she whispered. "They will be so far away, out of our sight—and we will have no way of helping them, when trouble they face."

And certainly they would. Maddek's quick laugh rumbled out. "This is what it must be like to have children."

She laughed, too, then bent her head back for a kiss, sighing softly as he moved his lips to the side of her neck. "Perhaps I should have gone, too."

"You are where you should be, my warrior-queen," he said, pinching her earlobe with his teeth, and with his sword hand he drew up the silk skirt of her robe. "You are the burning heart of this new alliance. They may fly far, but always they will know where to return for strength and for help. And so hot the heart of you is."

His fingers stroked through her wetness, and she trembled against him. "Maddek," she breathed.

"A fierce Dragon you seek to make for the western realms," he said, lifting her and sliding deep, so deep within her scorching embrace. "An alliance to protect all within, an alliance of claws and wings and fangs and sting."

She cried out as he pumped into her, deeper and deeper. "And armor."

"And armor," he echoed, his grunts harsh in her ear, his cock hard as steel within her. "For when the Destroyer arrives, these Dragons will gather and serve as a guard for all that we love—and you will be the burning heart."

As she was his.

Her back arched and she writhed upon him, then he held her so tight as they flew together. With ragged breaths they came down, and she turned within his arms, buried her face in his chest.

"So much pain the Destroyer left in our parents," she whispered. "And so much has passed to the children. I would never want our daughters and sons to know the horror that the children who lived through his terror did."

Because so many young ones were taken and enslaved, to serve in his army. "I would not, either," Maddek said thickly. "But we will defeat him."

She nodded against his chest, then pulled back slightly to withdraw a vial that she'd tucked into the linen wrapping near her wrist. The half-moon milk, that she'd taken in small doses as warriors did to force their menstrual blood to flow. For the past two years, they had traveled hard and often throughout the realms that made up the alliance, so she had not risked becoming pregnant again.

And because, he thought, of what she had just said. They would wait until the Destroyer was defeated.

Except now she tossed the vial over the side of the wall.

His warrior-queen looked up at him, her moonstone eyes shining. "The Dragon we gather will stop him."

So Maddek believed, too. "This is true."

"No. But we will *make* it true." She drew him down for the sweetest kiss. "So this is hope."

Turn the page for a special look at the next
Gathering of Dragons book by Milla Vane

A TOUCH OF STONE AND SNOW

Coming Summer 2020

LIZZAN

Many an innkeeper had woken Lizzan by tossing a bucket of water in her face. This morning marked the first time she was doused awake by a tree.

Or perhaps it was midday. When she sat up, sputtering, the source of the light filtering through the jungle canopy seemed too high for morning—and seemed too bright for eyes unshaded by sobriety. Though judging by the pounding in her head, she was *nearly* sober.

A sad state that Lizzan would soon remedy.

She uncorked the flask that was always as near to her hand as her sword—and was doused again when another broadleaf overfilled with rain and tipped out its burden.

The deluge poured over the top of her head. Sputtering again, her black hair hanging wetly around her face, Lizzan contemplated the effort of leaving the base of the tree where she'd made her bed. But all around her, the canopy dumped water as if making wet war on the world below, and many leaves were much larger than those above her. She would be no drier if she abandoned this spot.

And she would be no drunker unless she did. Only a few drops remained in her flask—and those tasted only of rainwater.

Groaning, she shoved the cork into the neck. A fine day this was. Such a very fine day.

Whatever day it might be. The last she remembered, her flask had been full. Usually at least two or three evenings passed before she had to fill it again.

Idly, she unsheathed her sword. No blood stained the shining blade. So she had likely not killed anyone in the time unremembered, or the blood would still remain. Lizzan was not the tidiest of warriors when drunk.

And now she was here. In the jungle. She had the vaguest recollection of a man with a gray curling beard saying that a group of bandits were plaguing travelers along the road between the villages of Dornan and Vares. Perhaps she had set out to hunt them.

If so, then a fool she was. Gladly would Lizzan collect bandits' heads. But she had no money and no horse—and now, no drink. Better to have waited until someone offered to pay for those heads.

A look through the rest of her belongings told Lizzan that at least her only foolishness had been chasing after brigands. Still in her possession was her purse—empty though it was—and her sword, which would fill the purse with coins again. She had not sold any more of her armor. Even with the sigil of the Kothan army scratched away, each piece was fine enough to fetch a fair price—her chain mail tunic alone could buy a horse and a year's worth of drink. But she was not yet so desperate. Or so thirsty.

A sniff told her that she also had a rather unpleasant odor. But the rain would take care of that.

Mostly.

Her leathers and boots were soaked through when the storm finally passed. Made from a northern falt's watershedding fur, her bedroll had been spared the soaking, but it was so muddied that nothing of the white pelt could be seen under the brown. The cursed heat in this realm would dry them all soon enough, but still she stripped down to her linens and boots before starting out in search of the road, so that her squelching would not draw predators, whether human or animal—and to spare herself the chafing.

Some days it seemed that everything she touched immediately began to chafe her skin. Everything rubbed the wrong way.

It was not skill that led her to the road, but the noise of the travelers already upon it. Out of sight amid a heavy growth of ferns, Lizzan studied the procession. A few dozen families—men and women, young and old. A few carts drawn by oxen carried supplies and the weaker among them. But most walked and carried their belongings upon their backs.

Except for the mounted figure at their head. Lizzan could only see her back, but the red cloak she wore identified her well enough. A Nyrae warrior—or so she would have everyone believe by wearing that cloak. Once, those roaming warriors guaranteed the safe passage of anyone who traveled the road with them, for only a fool would attack one of the goddess Vela's chosen. But few Nyrae warriors had survived Anumith the Destroyer's deadly march a generation past. Now, it was more likely to be a woman from one of these families—and that she had donned a red cloak in hope that bandits would not risk attacking a party led by a true Nyrae warrior.

But the deceptive practice had become so common that there was little protection in it anymore. Instead those who could afford the cost hired guards—which was how Lizzan earned most of her coin. Of late, she had escorted merchants and nobles fleeing east, as rumors spread of the Destroyer's return from the west. From the east, she had escorted merchants and nobles fleeing west to escape the tyranny of the warlords in Lith. And from the north came those fleeing unnamed terrors that stalked through the ice and snow.

This was the first party she'd seen fleeing north—usually the only escort in that direction was for merchants' goods, which were a prime target for bandits. More than all else, the destitution of these travelers might be better protection than any red cloak. For they had little to tempt thieves.

But brigands were often tempted by very little.

A few stragglers made up the tail of the party—likely those who had joined the primary group after it had already started out, for it was Vela's law that no one would be denied a Nyrae warrior's protection upon the road. Even if that warrior was truly only a farmer.

Lizzan waited for the entire procession to pass, then began to straggle after the stragglers. With her wet hair hanging lankly over the left side of her face, her armor and leathers wrapped up in her bedroll, she received little more than a curious glance or two from the others, and she remained far enough behind to escape any attempts at conversation.

But she did not escape notice. Lizzan had barely settled into the procession's slow pace when the quick tempo of hoofbeats announced the approach of the red-cloaked figure.

Oh, and no farmer was she. Not on a horse so fine. Sheer envy struck Lizzan's chest. Perhaps she would part with her chain mail tunic, after all.

Except this woman did not likely need it. A thick braid swept her black hair away from the proud set of her face. She was not a large woman—shorter than Lizzan and more finely boned—yet the eyetooth-studded belt she wore left little doubt of her skill.

There was also little doubt of her identity, for one could not step into an inn without hearing of how Krimathe's future queen had set out on the quest that would earn her the Ivory Throne. And all who quested for the goddess Vela also wore a red cloak.

Not a Nyrae warrior, but a Krimathean. So there was little difference.

And although Lizzan had little use for royals, the woman eyeing her now was no mere queen. For legend was that Hanan had fucked one of her foremothers, and that god's silver blood ran through her veins—and his strength through her limbs.

So Lizzan felt a little bit of a fool when she told the woman, "I have heard that bandits are preying the length of this road. I offer my sword and assistance if we happen upon them."

The woman's dark eyes swept Lizzan from drenched head to wet toe, and Lizzan did not think that piercing gaze overlooked a single scar or battle-hardened muscle.

No response did she give, except to cock her head—as if waiting for more.

Lizzan sighed and scratched the side of her neck. "And I would not ask these people for payment, but if the bandits are mounted, I would like first pick of their horses."

The Krimathean's eyes narrowed. As if she *knew* there was more.

And so there was. "Also their flasks."

The woman's lips twitched. Then she swept her forefinger over her left eyebrow.

Lizzan's chest tightened. Yet she could see no way around it. Had she still been in the north, or if it were winter, no one would think anything if she'd covered much of her face. Yet if she'd joined this procession wearing the mask she often used while working, she'd have immediately been thought a bandit. But her hair had not concealed her well enough.

With muddied fingers, she drew back the black strands, revealing the scars that raked down the left side of her face.

"Though it looks similar, it is not Vela's mark," she said thickly. "I am not cursed."

And of all people, this woman might know. For if the Krimathean failed in her quest for that goddess, she would bear Vela's mark—and be shunned by all. Driven from every village and city to live forsaken and alone. A woman to whom even a Nyrae warrior would not offer protection.

With the tip of her finger, the Krimathean drew a line down the outside of her cheek.

Relief lightened Lizzan's heart. For that line was where another scar would have been, had she borne Vela's mark. So this woman must have seen it before. So many others had not. And Lizzan had often known all the weight of the curse that she hadn't earned.

She *had* been cursed. And shunned. But not by a goddess. Instead a bastard prince had been the one to steal everything from her. Her rank. Her honor. Her heart. For not all thieves skulked in the forests.

Oh, but she prayed they came across bandits soon. For now that she had thought of him, her sword thirsted for blood.

Ready to find
your next great read?

Let us help.

Visit prh.com/nextread

Penguin
Random
House